THE
FORSAKEN

LISA M STASSE

ORCHARD BOOKS
338 Euston Road, London NW1 3BH
Orchard Books Australia
Level 17/207 Kent Street, Sydney, NSW 2000

First published in the US in 2012 by Simon & Schuster
First published in the UK in 2012 by Orchard Books

ISBN 978 1 40831 880 5

Text © Lisa M. Stasse 2012

A CIP catalogue record for this book is available from the British Library.

1 3 5 7 9 10 8 6 4 2

Printed in Great Britain by CPI Group (UK) Ltd, Croydon, CR0 4YY

Orchard Books is a division of Hachette Children's Books,
an Hachette UK company.

www.hachette.co.uk

For Alex McAulay

PROLOGUE

At first I think the hammering sound is the noise of waves crashing down on white sand. I'm dreaming I'm in Old Florida with my parents, before the government restricted all travel.

Then, as I start to wake, I realise the noise is something else. Something real. I pull a pillow over my head. But the hammering gets more insistent.

I finally realise that someone is banging on the front door of our apartment.

I wonder why my parents aren't answering. Usually they're awake late at night. But tonight, there's no sign of them.

'Get the door already, jeez,' I mutter.

I am ten years old.

I have no idea that tonight I will become an orphan.

The door to my bedroom bursts open, letting in a blaze of light. My mum rushes inside, frantic.

'They've come for us!' she hisses. I hear distant guttural voices barking out orders.

I sit straight up, pushing the covers back, my blood turning to ice.

The military police are here.

'Hide! Hide!' my mum whispers harshly. She grabs my

arm, hard enough to bruise it through my pyjamas, and yanks me out of bed.

We're halfway across my room when I hear a deafening crack. Our front door is beginning to splinter.

'Run!' my mum screams, pushing me into the hallway. I see my dad at the front door, desperately trying to barricade it with furniture.

There's no time to hide. No time to reach the kitchen and the hollowed-out space in the wall behind the refrigerator.

The front door gives way. Armed police barge into our apartment, knocking the smashed door off its hinges, ploughing the furniture out of the way.

My dad springs forward, tackling the first man who comes through the doorway. But another policeman strikes him in the mouth with his assault rifle. The police surround my dad and start beating him with nightsticks. All of them are wearing dark visors and black uniforms.

'Alenna!' my mum screams as policemen race towards her. 'You'll be OK!' But the look in her eyes says she knows the truth.

Our lives are over.

One of the policemen jabs my mum in the neck with an electric cattle prod. Her body seizes up. She goes crashing to the carpet.

'Mum!' I yell, rushing over.

My dad has already disappeared. Before I can reach my mum, officers grab her arms and start pulling her away too.

I cling to one of her ankles, but an officer smacks my

knuckles with his nightstick. I fall back with a gasp. My mum gets dragged across the carpet, right out the front door. It's over lightning fast.

I barely remember what happens next. It's just fragments, like a nightmare. Policemen stand in the doorway, blocking it so I can't run after my parents. There must be at least twenty of them crowding our apartment.

In numb shock, I walk back into my bedroom and crawl into bed. I pull the covers over my head, clutching my throbbing hand. *Now that they've taken my parents, what's going to happen to me?* I want to fight back, but what can a ten-year-old do against the government? What can anyone do?

Moments later, someone walks into my bedroom. I curl up in a ball as the covers are peeled away.

When I look up, an old man in a dark suit is standing over me, smiling warmly. Behind him, officers rummage through my father's frayed notebooks, slipping them into evidence bags in the hall.

'Alenna Shawcross, you are now a ward of the United Northern Alliance,' the old man says gently. 'Come with me, and our government will take care of you – despite the treasonous crimes of your parents.'

I want to scream at him for taking my mum and dad away. Hit him in the face and then run. But I'm so stunned that I do nothing. I just sit there and stare back at him.

'I'm not going to hurt you,' he says. 'In fact, I'll take you to your new home. Orphanage Forty-One in New Providence, about an hour down the Intercoastal Megaway.'

'Why can't I stay here?' I ask, biting back tears.

'You're too young to live on your own. Besides, there are lots of other girls your age at the orphanage.' He smiles again. 'Hurry up and put some shoes on. A car is waiting for us downstairs.'

A few minutes later, he leads me out of the apartment and into the narrow halls of our building. I've lived here, on the thirty-sixth floor of Tower G-7 in New Boston, for most of my life. I know that our neighbours must have heard what happened, but all of their doors remain closed.

'Today is the start of your new life,' the old man tells me. He puts a comforting arm around my shoulders. 'You're safe now, Alenna.'

I nod. But I don't feel safe.

And I can't imagine ever feeling that way again.

THE UNITED NORTHERN ALLIANCE

SIX YEARS LATER

As our bus approaches the Harka Museum of Re-education, I peer out the window at the soldiers standing in front in the sculpture gardens. The sculptures are just broken remnants, long ago smashed under combat boots. The flagpole flies our nation's flag, an eye hovering over a globe branded with the letters *UNA*, the abbreviation used by everyone for the United Northern Alliance.

The driver parks on a circular driveway in front of the museum's entrance, and I look up. Marble columns sweep fifty feet towards a pediment that still bears old scars from rebel mortar attacks.

There's only one day left until I'm forced to take the Government Personality Profile Test – GPPT for short – which is why our class is on this field trip. The trip is meant to show us what happens to kids who fail the test.

A heavyset woman in a grey uniform stands up near the front of the bus as the door opens. It's Ms Baines, our Social Reconstruction teacher. She ushers our class out of the vehicle and into the hot sun. We stand on the asphalt, a diverse throng of kids. Everyone, rich or poor, orphan or not, goes through the same public school system in the UNA.

'This way, class,' Ms Baines orders. We follow her up a wide stone staircase, towards the massive front door of the museum that beckons like a hungry mouth. Inside, it's dark and cool.

The Harka Museum once held some of our state's greatest works of art. Now, like most museums, it's a shrine to our government and its leader, Minister Roland Harka. Instead of paintings, the walls display digital maps of the United Northern Alliance's global conquests. Armies are rendered as colourful dots, and battles as pixelated cubes.

Being in this museum makes me think about our nation's complicated history. At sixteen, I'm too young to remember what a real museum was even like. I only remember reading about them, before most books and digital media were withdrawn from circulation. That happened when I was eight, two years before my parents got taken, and just three years after the formation of the United Northern Alliance – a merger of Canada, the United States and Mexico into one vast, chaotic nation.

From what my mum and dad told me, the citizens of those countries weren't in favour of the alliance. But food was scarce after a global economic meltdown, and people were turning to violent crime. So the government leaders made the radical decision to create the UNA.

When angry citizens rebelled, military police used lethal

force to stop the demonstrations. The demonstrations turned into riots, and then into total anarchy as people turned against their own government.

Every week our building would shake as a car bomb detonated somewhere, and I'd often fall asleep at night listening to the crack of gunfire. That was when Roland Harka, a charismatic four-star general, took office by force and appointed himself prime minster of the UNA. For life.

After that, everything changed. Minister Harka united the military by rewarding those who joined him with bribes, and imprisoning anyone who disobeyed. He imposed savage penalties for breaking laws and snatched away the freedoms everyone took for granted. All communication was restricted: no more mobile phones, personal computers or internet access.

Anything that could encourage subversion of the government, or simply draw a crowd – like religious gatherings – was outright banned. Then the nation's borders were permanently closed. According to Minister Harka, the entire country had to be united in isolation to achieve safety and prosperity.

He also mandated that all scientists immediately put their knowledge to use for the benefit of the government. For Minister Harka, technological supremacy became the key to conquering the globe, amassing plundered resources from other nations, and maintaining order at home.

'Move it, Alenna!' Ms Baines suddenly snaps, breaking my reverie and shooing me along a corridor. I'm lagging behind my classmates. We're heading towards a large display screen, thirty by fifty feet, hanging on a stone wall in the main gallery. This screen is the centrepiece of every Harka Museum. When I reach it, I jostle for position, looking up at the live digital feed.

There is a name for the place that we're watching – Prison Island Alpha – but nobody dares say it out loud for fear it might jinx them. Some call it the Land Across the Water, or the Land Beyond. To others it is simply the Forgotten Place. I stare in fascination at the footage of stunted trees and verdant plains now flickering in front of me.

The kids who get sent to this island are the ones who fail the GPPT, a test that predicts a propensity for criminal activity years in advance. It's administered to all high school students during the fall of their junior year, and can identify potential murderers, rapists, thieves and psychopaths before they act on their impulses. Because of this test, crime has virtually been eliminated in the UNA.

The test isn't something you can study for. It's not even a test in the normal sense. No one asks you any questions. Instead a serum gets injected into your veins, and then computers scan your brain, looking for abnormalities.

The kids who are found to have aberrant personalities – ones that will lead them towards a life of crime and violence – are labelled 'Unanchored Souls' by the government and shipped to the desolate prison island.

I continue to stare at the digital window into this harsh world, waiting for something to happen. On the grassy plain, between rows of crooked palm trees, stand the ruins of gigantic concrete buildings. Behind them is a massive stone spiral staircase, leading up into grey clouds that hang above the landscape.

A balding museum docent steps forward, speaking into a microphone. His reedy voice crackles to life in our government earpieces, the ones we have to wear each day from sunrise to sunset in our left ears. Sometimes the earpieces play classical music – like Wagner and Bruckner – other times, recordings of patriotic speeches delivered by Minister Harka.

We can't control the earpieces, so I've learned to ignore mine. But today I'm listening. I want to hear what the docent has to say.

'When Prison Island Alpha was first populated, more than two thousand video cameras were placed inside. We thought that the island would develop its own civilization – like penal colonies have in the past. Most notably Australia in the 1800s.' The docent pauses. 'Yet this never happened on Island Alpha. Instead, the savages who call it home destroyed most of our cameras. Only a few cameras remain, hidden in trees. We now rely on satellite imagery as our primary—'

'Can't you drop more cameras in there?' a boy interrupts.

The docent shakes his head. 'The inmates use the raw materials for weapons.'

'Doesn't the island get overcrowded?' another classmate asks. It's Melissa O'Connor, a brunette with perfect hair and teeth, courtesy of her wealthy parents.

The docent looks over at her. He has probably fielded

a million random questions from students like us. I wish I could come up with one he's never heard before, just to stump him.

'Overpopulation's not an issue,' he explains, 'because life expectancy on Island Alpha is only eighteen years of age.'

The crowd burbles.

Eighteen.

I turn that number over in my mind. I wonder what it would feel like to have only two more years to live. My chest tightens.

I haven't done any of the things I want to do with my life yet. I want to travel, but because of all the restrictions, I haven't left New Providence in years. And I want to write music. I've been playing guitar since my dad started teaching me when I was six, and the guitar was bigger than me, but I've never played in public, only at home. And I haven't even gone out on a date with a boy yet, let alone kissed one. For a sixteen-year-old, that's pretty pathetic.

I realise for the first time what being sent to the island really means – the total annihilation of hope.

I peer back up at the image on the screen. I don't see a single person. Just the desolate landscape, rotting under the sun. I wonder if the inhabitants are hiding.

'Can the prisoners escape?' a nearby girl asks the docent, sounding worried. 'Build a boat and sail it back here?'

'Sometimes they try, but they always fail.'

'What a bunch of losers,' Melissa mutters. Her friends titter, but not me.

I guess I just feel bad for any kid who gets sent to this place, even if I know they deserve it. Maybe it's because of what happened to my parents.

They never even received a trial. They just vanished. My dad had been a philosophy professor, and my mum had been a genetic engineer. At least before all the research facilities and universities were placed under government control. My mum quit her job because she said the UNA just wanted to use her research to develop biological weapons.

I never found out exactly why both my parents got seized when they did, although I assume it was partly because of my mum's refusal to cooperate. I was told their old jobs had just been covers anyway, and that they'd been plotting to form a terrorist cell and assassinate government leaders.

For a long time, I was certain this was a lie. But these days I'm no longer sure what to believe. I loved my parents deeply, and I still hate the government for what they did to them. But it's also true that the UNA succeeded in restoring order. There are no more bombs going off in buses, or people dying on the streets in rebel attacks. Perhaps accepting the inconvenience of being controlled by the government is actually the price of safety, like Minister Harka says.

Sometimes I feel angry at my parents for doing whatever it was that got them taken. They must have known I'd be stranded and sent to an orphanage if they got caught. Why would they jeopardise our family like that if they truly loved me?

I assume by now they're probably dead, because prison

conditions are harsh in the UNA. I often try to pretend that the first ten years of my life were a dream, and I was always an orphan. It's easier that way.

I sneak a look at my classmates watching the screen. For once they look excited, probably hoping to see some on-screen violence. Usually their faces are slack with boredom, their minds dulled from taking government-prescribed thought-pills. The thought-pills are meant to increase concentration and help us do well in school, although they just seem to make most kids sleepy. They've never had much effect on me.

In fact, I've always felt slightly different from most of my classmates. This is partly because orphans with dissident parents aren't too popular, but also because the things other kids bond over – like military parades and government war movies – just don't interest me much. And the things that I love, like music and books, don't seem to interest them.

'Oh my God!' Melissa yelps, startling everyone.

At the same instant, another girl shrieks, *'Look!'*

I stare up at the screen as a figure steps into view.

The instant I see his face, I gasp. I expected to see a menacing juvenile delinquent. Someone with a shaved head and blackened teeth, with curved talons for fingernails. Carrying a blood-spattered weapon.

Instead, I see a remarkably good-looking teenage boy staring defiantly into the camera lens. No weapon, no blood, no talons. His dark brown hair is dishevelled, and his eyes are a magnetic shade of blue, set above high cheekbones.

He's lanky, but muscular. Wearing beat-up jeans but no shirt, displaying his tanned, lithe torso.

The strangest thing of all is that the more I stare at the contours of his face, the more I feel like I know this boy from somewhere. But of course that's impossible. I instantly dismiss the feeling. He's just a random Unanchored Soul fending for his life on a prison island, while I'm here on the mainland, on a school-sponsored field trip.

Still, I feel oddly drawn to him for some reason. His blue eyes are piercing and intelligent.

'Ew, he looks so *wild*,' Melissa spits. 'Like an animal.' Other kids instantly chime in with comments.

'I bet he hasn't bathed in a month!'

'Or a year!'

'He doesn't even own a shirt…'

Our earpieces begin playing classical music to calm us.

'Quiet!' Ms Baines admonishes, but no one listens to her, least of all me. I'm still mesmerised by the boy.

He's gesturing with his hands as his eyes remain locked on the camera. At the same time, I see his lips start moving and I realise that he's talking. He looks intense and focused, like he's trying to convey an important message.

I speak up, startling everyone, including myself. 'Can you turn the volume up?'

The docent glances over at me. 'There's no audio. We can't risk inmates trying to corrupt innocent minds with their madness.'

'Yes, yes,' Ms Baines seconds, glowering at me for asking

an innocent question. 'This boy's probably speaking in tongues.'

'Someone should put him down like a rabid dog,' a chunky kid named Jonas mutters. He gets some murmurs of agreement.

'Stop it!' Ms Baines snaps. She glances over at the docent sheepishly, like our class is embarrassing her. Then she turns back to us. 'The island will take care of Unanchored Souls like this boy.' Her voice rises in pitch. 'The island knows what to do with savage teenagers who don't fit in!'

On-screen, the boy continues to talk and gesture fiercely. His hands dash and twirl, drawing complex figures in the air. I realise he's trying to use sign language to communicate his message, but I still can't understand.

It's then that another figure emerges from a cluster of trees behind the boy.

This second figure is huge and menacing – a good head taller than the first one – and he's wearing a long black robe. I can't see his face clearly.

'Whoa. They're gonna fight!' Jonas and his friends begin yammering. My heart starts beating faster.

'We can dim the screen,' the docent says, no doubt trying to protect our tender eyes. But Ms Baines interrupts him.

'Don't. It's important that they see this.'

I watch as the dark figure edges closer, head down, slowly moving up behind his intended victim. The blue-eyed boy is still looking at the camera, oblivious.

'I can't take it!' a girl cries. But she keeps watching, and so do I, the breath stuck in my throat. I'm surprised the boy hasn't heard anything yet, like the crackling of twigs underfoot. But the dark figure is moving forward with methodical precision, like he's done this many times before.

Now he's twenty paces away from the boy.

Now fifteen.

Now ten.

Now five.

At the very last second, the boy's eyes widen, and he spins sideways. Melissa and her friends scream. The attacker lunges forward, his mouth twisted into a toothy snarl. I now see that his face is painted blood-red, with black lines rimming his eyes and lips.

The blue-eyed boy raises an arm, and surprisingly, I catch a flash of something sharp and silver hidden in his palm. It looks like a knife. Almost like he was expecting the attack and was just biding his time.

Then the image pops and slips into a dizzying array of electronic glitches. Everyone gasps. The screen cuts to black.

The docent looks truly alive for the first time. My classmates start babbling:

'Dude, what happened?'

'We want to see!'

'Bring it back up!'

'We lose the satellite feed sometimes,' the docent explains, entering a code on a touch-screen pad. 'Not often, but it happens.'

Our class is getting noisier, and Ms Baines shushes

everyone. Our earpieces are practically blasting classical music now. A moment later the screen flares to life again.

But the blue-eyed boy and the dark figure are both gone. It's just the trees, the grassy plain, the buildings and that strange stone staircase, sitting there in a lifeless tableau.

Goosebumps run up and down my arms. The boy might be dead, unless he did indeed have a knife. Around me everyone is speculating about what might have happened.

The boy definitely didn't look like he belonged on the island to me, but supposedly no one can tell from appearances. An Unanchored Soul is invisible to the eye. Antisocial tendencies cut across skin colour, gender, looks, and everything else. Which is why the GPPT is so important.

At least I have nothing to worry about, I think. Of the millions of kids who take the test every year, only one thousandth of 1 per cent fail and get sent to the island. And I've never done a single thing that suggests I'm a burgeoning psychopath. In fact, I'm pretty much the opposite of an Unanchored Soul. I get good grades, I keep my head down, and I look forward to the future.

While life as an orphan in the UNA might not be perfect, it could be a whole lot worse. So I know that the GPPT will show I pose no threat to anyone – let alone society itself.

Our class moves on to make way for another. Yet something about the blue-eyed boy on the video screen continues to linger in my mind and unsettle me just a tiny bit. *What was he trying to tell us so desperately? And why did he look completely sane if he's supposed to be an Unanchored*

Soul? For an instant, I wonder if it's possible he got sent there by some fluke accident.

Then I put the thought right out of my mind. There'd have to be some kind of terrible mistake during the GPPT for such a thing to happen. And that would be inconceivable, because Minister Harka's government – as it so often reminds us – never makes mistakes.

SCANNED

When the next morning arrives, I slouch downstairs and sit at the long breakfast table at the orphanage, next to Sandy and Claudette, two other girls my age. I've lived with them for six years, but we're not as close as we could be. We orphans tend to keep to ourselves, even as we live on top of one another. All of us know how much it hurts to lose people you care about, and it's hard to risk forming close bonds again.

'Sleep well?' Sandy asks. I nod.

Sandy always smells like cherry lip balm and spends most of her time pining over government-promoted teen idols. Claudette is thin and studious with short black hair. Like many of the girls here, both of them lost their parents in the ongoing wars with Europe and Asia.

'Ready for our big day?' Claudette asks me, arching an eyebrow.

'I guess. You think anyone we know will fail?'

Claudette peers at me over her bowl of cereal. 'Well, they probably won't send any orphans to the island.'

'Really?' Sandy asks.

Claudette looks at her like she's stupid. 'Think about it. It'd be like the government admitting they screwed up if they sent one of us to the Forgotten Place. That they couldn't fix our brains. They've raised us since we were little. What would it say about them and their orphanages if we turned out to be Unanchored Souls?'

'Good point,' Sandy agrees.

After breakfast we line up with dozens of other juniors and head outside to board our bus. The local testing arena isn't far. Just a thirty-minute drive down the Megaway, the twenty-lane highway that cuts across New Providence like a thick grey ribbon. A decade ago the arena used to hold football games. But now it's been enclosed and subdivided into thousands of tiny cubicles, each one housing a scanning machine.

As we drive, I look out the window at all the UNA billboards. Most of them display images of Minister Harka's benevolent, smiling face. With his dark hair, hypnotic eyes and rugged good looks, he appears both attractive and paternal. Even the large diamond-shaped white scar on his left temple, sustained in battle, seems to enhance his appeal. But he also seems curiously ageless. Although I see new pictures of him every day in the government media, he looks exactly like he did when I was eight. Of course no one else seems to notice this, or if they do notice, they don't seem to care.

We eventually reach our destination and turn off the Megaway. In the distance, the covered testing arena resembles the hub of a small city. Doctors in white jackets lead teams of nurses into the gigantic domed structure, and mobs of kids cluster everywhere.

We drive down an access road and pull into the parking lot. Miles of buses and cars sparkle under the sun, as automated shuttles transport people inside. I hear a loud droning noise overhead, and I look out the window of the bus to see a military helicopter passing above us, flying low, its spiderlike shadow falling across the crowd.

On the surface everything seems disorganised. But as I look closer, I see there's a network of guards, teachers and social workers, guiding lines of kids along.

Our driver parks, and we disembark. Some kids look excited, while others look bored. I just feel vaguely annoyed that I have to take a test I already know I'll pass.

I wonder how that blue-eyed boy felt on the day of his test, which probably wasn't even that long ago. He must have suspected he was an Unanchored Soul, with malevolent, antisocial forces lurking inside his brain. I realise that even though he seemed lucid on-screen, it was probably some kind of act.

I gaze around, taking in the sights before me. I wonder how they even ship the few kids who fail the GPPT to the island. Planes? Helicopters? Boats? The whole system is shrouded in secrecy, but somehow it works.

We're led on to one of the shuttles, which comes to a halt several minutes later at an entrance to the arena. After we exit the shuttle, a guard takes us through a brick opening into a noisy atrium. The sound of the teeming crowd echoes off the walls.

Sandy, Claudette and I are shuffled into a long line. A

government official walks down it, handing out paper cards with absurdly long numbers and bar codes printed on them.

Another official appears, barking orders through a megaphone: 'Keep your GPPT scanning cards safe! Do not bend them. Do not tear them. These are important government documents! You will be led into a holding pen. When you hear the nurse call your number, you will follow her into your assigned testing cell!'

The man keeps walking. He repeats his speech all over again. I realise he probably spends his whole day dispensing instructions. A robot could do his job, and might even be nicer about it.

The line keeps moving relentlessly. Warm bodies press against me, reeking of sweat and perfume. Finally we reach a large octagonal waiting area decorated with framed photos of Minister Harka. I realise this must be one of the holding pens. I just stand there with Sandy and Claudette, getting jostled as more kids flood into the room.

But kids are exiting this room as well. On the other side of the vast space is a series of openings. They lead into narrow hallways lit with flickering fluorescent lights.

Every minute or so, a nurse appears from one of them and yells out a number. I check my paper card each time.

Sandy's hair is lank, and her face has gone pale. 'You'd think they'd have some soda pop machines in here,' she complains, twisting her fingers.

'You would think,' Claudette mutters. 'But they don't.'

I shift my weight from one foot to the other.

'Number 014-562-388?' an unsmiling nurse cries, poking her head out of a long hallway to my right.

She starts repeating the digits, practically screaming them. I glance down at my card and realise she's calling my number. I double-check it quickly, like an eager government lotto winner, then blurt: 'That's me!'

I wave goodbye to Sandy and Claudette, and I make my way through the crowd towards the nurse.

She leads me past rows of closed doors until we reach an open room. She takes my card, swipes it in an electronic reader, and gestures for me to go inside. I do as she indicates. She turns to leave, and closes the door behind her.

Not sure what to do, I sit in the lone chair, smoothing down my pleated skirt. The chair is bolted to the cement floor in the centre of the tiny room. I can still hear the noise of thousands of teenagers thrumming away in the holding pens outside, like I'm in an angry beehive.

I glance around my testing cell. It's cold, lit by an overhead bulb, with nothing on the walls but peeling yellow paint. It's like a cross between a dentist's office and a school bathroom.

A laptop computer and a large silver box with wires running out of it sit next to me on top of a storage cabinet. Electrical cables and a strange metal halo hang from the ceiling above my head, just under the light.

I hear a knock at the door as it opens. A tall man in a white lab coat appears. 'Alenna Shawcross?'

I'm surprised he's using my name instead of a number. 'That's me.'

He nods. 'Just making sure I got the right girl.'

As he walks into the room, I check out his government name tag. Oddly, there isn't even a name on it, just a bunch of cryptic symbols.

The man stands next to me, tapping keys on the computer and fiddling with knobs on the silver box. 'I'll be your scanning tech today, Alenna. Roll up a sleeve, if you don't mind.'

'You've done this before, right?' I babble, knowing it's a stupid thing to ask. But I can't stand getting shots or having blood taken. It always makes me nervous.

'Ten thousand times, give or take a few hundred.' He smiles and slips an electrode belt around my chest. I reluctantly roll up one sleeve of my blouse. 'Now take a deep breath and hold it.' He adjusts the belt. 'Now relax.'

Relaxing is hard, but I try to ignore the medical aspects of the GPPT. Then I notice that the tech already has a narrow syringe in his hand. *Where did that come from?*

'You'll feel a small poke,' he says as he suddenly sticks the needle into the crook of my left elbow.

'Ouch!'

He depresses the plunger and shoots the scanning fluid into me, and then withdraws the needle with a grin. 'C'mon. That wasn't too bad, was it?'

As I rub my arm, he dims the light and starts lowering the metal halo from the ceiling. Right away, I begin feeling drowsy, but soon the pleasant sleepiness morphs into woozy seasickness.

'I feel kinda weird,' I manage to say through numbed lips. 'Hard to talk...'

'Oh, that's normal,' the tech replies blithely. He brings the metal halo down further and places it around my head, gently pushing back my hair.

'I don't have to...do anything...right?' I ask, my speech slurred. I'm afraid I'm going to faint.

'Naw, the machine does all the work.' He adjusts the halo, tightening the cold metal around my skull. 'You can even fall asleep if you want. Most kids do, once the serum takes hold.'

'How long...does the test take?'

'Depends on the person.' He leans over and extracts an object from the top drawer of the cabinet. It looks like a candy bar. He unwraps it and hands it to me. It's made of green plastic, with the texture of spongy foam.

'Put that between your teeth,' he instructs. 'It helps calibrate the data.'

Groggy and unquestioning, I do what he says.

'What happens afterwards?' I ask, forcing the muffled words out around the plastic. 'Do I just go home?'

'So many questions.' The tech chuckles. 'You need to stop talking and start relaxing.'

The plastic makes it difficult to talk anyway, so I lean back in the chair. The tech taps a few keystrokes into the computer. I shut my eyes.

But in the final moments before the injection puts me under, I hear something unexpected – other voices inside the tiny room. I realise the door to my testing cell has been opened again, and that people are stepping inside.

I don't understand why they're here. *I'm probably just imagining things.* My eyelids are too heavy to lift now, and the metal halo has me immobilised. I sense that the voices are talking about me. *Is this normal?* They grow fainter, and I realise I'm about to sink into a drugged slumber.

Then, out of nowhere, an image explodes across my vision in the instant before the blackness claims me:

It's the blue-eyed boy from the island.

Beckoning me. Calling my name.

And behind him is that mammoth spiral staircase, baking under the tropical sun.

I try to ask the boy who he is, and what he wants. I try to reach out and grab his hand. But he dissolves into a million shimmering particles, like cosmic dust.

Then waves of silky blackness well up from all sides, and I succumb to the darkness.

FORSAKEN

One second later, I wake up choking and gasping, with the worst headache of my entire life.

I try to open my eyes, but blinding light stabs my retinas. I try to scream, but my lungs are filled with smoke.

My ears are ringing, and I realise I can barely hear. It hurts to think. My hands are numb, my face bruised and battered.

I must have been in an accident. Maybe a car crash on the Megaway. It's all a blank. My memory has been shattered like a smashed mirror.

I dare to open my eyes again, and the brightness causes a fresh surge of pain. But I manage to get on all fours.

What has happened to me?

I raise a trembling hand and touch my forehead. The skin feels raw. Singed and blistered. I'm beyond terror now. I just want to lie down until the pain goes away.

But something inside won't let me give up. I push up with both hands, like an animal rising to its haunches.

When I finally get my eyes to stay open, I'm looking at large green leaves and dense, lush foliage. This is obviously not New Providence, where everything is industrial and utilitarian. This place is tropical. I crouch for a moment, then manage to stand on shaky legs, trying to push past my pain and confusion.

Everywhere I look are ropy vines, exotic trees with intertwined branches and neon pink and blue flowers. The air is humid and dank. It smells like earth and decay.

Some of my memory starts to return: the testing arena, the scan, those voices in the room . . .

But it's not possible.

I stagger around in disbelief, seeking a three-hundred-and-sixty-degree view of my surroundings. In the distance, a huge stone structure ascends into the grey clouds. A broken spiral staircase.

I feel stunned.

Terrified.

Betrayed.

Somehow I am on the island.

The Land Across the Water.

I sink to my knees like I've been punched in the belly. I'm too scared to cry. How could this have happened to me? There's been a horrible mistake!

OK. It's probably just a hallucination brought on by the serum, I tell myself desperately, trying not to hyperventilate. *There's no way I've actually been sent to Island Alpha. I'm not an Unanchored Soul!* But the vegetation, the heat and the smell of the soil are too visceral to be the product of my imagination.

I crouch in the underbrush as my senses slowly return. Other than distant birdcalls, the island around me seems completely deserted. I touch my aching forehead again.

I shouldn't be here. I'm a normal, decent member of the UNA. I'm no different from any of the other orphans or kids at my school. *This is insane.* How did I even get here? There are no tyre tracks or roads. Was I tossed out of a helicopter? Doubtful. I don't have any broken bones, and the pain is already subsiding.

I check my skirt pocket for my government ID card. It's not there. There's no sign of my earpiece either. I feel shorn of my identity. I always hated the photo on my ID card because my hair looked so messy. And I hated my annoying earpiece, too. Now I'd do anything to have them back.

The camera! I suddenly remember that the museum's video screen is the only means of communication that I know of between the UNA and the island. It can't be too far away if I can see that spiral staircase. If I can reach the staircase, then I can find the camera and signal for help.

I'm aware this was what the blue-eyed boy might have been trying to do, even though he didn't seem as panicked as I feel. But no one could understand what he was saying. I won't make the same mistake. I'll write a message somehow and prove I'm not some crazy savage. I'll let them know they've made a huge error. Hopefully they'll send someone out to rescue me right away.

Of course I'm scared that a monstrous figure with a painted face will burst out and grab me before I can reach the camera. For all I know, someone is tracking me already.

Still in shock, I start hobbling through the dense forest in the direction of the giant staircase, moving as fast as I can.

But I don't get very far. I make it only fifteen paces before I see a pale object sticking out from a thick tangle of underbrush.

I stop moving and crouch down, trying to figure out what it is, and whether it's dangerous to walk past it or not. It takes me a second to realise it's a human hand.

I'm instantly terrified, but the hand isn't moving. Maybe its owner is already dead. *Or maybe it's a trap.*

I stand up warily, ready to move on.

Then I hear a voice gasp: 'Help me—'

I freeze, too scared to move. The voice is coming from inside the underbrush.

'Help me!' the voice gasps again. 'Please—' The hand disappears, and the brush starts shaking.

As I back away, a boy slowly sits up. He's dazed and covered in leaves. He looks like he's in pain. His short black hair is scruffy, and he has a horizontal burn mark across his forehead. He's skinny, with a nose that's slightly too large for his angular face. His almond-shaped eyes squint against the light.

He starts coughing, struggling to breathe. I realise he's probably waking up here for the first time. Just like me.

I watch him in fear, prepared to run. Most likely he's a malevolent psychopath. Someone with madness and chaos inside him waiting to flower on the island. An Unanchored Soul. But of course I'm here, and I'm not crazy, so maybe he's normal and there's been another mistake. *But what are the chances of that?*

'Stay away from me,' I say, my voice cracking.

The boy tries to stand, but staggers and falls back down.

He looks up at me with dark eyes. 'We're on Island Alpha, right?' he croaks. He sounds scared, but not surprised. I don't answer at first. But he keeps staring at me.

'There's been a mistake,' I say finally, as I begin backing away. 'I don't—'

'You're from New Providence,' he interrupts.

I stop moving, startled. 'How did you—?'

'I am too. I just figured they'd dump us near each other. There are probably other kids somewhere around here – unless we're the only two who made the cut today.' He finally gets to his feet and stands there swaying. He's only a couple of inches taller than I am. 'I was afraid this would happen to me.'

'Why?' I ask nervously, muscles still primed to sprint away from him.

'Because I don't trust the government, that's why. I'm not an Unanchored Soul, and I'm betting you're not either. I've heard stories about kids getting sent here just for criticising Minister Harka.' He hesitates. 'And I've heard worse things too. That every now and then the government sends some normal kids here for the crazy ones to hunt for sport. Just so they don't cause trouble.'

I don't respond. Back home, antigovernment talk like that could get you locked up. Of course, now we're in the worst situation I can imagine, so what we say probably doesn't matter any more.

'I'm David,' the boy says, extracting himself from the brush. 'David, not Dave. I hate nicknames. You?'

'Alenna.' I still don't trust him. 'Don't get too close to me or I'll run. Are you really from New Providence?'

'Yeah, centre city. Franklin Street.'

I nod. 'I'm from Thayer Corridor.'

'That's not too far from where I live.'

I watch him closely, looking for any signs of aberrant behaviour. I don't see any, at least not yet. 'I'm heading for the camera,' I finally tell him. 'The one that's linked to the Harka Museum. There's obviously been a mistake, so I'm going to signal for help.'

'I doubt anyone's gonna help us.'

'Why's that?'

He doesn't answer.

'You have a better plan?' I look around, thinking about all the awful things that might happen to me if I keep standing here talking.

'Honestly? No.' David bends down. 'Can't find my glasses.' He starts rummaging in the underbrush. 'Ah, here they are.' He lifts them up and puts them on, adjusting the black plastic frames.

'We need to move,' I tell him, edging away. We're in so much danger, the last thing I want to do is waste time. I'm not even sure if this boy is an ally for real, or if he's putting on an act.

'Wait. I'm coming.' He takes a few tentative steps forward and winces. 'I hurt my foot somehow. It's been killing me ever since I woke up.'

In a way, I'm relieved to know he's injured. He's less of a threat if I can outrun him. He takes another step forward, limping.

I think about trying to ditch him in the forest. But for the moment it feels better to be with someone else than all alone. I'll just have to keep my guard up. I still can't believe that I've ended up here.

We start hiking in the direction of the camera. I push my aching body forward, climbing over fallen tree branches and rotting logs. David lags behind. The ground is spongy beneath my feet, marshy and wet. My shoes are already soaked and muddy. Mosquitoes and gnats swarm my mouth and eyes, buzzing against my ears.

David and I don't talk much. It's hard enough just to keep going, and the thick, damp air makes it tough to breathe. Both of us are panting.

'Alenna, stop,' David suddenly whispers.

I look back at him. 'What?'

'Listen.'

It's then that I hear the howling noise:

Aooooooooooooo!

It's a plaintive, animalistic wail that echoes through the trees.

My body stiffens. The sound isn't close, but it's not too far away either. I move backwards and press myself against a tree trunk, holding my breath until the noise stops. I exhale slowly. I look over at David. He's crouching low to the ground.

'What was that?' I whisper.

'Don't know, but it didn't sound good.'

We wait another minute.

Only silence.

Eventually we resume our desperate hike.

Fifteen minutes later, we finally reach the clearing in front of the spiral staircase. After a few seconds of anxious searching, I spot the museum camera, wedged up fifty feet high in a thick Plexiglas box, between the *V* of two massive tree branches. Its lens points directly down at us.

I'm now in the exact same place where I saw the blue-eyed boy. Even though it's sweltering in this jungle, I instantly get the chills. I try not to think about the robed figure. I suppress my fear – I can't let it overwhelm me. David and I stare up at the camera as I listen to the blood rush through my veins.

The camera glares back at us with its cold, dead eye. I can see our reflections in the Plexiglas box. I already look filthy, small, and terrified – which is exactly how I feel.

David just stands there, looking resigned, with his shoulders slumped. Like he expected this would be his fate. *Like he knows he's guilty of something.* But what? He seems like the shy, studious type. Maybe he was planning on doing something awful, and the GPPT detected his mental aberration, just as it should?

'I gotta find something to write with,' I explain. I kneel and look for a thin twig. I find one almost instantly. But it's harder to find something to gouge letters on to. My fingers plunge around until I discover a large, damp, waxy leaf, the size of my hand. I stand up in view of the camera.

'I'll keep watch,' David says. 'Make sure no one sneaks up from behind.'

I take the stick and start writing on the leaf. It doesn't work too well, but I keep at it until letters are marked into its surface, like messy etchings.

I manage to fit two words on the leaf: 'HELP!' and 'MISTAKE!' I hold the leaf up to the camera, point at myself, and then at the words. If anyone's watching, I'm sending a clear message. I toss that leaf down, find another larger one, and write my full name on it, trying not to tear the leaf. The letters are small and jagged, but the docent, or whoever controls the camera, can probably zoom in if he wants.

'What's your last name?' I ask David, trying to be generous and give him the benefit of the doubt. He's still keeping lookout. 'I'll write something for you. Maybe they'll come rescue both of us.'

He turns towards me. 'You really think someone will come, don't you?'

'Maybe.' The truth is, I don't know. I've never heard of anyone being rescued from Island Alpha, or any mistake of this magnitude being made. But I'm not going to let that stop me. 'I guess it feels better to try than to just stand around doing nothing.'

David sighs. 'Aberley,' he says. 'That's my last name.' He spells it for me.

I find another leaf and write it down for him. Then I hold it up to the camera and point in his direction. If he's sane like me, then this might help him get rescued. At the same time, if he's an Unanchored Soul, then maybe putting his name on the leaf will hasten my own rescue – because the authorities will be worried about my safety.

I know that if I'm still on this island when night falls, it's going to be a struggle to survive. I'm a city girl, used to my familiar routines at school and the orphanage. And now I'm on an island with thousands of violent, potentially psychotic teens, with David as my only companion.

I lower the leaf, feeling a little stupid that I even tried. We don't need to be standing here in the open, waiting for some frightening apparition to explode from the trees and snatch us. So I stick the leaves on branches, check to make sure they're in camera range, and then David and I head back towards the forest.

I try to imagine what my dad would tell me to do. Until the day he got taken, he was always good in tough spots. He'd probably tell me to find a safe hiding place, keep an eye on David, and try to think my way out of the situation.

I'm about to re-enter the trees, when I hear the faint rustle of nearby branches. The sound is so soft that anywhere else I probably wouldn't have noticed it.

I stop moving. The sound comes again.

'David?' I whisper. He's already heard it too.

I look back at the camera. No doubt it catches the terrified expression on my face. But the camera can't help me. The rustling noise gets louder, like someone's headed straight in our direction.

'Don't move,' David cautions softly. 'Don't make any noise.'

My first instinct is to run, but I know once I get into the depths of the forest, I'm going to get lost pretty quickly. My eyes flick towards the spiral staircase. I'm too far away to make a dash for it. And besides, it doesn't lead anywhere. Someone could trap me up there if they wanted to.

David sinks down to the ground, motioning for me to do the same. So instead of running, I crouch down near a fallen tree covered with lichens.

I press myself flat in the underbrush behind it, trying to make myself invisible. David is a few feet to my left. I take shallow breaths, even though my chest is pounding. The rustling sounds grow louder. I peek through the underbrush above the fallen tree.

Standing at the edge of the clearing is a four-legged animal, the size of a large pig. But it's not like any pig I've ever seen. While its body is stocky and its legs end in cloven hooves, its head is sleek and vicious with a narrow, pointed snout.

The animal sniffs the air, revealing rows of tiny sharp teeth. It doesn't see me or David yet. Its yellow eyes are wild, almost mad-looking.

It roots in the earth like a boar, digging its teeth into the mud as it grunts.

Suddenly, it tosses its head back and opens its mouth

wide. A loud, screeching explosion of noise bursts forth. Unable to stop myself, I let out a startled gasp.

David shoots me a warning glance. The screeching stops instantly. *Did the animal hear me?* I'm too scared to look up and find out.

Then I hear another sound, faint but distinct. A harsh, guttural shriek. I realise that somewhere out there is a second one of these animals. David signals at me to start moving backwards.

I risk a terrified peek again, thinking that the creature will probably be looking for its companion now.

But I'm wrong.

The animal is staring directly at me, its yellow eyes locked on mine.

It sees me. Knows exactly where I am. I start inching back slowly, my belly still on the ground.

The animal raises a hoof and takes a step in my direction. A silvery rope of saliva hangs down from its black gums. I start wriggling away from it faster, arms and legs moving frantically. The creature bares its teeth, taking another step. Then another. It swings its head in David's direction. Now it has seen both of us.

I finally scrabble to my feet. David does the same. In the second before we turn to flee, I catch a flicker of movement from the corner of my eye, headed our way.

At first I think it's the second animal. But then I see that it's a dark figure with a painted face – *exactly like the figure who attacked the blue-eyed boy*. The figure blazes a trail directly towards the creature in a rapid, swirling frenzy.

The animal hears the person coming and arches its neck, emitting that horrible screech again. At least it has lost interest in me and David. It pivots and bares its fangs, still screeching. But it's no match for the whirlwind heading towards it at maximum velocity. I see the flash of metal blades in the figure's hands as it descends on the animal.

Everything happens in a blur as knives plunge into the animal's flank. I can't see the figure's face now because its black robes are flying and fluttering all around it.

The figure rides the animal downwards as it plummets headfirst into the earth. A long metal blade churns its way through the animal's throat, blood arcing outwards and spattering on to the leaves.

'Run! C'mon!' David screams at me.

I finally turn and race blindly through the forest, branches whipping at my face and hands, lashing the skin. I trip over gnarled roots and fallen vines, but keep scrabbling forward. I hear David hobbling behind me.

The life expectancy here might be eighteen years, but I won't even have lasted one hour! I always thought I was smarter than a lot of the kids back home. Yet my classmates and fellow orphans are probably safe right now in the UNA, and here I am on the island, about to die.

It takes another fifteen minutes of running before I realise that I don't hear anything behind me. The animal's screeches have ceased. I assume the figure killed it. I wonder if it's possible that he didn't see me or David, but that seems unlikely. It's more like he just waited until one of us distracted the creature before going in for the kill. Like he was using us as bait.

I finally stop running when I reach another clearing. I'm gasping for air like I'm surfacing from a deep sea dive. I stagger around, trembling, looking behind me. Above the canopy I can still see the upper portion of the broken stone staircase, which means I'm not lost. At least not yet. But I don't see David anywhere.

'David?' I call out softly, afraid to get too loud in case someone – or something – hears me. 'Where are you?'

It takes a moment, but I finally hear a faint reply. 'Over here.'

I see him emerge from the forest. I move towards him. He's limping severely now, like he can barely put any weight on his injured foot. Unanchored Soul or not, he's got to be safer for me to be with than those creatures or the robed figure.

'So, it's not safe on the ground.' He takes a deep, shuddering breath and then exhales. 'When it gets dark, we're gonna have to climb a tree and sleep in the branches. We can take turns keeping watch.'

I feel sick. 'Who do you think that guy with the knives was?'

'No one we want to meet. Hopefully he's preoccupied with his kill. We need to start a fire and make some torches.'

'That'll give our position away,' I point out.

'I'm pretty sure he saw us already, and we need some kind of weapons. Besides, torches will keep any animals at bay.'

'We don't have a way to start a fire,' I tell David, looking around. I'm afraid the robed figure will reappear. But David is already scavenging in the underbrush. He brings up a pair of thick, dry branches.

'Perfect,' he says.

'We have to keep moving,' I remind him, but he limps over to a tree and begins peeling strips of dead bark from its trunk. 'What are you doing?'

'Making our torches.'

David wraps the bark in loops around the end of each branch. Then he tucks one branch under his arm and fiddles with the other one. To my surprise, moments later I see a flash of light appear. I realise that somehow, impossibly, he has started a fire. He holds the lit torch in front of him and inspects it.

'How did you do that?' I ask, startled by his acumen out here in the forest.

He looks over at me and arches an eyebrow. 'Magic.' It's only then that I see he's clutching a handful of matches. 'I sewed these into my back pocket, just in case. Figured they might not find 'em.' He passes me the unlit torch and lights the end of it. 'It won't burn for long.'

'Thanks.' I hold my torch out in front of me like a sword.

'So, why do you think you got sent here?' David asks as we start hiking again. 'You honestly believe it's all just a big mistake?'

'Of course,' I tell him. 'Why, did you do something?'

He shakes his head. 'No, I told you.' He peers around.

'We're exiles now. It doesn't matter if we're innocent or not. The UNA doesn't care about us.'

'I hope you're wrong.' We keep walking.

I'm still amazed at how desolate this place seems. It feels like David and I are the only two people alive right now. *Other than the robed figure and the creatures trying to kill us.*

David gestures up ahead. 'Look.' For a moment, I think he has seen someone else, and I feel a surge of fear. But then I realise he's pointing at a huge oak tree, at least sixty feet tall, with a stout trunk. 'That's the kind of place we could sleep in.'

I don't really like the idea of climbing a tree and sleeping in it, because I'm afraid I'll fall out. I also don't like the idea of falling asleep around David, although so far he has only done things to help me.

He hobbles over to the tree. 'You any good at climbing?' he asks.

I shake my head.

'Yeah, me neither.'

I walk over and join him at the tree.

'Hand me your torch,' he says. I give it to him, gazing up at the branches. 'My foot's busted. Can you test it for us?'

'You mean try climbing it? Now? Are you serious?'

'If we test it now, we can find out if it's safe. If it is, then we'll come back later today. Make this our base camp until we figure out what to do next, and where to go. We also need to find some fresh water. Maybe we can spot a river or lake from the tree.'

'Fine, but I'm wearing a skirt, so don't look.' I gingerly put my foot on a low branch and hoist myself up. The branch holds my weight easily. 'This might actually work.' I grab hold of another branch above me and pull myself up faster.

'Can you see anything from up there?'

I gaze out into the endless green landscape. 'Just more trees.' I pull myself up higher. Luckily, the branches remain sturdy.

David is walking around the tree. 'Looks good. I guess we know where we'll be spending the night.' He sticks one torch into the earth, and then the other, so that they stand upright. 'I better get up there too. See if it can hold both our weights. Can you help me?'

I'm about to climb down and help him up, but right as David finishes speaking, what I've been dreading all along finally happens.

A robed figure steps out from the trees, just twenty paces from us.

It's not the one who attacked the animal earlier today. This one is even larger, and he's wearing a scowling metal mask daubed with orange war paint.

There's nowhere to go.

David and I are trapped.

'Keep the hell away!' David immediately calls out, grabbing both of our torches. I clamber down from the tree, and he stands protectively in front of me. With shaking hands, I take my torch back from him. 'Don't come near us! I mean it.'

The figure doesn't answer. He just keeps watching us from behind his implacable mask.

I risk a glance behind me and flinch. Two boys with painted faces lean against other trees. *Where did they come from?* I hear more noises in the distance. Footsteps approaching. We're being surrounded.

I turn back to the masked figure, panicked. 'Who are you?' I call out. 'What do you want with us?' My voice is close to breaking. 'I don't even belong here!'

I can hear the boys behind us moving closer. They could kill us right now. Everything starts becoming dreamlike and floaty as the blood rushes from my head.

A muffled voice suddenly speaks from behind the metal mask. It's deep. Ominous. But it definitely belongs to a teenage boy. 'We own you.'

'Wh-what?' I stutter.

'You're in our sector. We found you. That means we own you.'

The boy's companions continue moving towards us. More figures emerge from the trees. Twelve in total. All with painted faces and black robes.

'I've got a knife!' David lies, sounding pretty convincing. He swings his torch wildly. 'If you touch me or the girl, I'll stab you. Don't mess with us.'

'We're taking both of you to see the Monk,' the masked boy continues, ignoring David completely.

I sputter, 'I'm not going anywhere with—'

Right then, one of the other boys lunges forward and grabs my arm. He knocks the torch right out of it. I try to swat his hand away, but his jagged fingernails bite angry crescents into my flesh through my blouse. I cry out in pain, but he doesn't loosen his grasp, even when David tries to push him away with his torch.

'Quit struggling!' the robed figure hisses at me as another boy reaches us. I start screaming and fighting. But they keep grabbing at me, their robes flapping. I feel like I'm being battered by ocean waves, and I fight against the tide.

'Get off me!' I scream.

Figures surround David too, as he curses and tries to punch at them. I see one of them rip the torch from his hands and extinguish it.

'The Monk will tell us what to do with you,' the boy in the metal mask intones loudly. And then, clapping his hands together, he addresses the others: 'Quick! Take our new slaves to the Monk!'

'No, wait! Stop!' I shriek, continuing to fight and claw at their faces. I hear David scream as one of the boys stomps on his damaged foot. The boys surround and overwhelm us, chattering and raving. Their rough hands grasp me tight as they begin to propel me through the trees.

Then a voice cuts through the hubbub like a sharp blade, and everyone stops what they're doing. This new voice is loud, female and angry:

'Let go of them right now, you ugly bastards!'

A girl is standing on top of a nearby hill in the forest, staring down at us through the trees. She looks fierce, with streaks of blue dye in her hair, and metal piercings in her nose, ears and lip. A sleeve of homemade tattoos runs down her left arm. She's wearing jeans and a tank top made out of tanned animal hide.

In her hand is a weapon. It looks like an old-fashioned shotgun, but I'm not certain. All guns are banned in the UNA, except for the AK-47 assault rifles carried by the police.

'If you let 'em go right now, there won't be any consequences,' the girl calls down to the masked boy.

He looks up at her hungrily. 'Maybe we can make a trade.'

'No trades.' The girl carefully steps a few paces down the hillside. She's tall and athletic, with a feral look in her brown eyes. She's maybe a year or more older than me. She keeps her gun pointed straight at the boy's chest. 'You know the rules. New arrivals belong to us. You can't take them if they turn up in the blue sector.'

'They weren't in the blue sector. They were over by the stairs—'

'Well, they're in the blue sector now. And this sector is *ours*.'

The boy just sneers at her through his mask. To my horror, I see that his teeth have been chiselled into sharp points. 'The rules are changing, Gadya. Every day the Monk grows stronger—'

'You wish,' she interrupts. 'But these two are mine.'

I realise they're bartering over us like we're pieces of property. 'Hey!' I yell. 'I'm right here! I don't belong to either of you.'

'Neither do I,' David adds, shoving one of the robed figures away from him.

'Shut up!' Gadya snaps at us. She turns back to the masked boy. 'I'm taking them to our village, whether you like it or not.'

The boy looks around at his companions. All of them are silent, but I sense their bristling hostility.

'Soon your village will be meaningless,' he growls. 'The Monk will control this entire island. North and south. East and west. Then where will you go? Into the ocean?' He raises his right hand, showing off a short, curved blade.

Gadya ignores his jibes. 'Get your asses up here,' she hisses at me and David.

We exchange glances. It's not much of a choice. Neither of us knows what's going on, but we're not about to question our good fortune.

We head up the hill towards Gadya. None of the boys stop us, although I can feel their eyes heating my back.

'I'm gonna tell the Monk about this!' the masked boy threatens Gadya. 'You've got no idea how powerful he is now!'

I glance back and see that the boy's hands are shaking with anger and frustration. Or maybe just from crazed devotion to the Monk – *whoever that is.* The boy's cohorts draw closer, like they're preparing to gang up and fight us.

Gadya looks down at us from the hill. 'Hurry!' she snaps.

I scramble up the rest of the hillside, with David limping behind me. We finally reach Gadya and look back at the boys. They stand there clutching knives, hatchets and other primitive weapons.

The masked boy turns and mutters something inaudible to his companions. I hear angry murmurs of agreement as they brandish their knives. I don't think these boys are going to back down. Apparently neither does Gadya.

She raises the gun to her shoulder, taking aim again. 'You and your friend better be fast runners,' she whispers to me, sounding worried for the first time. 'Or you're gonna get us all killed!'

GADYA

A split second later, the boy at the bottom of the hill pivots towards us and tears off his mask. Underneath, I see an acne-scarred face with a wide nose, contorted into a grotesque scowl. 'In the beloved name of the Monk, we're claiming this girl and this boy as our slaves!' He storms forward up the hill, followed by the others.

Gadya raises her gun. For a second, I think she's going to fire. Instead, she flings the weapon as hard as she can at the scowling boy's face. The butt connects with his nose with a sharp crack. He flails and careens backwards down the hill, losing his balance.

Gadya jerks me sideways, pulling me into the forest. 'This way!' she yells as David grabs for my other hand.

Another robed figure reaches the top of the hill, faster than I expected. I turn around, and he's almost on me and David. Gadya has let go of my arm. She's a few feet ahead, and she can't turn back in time. The figure lunges forward, and I scream in terror.

Then, suddenly, he gets knocked right out of the way, and crashes forward on to his face. It takes me a second to realise what happened. It's David. He's thrown himself at the figure, tackling him by the legs and bringing him down.

'Run!' he screams at me. 'I can't make it anyway, 'cause of my foot! If you survive, come back for me!'

'David!' I yell, hesitating. I can't believe he'd sacrifice himself like this for me. These are not the actions of an Unanchored Soul.

I hear other boys rushing up the hill and through the trees, calling out violent threats. If I wait one second longer, I'm going to get taken. 'I'll come back and rescue you!' I call out to him. 'I swear it!'

As other figures reach him, I start running as fast as I can, chasing after Gadya. She's barely visible in the forest ahead. 'Gadya – wait!'

'Pick up the pace!' she screams back at me. 'Or you'll end up like your friend.' She takes a hard left on to a narrow dirt trail. I follow. She moves with incredible grace and speed.

'Please—' I gasp, but she doesn't slow down. I'm terrified of losing her among the trees. She's just a faint flash ahead of me. I keep running.

We're putting space between ourselves and the boys. Maybe their bulky robes are slowing them down. And obviously a lot of them have surrounded David already. *But what will happen if we stop running?*

Then, suddenly – horrifyingly – I realise that I've lost Gadya. I didn't even look away. She was directly ahead of me one second, then gone the next. How could she disappear like that?

'Help!' I yell wildly, not caring that the boys might hear. 'Gadya!' I keep plunging forward out of sheer momentum.

Then the earth gives way under my feet.

For a second, I'm suspended in air, running through space. The ground is disintegrating beneath me like I've leapt off a cliff.

My shins collide with something hard, and I cry out in pain. Rough hands drag me down into some kind of earthen hole. An object slides over the top of my head. It's a woven blanket of leaves and twigs.

I look around and see Gadya sitting there, staring back at me. I'm panting like crazy, completely disoriented. I slowly realise that I've fallen into a deep hole dug in the trail, now masked by the leaf blanket above us. It's like a grave, but square. It smells like bamboo.

Gadya shoves her hand against my mouth and pushes me hard against one side of the hole.

'I didn't know you'd cause me so much trouble!' she whispers angrily. 'I didn't think they'd chase us this far!'

I can't respond because her hand is covering my mouth. In the distance, I hear boys' voices.

'Don't worry. No one will find us.' Gadya finally lets me go and starts digging around in the dirt. 'But if they do, I've got a nice surprise for 'em.' She pulls up a knife in a leather sheath, and tugs it out with her teeth.

I swallow hard, gasping for air. 'What is this place?'

She stares at me as she plays with her knife. 'A spider hole. I helped dig it three months ago. We've dug them all over this sector.'

'Your gun—' I begin, curious why she'd trade such a

powerful weapon for a simple knife. 'Why didn't you shoot?'

'No bullets. We haven't had them for months.' She pauses. 'And most of the guns don't work either. The Monk's drones don't know that yet.' She cocks her head to listen. The voices outside are fading as the boys move on. 'Besides, it's not our way to kill. Unless we have to.'

I try to make my legs more comfortable. My ankles are throbbing. 'What's going to happen to David?'

'Why do you care?' Her eyes narrow suspiciously. 'Do you know him from back home or something?'

'No, I just met him. But we're both from New Providence, and he saved my life.'

'Don't worry about him. Just worry about yourself.'

'I told him we'd come back and rescue him.'

'Then you lied. Accept his fate and move on.'

I can't accept it, but I don't want to argue with her. 'So are we trapped here?' I whisper. 'In this little hole?'

This little hole, Gadya repeats mockingly. 'You'd be dead without it.'

'I'm not criticising it. I'm grateful.' We sit in awkward silence. I keep sneaking glances at her. Beneath the piercings and tattoos, and the mane of blue hair, I can see a regular teenage girl. Not too different from me. She catches me looking at her, so I glance away. Now I hear only the cries of tropical birds above us. The robed boys have completely passed us by. 'So, your name's Gadya?' I finally ask.

She nods sharply. Doesn't offer a last name.

'I'm Alenna.'

She nods again, less sharply. So I finally dare to ask the question that's on my mind. 'No one's coming to rescue me, are they? I mean, no one from back home.'

Gadya shakes her head. 'Nope.'

'Then why did I get sent here? And why are kids like you and David here? I thought everyone on this island was supposed to be an Unanchored Soul. But David and you seem so—'

'Normal?' she interrupts. 'Of course we are. Just like you. Nothing they told us in the UNA is true. Not about Island Alpha or anything else.'

'Then tell me what's really going on. Why were those boys chasing us?'

She glares at me. 'Doling out reality checks isn't part of my job. Our leader will explain everything to you when we get back to the village. My job was just to find any new arrivals and bring you in.' She runs a hand through her blue hair. 'Guess I only did the job half right, seeing as your friend didn't make it. But it doesn't matter much. Kids always turn up around here, so we take turns searching the area every day.' She sheaths her knife and hides it in the dirt floor of the spider hole, presumably for the next person who needs it.

Then she lifts the roof of our enclosure and peers out. 'All clear,' she declares, pushing back the roof the rest of the way, letting light filter in. 'I need to get you to the village right away. Get you vaccinated.'

I look at her, startled. 'Vaccinated?'

'I bet you only have another hour. After that, it'll be too

late.' She puts her hands on the edge of the hole and pushes herself up and out, in a smooth, practised gesture. Then she brushes herself off and extends a hand. I take it and struggle my way out, feeling awkward and oafish. I crawl on to the trail and stand there on wobbly, aching legs. Gadya kicks the roof back over the hole.

'You're scaring me,' I tell her. 'Vaccinated against what?'

'You talk too much. You ask too many questions. That's not a good trait to have here.' Gadya starts heading down the trail again. I start jogging along behind her.

'Then give me some answers. Don't treat me like I'm a moron.'

'I don't think you're a moron. You're just green.' She lets out a frustrated sigh. 'Being green can get people killed.' She lifts up a vine as thick as my wrist, and we pass underneath it.

'At least tell me about the vaccine.'

Gadya looks back at me. 'It prevents disease. Trust me, you need it.'

We reach a wider path, lined with magnolia trees. Gadya pauses for a second, listening. All is silent. We start moving again, wading rapidly through the tangled underbrush.

'And the island?' I press, trying to gather as much information as possible. 'Where are we exactly? The Atlantic? The Pacific?'

'First of all, no one calls this place "the island". We call it "the wheel", because it's divided into misshapen triangular sectors. Like pie slices. There are six of them. Don't ask me why – I didn't make the rules. The UNA did. The Monk controls four sectors – orange, purple, yellow and red. Our tribe controls one – the blue sector. The sixth one's called the grey zone. Bad things happen in there.'

Her grim tone gives me a momentary chill.

'We used to control the orange sector,' she continues, 'but the Monk's been expanding his territory. More and more kids keep joining his gang, or religion, or whatever he calls it. You picked a hell of a time to turn up here. We're in the middle of a war. And we're losing.'

My head is buzzing as we walk, filled with a million more questions. 'A war against the Monk? Who is he?'

'An old man who's been here longer than anyone else. He claims he has supernatural powers. He tells everyone that the wheel is a test, and if they do what he says, they'll get off it one day – or find their reward in the afterlife. Crazy, desperate kids turn to him, looking for meaning.' She lowers her voice. 'We call him the Cannibal Monk.'

I stop in my tracks, horrified. '*Cannibal?* As in, like, he eats people?'

Gadya chuckles. 'Not flesh. Souls. That's what he's after.' She glances back and sees the stricken look on my face. 'It's a figure of speech.' She increases her pace. 'C'mon.'

The path is wide enough to walk shoulder to shoulder, although it's hard keeping up with Gadya. 'So how long have you been here?'

'Fourteen months,' she replies, like that's nothing. Then she points up ahead. 'Look, we're almost at the village. We're rebuilding from a night-time raid. If we build huts, eventually the Monk's drones burn 'em down.' The trees thin as we crest a ridge and approach a grassy clearing the size of a baseball diamond. 'This island is allergic to civilization. The Monk makes sure of that.'

I don't fully understand, but I'm too dazed and distracted to ask any more questions. We've reached the edge of the trees and I'm gazing out at the clearing. I see about a hundred teenagers, my age or older, hammering and assembling makeshift shacks around the edges of the clearing. Hammocks hang between crooked palm trees. *So this is how exiles live.*

Most of the kids are dirty and unkempt, with ragged hair. A few even have wispy beards. But none look particularly crazy or dangerous, not like the boys in robes. These kids are mostly wearing T-shirts and jeans, or shorts. I wonder if the blue-eyed boy will be among them, if he's still alive, and if this is his village. I look for him, hoping to see him, but don't find his face anywhere.

A huge stone fire pit sits in the centre of the clearing, about twelve feet in diameter. It holds only ashes at the moment, but the odour of smoke and greasy barbecued meat hovers in the air.

As Gadya and I emerge, some of the villagers stare in our direction.

'Took you long enough!' a boy yells at Gadya. He's got muscular shoulders, and he's lugging a large sheet of warped plywood. Gadya flicks him off with a calloused middle finger. He laughs. I barely know Gadya, but I already wish I could be as confident and brash as she is. Especially here on this island.

I'm surprised there aren't more people at the village. The island is supposed to hold tens of thousands of Unanchored Souls. So where is everyone? Maybe they've joined forces with the Monk already. Despite Gadya's advice to forget about David, I'm worried about what's happening to him right now. He probably needs the same vaccine that I'm about to get.

'I know what you're thinking,' Gadya murmurs. 'This village is small, and it looks like crap, right?'

I don't reply.

'There's more of us in the blue sector than just these kids,' Gadya elaborates. 'But it's safest to keep each village small and spread out. Easier to mobilise, and easier to move and rebuild. There's another village thirty miles east. Another thirty miles south. There are fifteen villages total in our sector, but we don't communicate with them much unless we need to. Each village is pretty self-sufficient.'

I'm half-listening, distracted by thoughts of the vaccine, and also by the sight of a boy and a girl fast approaching across the clearing. Both are fair-haired, slender and attractive. A few years older than me. The girl is wearing a white sundress, and the boy is wearing a white T-shirt and slacks.

The boy waves at Gadya as he nears. 'Trouble?'

'Nothing I couldn't handle. Just some drones. I set 'em straight and—'

'Where's your gun?' the girl interrupts, frowning.

Gadya glares at her. 'Up a drone's ass. Why?'

The boy laughs, but the girl keeps frowning. I want to speak up for Gadya and explain that if she hadn't thrown the gun, we wouldn't be here right now. But I stay quiet.

The boy and the girl scrutinise me. I'm struck by the way their pale skin seems to glow. They both have delicate features, straight noses and expressive blue eyes. I wonder if they're siblings – maybe even twins.

'We've been waiting for you,' the boy says. 'Well, not you specifically, but for the next arrivals.'

'There was another one, but the Monk's drones got him,' Gadya explains. 'He's either dead already or the drones are brainwashing him into joining 'em. It's too late to go back for him.'

'Pity. I'm sure you'll do better next time.' It takes me a moment to place the unusual lilt in the girl's voice. The boy has it too. Then I realise they must be from far up north. The place once called Canada.

The boy extends his hand to me. 'My name's Matthieu Veidman,' he says. 'I run things around here.'

I tell him my name as I return his handshake. His grip is firm and dry, despite the heat.

He gestures at his companion. 'This is Meira.'

The girl extends her hand coolly, and I shake it, too. 'Did Gadya explain about the vaccine?' she asks.

'Kind of.'

'My predecessor discovered how to make it,' Veidman says. 'It prevents a malarial fever that used to be common around here.' He pauses. 'Come with me to my cabin, and I'll get you sorted out.' He turns to Meira and Gadya. 'Bring me ten ml's of the new batch.'

'Sure,' Meira says, heading away at once with Gadya. I'm pretty surprised they even have needles and vaccines here.

Veidman calls after Meira, a few final words in French. Then he turns back to me. 'I'm from Montreal – in Quebec,' he explains. 'I mean, before it all became part of the UNA and Minister Harka renamed everything.'

Sensing that he probably has a lot more answers than Gadya, I blurt, 'So tell me everything I need to know about this island! Is there any way to get off it?'

Surprised by my outburst, he laughs. 'Look, on the wheel you have to learn as you go. That's how most of us have made it this far.' He cocks an eyebrow at me. 'You gotta use your wits. I'm nineteen and a half. That's one year and six months beyond my life expectancy, and I don't plan on dying anytime soon.' Veidman puts a gentle hand on my shoulder and starts steering me towards a shack about a hundred paces away. 'But feel free to ask me whatever questions you want.'

I don't know where to begin. 'I thought only Unanchored Souls got sent here. But I'm not like that. And neither are any of you. Why would the government lie?'

'We don't know. There are definitely some evil people here on the wheel, but a lot of regular ones as well. It's not too different from back home, I guess.'

'Gadya told me about the Cannibal Monk,' I say. 'That you guys are at war with him.'

'The boys you met in the forest today are the Monk's warriors, his hunters,' Veidman tells me. 'We call them drones. They're like worker bees protecting the hive. Other

62

groups exist in the sectors controlled by the Monk, like gatherers, builders and cooks. His people worship him, and they've been taking over the island one sector at a time for years. We're the only sector of kids left who oppose him.'

We reach some colourful blankets on the ground outside Veidman's shack. We both sit down, cross-legged.

'Actually, we think some drones might have infiltrated our sector,' Veidman continues. 'That they're living among us, maybe even in this village, pretending to be on our side. But waiting for the perfect moment to sabotage everything...'

His words trail off as Meira and Gadya reappear. Meira is holding a medical syringe in her left hand. It's just dangling there, filled with dark fluid. Red, like blood. She walks over and hands the syringe to Veidman.

Veidman glances over at me. 'I was planning on becoming a doctor before I got sent to the wheel.' He holds up the syringe and squirts a little liquid into the air. 'Now I just get to play one.' He smiles. 'Show me your arm.'

Suddenly I'm back in the scanning cell, with the tech in the white lab coat leaning over me.

'Flashback,' I croak, breaking out in a cold sweat. I feel woozy. Faint. And embarrassed.

'Happens sometimes.' Veidman leans forward, pushing up my right sleeve. He taps the inside of my arm, searching for a vein.

'You know why you felt like crap when you landed here?' Gadya asks from behind me.

Veidman frowns. 'Probably not the best time—'

Gadya keeps talking: 'Why your head hurt? Why your thoughts were all fuzzy?'

I glance back at her over my shoulder. 'No. Tell me.'

'Gadya.' I hear a cold note of warning in Meira's voice. But I don't want Gadya to be quiet. I want to know what happened to me. It's my body. I have a right.

Gadya moves forward into my view. 'Ever heard of ECT?' she asks. 'Also known as electroshock therapy? That metal band in the testing cell didn't scan your mind. It delivered an eight-hundred milliamp jolt of electricity, right into your frontal lobes!'

I yank my arm out of Veidman's grasp, horrified. 'Electroshock! But that was banned years ago!' Tears spring into my eyes. The government tried to fry my mind?

'It's no big deal,' Veidman says, sounding resigned. 'Happens to everyone who gets sent to the wheel. They use a low dose to disorient us. To make us forget how we got here.' He pulls my arm forward again, ignoring my dismay. Before I'm even ready, he jabs me with the needle on the inside of my elbow. *Just like the scanning tech.*

Veidman stands up and hands the empty syringe back to Meira.

'So what happens now?' I ask. 'Am I going to be OK?'

Veidman looks down at me. 'Well, I've got good news and bad news.' His tone is fairly jocular, but his eyes are distant and veiled. I look over at Gadya and Meira. Meira is now half shrouded in the shadow of a tree; Gadya is still watching me closely.

'I'll take the good news first,' I mutter. I try to stand up, then realise that my whole body feels heavy. I sit back down again as a sensation of heat rushes through me. 'Does anyone ever have an allergic reaction to this vaccine?'

Veidman is about to speak, but Gadya cuts him off. 'It's not a vaccine!' she exclaims, like she's unable to stay silent. I look up at her, confused, as my head starts swimming.

'Gadya, keep your fat mouth shut,' Meira warns.

'It's not a vaccine. It's a truth serum!' Gadya continues. 'They're gonna ask you questions and find out who you really are. They think you're a secret spy for the Monk. They think you've been sent here to kill us all!'

THE VILLAGE

Five minutes later, the truth serum – or whatever it is – has completely taken hold. I'm caught in a weird state between waking and sleeping. I've been dragged inside Veidman's cabin and stretched out on a hammock. Veidman, Gadya, Meira and several other villagers cluster around me.

The questions come in rapid succession from a chorus of voices. They ask me what my real name is. Where I'm really from. Who sent me here, and why. What I know about the wheel and about the Monk. They ask me about David. And if I'm here to hurt anyone, among a hundred other things. For once ignorance truly is bliss. I know nothing. Less than any of these kids do.

But the questions don't stop. Veidman and Meira are certain I have secrets. Their voices grow as sharp as knives, slicing deeply. They think I'm lying, despite the truth serum.

'You're an orphan,' their voices insist. 'You claim your parents were dissidents, so what did they do? Tell us!'

But of course I don't have an easy answer for that one. I never have. I can hear my own voice explaining all of this, calm but deadened, inside an echo chamber of numbness. I tell them I was only ten when my parents got taken away. If they did anything radically subversive, beyond minor infractions, then they hid it from me.

Finally, after what feels like hours, my interrogators begin to sound tired. The questions wane.

'She doesn't know squat,' I hear Gadya mutter. 'Just like I figured.' She's the only one who hasn't asked me a single thing. 'She's not the one you're looking for, Veidman.'

'Maybe,' I hear Meira say, still unconvinced.

Gadya and another girl eventually lead me out of the hut and back into the grassy clearing. The sun is lower on the horizon, the sky a deeper shade of blue. I sit down. The girl splashes cold water across my face before heading away with a dismissive glance. I'm still groggy, but starting to come around.

'I told you I didn't know anything,' I murmur to Gadya.

'I know, but I don't make the rules, remember?' She forces a plastic water jug into my hands. 'Drink. It'll help you pee the serum out faster.'

With trembling fingers, I raise the jug to my lips and take a sip. Then I lower it. 'You tricked me.' As my senses return, I'm starting to get angry. 'You lied about the vaccine.'

'I didn't have a choice. There was no way to know if you were a spy or not. You and David could have just been pretending to be new to the wheel.' She crosses her arms. 'It wasn't my idea, if that helps any. Veidman and Meira are the ones who figured out how to make the truth serum – from henbane seeds and grain alcohol. They're crazy smart. They know things we don't, and they've been here longer than anyone else in our village. They've started using their truth serum on every new arrival.'

I take a deeper sip of water, feeling it trace a cool path down my throat. 'So now that you know I'm not a spy, tell me why you think I got sent here. Give me that much.'

Gadya takes the jug from my hands and swigs from it, and then wipes her mouth on the back of her arm. 'None of us know why we're here. Personally, I think the wheel is just a place where the government sends any teenager it wants to get rid of. I don't even know if the GPPT tests for anything at all.' She pauses. 'In your case, you told us under the serum that people came into your cell and administered ECT before the test could even take place. That means the government had marked you as an Unanchored Soul from the get-go. But it doesn't always work that way for everyone... Look, we'll fill you in on what we do know at the campfire meeting tonight, with Veidman and Meira.'

'I don't think they like me.'

'Those two don't like anyone except each other. Canadians are weird.'

'Are they twins or something?'

Gadya stifles a grin as she passes me the water jug again. 'Don't let either of them hear you say that. They're a couple – they just look alike.' She watches as I chug more water. 'How are you feeling?'

'Like I just got tricked and drugged,' I mutter. 'Other than that, fine.'

Gadya smiles. 'I'll take you on a tour of the village,

introduce you to some other kids. When I first got here, I felt really alone until I made some friends.' A shadow falls over her eyes. 'A lot of those friends aren't alive any more.'

'They got killed fighting the Monk?'

'That, or they were taken by—' She breaks off, standing up. 'If I say too much now, Veidman and the others will get mad.'

As we start walking around the edge of the clearing, I take in my surroundings. Sloppily constructed cabins are clustered beneath the trees. They're made of mouldy wooden slats, propped up with stones. The roofs are either thatched or made from sheets of corrugated metal, like the shantytowns I've seen in government-sanctioned depictions of Europe and Asia. The village looks ramshackle and filthy. I remember what Gadya said about the drones constantly destroying everything. This is probably the best the villagers can do, given the circumstances.

I'm reminded of a book of mythology that my dad gave me when I was six. *D'Aulaires' Book of Greek Myths*. It was mostly drawings, which was why I liked it so much at the time. My dad would read the text while I looked at the pictures.

One of the myths was about Sisyphus, who had to roll a boulder endlessly up a mountain – only to have it crash down on him whenever he neared the top. Then he'd have to start his journey all over again. He was locked in that cycle for eternity, as punishment for offending the gods. I told my dad I thought it was a pretty discouraging myth, and that I felt sad for Sisyphus.

'Ah, but the key is to imagine Sisyphus *happy*,' he earnestly explained to my six-year-old self. 'If Sisyphus is happy, then the story isn't sad. Maybe he finds a lot of meaning in rolling that boulder up the mountain, even if he seems doomed to us. If Sisyphus ever lost his boulder – or succeeded in getting it over the top – he'd probably lose his entire purpose in life!'

I keep that story close to my heart as I trail Gadya past all the kids rebuilding their shacks. *To imagine Sisyphus happy. Is that really possible?*

Some of the kids start noticing me, and they stop what they're doing. All of them are grubby and tousle-haired, smeared with dirt like they've been playing in the woods. But I know that none of them have been playing. Their eyes burn with concentration and fear.

'Where'd you find this one?' a red-headed boy calls out to Gadya.

'Yeah, what's her name?' yells a frowning girl, sounding worried. 'Is she safe?'

'My name's Alenna,' I say, before Gadya can speak for me. I want to stand up for myself. If I have only two more years to live, then I don't want to spend them living in the shadows.

'She passed Veidman's test,' Gadya tells them. I notice shirtless boys lurking nearby with wooden spears. Many of them have dark tans, but their skin tones vary. It looks like a mix of kids and ethnicities from all over the UNA. Again, I seek out the blue-eyed boy, but he's not among them. *Maybe he's from a different village, and was just passing through this area.*

A lot of the kids hang back. Others shoot me hostile, challenging glares. An Asian boy with long black hair finally breaks away from the pack and strolls over.

'Hey, new fish,' he says. He's wiry with a gleam in his eyes. Cocky, but at least he looks lively and intelligent, which is different from a lot of the kids back in New Providence. The boy sticks out his hand, and I shake it firmly.

'My name's Assassin Elite,' he says with a straight face.

I take my hand back quickly. 'That's a pretty messed-up name.'

Gadya rolls her eyes. 'A lot of kids make up new names here. Island names. Especially the boys.'

'Yeah, we're not all born with awesome names like Ga-dee-ya,' he drawls sarcastically. 'And we don't all dye our hair blue with berries.'

'Shut up, or I'll tell her your real name – so she can make fun of you like everyone else does,' Gadya snaps. Other kids laugh in the background as the boy glowers. To me, Gadya adds, 'He's showing off. Probably means he likes you.'

A few other kids step out and introduce themselves, including a heavyset blonde. 'I'm Edie,' she says with a distinctive Canadian lilt. 'How long have you been on the wheel, eh?'

'Long enough to know that it sucks.'

'A day? A week?' She sounds suspicious.

'More like hours,' I reply.

I want to ask these kids some questions, but Gadya keeps moving, like she's enjoying her role as tour guide. She swans past the group with me in tow, saying, 'See you at chow time, guys.'

We walk down a narrow trail nearly overrun by brambles. I notice we're moving further from the central clearing and the shacks.

Along the way, we meet a few other boys and girls. All of them wear the same guarded look in their eyes. I can tell they're curious about me, but they're not about to open up to a complete stranger. I wonder how frequently they get a new arrival here. It can't be too often, or they wouldn't be interested in me.

Gadya gestures to some horizontal slats of wood, just off the trail, with circular holes cut into them. 'Our toilets. We use dried leaves for paper.'

'And I thought the orphanage was bad,' I mutter.

Gadya laughs. 'A lot of kids here are orphans.'

So much for Claudette's theory. 'Are you an orphan?'

She shakes her head. 'I wish. Both my parents are really conservative pro–UNA types. Or at least they were before I got sent here. Who knows if that changed their minds.'

As Gadya and I keep walking, she points out other sections of the village – an area of flattened tree branches where food is being prepared, an enclave of woven hammocks where people rest between trees, and a shallow tributary from which the villagers draw their drinking water.

It's only near the end of the tour that Gadya pauses. 'Now that you're gonna be living here, I want to show you something else. But I really don't want to scare you.'

'I'm getting used to feeling scared.'

Gadya glances around, making sure no one's watching. 'We gotta be quick. I'm not supposed to show you this yet.' She points down a narrow, muddy trail that leads even further away from the main camp. 'Follow me.'

Together we walk rapidly down the trail. 'Where are we going?' I whisper.

'To see the Ones Who Suffer.'

'Who?'

'*Shhh*. No talking. I don't want to get in trouble.'

A few minutes later, we turn a bend in the trail. A separate clearing looms fifty feet in front of us, at the end of the path.

But there are no cabins or fire pits here. Only writhing bodies sprawled in hammocks and lying on stained blankets. I hear moans and wracking coughs. A sickly odour reaches me, dancing on a gust of wind. It's the stench of putrescence. These kids are dying.

I stop moving, instantly terrified. 'What's wrong with them?'

'We don't know. No one does. It's not contagious, at least.'

'You sure about that?'

'Not a hundred per cent. But the disease acts more like food poisoning than a virus. At least that's what we think. For some reason, it usually only affects kids who've been here for a while.'

I see healthy boys and girls moving among the sick ones, tending to them, wiping sweat from their faces. Getting seriously ill on an island like this would be a death sentence.

No doctors, no hospitals, no medicines – unless Veidman can cook up antibiotics in addition to his truth serum.

I feel light-headed. 'They all look so sick.'

Gadya flinches. 'Don't use that word.'

'Sick?'

'Yeah. Veidman doesn't like it. Says it causes panic. That's why we call them the Ones Who Suffer.' She pauses, reading my face. 'The situation creeps me out too, OK? All we have right now are theories. The illness could be something natural, like toxic mushrooms or berries. Or bad meat. But I doubt it. I think the Monk's drones are deliberately trying to poison us.'

I'm watching the bodies in the hammocks. An emaciated boy about my age whimpers in pain, his eyes swollen shut. Crusts of dried blood speckle the corners of his mouth. I glance away.

'The Suffering is one of the real reasons most people don't live past eighteen here,' Gadya says. 'I bet no one told you that back in the UNA.'

I nod. 'What are the symptoms?'

'Fever. Tiredness. Bleeding out of places you shouldn't bleed from. After that you just fall apart and die, like you've got the plague.' Gadya turns away. 'Don't tell anyone I showed you this place. Veidman usually makes me wait a few more days.'

'I can understand why,' I mutter.

We start walking back up the trail in silence, the wailing and coughing sounds receding into the distance. I'm stunned, and I feel terrible for the victims of this disease.

'Can I do anything to avoid ever catching it?' I ask Gadya.

'Watch what you eat. But it's not like there are too many options on this island. Other than a few kinds of fruits and vegtables, hoofers are pretty much it.'

'Hoofers?'

'A type of wild boar. The whole island is crawling with them.'

'I think one almost attacked me and David, before you found us.'

'Attacked you?' Gadya scoffs. 'Doubtful. Hoofers are scared of humans. We hunt 'em for food. They shriek like the devil, but it's just noise.'

'Good to know.'

'And another important thing about the wheel, before I forget.' She pauses as we reach the edge of the main clearing again. 'We've got a rule – no hooking up with guys. I mean, kissing's OK and stuff, but no sex.'

I want to laugh. I'm grimy, sweaty, exhausted, and my dark brown hair is a tangled mess. I can't imagine anyone wanting to touch me, let alone hook up with me. 'That's not gonna be a problem.'

'Good, 'cause hookups lead to babies, and no one wants that.'

I don't ask what the penalty is for breaking this rule, but I have no doubt that kids probably sleep with one another all the time. Still, I don't see any babies anywhere, so maybe not.

'Is there any place to bathe?' I ask, suddenly aware of how much my skin is itching.

'The big river. It runs along one edge of the village. Us girls made some bathing shacks out of plywood so the boys can't watch us. They always try.'

'So the water's safe here?'

'As safe as anything else.' She sighs. 'The wheel is a harsh place, Alenna. You either learn to adapt or it'll eat you up and spit out your carcass with a burp.' She sees my glum look and grins. 'But at least there's no more school. Or earpieces. Or thought-pills. Or any of Minster Harka's re-education crap. We've got more freedom here than the kids back home can ever dream of.'

'True. We just can't do anything with it.'

'Not yet,' she says softly. Before I can ask what she means, she adds, 'I'll take you to the river so you can clean up. I'll get you some fresh clothes too. Then it'll be time for our nightly meeting and dinner. We have it round the fire pit before sunset. You're our first new arrival in three weeks, so everyone will be curious to meet you.' She looks me up and down, like she's seeing me for the first time. Almost begrudgingly, she says, 'You're pretty. You're gonna get hit on a lot. Especially when you clean up and fix your hair.'

'Thanks, but no way,' I protest. 'Back home I was totally invisible to guys. To everyone, really.'

'So were a lot of us. It's different on the wheel for some reason.'

Gadya leads me along an overgrown path running parallel to the main camp. We stop at a supply shack, and she rummages through it, taking out a pair of jeans, a plain black tank top and a pair of boots. I don't ask who these clothes belonged to, because I'm afraid their previous owner is a corpse.

Then Gadya takes me down to the bank of a large grey river. The water's moving rapidly. I see the bathing shacks standing near the edge, jutting out of the muddy bank like crooked teeth.

We walk to the edge of the choppy water. 'The River Styx,' I murmur, thinking of those Greek myths again. 'The river from hell.'

'And you haven't even felt how cold it is yet.' Gadya walks over to one of the bathing shacks and yanks open the door. A grey towel spotted with mildew hangs on a hook inside. 'No shampoo, only homemade soap from hoofer fat,' she says, rummaging around.

I walk over, and she hands me a white lump of soap. It feels disgusting, like congealed snot. 'Thanks.'

'I'll be tending the fire. Come find me when you're done.'

I nod.

She leaves me there and strides back up the riverbank, disappearing into the trees. I'm very conscious of the fact that I'm all alone now in this strange domain.

It doesn't seem possible that my life has come to this. I never thought I'd be homesick for the bland amenities of government-controlled life in the UNA. Yet here I am.

I strip down, hanging my old clothes and bra under the towel. I bathe quickly in the icy water, kneeling and splashing to wash grime off my skin and grit from my hair. Then I dry myself and get dressed, slipping back into my panties and itchy bra, and then my new jeans, tank top and boots. The jeans are baggy, and the tank top has a few holes in it, but at least these clothes are clean and dry. I smooth back my wet hair with my hands. My arms are already covered in mosquito bites.

Although I still feel like I'm living inside a surreal nightmare, I know I'm going to have to shake that feeling pretty fast. I need to make friends, find out what's really going on here, and figure out if there's a way to get off the wheel before something bad happens to me, like it already did to David. I wish I could somehow find a way to honour my promise and go back for him. I owe him my life. But there's no way to reach him right now.

I leave the towel on the hook, tuck my old clothes under my arm, and rapidly head up the riverbank to the village, in search of Gadya and more answers.

THE NIGHT RAID

When I finally reach the main clearing, a fire is already roaring in the pit. Yellow flames dance upwards into the darkening sky. Occasional gusts of wind blow the flames sideways, scattering orange embers across the dirt and grass.

There's no sign of Gadya. I feel awkward and vulnerable without her around. Two rugged boys I don't know yet are feeding the fire with dead branches. They look up as I near.

Then I hear footsteps behind me. I turn around, expecting to see Gadya. Instead it's Assassin Elite.

'What do you think of this place?' he asks.

'I'm just grateful to be here, let's put it like that.'

He laughs. 'It's a dump. A total hovel. We all know that.'

I hear a sharp voice to my left: 'Alenna!'

To my relief, it's Gadya, trailed by a freckled girl I haven't seen before. This girl is short and a little heavy, wearing overalls and a necklace made from seashells. Probably just a bit older than I am. Her auburn hair is in braids, and she's wearing glasses.

'Is this idiot bothering you?' Gadya calls out to me.

'C'mon, I'm just being friendly!' Assassin Elite – or whatever his real name is – retorts.

'Yeah, I'll bet,' Gadya snaps. 'Get lost before I give you a pounding.'

'Sounds hot. Is that an invitation?' But he turns to leave, smirking. 'I gotta get back to doing something useful.'

'That's right, keep walking,' Gadya taunts.

She and the freckled girl reach me as the boy retreats. Unexpectedly, the freckled girl steps forward and hugs me. 'You've probably met enough new faces already – but I hope there's room for one more? I'm Rika.'

'Alenna.'

She steps back. 'You're famous around here. The new arrival. But don't worry. Your fame's only gonna last until someone else new turns up. Then everyone will forget about you. That's what happened to me!'

'Good. I don't want to be famous.'

'We better get moving,' Gadya points out. 'It's almost time for the meeting.'

I'm swept along in Gadya and Rika's wake as they walk around to the other side of the fire pit. Despite their divergent appearances, I can tell that they're good friends.

The flames are now raging inside the pit like a living animal, fifteen feet high. I can feel the fire's brutal warmth. The same two boys are still stoking it. The sky is growing darker; it's now an ominous shade of purple-blue. Kids are streaming out of huts and from the forest, to congregate around the pit. The night is cooler, so some wear hoodies, and others have shawls and blankets around their shoulders. I notice several kids wearing shirts with defaced UNA logos on them.

'How many people live in the village?' I ask as Gadya hands me a spare blanket.

'We haven't done a head count in months,' Rika says. 'Kids keep turning up, but then there's the Suffering, and the war with the Monk... It all evens out, I guess. Maybe a couple of hundred?' She looks at me. 'I'm a pacifist, at least most of the time. So I'm a cook. That's what I do here. How 'bout you?'

'I don't know yet.'

'You got anything you're passionate about?'

'Music,' I tell her. 'Playing guitar.'

'We need more of that here,' Rika says, nodding her approval. Gadya just snorts.

The three of us eventually perch on some granite rocks near the fire. The crowd isn't exactly noisy, but it's not quiet, either. In the flickering light I recognise the few kids I've already met, plus many more. I see Assassin Elite among a group of athletic, shirtless boys to my left. By their spears and primitive bows, I deduce that they're the hunters and warriors who protect this village.

Most of the kids sit on the ground, but some rest in ancient leather lounge chairs. The seats are cracked, with yellow stuffing poking out. I wonder how these chairs even came to be here. Or how anything else on the island got here. Like the giant stone staircase, these random items are out of place in this desolate wilderness. *What did this island used to be?*

I finally see Veidman and Meira heading through the crowd towards the fire. Conversations slowly cease. Even in the pale firelight, they look so clean compared to everyone else here. Like dirt doesn't stick to them. I feel mixed emotions. I'm still mad at Veidman for tricking me, but I guess I understand why he did it.

Veidman stands up on a gnarled tree stump. Everyone's quiet now, watching him. The only sounds are the crackling and popping of the fire. 'Greetings,' he says, sounding oddly formal.

'Greetings,' the group echoes back, like a church congregation. I wonder if this is some kind of strange village ritual.

'As you know, we got a new arrival from the UNA today,' he continues, his gaze drifting in my direction.

My stomach instantly clenches up.

Please don't mention my name!

I want to remain anonymous, at least for a little while longer. But obviously that's not going to happen. Everyone's eyes are glued to me now.

'Her name is Alenna Shawcross. Gadya found her near the eastern stairway, along with a boy that we couldn't save. Alenna passed the truth test, so she's one of us now. Make her feel at home.'

Everyone just keeps staring at me. I wave awkwardly at the crowd like an idiot. A few kids wave back, but most of them keep staring. *Am I supposed to say something? Make a speech?* That's not going to happen.

Meira steps up beside Veidman on another rough-hewn stump. Her voice rings out over the crackling fire: 'We finally have some news about the grey zone too.' All eyes turn to her.

'About what Liam found there last night.'

The crowd starts chattering with excitement and anticipation when they hear his name. I glance over at Gadya, eyebrows raised. 'Who's Liam?' She either doesn't hear or pretends not to.

'Spit it out, Meira!' a boy's voice bursts from the crowd.

'I don't need to. Liam has recovered enough to speak for himself.'

At Meira's words, the lithe silhouette of a boy emerges from behind her and Veidman. Most of the kids start clapping. Some even stand up. They all seem to love this boy, whoever he is. His silhouette moves closer to the light. Meira steps down from the tree stump so that he can take her place.

The boy's face finally becomes visible, the flickering flames illuminating his chiselled features as he steps up on to the stump.

For a second, I just stare. Then my heart literally skips a beat, losing its rhythm for an instant.

It's him.

The blue-eyed boy from the museum screen.

I can't believe it.

I don't know what to do. Not in the slightest. So I just sit there watching him, my mind racing madly. I feel overwhelmed.

In person, the sense of some kind of weird connection with him is even stronger. I feel even more drawn to him, and not just because he's so good-looking. It's different from that, but I don't know how to explain it. He starts talking before I can puzzle out what I'm feeling.

'Hey, everyone,' Liam says, one hand jammed into the pocket of his jeans. His voice is low and husky. He's wearing a grey T-shirt, and his left arm is in a sling. 'Like Meira said, I've got news.' He looks around. Surprisingly, given his obvious status in the village, he seems a little uncomfortable with the attention. 'Last night I was in the grey zone, right before the tunnel collapsed. And I finally saw what we've been looking for all this time. An aircraft overhead—'

The hubbub of the crowd grows louder again, drowning him out.

'Anyway,' Liam says, talking over the noise. 'I tracked it in the sky for a few miles through the grey zone. I saw its lights. I think it was landing—' He breaks off.

The crowd has gone completely nuts. Some of the kids high-five each other as they hoot and holler.

I turn to Gadya. 'What's this all about?' I ask.

'It might be our ticket off the wheel,' she says, eyes shining. 'We've been trying to spot a UNA transport aircraft for as long as I've been here. And it sounds like Liam might have seen one, and maybe even found where they land and take off from.' Before I can ask another question, Liam starts talking again:

'I tried to keep after it, but there were too many drones in the trees. They must have followed me through the tunnel. I had to hide for a couple hours before things cooled down… You all probably know what happened on the way back. The tunnel got detonated by some crazy drones, and I barely made it out alive before sunrise.'

I'm still trying to understand what Liam is talking about, when Veidman speaks up. 'Now that the tunnel's gone, we need to find another way back into the grey zone as soon as possible, to learn where the landing strips are. If we can figure out how to hijack one of these aircrafts, then we can start—'

A sharp pop interrupts him.

At first I think it came from the fire. But then it comes again, an instant after a distant flash of light. My heart starts beating faster. I recognise this sound from back home when I was young.

Gunfire.

'The Cannibal Monk!' a boy yells, his voice taut with panic. I hear distant screams and more popping sounds. Kids start jumping to their feet all around me, grabbing homemade spears and bows. Preparing for battle. I see Liam hop down from the stump, snatch up a spear with his good arm, and dart forward in the direction of the sounds. The other hunters follow.

The dark sky above us suddenly lights up with a starburst of colourful red and blue embers.

I stand up, finally realising what those popping noises actually are. It's not gunfire at all. *It's fireworks.*

Back in the UNA I saw them in patriotic commercials about national pride and military service. But never once in real life. Fireworks, like so many other things, were banned back home.

I'm about to breathe a sigh of relief, when an object whizzes past my head like a rocket. I scream and duck.

It detonates in the trees at the edge of the clearing, instantly setting the branches on fire in a shower of sparks. Everyone is yelling and running past me. Some of the underbrush is alight, and the flames are spreading fast.

'Keep your head down!' Gadya calls out to me over the chaos.

A spider burst of sparkling lights explodes overhead with a boom. The air is quickly filling with acrid smoke.

'It's a firework attack!' Gadya yells at me. 'The Monk's drones do this every couple weeks to start fires in our village.' A concussive blast drowns out the rest of her words.

Another group of shirtless warriors runs past, whooping as they plunge into the forest. They're moving in pursuit of the invisible drones.

I hear more loud cracks as bottle rockets fizz and sputter, and smoke bombs detonate nearby. My ears are ringing. Rika gets down and presses her chunky body flat on the dirt. I do the same. Gadya remains standing.

A boy runs past and tosses her a spear. She grabs it easily, the metal tip flashing in the firelight. 'I'm gonna get these psychos!' she cries. 'Stay here. I'll be right back.' Then she rushes off into the forest after the other hunters.

'Is Gadya crazy?' I whisper to Rika, my head close to hers. 'Where's she going?'

'To fight. Gadya's a warrior. We're just survivors.'

From our vantage point, Rika and I can see boys and girls

racing everywhere. A group of them pours buckets of river water on to the burning underbrush, trying to extinguish the flames.

Fireworks keep exploding above us. I jam my fingers into my ears. Showers of multicoloured sparks fall down like rain, forming pinprick afterimages that dance on my retinas.

I still can't catch any real glimpses of the drones. They're just shadowy figures dashing through the trees at the edges of the clearing. They hoot and cackle as they run, using slingshots and mortar tubes to shoot off aerial shells like grenades.

A particularly loud explosion makes me and Rika flinch. I blink and look back up from the ground. And when I do, my mind goes totally blank for an instant.

A pair of feet has appeared directly in front of us.

I'm hoping somehow it's Liam, or Gadya, or one of the other hunters.

But I find myself staring up at a drone clutching a metal spear. Red war paint obscures his features, making him look demonic.

Rika instantly shrieks, 'Interloper!' She rolls sideways on to her feet, surprising me with her speed. I stagger up ungracefully, several beats behind her.

We turn to run, but then I hear a familiar voice call out, 'Alenna! It's me!'

I turn around, stunned, staring at the painted drone. *'David?'*

'Wait? You know this lunatic?' Rika practically screams.

David moves closer, limping, as he lowers the spear. Now that I can see his eyes, I know it's him for sure. He's not wearing his glasses.

'I thought you were dead!' I say.

'I talked my way out of it,' he replies, speaking fast. 'Told them I'd join their cult. Said everything they wanted to hear. But they're all insane! They painted my face and said that tonight is my initiation rite. I have to kill a villager to prove I'm for real, or else they're going to kill me!' He moves closer. 'I don't want to kill anyone. Let me hide in your village. I can—'

'There you are!' a voice booms out. I spin around.

There's another drone standing right behind us.

This one's face is painted lime green, like a lizard's. He's holding a cigarette lighter up to the short wick of a massive cylindrical firework, as large and dangerous-looking as a bomb. He also has a knife strapped to his leather belt. We're trapped.

'Hey, this is our sector!' Rika yells at him.

'We control this entire island,' he spits. 'You girls just don't know it yet!' He looks over at David. 'Raise your spear, punk. Look alive.'

Rika stares down the lizard boy. 'You better not light that firework. You'll blow us all to kingdom come.'

'Good.' He starts baying like a wolf, and I see that his tongue is split down the middle, the two sections moving separately like worms. He stops baying and gestures at David again. 'Take care of these girls, like I told you to.'

'We're taking you back with us to the orange sector,' David says to me and Rika, halfheartedly brandishing his spear. He's just playing a role. I look around for someone to help us, but everyone's fighting or putting out fires.

'Draw some blood,' lizard boy coaches David. 'That'll get their attention. Go after the fat one first. That'll scare the other one into doing whatever you want.' He grabs his crotch, making his meaning clear. 'She'll come back to our camp if she knows what's good for her.'

'We're not going anywhere with you,' I tell him, revolted. But my voice warbles with fear. I feel pathetic. Useless. He knows I'm scared of him.

I move closer to Rika. If it weren't for the gigantic firework and the knife, we'd just run into the forest.

'Are you a coward, or a killer?' lizard boy starts yelling at David, seemingly enraged at his inaction. 'Tonight's your only chance! Show these villagers that you mean business!'

David lunges forward awkwardly on his injured foot, and grabs me around the neck, putting me in a loose choke hold. 'Play along,' he whispers. 'Maybe we can take this guy down before he does something really crazy. Just promise me I can seek shelter here and join your village?'

'Of course!' I whisper. 'I wanted to come back for you, but—'

Suddenly, I see lizard boy race behind Rika, grab a fistful of her braids, and yank hard. Rika turns and fights back, kicking and punching her assailant with surprising fury for a pacifist, making him drop his cigarette lighter and back away. 'Don't mess with my hair!' she snaps.

For a second, it seems like we might have the upper hand. But right then, a third drone appears, also clutching a spear. He's thick-necked and thuggish, with painted zebra stripes crisscrossing his face. He holds up his weapon, like he's about to attack.

'This initiate is a wimp!' lizard boy yells over to him. I realise he's talking about David. 'He won't draw first blood!'

'It'll be my pleasure to do it for him.' Zebra-face lashes out and catches my arm, pulling me away from David. I stumble and nearly fall. His fingers tighten. He starts laughing like he's enjoying himself.

His laughter makes me angrier than anything else. With a surge of energy, I rip myself free of this drone's grasp, lashing out with my fist. The blow glances off the side of his jaw, smudging his face paint.

'Stay away!' I warn. I spin around and see that Rika is battling lizard boy again. David is trying to help her without making it obvious whose side he's on. I turn back just in time to see zebra-face moving forward again. His chiselled teeth are bared like a wild dog. He's not laughing any more.

'You're mine!' he spits, raising his spear. 'I'm gonna take you back to my sector. Make you bow down to the blessed Monk.'

A hundred paces away, a bevy of village kids suddenly tumbles out of the trees.

'Help!' Rika screams at them, but they don't hear. She has

managed to get away from lizard boy. Her shirt is torn. We exchange a scared glance.

I know that lizard boy and zebra-face aren't done with us yet. I look around as the pyrotechnic display continues overhead. There's nothing to use as a weapon nearby. And even if David lunged at the drones with his spear, they're larger and more skilled. They'd probably kill him before he could get in a blow.

Wordlessly, lizard boy leans down and picks up his cigarette lighter from the leaves. With a casual flick, he sets the short wick of the firework alight. Before I can do anything, he swings back his arm and pitches the explosive into the night sky. A moment later there's a deafening crack, and the sky flashes with a multicoloured palm-shell burst.

He and zebra-face start laughing like maniacs as embers slowly drift downwards towards the treetops.

'You're crazy!' Rika yells.

Right then I hear another sound, a high-pitched electronic squeal, like a sonic buzz saw. The boys hear it too, and they instantly stare upwards. Their painted faces reflect the light from the fireworks.

Rika grabs my arm. I don't understand what's going on. *Is this some other form of attack? Some new kind of weapon?* David looks confused too.

My head starts feeling funny, like everything inside is vibrating. The noise increases in intensity. My eyes and teeth throb, and I clutch my face.

Right then I spot Gadya racing out of the trees ahead of

us. Behind her come more hunters from the village. They're heading in our direction, streaming towards us.

We've been rescued.

The fireworks cease, but the strange noise continues. Its pitch and volume make it hard to think.

'Whatever you do, don't move!' Gadya yells at me, as I start to realise we haven't been rescued at all.

Zebra-face turns to run, outnumbered and evidently frightened by the noise above us. David tries to rub the red paint off his face, but it just smears. And even though he has dropped his spear to show his peaceful intentions, I know that the villagers don't realise his identity. They start racing towards him, weapons drawn, about to attack.

Unless he starts running too, someone is going to kill him by mistake. They think he's a drone, instead of a normal kid who was forced to act like a drone in order to stay alive and reach our camp.

'It's OK! He's one of us!' I yell, but nobody is listening to me. 'He's on our side!'

Then, inexplicably, both lizard boy and zebra-face fall to the ground, like an invisible force has shoved them down on to the dirt. David scrambles sideways, trying to get to the safety of the forest before a stray arrow from a villager can hit him. Zebra-face manages to do the same thing, scuttling away towards the trees.

But lizard boy remains frozen. Pinned to the ground, seemingly by fear. I stand there watching in horror, pressing both hands against my ears.

'No!' lizard boy screams into the air, like he's talking to some invisible entity. 'Not me! I didn't do anything!'

I glance back at David. Zebra-face has found him and is dragging him away into the forest. There's no way to rescue him. My only hope is that zebra-face and the other drones don't kill David, and he's given another chance. Whatever is going on has brought an early end to the raid. With no more fireworks in the sky, the flames in the fire pit are the only source of illumination.

In addition to the high-pitched sound, I suddenly hear the clatter of military helicopter rotors above us. I glance up but can't see anything.

A stark white beam of light abruptly appears. It's a spotlight, blazing down from a point of unknown origin in the sky. It fixes itself directly on lizard boy.

'God – no! Please – I'll go back!' the boy starts screaming loudly. 'Just don't – just don't take me!'

I peer at lizard boy through the beam of white light, squinting to see better. In the brightness, I can see all the holes in his tattered clothes. His emaciated arms are like sticks, and there's dirt all over him. His hollow cheeks make him look half starved.

His green face paint glistens in the burning white spotlight. The noise of the rotors is even louder now.

As I watch, a thick black wire – almost like a tentacle – uncoils from the shaft of white light and races down towards the frozen figure. Another one follows it. Then another. And another.

Lizard boy has stopped screaming. He's just gaping in horror at whatever he sees above him in that white light. I wonder why he doesn't try to run, but obviously he's panicking. I can't tell if the tentacles are alive or mechanical. They move with terrific speed, like writhing snakes in search of prey.

The tentacles wrap themselves around the boy in one second flat, pinning his arms and legs tightly to his body, immobilising him. He starts sobbing, words giving way to cries of pain and fear.

The tentacles tighten even more. In an instant he's jerked upright. For a moment, he dangles a few feet above the ground, like a spider at the end of its web. He opens his mouth to scream, but he can't get enough air.

'No,' he mouths.

Then he's whipped straight upwards into the beam of light, right towards its source.

The spotlight immediately cuts off.

The rotor noises diminish, as does the high-pitched whine. Within thirty seconds, the night sky is calm and peaceful again. I hear only a distant thrum as whatever it was moves rapidly onwards.

I sink to the ground, shaking and dizzy. I don't understand what I just saw.

What were those tentacle things?

Why did they kidnap the drone?

Gadya crouches down next to me. 'You OK?'

'No.' My lips are numb, and my mouth is dry. 'What the hell just happened?'

'We got attacked by the Monk's drones. From the looks of it, three of 'em almost got you and Rika.'

'No, one of them was David. The drones made him paint his face red. Told him he had to kill someone.'

'An initiation rite. He's lucky to still be alive.'

'But what was that other thing?' I ask. 'The thing in the sky.'

Gadya doesn't answer. She just asks, 'Can you stand?'

I struggle to my feet. Two hunters are already questioning Rika. I can tell she's explaining everything to them.

'Buck up,' Gadya tells me. 'Maybe we'll get another chance to save David.' She looks me up and down. 'I'm glad you fought back. Or tried to. That means there's a chance you'll live longer than a week.' She sticks her spear into the earth, where it stands upright. 'The passive ones? The weak ones? They're only good for a few days.'

'But what was that noise? And those tentacles...' I swallow hard. 'You have to tell me.'

She looks at me. 'I'm sorry you had to see that on your first day. I was on the wheel for two weeks before I saw someone get taken.'

'*Taken?*'

'The light, the noises. The whole shebang.' She pauses. 'We don't call them tentacles, though. They're not alive. They're robotic filaments, attached to the bottom of some kind of helicopter, probably unmanned. We call them *feelers*.'

My hands are still shaking, so I cross my arms and bury my fists in my armpits. 'Where do the feelers come from? What do they want?'

'No one knows. But once someone gets taken, we never see them again. We don't know where they go, or what happens. They just never come back to the wheel. We figure they get killed.'

Rika walks over to us. Her glasses are askew, smeared with mud. 'Scary, right? You did good.'

'Thanks,' I say, feeling empty and quavering inside.

'Look on the bright side,' Gadya declares. 'Now we've got one less drone to worry about.' She bends down and picks something up. It's lizard boy's lighter. She flicks the flint, and a yellow flame appears. 'Nice.' She slips it into her back pocket.

'How do I know one of those feelers won't come after me?' I ask.

'The odds of getting taken are pretty small, if you play by the rules. It mostly happens to people when they cross from one sector to another. Our best guess is that it's a UNA enforcement mechanism, to make us stay where we belong. We don't know why the UNA even cares about the sectors, but if we cross over into the Monk's sectors, or his drones cross into ours, this kind of thing tends to happen. Not all the time, and obviously not to everyone.'

'We cut off part of a feeler once,' Rika adds. 'Well, I mean, Liam and some of the other hunters did, with a knife. It just looked like a piece of electrical cable with tiny wires inside.'

Gadya and Rika exchange looks. I get the sense they know some things they're not sharing with me yet, but I don't press them.

We start walking back to the fire pit. I'm trying to mask my total horror over the feeler attack, as well as my inability to help David. 'Tell me about Liam,' I say, hoping to focus on something positive. But I don't get a good reaction from Gadya.

'He's the best hunter and tracker in our village,' she replies tersely, her shoulders tensing. 'Let's just leave it at that, OK?'

Rika pipes up. 'Liam and Gadya dated for a while—'

'Shut up!' Gadya snaps. 'Remind me to kick your butt later.'

Rika cackles. She seems a little giddy now that the battle is over. Meanwhile, I'm more frightened than ever. And because Liam is obviously a sensitive subject, I don't know what else to say.

'Get some rest,' Gadya tells me. 'The drones won't attack us again tonight. They get tired too.'

I look around and see other members of the village already cleaning things up. They're getting the camp together again and tending the fire. Hammering splintered cabins back together with homemade tools. It's like they've just accepted the drone attacks – and the risk of getting taken – as normal parts of everyday life. *Maybe I'll end up feeling the same way, if I live long enough.*

'Come on,' Gadya says, taking my arm and pulling me towards a row of vine hammocks slung between trees. 'If you can't sleep, at least lie down. You look like you're going into shock. We usually take turns keeping watch and doing chores, but don't worry about it tonight. You get a free pass for being a newbie.'

Rika nods in agreement. 'I can bring you something to eat. The drones trashed our stew and ruined dinner, but we've still got fruit. Strawberries and coconuts.'

I feel too sick to eat. Up until the feeler attack, I thought I was doing OK, given the circumstances. Now I'm not so sure.

'Listen, there's no way I can sleep or eat,' I say. 'Not after what I saw. So let me help. Give me something useful to do.'

Gadya looks surprised. 'Sure. You can help gather wood for the fire. But stay inside the camp's perimeter. Rika will go with you. I gotta go talk to Veidman about something.'

Rika nods. As we start walking, I wonder if I have what it takes to survive on the wheel. If not, I wonder if I can learn the skills I need and find the heart to keep going.

I think about David, stuck out there with zebra-face and the other drones. I'm scared for him. And I think about Liam. He was the boy I saw on the museum screen, out of all the kids on the entire wheel. I'm not hugely superstitious, but I still think there's something significant about that. I wonder what his first night on the wheel was like, if it was anything like mine. Today he rushed off so bravely to fight the drones. Was he always like that, or did the wheel help shape him?

Rika and I start bending down, picking up branches, gathering the firewood. I make an effort to calm down and focus on the task. I try not to think about what fresh horrors the wheel might have in store for me tomorrow.

THE INTERLOPER

Later that night, after gathering firewood and eating some berries with a group of other villagers, I finally lie down in one of the surviving hammocks. My body instantly succumbs to exhaustion and battle fatigue. The rest of the night passes in what feels like one second.

When I wake up early in the morning, I lie there for a moment in the heat before I sit up. It must be ninety degrees already, even in the shade. My hair is matted with sweat, and my muscles are cramped and knotted. I see slices of cloudless blue sky between the palm fronds above me. All around, I hear the noises of the village.

I was dreaming that I was home. Not at the orphanage, but back with my mum and dad when I was a little girl. Running around with other kids, when we would go on vacations to Old Florida. Back when books and computers and everything else were still allowed. Back before the UNA became something larger than the people it was meant to represent. Before Minister Harka took total control.

I wish I could crawl back into the world of my dream and turn it into reality. I want to relive those lazy days with my parents: eating good food, watching TV, reading books, and playing games with neighbourhood kids. I didn't think those things would ever come to an end.

But those days are gone, I tell myself bluntly. *They were all just a pleasant dream – so get over it.* My mum and dad are never coming back home because they probably died long ago. And I'm never going back home either. Home has been obliterated. I'm probably fated to spend the rest of my days on this island, fighting to stay alive. So the sooner I get used to it, the better for everyone. At least I have girls like Gadya and Rika on my side.

I swing myself out of the hammock and pull back my hair, wishing I had a rubber band to keep it out of my face. I walk into the sunlight. It's even hotter here. The odour of grilling bacon hangs in the air.

A figure steps into view. It's Veidman.

'Sleep well?' he asks.

I immediately feel self-conscious. I don't need a mirror to know how bad I look. But I try to play it off. 'Better than I thought I would.'

'Listen, I'm sorry about the whole truth serum thing yesterday.' He almost sounds sheepish.

'It's OK.'

'Good, 'cause I need to talk to you about last night.'

We start walking together along one edge of the clearing.

'Have they got you pulling chores yet?' he asks as we stroll past some other kids. Most of them are already awake, starting their workday repairing damage from the drone attack.

'Who do you mean by "they"? I thought you were in charge. You and Meira.'

He laughs softly. 'In some ways. Not all.' He pauses for a second. I try to smooth down my tangled hair. 'You drink coffee?'

I stop walking. 'Wait – You have coffee here?'

'We roast our own. Come with me.' Veidman and I walk along a narrow path at the edge of the camp. 'So, I didn't see the incident last night,' he finally says. 'I was fighting in the woods. But Rika says you watched someone get taken?'

'I've been trying not to think about it.'

'The first time I saw something like that, I was afraid it was going to happen to me next. I'd wake up in the night. Panicking. Sweating. Freaking out.'

'It's hard to imagine you like that.' Veidman has an aura of authority, like an adult.

'You'd be surprised,' he replies.

He takes me over to one of the thatched huts, which is stocked with rudimentary provisions. He pours a pungent liquid from a decanter into two chipped ceramic mugs and hands one to me. I take a sip. It's sludgy like molasses but tastes delicious. We sit down in homemade wooden chairs near the door.

'This better not have any truth serum in it,' I only half-joke as I hoist my mug.

'The only drug in there is caffeine.' He takes a swig from his cup. 'See? Totally safe.' His eyes dance. 'Like I said, I'm sorry I had to test you yesterday, but not everyone on the wheel is who they appear to be.'

'I know. Gadya told me.' I take another sip. 'Why don't

you just give truth serum to everyone in this village and find out who the spy is? I mean, if there is a spy.'

Veidman looks off into space for a moment. 'Meira won't let me. I wanted to, but she made a case against it. Said if we forced people to take the truth serum, it would make us as bad as Minister Harka and the UNA. A lot of kids agreed with her.' He glances down at his coffee mug in contemplation. 'We made a compromise. We agreed to test the new kids who arrive, and just watch everyone else really closely.' He shrugs. 'Who knows? Maybe I'm wrong to use the serum at all.' Veidman's eyes have a faraway look in them.

'So you've been on this island three and a half years?' I say, to keep the conversation going.

'Just about.'

'And somehow you've stayed sane.'

'The wheel gets easier with time. The rules are simple: Just fight the drones and avoid the feelers. You can survive and make a new life for yourself in our village. No ID cards. No earpieces. You can reinvent yourself. Become whoever you want to be.' His eyes grow even more distant. 'Some days I'm not even sure we should be searching for a way off the wheel – but don't tell anyone I said that.'

'You really think there's a way off?'

He peers at me over his coffee mug. 'Yes. The aircrafts in the grey zone hold the key.'

We suddenly hear footsteps crunching down the path towards us. A second later, Liam appears at the doorway. He doesn't look like he did the night before. In fact, it takes me a second to even recognise him. He's shirtless, hair back in a bandana, and his face and muscular torso are smeared with dried blood. His arm is still in its sling. He looks savage, like some kind of ancient gladiator, or mythological warrior. I can feel my heart start beating faster.

'What's up?' Veidman asks, a trace of annoyance in his voice.

'You need to come right away,' Liam tells him. 'We found someone during the morning hunt.' He glances at me and adds softly, 'Hey, Alenna.'

I'm startled that he knows my name. It almost makes me blush. 'Hey,' I tell him back.

I'm struck by the contrast between his fierce appearance and his gentle tone. And of course I'm struck by his physique. I can't help it. My eyes drift over his olive skin.

'You've been out hunting?' I ask, trying to ignore the way he makes me feel.

'We took down two hoofers, and it's not even nine o'clock.' He smiles crookedly. 'Me and four other hunters. We tracked 'em for a mile, then hauled their carcasses back here. We're gonna bury one in mud to keep it cool.'

'Great,' I say lamely, taking another sip of coffee to cover my awkwardness. I'm no good at talking to boys.

'I heard you volunteered to help with chores last night,' Liam says. 'Even after the raid.'

I nod.

'Cool.' He sounds impressed, and I feel my face flush again.

'Liam, can you be more specific about *who* you found and

why you're bothering us right now?' Veidman interrupts. 'Alenna and I were talking before you came along.'

'Oh, yeah. Sorry. A lost drone. We've got him tied up in the fire pit.'

Veidman puts down his mug. Looks at me. 'Guess we better check it out.'

'I guess so.' I feel weird, but in a good way. For once, two attractive boys in close proximity are actually looking at me instead of completely ignoring me.

Veidman and I get up and begin heading back to the fire pit with Liam.

I want to pepper both of them with questions, but I glance over at Veidman and see that he's looking straight ahead, preoccupied. There's no chance to talk to Liam either, because he's walking a few paces in front of us. I notice that even his back has muscles.

When we reach the fire pit, a small crowd is gathered around it. The fire is out, and the pit has been cleared of last night's wood. A figure, wrists bound with rope, is sitting in the centre on a bed of ashes, his back to us.

The crowd watches the figure in silence. I expected them to be taunting or insulting the drone, but they aren't doing any of that. They're just staring as he sways back and forth in the pit. I spot Assassin Elite in the crowd, but other than him, these are mostly unfamiliar villagers.

Veidman immediately strides away from me and Liam, directly towards the fire pit. He walks halfway around it, stopping in front of the drone.

'What's your name?' he asks sternly, but he receives no answer.

I hang back a little with Liam.

'We dragged him here with the hoofers,' Liam whispers to me. 'He's one of the drones who attacked the village last night.'

As we start walking around one side of the pit, I look closer. It's only then, as I see the red face paint, that I realise this is no typical drone. 'Oh my God, that's David!' I exclaim, rushing forward.

I reach the edge of the pit a few seconds later. Most of David's paint has been scraped off. He looks exhausted, all the energy kicked out of him. He's dirty and bruised, and his clothes are just rags. His left foot is badly swollen. He looks over at me, and his eyes brighten with recognition.

'Alenna!'

'This is David,' I say to the crowd, looking around at everyone. 'David Aberley. The kid who I woke up next to yesterday when I got here. He's not a drone. He's one of us. Let him go!'

The crowd eyes me like they think I'm crazy. I look around for Gadya. She could help confirm my story right now, but there's no sign of her.

'All I want to know is what you're doing in our sector,' Veidman says to David, ignoring me. There's no warmth in his voice. His face is twisted into a scowl, making him look almost ugly – something I would have thought impossible just minutes earlier.

'Stop,' I plead.

I feel a hand on my shoulder. It's Liam. 'Alenna, whether he's new or not, the drones might have threatened or bribed him last night. He might be corrupted already. Just let Veidman talk to him.'

'I was a drone for less than a day!' David cries out hoarsely, like he's overheard us. 'I was actually trying to get away from them! I got lost.'

It's obvious that most of the crowd doesn't believe him.

Assassin Elite steps up on the stone rim of the fire pit and stares down at him. 'Lost? I thought you drones were supposed to know this forest. What's your Monk gonna think of you now, chump?'

'I couldn't care less, because I'm not a drone,' David insists. 'This is ridiculous.'

I look around at the crowd. 'Why not just give him some truth serum?'

Veidman doesn't reply.

'I want to be here with you guys, not with the drones,' David says. 'I mean, am I acting like a drone right now? Think about it.'

Veidman crouches down at the edge of the pit, directly in front of David, at his level. 'OK, I hear you. But try to see it from our perspective. It's difficult to trust someone who attacked us last night, wearing face paint and holding a spear. So just tell me what happened, and then I'll decide what to do with you.'

'Last night, after that thing in the sky came down,

I managed to ditch the other drones who brought me here,' David says. 'But then I got turned around in the forest, and—'

'Couldn't find your friends!' a girl in the crowd yells. 'Couldn't burn down our village and capture any of us!'

Voices rise up in support of her words. Whether David is a drone or not doesn't matter to these villagers. The fact that he looks like one is enough for them to take their anger out on him.

'Quiet!' Veidman admonishes. He addresses David again: 'Keep talking.'

'I lost my way in the dark,' David murmurs. 'I couldn't find anyone. So that's why I hid in the forest all night and waited until daylight.' He shuts his eyes. 'When I got found by your hunters, I thought I was being rescued. All I want is to come and be part of your tribe, or whatever it is. I never wanted to go with the drones to begin with. They forced me to. Alenna and her friend – the girl with the blue hair – can clear all this up for you.'

'Not if you're secretly a spy!' an onlooker hisses.

The assembled crowd is growing larger, and they're muttering ominously among themselves. Someone throws a clod of dirt. It barely misses David's face.

'What are you gonna do with me, then?' David asks. 'I'm not the enemy, and I'm definitely not a spy.'

Liam steps forward. 'He's probably telling the truth about that part, at least. We found him one mile east of here, hiding up in a tree. If he's a spy, he's a pretty bad one.'

Veidman sighs. Then stands up, still looking at David.

'Until I can talk to Gadya and get some truth serum into you, I'm gonna have to lock you up for a little while, unfortunately. In one of our prison kennels. It's our policy to do this to anyone who turns up looking like a drone.'

'Great,' David mutters. 'Guilty until proven innocent. Just like in the UNA.'

'If our hunters hadn't found you, would you really have joined our village of your own free will?' Veidman asks. 'I can't be sure of that yet.'

David's shoulders slump. 'Fine, then. Just hurry up with your truth serum.'

Behind Veidman, I see a couple of hunters make slicing motions across their throats, like they want David dead. Veidman doesn't notice, but Liam does.

Concerned, Liam moves closer to David, stepping down into the fire pit. 'I can take him to the kennels if you want, Vei. Might be safest for him until we get this straightened out.'

'Fine,' Veidman murmurs. 'Meira and I will meet you there.'

Liam grabs David and helps him out of the pit.

'It's gonna be OK!' I call out to David, wanting to help him like he helped me.

Assassin Elite steps from the front of the crowd and takes David's other arm. Slowly, he and Liam lead David away up one of the trails.

The group begins to disperse. Gadya walks up beside me, appearing from out of nowhere.

'Where were you?' I ask, startled.

'Watching from the back.'

'Why didn't you say anything? You recognise him, right? Just talk to Veidman.'

Gadya holds up her hand. 'I'm not saying anything to Veidman yet. David's been out of our sight for most of a day. We don't know what happened to him when we weren't watching.'

'It just seems really paranoid to treat him like a full-fledged drone, when we know he isn't.'

Gadya looks irritated. 'Hey, if you don't like how we do things, then go back into the forest and stumble around alone. See how long you last!'

The force of her words backs me off a step. 'Look, I'm just trying to learn the ropes here. Don't get mad at me.'

'I'm not.' She takes a deep breath and then exhales slowly. Finally she says, 'All right. Maybe you touched a nerve.'

I nod, trying to understand.

'When I first got here, I didn't find Veidman and the village right away.' She grimaces in disgust. 'I got found by two drones instead. I didn't know who, or what, they were. They said they'd just arrived on the wheel themselves, so I trusted them. I was green. I let myself get taken advantage of.' Her eyes go distant. 'Every day I think about getting revenge for what those bastards did to me.'

I touch her arm gently.

She looks down at my hand. 'The Monk's people don't live by any rules,' she continues. 'Their society's based on his crazy religious teachings and his desire for power. His drones are drunk on fermented berries half the time, and always planning trouble and destruction. The Monk tells them the first step to getting off the wheel is conquering all the other sectors – at any cost. So even though I don't agree with some of Veidman and Meira's decisions, their rules keep us safe. And they keep us human.'

I picture lizard boy, dancing like a lunatic in the spray of fireworks last night. Completely out of his mind, like an animal. *Gadya's right. Those kids are nothing like us.* But I also know that David isn't one of them.

'Where are the kennels? Can I go visit him?'

'Maybe later. It'll take a while for Veidman and Meira to interrogate him.' Then, deliberately changing the subject, Gadya asks, 'Wanna help me and Rika prepare lunch?'

I nod, deciding not to push the David issue right now. I know Gadya's not going to back down. I feel guilty that I haven't been able to do more for David already. *At least he's in our village now, instead of out in the forest.* I'm confident that Veidman will quickly figure out he's telling the truth and set him free.

'So I'm guessing lunch is hoofer stew?' I ask Gadya.

'Yeah, but with some grubs and worms mixed in for protein.'

'Seriously?'

Gadya smiles, unable to keep a straight face. 'Just messing with you. See, you're still too gullible. We gotta work on that.' She spits on the ground. 'It'll be a cold day in hell before I eat an insect.'

We head over to a makeshift cooking area forty paces from the fire pit. Around us everyone seems busy, although I'm not exactly sure what they're doing. Cooking pots hang from triangular frames made from tree branches, over low flames.

I notice Rika standing next to a tureen made from a hollowed log. She waves as we approach.

Behind her, two boys are carving up a hoofer carcass, cutting the marbled meat with razorlike blades that must have been sharpened on rocks. The boys work quickly and efficiently, slicing the meat into thin strips and hanging it on branches to cure in the sun.

'Rika takes cooking seriously, and she's really good at it,' Gadya tells me as we near. 'If it weren't for her, things would be worse in the village. It's hard to fight on an empty stomach.'

When we reach Rika, she's stirring a thin brown liquid with a stick. Lumps of greasy hoofer meat bob near the surface. It looks revolting, but smells surprisingly good. 'Grab a stick and start stirring,' Rika tells me.

Gadya leans over and sniffs. 'Not bad.'

'Considering what I have to work with, it's a frigging gourmet masterpiece. Now someone help me stir already.'

I rummage on the ground, find a stick, and wipe it down. 'Will this work?'

'Yup.'

I take over the stirring duties as Rika begins chopping up a green cabbage-like plant. The smell of the stew makes my mouth water. I hold the stick up and lick it, sneaking a taste. It's tangy, like sweet-and-sour sauce.

I hear Rika and Gadya start laughing. They've been watching me. 'Thumbs up or thumbs down?' Rika asks. 'Be honest.'

I give her a thumbs up.

'Feel free to keep sampling. I always do.'

I stick my finger in and lick it showily. Rika laughs again.

So I stand there with the two girls, talking and laughing as we prepare the stew together. Other kids stop by and help. I try to catch their names, but there are so many of them that they tumble together into a blur of tanned faces and shaggy hair.

I realise that I almost feel safe, despite what happened last night, and despite the fact that David has been imprisoned. The wheel is definitely a terrifying, violent place – fraught with danger – but right now this village is a place of refuge, and I'm grateful to have found it.

TIGER STRIKE

Two hours later, almost all the members of the village are sitting around the fire pit, scarfing down Rika's stew for lunch. Veidman has returned from administering the truth serum to David. I was hoping that David would join us, but there's no sign of him.

'David was telling the truth even before we gave him the serum,' Veidman says, standing up on his tree stump to address the crowd. 'Or at least he seemed to be, at first.'

Everyone starts murmuring.

'Where is he, then?' a boy calls out.

'Still in the kennels.' Veidman runs a hand through his blond hair. 'Although he passed the truth test, Meira and I still thought his story was suspicious. We think he might be a different class of drone. One who's been prepared in advance to answer our questions and endure the serum, or maybe – through hypnosis or other means – he has had some kind of secret agenda implanted in his mind. Until we have time to interrogate him further, we're going to keep him locked up.'

Hypnosis? The whole thing seems completely implausible to me. 'But—' I begin to say. Heads immediately turn in my direction. I fall silent.

I'm nervous to speak in front of such a large gathering, and I also don't want to say the wrong thing. I know that David is genuine, and I'm worried for him, but I have to tread carefully. I clear my throat. 'If he passed the truth test, then I don't understand why you still don't believe him.' I ignore the scowls that come my way. 'What's the point of the test if you don't think it works?'

'It's more complicated than that,' Veidman continues smoothly. 'We're hoping to get more information from him soon. One way or another.'

'Did you ask him about the Cannibal Monk's face?' a girl's voice calls out.

I'm not sure what she's talking about. I glance at Gadya. She anticipates my question:

'None of us have ever actually seen the Monk,' she whispers. 'And none of the Monk's drones we capture will tell us anything specific. Supposedly the Monk always wears a wooden mask. Always. Some drones wear metal ones to emulate him. And the Monk never walks. He's carried everywhere by four drones.'

'Who knows if he even exists?' Rika chimes in from my other side. 'Some kids think he's a mass delusion.'

Gadya shakes her head. 'I just think he's smart enough to keep a low profile. But who knows? Maybe he's dead, and his own people don't know it yet. They just keep on fighting anyway.'

Our whispers trail away as Meira appears from the trees. She alights on a rock near Veidman, like an exotic species of bird. Her clothes are so clean and white, I don't know how she keeps them that way. Whenever I see her, I get embarrassed about how shabby I look. My sweaty clothes and underwear stick to my body, and the skin under my bra chafes. But of course most of these kids look more like me than like Meira. So maybe she's the one who should feel out of place.

Meira stands up, displaying the fluid grace of a UNA fashion model. She speaks where Veidman left off. 'The good news is, we don't think David knows about Operation Tiger Strike yet. This could mean the spy in our village hasn't had a chance to share any recent intel with the Monk.'

'Or maybe there *is* no spy, like a lot of us have been saying,' Edie adds.

'Operation Tiger Strike?' I mouth at Gadya.

'I'll tell you about it,' a soft voice says in my ear, making me jump. It's Liam. He has moved up behind us, silently and stealthily.

Gadya tries to pretend he's not there, but I glance back at him. He's cleaned up nicely and put on fresh clothes – jeans and a faded blue V-neck.

'It's the code name for a secret expedition,' he whispers to me. 'A small group of us hunters are going to look for another way into the grey zone, now that the tunnel's gone. The whole zone's surrounded by some kind of gigantic high-tech barrier, but if we can make an opening and get inside, we're going to keep exploring the zone, find out where the aircrafts are, and hijack one of them.'

'That sounds dangerous… I mean, kind of—' I stutter.

'Can you two be quiet?' Gadya hisses in annoyance. I fall silent, but Liam doesn't.

'Gadya agrees with me, even if she won't admit it. Eventually we're all gonna die in this village. Taken by the drones or the Suffering or the feelers. We can't stay here forever, because forever isn't very long on the wheel. We need to send an expedition party to find a way off. Then we'll come back and get everyone else.'

The thought of people leaving the village frightens me. And I don't want Liam to go anywhere, not before I can talk to him more. I'm about to respond, when I realise Meira has stopped addressing the gathering. I look up and see that she's staring at Gadya, Liam and me. So is Veidman.

'Liam, you got something to say?' Veidman asks.

Liam shakes his head. 'Nope.'

'You were telling Alenna about Operation Tiger Strike, am I right?'

Liam nods. 'Yep.'

Veidman turns his eyes to me. 'Our village is divided. Some of the hunters want to form a group and head into the grey zone right away to find the aircrafts. But other villagers are afraid of—'

'We're not afraid!' a girl's voice says vehemently right next to me, and I'm surprised to see that it's Rika. 'We just think it's a stupid idea to split up the village and lose our best warriors. It puts everyone at risk!'

Voices call out in support of her. Mostly female. But some

of the hunters start pounding homemade spears against rocks, making a din.

Assassin Elite holds up a spear excitedly. He looks ready to leave the village this instant and go on a rampage. 'It's stupid to stay here and wait for the next attack!' he yells. 'All of us can't go anyway. Too many people. So let the stupid people stay, and everyone else leave!'

His words get drowned out by the crowd.

The argument lasts for the next half- hour. I stay silent the whole time, just watching and listening.

What I learn is this: most of the camp wants everyone to stay at the village. They feel like it's their home. They've made a life here, even if it's an imperfect one. They're also worried about the Ones Who Suffer, and don't want to abandon them. And they're scared about what the hunters will encounter in the unknown heart of the grey zone, assuming the hunters can even get back inside now that the tunnel is destroyed.

A minority of the camp – comprised mostly of hunters and warriors – wants to leave the village as soon as possible and go on the expedition. This vocal contingent of boys wants to search, and fight, for a way off the wheel.

Nothing gets resolved by the end of the debate around the fire pit. I'm hoping that maybe no decision will get made for a long time, not until some crucial event tips the balance. I just got to this village. I don't want to see it disintegrate around me. And I need to help David. I wouldn't be alive if it weren't for him.

As the group begins to disperse, Gadya and I stand up.

Liam has already disappeared into the forest barefoot, completely at home in the outdoors. After spending my whole life in the concrete and asphalt of New Boston and New Providence, the natural world still feels like a stranger to me.

I turn to Gadya. 'What do you think about Operation Tiger Strike? And why's it called that, anyway?'

'I dunno. Stupid crap the boys thought up,' she answers absently.

'So do you agree with Liam, like he said?'

'I don't see eye to eye with Liam on *anything*.' She stares at me long and hard. Too long. She's scrutinising my face. 'You like him. I can tell,' she finally mutters. 'Wonderful.'

'What? I barely know him.'

'Just don't pursue him. He's off-limits to you.'

'Fine. No problem. I know that you guys dated, but I thought—'

'Rika should have kept her mouth shut,' Gadya snaps. 'She doesn't know what went on between me and Liam. No one does. It doesn't matter if we're together right at this moment. It just matters that you stay away from him.' She's starting to sound pissed off at me, for no reason. 'You can't just flounce in here with your wavy hair and your pale skin and try to go after all the guys, y'know? It doesn't work that way.'

'I'm not doing anything but trying to stay alive!' I sputter. 'Liam talked to me. I didn't talk to him.'

Gadya isn't appeased. 'Let's just see how you look after a year on the wheel. After a bad diet, and all the stress, and all the battles. You'll look like a ghost of yourself. A wretched, skinny, beat-up ghost!'

I feel like bursting into tears. If I were alone, I probably would. But I refuse to cry in front of Gadya. I'm mad at myself for even feeling like I want to.

I glare back at her. 'So what if boys are giving me attention? Back home I was invisible for the first sixteen years of my life. Boys never gave me the time of day. *Ever.* I was just a random orphan girl.' I swallow hard, to stop from getting teary again. 'Here, I feel different, like I've found people who don't look through me. Like you, Rika, Veidman, and yes, Liam too. But I am *not* going after him, or anyone else, OK? So back off.'

Gadya blinks a couple of times, keeping up a hard face to mask the emotions roiling beneath the surface. 'That's exactly how I felt before I came here,' she finally mutters. 'Invisible, I mean. I guess it's been so long that I forgot how it was back home. I could never get along with anyone. I don't even know why things are so different here.'

I keep glaring at her.

She pushes a strand of hair behind her ear, her face softening. 'Look, I'm an idiot, OK?' Words come tumbling out like a painful confession. 'Maybe I'm used to getting a lot of attention from the guys. Not as much as Meira gets, of course, but Veidman scares everyone away. And yeah, I do remember what it was like to feel unwanted in the UNA, like you're just part of the wallpaper. Or a crummy piece of old furniture. A number instead of a person.' She exhales shakily. 'So do you forgive me for acting like an idiot?'

'Yeah,' I say, relieved. 'Of course.'

She steps forward, and we hug. Then she lets go of me. 'I guess I still haven't gotten over Liam, huh? Pretty dumb to get hung up over a boy.' She pauses. 'And for what it's worth, I dumped him because he wouldn't spend any time with me. He's only interested in hanging out with his buddies and talking about hunting. But it still hurts.'

'At least you guys had a relationship. I've never even been on a single date,' I confess.

'You will soon, with the way boys look at you here.' Gadya grins at me.

Our argument has ended as quickly as it began, like a summer rain shower.

Just as we move to the edge of the clearing and start walking up one of the trails, I hear a sudden crash. Assassin Elite comes running out of the forest. I gasp, startled, banging into Gadya.

'Boo!' he yells, cackling wildly.

'Moron!' Gadya yells back. 'Were you eavesdropping on us?'

'You wish!' He laughs as he playfully dodges a blow from Gadya's fist. 'Your girl talk doesn't interest me. But it might interest Liam!' He laughs again as Gadya tries to kick him between the legs.

'Get out of here, you perv!' she yells. Still laughing, he races up the path away from us. Gadya looks like she wants to chase him, but she just sighs. 'He's a good hunter, but he's so immature, he drives me crazy.'

I hear him cackling in the distance. 'He's the kind of guy who makes girls *wish* they were still invisible,' I say.

Gadya laughs. 'No doubt.'

'What's his real name, anyway?'

'Sinxen Ro,' Gadya says, spelling his first name out for me. 'He's really touchy about it, probably because it's so freaking weird. Everyone calls him Sinxen anyway, instead of Assassin Elite.'

'Good to know. I like it better.'

We keep walking, ducking our heads under branches. I'm not even sure where we're going. 'So, what do you think about David?' I finally ask. 'He seemed really normal to me. And last night he actually tried to help me and Rika when the drones attacked.'

'I trust Veidman. If he thinks something fishy is going on, then I believe him. But if David's who he seems, then he'll become part of our village, just like you.'

I nod. 'And what about Tiger Strike? What do you really think about it?'

'Honestly? Rebuilding sucks. I'm burned out. We need to find a way off the wheel before it's too late.'

'So you'll go with the expedition party? I mean, if they leave?'

'Yup, with the rest of the hunters.'

'I guess I'll just stay here in the village with Rika,' I say glumly.

'If enough hunters go, there might not be much of a village left.'

I don't reply. Obviously I'm hoping a lot of hunters decide to stay, because I don't want to get slaughtered. But I also realise that on the wheel, I might not have the luxury of keeping my hands clean. If I want to stay alive, I might have to get down in the dirt. *And fight.*

THE CAPTIVE

That afternoon, I volunteer for another assignment. Veidman needs someone to bring a tureen of vegetable soup to David and the other prisoners, so I tell him that I'll do it. This is partly because I want to feel useful, but mainly because I want to check in on David and find out if I can help him.

The tureen is a large, heavy copper drum with a lid on it. Gadya and Rika help me get it into a backpack made from dried hoofer skin, and I hoist the pack over my shoulders. I have a walk ahead of me. The prison kennels are set half a mile from the main camp for security reasons.

'Watch your back around the prisoners,' Gadya advises me. 'Even if David turns out to be OK, the others definitely aren't.'

'Yeah, just give the soup to their guard, and he'll dole it out,' Rika adds.

'Who's their guard?'

'Markus Horvath. He's from New Portland.'

I try to loosen the vine straps over my shoulders. They're biting into my flesh, but I don't complain because I don't want to sound like a wimp. 'How many prisoners are there?'

'Fourteen. We had fifteen, but one ran away a month ago. It was a big relief actually, because then we didn't have to waste food on him any more.'

'Gadya likes to pretend she's heartless,' Rika adds, giving my backpack a pat. 'If you haven't figured that out yet.'

'I'm not pretending,' Gadya retorts.

With a wave, I start heading up the path leading to the kennels.

'Be careful!' Rika calls after me.

I hike through the forest, my feet crunching on twigs and dried leaves. Thick vines hang overhead, crisscrossing the path like electrical cables. Sometimes I have to crouch and duck underneath them. Tall trees on either side form natural walls of foliage, as dense as a hedge maze in places.

I realise this is one of the first times I've been alone since arriving at the village. Every sound is magnified, my senses on high alert. I quicken my pace. The backpack grows heavier, but I settle into a good hiking rhythm.

Strange birds trill and call to one another overhead. I tilt my head up and catch a glimpse of multicoloured wings fluttering past beneath the canopy of trees. *No place with such beautiful birds can be all bad,* I tell myself. But I'm not sure I believe it.

Eventually the path ends in a small clearing that houses the kennels – two long rows of bamboo prison cells, about thirty in all. There's no sign of a guard.

Worried, I slow down. From my angle of approach, I can't even see who's inside the bamboo cells.

'Markus?' I call out.

There's a shuffling noise nearby, and I startle, making the liquid in the tureen slosh. All kinds of awful visions dance through my mind. *Maybe the prisoners escaped and they're planning an attack!* I glance around in jittery panic, prepared to dump the soup and run.

Then I see a figure stumble out of the trees. It's a tall boy with curly blond hair. Markus. He's not overweight exactly, but he's large and fleshy, with big hands. He's zipping up his pants and looking around.

'Hey!' I call out.

He turns to me. 'Alenna, right? Sorry. Just taking a leak.' He motions to my backpack. 'You got my soup in there?'

I nod. I swing the pack off my shoulders and gently lower it to the ground. Markus walks over and scoops up the backpack easily in one hand. He doesn't look particularly friendly.

He takes the pack over to a dilapidated wooden picnic table at the edge of the clearing and unloads the tureen. I keep glancing at the kennels, but the prisoners are hard to see in the shadows, silent and still.

Markus turns to me as he opens the tureen. 'Wanna help me feed these bastards?'

'Sure,' I say. 'I can start with the new guy.'

'Oh yeah, David-something-or-other. They're all the same to me.' He picks up a wooden ladle and a green ceramic bowl from the table and thrusts them at me. 'Knock yourself out.'

I begin filling the bowl with the thin watery soup. It smells like potatoes.

'He's in the isolation cell,' Markus instructs. 'It's at the end of the row on the left, set off from the others. We keep the new prisoners in isolation for a week, just in case they're real crazy. I'll start feeding the rest of 'em.'

Carefully holding the bowl, I move towards the bamboo cages. Thin, sturdy stalks of green bamboo form the sides and ceilings of the cages, woven together to create a strong mesh. Vertical bamboo sticks are dug deep into the dirt at the bottom to keep the prisoners from digging their way out.

The densely woven bamboo slats make it hard to see inside. I squint as I get closer. I thought the prisoners would be noisily clamouring to get out. But they're oddly quiet.

I glance down to keep the soup from spilling out of the bowl. When I look up again, I'm almost at the first row of kennels. I pause, nervous. Inside the nearest cell I see a thin dark figure sitting against the back. The cell is too small for him to stand up in. I can't tell if he's asleep or secretly watching me.

I pass him by. The other kennels also hold silent, motionless figures.

'They wake up at night,' Markus calls after me. I glance back. 'They sleep most of the day. The heat, I guess.' He gestures at the cages. 'After sunset they'll be screeching and banging on the bamboo like monkeys. But the new guy's different.' Markus points at the isolation cage, that lone bamboo cell near the edge of the clearing. 'He's awake now because he hasn't fallen into their pattern yet. But he will.' He doles some soup into a bowl for another prisoner. 'Oh, and watch your hair. They like to pull it.'

I turn back and walk the rest of the way to the isolation

cage. I can finally see David crouching inside, a shaft of light illuminating his eyes through the bamboo slats. He looks a bit groggy. Maybe it's from the after effects of the truth serum.

'David, it's me,' I say, kneeling in front of his cell. I hold the bowl up. 'I brought soup.' I lean down and push the bowl through a rectangular opening at the bottom. 'You'll feel better after you eat this.'

'Alenna.' He hunches forward. More light falls on to his face. His eyes are red, like he's been crying. 'You gotta get me out of here.'

'I'm working on it.'

'Why am I still locked up? I told them everything I know.'

'They think you've got some kind of secret plan, maybe put there by hypnosis. That you're working for the Monk. It's crazy, I know.'

He shakes his head. 'I barely spent any time in the drones' camp. I didn't even pass my initiation rite with them, because I didn't kill anyone. And they definitely didn't hypnotise me.'

'I believe you.'

'So what are the villagers planning to do with me?'

'Veidman said they want to ask you more questions or something.'

'So the drones are after me, and the villagers don't trust me. No side wants me.' He looks down at the bowl, and then back up at me. 'I just don't wanna end up like *them*.' He points at the occupants of the other cells. 'There's something wrong with the prisoners, and not just because they're drones.'

'What do you mean?'

'I think they're being drugged with more than truth serum. They're acting like zombies. Don't you see that?'

I glance behind me. Markus isn't watching us. He's ladling soup into bowls. 'Tell me more.'

'Maybe someone's putting drugs in their food to keep them docile.'

'Well, no one put anything in your soup. And you're probably safer in here than anywhere else on the wheel.'

'I doubt it.' He leans closer. His cheekbones catch a flash of sun. His skin is tight across them. Dirty, bruised. He moves closer still, pressing his face against the bamboo, talking softly. 'I just want to be free.' His black hair is matted. 'And I can barely see. My glasses got smashed by the drones, right before they attacked the village.'

'I'm—'

Without warning, one of his hands lashes out of the opening at the bottom of the kennel.

I try to leap back, stunned. But I'm not fast enough. David's thin fingers grab me around the wrist.

The soup bowl spins sideways with a clatter, spraying its contents over the earthen floor of the cell. David must have been creeping his hands closer to the opening the whole time he was talking to me.

He yanks me forward, off balance. I tumble against the bamboo slats, slamming my face against them. I open my mouth to scream for Markus. David's fingers tighten like claws.

'Don't yell,' he whispers, his breath hot in my ear. 'Just listen.'

But Markus has heard the noise and is already rushing over from across the clearing. I try to pull away, but David won't let me go.

'There's something you don't know about the wheel! Get me out, and we can figure things out together! I can help you.'

'I'm not the one who needs help!' I yell at him, still shocked at what he's doing.

'Yes, you are. You just don't know it yet.' He presses himself against the bamboo, his words rushing out: 'Nothing here is what you think it is! I heard the drones talking when I was in their camp, after they interrogated me about my arrival on the island. I mentioned your full name – I saw it when you wrote it on the leaf. They went crazy when they heard it. They asked me a million questions. I think your parents were—'

'My parents? What are you talking about?'

Suddenly Markus is there, towering over me, screaming at David. He's holding a thin pointed stick. He jabs it between the bamboo slats just as David releases my arm. The stick catches David in the shoulder and tosses him back against the other side of the cell.

Markus puts his hands under my armpits and yanks me to my feet. 'Did he hurt you?'

'I'm fine,' I say, although I'm shaken and my mind is spinning.

Your parents. That was what David said, unless I heard him wrong. What could he possibly know about my mum and dad?

Markus lets me go. We both step back from David's cell. 'I told you to watch yourself,' Markus says sharply. 'Drones are like animals.' He stares into the cell, brandishing his pointed stick. 'Touch her again and I'll thrash you, understand?' Markus pokes the stick through the slats again, trying to prod David. But David suddenly grabs hold of the stick and starts a tug-of-war.

'Let go!' Markus yells, but David keeps holding on. Long enough that he has time to stare directly at me.

'I think your parents got sent to this island!' he starts yelling. 'Thomas and Leah Shawcross, right? Dissidents like them were shipped here after the UNA got formed.' Markus wrenches the stick back and cracks David across his forehead. David yelps and tumbles back, hands pressed to his head.

'Shut up with your nonsense!' Markus yells at him.

'Let him speak,' I plead. But Markus keeps jabbing him.

'All drones do is lie,' Markus says. 'They're liars and thieves and scumbuckets!'

'But how could he know about my parents?' I ask desperately. 'I never told him their names.'

'I don't know, and I don't care.' Markus turns back and slams David with the stick again.

'Stop – Don't—'

Markus isn't listening.

David is gagging. One of the blows caught him in the throat. I see that his lip is split.

'You really hurt him,' I tell Markus as he steps back, sweaty and breathing hard.

'Good. Us villagers are trying to make the best of things on the wheel. His kind are trying to make the worst.'

'He only fell in with the drones because they caught him when he helped me and Gadya escape. Don't torture him!'

'Torture?' He sounds incredulous. 'Veidman gave him the truth serum and still doesn't trust him. They're working on a stronger serum to give him next. And there'll be a stronger one after that, believe me.'

'Just let me talk to him one more time, OK?'

Markus steps back, rolling his eyes like I'm an idiot. 'Be my guest.'

I kneel down. David is still choking, trying to get his breath back. I whisper, 'I'll make sure you get out of here. I don't think you're a drone, or a spy, or anything else bad. Just tell me what you heard about my parents.'

The choking sounds resolve into words, forced out between gasps of air. 'I think your parents were here – years ago, on Island Alpha. It's not just for us kids.' He coughs and hacks, spitting out blood. 'Grown-ups got sent here once… I heard drones say that your name is carved on rocks. Near where they all break through the barrier into the grey zone – part of an old prison colony.'

His words have become indecipherable to me. Fractured and incoherent. 'A prison colony?' I ask.

'He's messing with your mind,' Markus interrupts, sounding frustrated and exhausted. 'Alenna, I need you to head back to the fire pit now.' It sounds like an order. 'And get your arm looked at too. Infections happen fast out here.'

I don't know what he means until I glance down and see that David's fingernails have torn my skin. Droplets of blood dot my wrist like a red bracelet.

I want to stay and help David, but Markus is firm about my leaving. There's nothing I can say to make him change his mind.

I decide not to press my luck right now, because I'm new to the village. Instead I just decide to lie.

I look Markus square in the eyes. 'Maybe you're right, after all. Maybe he is just a crazy drone. He's not making a whole lot of sense.'

Markus seems relieved by my sudden change in attitude. 'Exactly. All we gotta do is feed 'em and not think too much. If I still had my UNA earpiece, I'd wear it around the prisoners. I'd rather listen to Minister Harka's propaganda than these drones.'

I start backing away. 'So, I'll go back to the fire pit, then. Wash my arm. See if Rika needs help with anything.'

'Good call.' Markus is breathing freely again.

But he wouldn't be if he knew my real plan: to sneak back to the kennels later on, tonight. When Markus hopefully isn't on duty. I need to ask David more questions – and figure out how to convince the others to let him go free. I can't decide yet whether I should tell Gadya about the things David said.

Of course, I'm not sure I actually believe that my parents were ever on the wheel. I've never heard of Island Alpha housing anyone except kids who failed the GPPT. And there's no sign of any adults here. But I definitely believe that David learned a lot more about the wheel from the drones than I've learned so far from the villagers.

I wonder if Veidman knows that Markus beats the prisoners. If Veidman were considering letting David out, would he really let Markus treat him that way? But then again, if Veidman is drugging the captured drones like David claims, he probably doesn't care.

I keep all of these thoughts wrapped tightly inside my head as I say goodbye to Markus. With a final glance at David's cell, I make my way back to the trail.

As I walk down to the main clearing, I barely notice my surroundings. I'm thinking about my mum and dad. I miss them so much, it still hurts like a physical pain in my chest whenever I picture their faces – especially my dad. I was always closer to him than my mum, mostly because my mum spent so many hours away from home at the genetics lab. But David's words have conjured my parents in my mind again, at least for a moment.

Grown-ups on the island. My name on rocks somewhere, hidden inside the grey zone. Some kind of prison colony . . .

I know I have to learn the secrets of the wheel before it's too late. Before those secrets rise up and engulf me, and my chance to learn the truth gets ripped away forever.

Deep down I know that David holds a key to surviving and outsmarting this island. We need to share what we know. I wouldn't even be here if it weren't for David, so I'm definitely not going to let him rot in a prison kennel. I vow to return and help him before the night is over.

LIAM

When I reach the fire pit, I don't see Gadya or Rika. Instead, I see Liam. He sits against a nearby tree, whittling fresh arrow shafts from branches with a pocketknife. I notice that the sling is off his arm already. And for once, he's alone.

I hesitate for a moment, trying to compose myself after my encounter with David. I remember Gadya's warning that Liam is off-limits. Even though he's definitely attractive, I force myself not to think about him in that way. It would be easiest in some ways to completely avoid him. But I have a legitimate reason to talk to him right now, because he's been inside the grey zone. There's a good chance he knows something about the rocks that David was talking about.

I smooth down my hair, take a deep breath, and decide to walk over to him.

Liam hears me coming, glances up, and breaks into a smile. His teeth are very white. I wonder what people use for toothpaste on the wheel, because my teeth feel furry. I smile back at him, keeping my lips closed.

'Hey,' Liam says.

For a moment, I'm not sure what to say in response. I should have figured out some kind of opening line. Then I notice a pile of branches on one side of him, a stack of wooden shafts on the other, and a bowl of flint arrowheads nearby. 'That's a lot of arrows,' I say. I don't mention anything about my parents, or David, or how I saw Liam on the museum screen back in New Providence.

He stops whittling for a moment and flexes his hand. 'I hate doing stuff like this. I hate sitting still.'

'Really?'

'Yeah. I only feel like myself when I'm moving. But I gotta take it easy sometimes, until my arm heals. It's almost better. I broke it for the third time two months ago, and then I sprained it again in the tunnel collapse.'

'Ouch.'

He smiles, his eyes warm but guarded. 'I've been breaking bones since I was a little kid – mostly my own. My dad called me *Pequeño Demonio*. Little Terror.'

I laugh. 'Nice. I've never broken a bone in my life.'

'Then what do you do for fun?'

I laugh again. 'Play guitar. Write songs. That sort of stuff.'

'Cool. Acoustic guitar or electric?'

'Acoustic.'

He nods. I desperately want to tell Liam about everything, but I don't want to sound crazy and freak him out. Besides, I think I'm still in shock over what David said. 'Tell me about your family,' I say, sitting across from him on the grass. Near, but not too close.

'There's not much to tell. I've got five brothers, all still back in the UNA, as far as I know. My mum kept trying for a girl. Never happened.' He pauses. 'We moved around a lot because my parents were rebels. My dad's originally from Nuevo Tijuana, and my mum's originally from London, but she immigrated to Central UNA when it was still called America. I'm a mutt, I guess – half Latin, half British. My dad died when I was nine. Taken in an antigovernment demonstration.'

'Wow. That sucks.' I wonder how many kids on the wheel share the same experience. 'My parents got arrested when I was ten. They were rebels too, I guess.'

He pauses. 'Both of them?'

I nod.

'Tough.' He shakes his head. 'Any siblings?'

'Just me.' I push back a coil of hair. 'So, you probably miss your mum and all your brothers.'

'Yeah.' He doesn't say any more, but he doesn't need to. He looks down. He has started whittling again, his hands moving automatically.

'Maybe you'll see them again one day.'

'Not on the wheel, I hope. But yeah, someplace else.'

He holds an arrow shaft up to the sun, nearly finished. It's smooth and polished like it's been put on a lathe. He squints at it. 'Looks good, right? Wanna help me put the fletching on?' He picks two long black feathers out of the bowl, raises the knife, and slices them perfectly in two. Then he hands the pieces to me. From another bowl he takes a gluey substance and slathers it around the blunt end of the arrow's shaft. 'You put the feathers on like this, see?'

He guides my hand, sticking the feathers on to the wood.

The substance is already drying, fusing them in place. 'What is this gunk?' I ask.

'Pine sap.' He plucks the arrow out of my hands and holds it up again, rolling it between his hands. 'Nice.' He tosses it into a pile with the other arrows, awaiting their flint heads.

'I can help more.' I have the urge to be useful around him. Show him I'm not just some spoiled city girl who arrived here and expects to be taken care of.

'Good. I need all the help I can get.'

We sit there working together. A few minutes slide by in silence. It's a little awkward at first, but then it grows increasingly comfortable.

There were no boys like Liam at my school. Not many like him in all of the UNA, for that matter. Everyone back home seems dull and complacent in comparison. There's something special flashing behind Liam's eyes. He has substance. Charisma. I can see why Gadya would have trouble getting over him.

'How'd it go with Markus and the prisoners?' he finally asks.

I hedge, wishing I could tell him about David, but not wanting to give anything away yet.

'Markus kept beating on David with a stick.'

Liam frowns. 'He's not supposed to do that.' He looks around, like he doesn't want anyone to hear what he's going to say next. 'Markus has changed a lot from when I first met him. His girlfriend Chloe got taken four months ago. Not by drones, but by feelers. After that he was different.'

'Different how?'

'Before then, he'd give people the benefit of the doubt. What happened to Chloe messed with his head. Now he gets mad really easily, and he takes it out on the prisoners.'

'Veidman lets him?'

'He looks the other way. Maybe even encourages it sometimes.'

'I guess it doesn't matter,' I say quickly. I don't want to seem too interested in the prisoners, given my plan. 'So what's the grey zone like?'

'It's the worst sector on the wheel. And before it collapsed, the tunnel leading into it was a good place to get ambushed. There's so many stories I could tell—' He breaks off. 'All I'll say is that you see weird things in the grey zone. Huge stones with etchings on them. Remains of lost towns. And there are old gravestones too. It doesn't really make any sense.'

I instantly get goosebumps all over, and the hair on the nape of my neck begins prickling. I'm thinking about what David said. *A prison colony*. Inside that treacherous, forbidden zone. *Were my parents really sent to this place, just like me?*

Liam keeps talking. 'The air's different too – way colder all year round. So cold you have to wear jackets and gloves in there. No one knows why it's like that.'

'That's really weird.' I'm trying to imagine how a person could ever be cold on this sweltering island.

'I think the grey zone is where we first arrive when we

get sent here, even if we don't remember it,' he continues, looking over at me. 'Think about it. You just went to sleep in a testing arena, and woke up on the wheel, right? In the middle of nowhere.'

I nod.

'Even if an aircraft brought you to the wheel, what could have deposited you so far inland, right near our sector?'

It takes a second, but then the pieces suddenly snap together. 'The feelers!' I blurt out. 'They take people, but I bet they also bring us here, don't they?'

'That's my theory. I think there's some kind of landing station inside the grey zone. One that unloads us from the aircrafts and turns us over to the feelers. We have to get to that station, find out how it works, and then report back to the village. If we know what we're up against, we can figure out how to fight it.'

'How far do you think the wheel is from the mainland?'

'Veidman told me that some kids built a boat a few years ago. They sailed out for eighty miles. Nothing but ocean. They barely made it back alive. Veidman thinks we're thousands of miles from dry land.'

I mull this over. 'But if any of us ever do escape somehow, won't they just send us back here when we get home to the UNA? Or worse?'

Liam grins. 'Who said anything about going home? There are other countries on the globe. The European Coalition. Allied West Africa. Asiana. Most of them are at war with the UNA. Think of all the inside info we have that we could trade for new lives. And if it doesn't work, at least we tried. We didn't just sit around waiting to die before we turned eighteen.'

He reaches out and touches my knee. The gesture is sudden. I don't expect it. I feel a rush of longing to clasp my fingers over his. The feeling takes me by surprise. I want to tell him everything right then and there. But I can't. Not yet.

I see the passion to take action burning in his eyes, and I realise this is why he's a hunter and a scout.

I also know he's right. There are already so many ways to die on this island that getting off it can't be much worse. I realise my eyes are locked with his, so I look away, breaking the intensity of our gaze. I'm not a particularly romantic girl, but I have to admit that Liam is getting to me.

It's then that I see Gadya emerge from the forest, heading our way. I glance back at Liam. He takes his hand off my knee. I feel embarrassed, like I'm doing something wrong. I owe Gadya so much. The last thing I want to do is accidentally flirt with Liam, especially since she asked me to back off.

I stand up quickly and say, 'Hey,' as Gadya reaches us.

She holds out part of a plastic label, the kind you might find on a bottle of government-issue soda pop.

'Check this out,' she says to us. 'Edie just found it in the stream.'

Liam takes the wrapper and scrutinises it. There are rows of numbers and figures printed on it. A few nonsensical words.

'What is it?' I ask.

Liam hands it to me. 'See these drawings?' he asks, pointing at the wrapper. 'They're chemical formulas. And those words? Again, lists of chemicals.'

He and Gadya exchange a look. I can read the look well. It says, *How much should we tell the new girl about what we know?*

'It's fertiliser, or some kind of drug,' Liam finally says. 'These labels must come from its packaging. We keep finding them in the underbrush. We know they're fresh because they're stamped with this year's date.'

'The chemicals could be causing the Suffering,' Gadya adds.

Liam takes the wrapper back. 'Veidman thinks the feelers dispense chemicals in the atmosphere, and sometimes these labels accidentally get dropped too. No one's ever seen it happen, though. Or knows why.'

'Maybe they're just dumping garbage here,' I propose. 'The wheel could be one big trash heap for the UNA.'

Liam stands up. 'I'm gonna jet this over to Veidman. I think he's started collecting them.'

Gadya nods.

Liam leaves his pile of arrows and heads off rapidly into the forest. I stand there for a second, watching him disappear.

Gadya is about to say something to me, but right then we both hear a loud scream. It comes from deep within the forest, opposite from the direction that Liam went.

Then we hear another scream, and I realise that they're

not screams at all but war whoops. *Deranged cries of elation,*
coming from an army of drones.

'Crap,' Gadya mutters.

Warning calls go out around us as the village explodes
into action. Kids burst from trees, shacks, hammocks and
from around the fire pit, shouting orders. Boys rush around,
getting ready to fight and defend the village.

'I thought the drones only attack at night!' I yell.

'Guess someone forgot to tell 'em that.' Gadya grabs my
arm. 'Quick. This way.'

I catch glimpses of menacing shadows racing through the
trees. Painted bodies clutching spears. Gadya and I dash over
to a stash of bows, spears and other weapons hidden in a
trench near the base of a eucalyptus tree.

'Grab something!' she yells at me.

I have no clue how to fire an arrow with any accuracy, so
I snatch up a heavy wooden spear.

Gadya goes for a bow. She already has a knife strapped in
an ankle sheath. My chest tightens with panic, but my mind
remains clear. I've been through one of these attacks already.
I can get through another.

'You don't know how to fight, do you?' Gadya asks. 'Hand
to hand, I mean.'

My heart pounds faster now, beating out a staccato
rhythm. I feel the blood pumping through my veins. 'No, of
course not.'

'Then you better learn fast. I told you the wheel isn't for
wimps.' She glances at me. 'Grab that spear tighter. Use both

hands. Make it clear you can't be messed with. Get *fierce*!'

She notches an arrow into her bow, holding the weapon like a natural extension of her body. I know that if a drone comes through the trees, she'll let him have it right through the chest.

Yet despite all the screaming and running, no one comes barging out. In fact, the sounds are already lessening a bit. Like the drones are moving onwards. Maybe another distant village in this sector is their target today, not us.

Gadya keeps her eyes trained on the verdant wall of trees surrounding our side of the clearing. Behind us I see other kids doing the same, bows ready. I'm just relieved that the drones are heading away from us. I lower my spear, resting the tip on the dirt.

Then Gadya says, 'We can't let them get away.'

I hesitate. We're safe here. Or as safe as anyone can be on this island during the middle of a battle.

Gadya notices my reluctance to give chase. 'C'mon, what do you have to lose?'

'My life?'

'If it weren't for those of us who fight, you wouldn't have a life! Don't be like Rika and the other girls who let boys fight all their battles.'

Kids start flocking past us into the forest, weapons drawn. Some remain behind, probably to guard the fire pit and the Ones Who Suffer, but most head in pursuit of the drones.

'Come on, Alenna!' Gadya yells, plunging into the foliage. 'Do or die!'

I have a choice to make. Gadya has thrown down the gauntlet, and it's up to me whether I accept the challenge. For a second I swear that I'm going to stay behind.

Then I realise I don't want to be anonymous here, like I was back in the UNA. I want to be part of something bigger. I want Gadya and Liam to respect me. And I also want to survive. So I yell, 'Hey! Wait up!'

Then I take a deep breath and plunge into the trees after Gadya.

BATTLE CRY

I can hear kids all around me running, yelling and laughing maniacally in the thick foliage. I feel like I'm in the middle of an invisible stampede. It's hard to even see Gadya, and she's only a few paces ahead of me.

I slip and almost fall, banging my spear against a tree trunk. The blow reverberates up the weapon and makes my hands throb. But I keep my grasp. I smell smoke, but I don't know where it's coming from.

Gadya stops abruptly.

'Wait!' she says. We're both gasping for air. The whole time we've been running, she has kept her bow ready.

'What?'

'Up ahead – Between those trees.' We creep forward through the brush.

I follow her gaze and see nothing but green leaves. Then I hear heavy footsteps thundering towards us, and branches begin to rustle.

'Hey!' Gadya calls out, aiming her bow. 'If you don't stop moving, I'm gonna put an arrow between your eyes!'

The footsteps don't stop.

A second later, a large figure shoves branches out of its

way and stands before us. It's a robed drone, but this one looks nothing like the ones I've seen so far.

This drone is a girl.

Her head is shaved down to blonde stubble, and her face is painted zombie white, with black markings under her eyes. She's also about six inches taller than either me or Gadya. I've never seen a girl who looks like this, like some savage Amazonian warrior. She's holding a homemade axe with a chipped, rusty blade.

Even Gadya looks taken aback, but she keeps her bow steady. 'Are you deaf? Didn't you hear what I said? Back the hell off.'

The girl bares her sharp yellow teeth. She looks monstrous, terrifying. I almost hope that a feeler drops down from the sky and snatches her up. But it doesn't happen.

Gadya flourishes her bow. 'I've killed before. I'll do it again.'

I realise I should say something too. Yet I'm too scared to even speak. So I just raise my spear and point it at the huge girl, even though she could probably swat it away in a second. She raises her axe.

'I'm giving you fair warning,' Gadya says, her voice like steel. 'Three seconds to turn around and leave. I don't want to kill you. That's not my way. But I'll skewer your heart and send you straight to hell if you make me.'

The big girl looks in my direction, still silent. I try to hold the spear steady, but my hands are shaking.

Gadya begins her countdown: 'Three…two…'

The big girl doesn't look frightened. The corners of her mouth curl upwards to display even more of her teeth.

Gadya begins to mouth the word 'One'.

I'm watching the drone closely, and I see the muscles in her jaw ripple. It's a subtle movement, but I can tell that right then she's planning to spring forward and leap at us with the axe.

I have to do something. Gadya's preoccupied with aiming her arrow. Time slows down to a crawl. This drone is not going to turn around and leave. *She is going to hack us up into little pieces.*

Before I can think too much, I fling my spear right at her deranged painted face.

At the same instant, the girl makes her move and lunges forward, which means my spear misses its target. The wooden shaft rebounds harmlessly off her muscled shoulder. But the blow is enough to distract her and momentarily slow her down.

That split second gives Gadya an advantage. The arrow flies from her bow with a twang and sinks directly into the centre of the girl's chest. The girl unleashes a scream that sounds like a wounded lion. She staggers sideways, dropping her axe. Her hands grasp at thin air.

'Run!' Gadya yells at me, as if I need encouragement. We tear away through the trees. I hear the girl screaming and growling behind us as she tramples the foliage. I realise Gadya's arrow must have missed her heart, but it has given us time to escape with our lives.

'Nice shot!' I finally gasp, once we stop running a few minutes later. Somehow we've managed to shake the injured drone.

'That was *way* too close,' Gadya replies. 'And that girl was bigger than most of our hunters.' She slots another arrow into her bow. Brushes blue strands of hair out of her eyes. 'We have to keep moving.'

'I don't have a weapon any more,' I point out.

Gadya reaches down and extracts the knife from her ankle sheath. She hands it to me silently.

I take it, and we press forward again. I can hear screams and battle cries, but they're fainter than before. I realise our warriors must be forcing any stray drones away from our village. Moving cautiously, Gadya and I finally reach one of the narrow forest trails.

I hear a voice suddenly calling out, 'Gadya! Alenna!'

It's Markus. He stumbles out of the trees, about thirty paces in front of us. A bow dangles from his left hand. 'Come with me. You gotta see this.'

'We're busy right now!' Gadya yells back. 'Or haven't you noticed?'

'The attack's over,' he says, lumbering in our direction. 'They got what they came for.'

'How do you know?'

'They went after the prisoners,' Markus says, sounding stupefied. 'They set fire to the kennels and killed most of 'em!'

My heart sinks in horror.

David.

Gadya looks equally shocked.

'Is David OK?' I ask numbly.

Markus just gestures at us to follow him.

We do so, dazed, stopping only when we reach the clearing that once housed the kennels. The air is thick with roiling clouds of dark, putrid smoke. The kennels have been obliterated. Transformed into smouldering ruins. Some of the trees in the clearing are burned too, their trunks blackened. I avert my eyes from the corpses inside the remains of the cells.

Gadya surveys the damage, shaking her head in disbelief. 'Looks like they used powder from their fireworks as an accelerant.'

'I thought it was a rescue mission at first,' Markus explains. 'I thought they were going to free the prisoners. I never thought they'd do this.'

I walk forward into the clearing. There's no sign of David anywhere. I can barely believe it. One second he was alive and telling me about my parents. Now he's probably dead – and right after I promised to help him. He never even deserved to be imprisoned here in the first place.

But as I peer out over the field of ash, bodies and charred bamboo, I realise that beyond the smoke one kennel is still standing in pristine perfection, untouched by flames.

It's the isolation kennel. *David's kennel.*

And its door is hanging wide open.

Markus sees me looking. 'Yeah, only one of 'em got away.' He walks forward and kicks at some smouldering ashes glumly. 'Bet you can guess who.'

Gadya looks over at me. I feel like she's eyeing me with suspicion.

'What happened?' I ask Markus, trying to make sense of the situation. Mostly I just feel relief that David didn't die in the fire.

'A bunch of drones burst out of the trees. Too many for me to fight them, so I ran and hid in a spider hole. When I came back, David was gone and the other prisoners were dead or dying. David obviously fled with the drones who rescued him.'

'Or else they kidnapped him,' I point out. 'You don't know that he went willingly.'

'I bet David was a high-level drone, just like Veidman and Meira thought all along,' Gadya mutters.

We look at each other, desolate in the smoky haze. I don't believe her.

'Listen, Veidman was already here, and he told me not to say anything,' Markus continues softly, 'but there's more.' He scans the ruined kennels. 'Off the record, another one of the drones is still alive. Barely. He's probably the only one who actually saw what happened. But he's not talking.'

'Where is he?' Gadya asks.

Markus points at a pile of palm fronds on the ground near the edge of the clearing. 'I dragged him over there. Put the palms on him to hide him, like Veidman told me to. He's not gonna live much longer.'

Markus is still talking, but I'm rushing in the direction of the palm leaves. As I grow closer, I see the shape of a body under them.

'Don't!' Markus hisses after me. 'Veidman'll be back any second! He went to get Meira. He doesn't want anyone to know there's a survivor. He wants to question him in secret.'

I ignore Markus, crouching down and tearing the palm fronds off the drone's body. I expose a charred arm. Then part of his chest. Finally, a face.

Markus wasn't lying. This drone is badly burned, his skin charred and swollen with blisters. His eyes are open, staring, and I realise his eyelids have been burned away. At first I think he's dead for sure, but then his eyeballs swivel in my direction.

'I'm dying,' he whispers. His voice has become a croaky old man's rasp of pain.

'You're gonna be OK,' I lie. I've never counselled a dying person before. It's hard to be close to this much agony. I can hear Gadya heading over to us. The last thing I want to do is interrogate this boy in his final moments, but I need answers, or my life and the lives of everyone else in the village might be in jeopardy too.

'What happened to David Aberley?' I ask. 'The boy in the isolation cell. Is he OK? Did he get taken? Or did he go with the drones willingly? Please. I'm begging you.'

For a moment, I think the drone has passed away. But then I feel his broken breath on my cheek. 'You're Alenna Shawcross.'

I recoil. 'How do you know my name?'

'I heard…David say it.' He coughs. I just stare at him. 'There are messages for you…on the rocks beyond the barrier… Messages from your parents.'

Right then Gadya reaches me. 'Don't get too close to him!'

I turn around. Markus is directly behind Gadya. And twenty feet behind him, I see Veidman and Meira moving up the trail.

I turn back to the drone. He opens his blackened lips again like he's going to speak. Instead of words, a choking gasp forces its way out. *A death rattle.*

'No!' I cry. 'Please!' I want to force the life back into him. But it's too late. He's gone.

'Well, I guess that's for the best,' Markus finally murmurs, looking down at the drone's ruined body.

'What did he say to you?' Gadya asks me, sounding suspicious. 'I heard you asking him about David.'

'He was just—' I find myself speechless, biting back tears. Am I crying for this anonymous drone? Or am I crying for myself? I don't even know. I feel scared. Selfish. 'He wasn't making any sense,' I finally say. 'Just nonsense stuff about the Monk.'

I stand up, ignoring Gadya's gaze.

'Is that drone still alive?' Veidman calls out as he reaches us.

Markus shakes his head.

Veidman curses and shoots Markus a stern look. 'I told you not to say anything. We'll talk about this later.'

Markus nods. We all stand around and look down at the

body, still partially covered with palms. I don't know why Veidman wanted to keep this drone's survival a secret.

'We should bury him,' I say at last.

'No,' Meira replies quickly. 'He's not one of us. He's an interloper. He can't be buried in this sector.'

'So you're just going to leave him out here?' I ask.

'I'll start a fire,' Markus says tiredly. 'Finish the job.'

Meira turns to me. 'Only members of this village get buried here. It's an honour that drones don't deserve.' Her eyes have gone cold and glassy, like a doll's eyes.

More villagers stumble out of the trees. The battle is over. It's clear to me the drones just came to burn down the kennels. And either free or recapture David Aberley.

I'm overwhelmed with questions. What if the Monk somehow knew that David would tell me, or other villagers, secret things? I don't want to tell anyone what the dying prisoner said to me, in case they start suspecting that I'm involved with the Monk somehow.

'We'll convene at the fire pit tonight,' Veidman calls out sharply, turning on his heel to leave. 'Spread the word.'

Meira follows without a backwards glance.

Gadya sighs. 'Now you know why I have to leave the village and go into the grey zone. We can't live like this much longer. Things are getting too crazy. The drones aren't just killing us – they're killing each other.' She looks me hard in the eyes. 'And for the record, I think David tricked you. I think he's been working for the Monk all along. He's probably been on the wheel for months.'

I just can't accept that. 'He's done nothing but try to help us and be part of this village.'

'Yeah, probably so he could get invited inside and spy on us! You're too trusting, Alenna.'

I don't want to argue, so I stop talking. I look down at the drone's corpse a final time. Despite his burns, he seems oddly peaceful. He's not in pain any more.

I pull my hair back from my face. Gadya shoulders her bow and arrow. I sense the tension between us. Other kids are heading our way, but I don't feel too sociable.

'I need some water,' I tell Gadya.

'Go get some, then,' she retorts.

I walk away from the drone's body, giving both Gadya and the ruined kennels a wide berth. So many kids died here, burned alive while Gadya and I battled the giant girl. Life on the wheel is beyond cheap, I realise. It's meaningless.

I'm reminded of Sisyphus again. *The trick is to find meaning in such pointless, repetitive suffering.* Maybe that's impossible.

Now that David is gone, I know that the only way to find answers about my parents is to leave this village. The dying drone said that my mum and dad left messages for me. And David even knew my parents' names and that they were dissidents. No matter what, I need to try to find those messages – assuming they actually exist and I'm not just a pawn in the war between the villagers and the drones. I must become part of Operation Tiger Strike and plunge into the grey zone looking for answers, with Liam, Gadya and all the other hunters at my side.

THE DECISION

Hours later, the entire camp – except for some perimeter guards and the Ones Who Suffer – is gathered around the fire pit. Low flames crackle as damp branches pop in the fire. Some kids hold out sticks, roasting chunks of hoofer meat. Others just bask in the warmth. It's nearing twilight now, and the air is getting cooler.

Torches are set up around the edge of the clearing, casting flickering yellow shadows. I wrap an old shawl from the clothes pile around me, curling myself into its cocoon.

Liam is sitting with the other hunters. They're gathered in a group on one side of the fire pit. I've noticed they close ranks after an attack. I wonder if Liam killed any drones today. *Probably.*

Veidman gets up on his tree stump. As always, Meira is nearby, his second pair of eyes and ears.

'You all know why we're here,' Veidman says as everyone falls silent. 'We've been facing this decision for a long while. But now it's time to stop thinking and take action.' Some voices rise up, but he keeps talking. 'Today the Monk sent his drones to attack us in daylight, for the first time. He killed the prisoners – his own people – and rescued one of them. The drone who called himself David Aberley.' He pauses.

'I have no doubt David was sent here as a spy, and that when we suspected and imprisoned him, the drones came here to set him free. He was probably too valuable to lose.' The crowd rumbles. 'I've heard that other villages are crumbling one by one, overcome by chaos and destroyed from within by interlopers. It doesn't matter how many drones we scare off or kill. More will arrive tomorrow. And even more the day after that.' He stares around at the assembled throng.

'Tell 'em!' one of the hunters yells.

'We can't wait any longer,' Veidman continues. 'Meira and I have discussed it. We've been consulting with the leaders of the other surviving villages. They're staying put for now, but we're going to send out our exploration party as soon as possible.'

The hubbub of noise grows louder in response.

'Please.' He holds up his hands. 'Listen.' I wonder how much older Veidman really is than the rest of us. In the soft firelight, he looks young. Vulnerable. I never thought of him like that before.

'The drones are filthy beasts!' a hunter yells. 'Let's go into the grey zone and kill as many as we can!' His words get cheered.

Veidman raises his hands again. The crowd grows quiet. 'Like I said, the attacks are going to get worse. So we're forming our expedition party now. Many of the hunters will be going, but we need volunteers to support them too. Kids who aren't afraid to risk their lives. The more people we send into the grey zone, the greater the chance of success.'

Meira steps forward. She takes Veidman's hand, her pale fingers clasping his, the hypnotic firelight playing over her delicate features.

'Veidman is going to lead the expedition. I will stay here and keep things running while he's away.'

'You're risking all our lives by leaving!' a boy yells at Veidman – a hut builder, not one of the hunters.

'We risk our lives every day on the wheel,' Meira retorts. 'Now we'll be taking control of our destinies. Owning the risk.'

Rika stands up. 'How do we know this isn't part of the Monk's plan? Have you thought of that? What if he's intensifying his attacks so we do something stupid, like split up the village? Maybe he's planning to attack us right after our best hunters leave, or to ambush the hunters on their way to the grey zone.'

'It's been decided already,' Veidman declares, heading off any debate before it becomes a mutiny. 'We've run this village and kept all of you alive for the past three years. So we make the decisions. Operation Tiger Strike is a go. The exploration party will be leaving in nine days, in search of the aircrafts. I promise you, this will be the first step towards gaining our freedom.'

'But we're free right here!' a girl yells.

'Free and alive!' another voice seconds.

Veidman turns, squinting to see in the firelight. 'Freedom means more than just struggling to survive. Freedom is our *right*. Our destiny. We have to take this chance while we still can. Before they send more drones like David Aberley. Before they kill more of us.'

Voices rise up again, expressing agreement and dissent in equal numbers. Veidman and Meira quickly make their exit from the fire pit, disappearing into darkness as they step away from the flames. It's like they've just dissolved into the cool night air.

Had this exact same meeting taken place a day earlier, I never would have considered joining the expedition into the grey zone. But after what David and the other prisoner said, I can no longer imagine staying.

'Whadda you make of this mess?' Gadya asks me. The camp is still buzzing with conversation and arguments.

'Honestly? I think it sucks.' My mind is still on David. *Could I really have been so wrong about him?* My gut tells me that he wasn't lying about my parents. But I don't know if I can trust my gut. It also told me that I'd never fail the GPPT. Still, it's impossible for me to believe that David tricked me.

'Staying won't be so bad,' Gadya replies. 'Maybe now that they've killed the prisoners, the drones won't attack for—'

I cut her off. 'I'm not staying. I'm going with you.'

She looks shocked. 'With me?'

'Yeah. Into the grey zone. I changed my mind about Operation Tiger Strike.'

Her shock rapidly turns into bewilderment. 'You sure that's a good idea? I don't think you're really cut out for this kind of thing.'

I want to challenge her. I want to ask, *And why not?* But

I know she's right. If it hadn't been for what David told me, I'd be happy to be a coward. So I just say, 'I have my reasons.'

'You mind sharing them?'

'I just don't want to stay and be a burden. And I want off the wheel.'

'You sure there isn't something else?' For a second I'm scared she knows my secret. But then she adds, 'Is this about Liam?'

'It's got nothing to do with him,' I tell her honestly, wanting to clear the air. 'Obviously, he's cute. I won't deny that. But I listened to what you said.'

'Good, because if you fall for him, not only will I kick your ass, but he'll end up breaking your heart. Girls come second to hunting for him. I can promise you that.'

'Look, I've got bigger things to worry about, like getting killed. I've got your back if you've got mine.'

'Have you told Veidman you're going?'

'Not yet.'

'It'll make his day. Then he can say, "See, even the new girl is ready to fight and die for our village, eh?"' Her impression of his Canadian accent is pretty impressive, and I smile.

A thought suddenly occurs to me. 'Can you teach me what you know? I mean, about defending yourself and stuff, and how to aim a bow?'

'In nine days?' Gadya scoffs, openly laughing. Then she realises I'm serious. 'I can't promise miracles, but I guess I can try.' She stands and stretches her lower back. 'You really think you're up for this?'

'No. That's why I need you to teach me.'

She bites her lip, lost in thought. 'OK, then. We'll start training tomorrow morning. But don't expect me to go easy on you just 'cause we're friends.'

'Deal.'

My eyes drift over the crowd. I notice Liam, still entrenched with the hunters. I wish I could get more information from him about the wheel and Operation Tiger Strike. Maybe I could put it together with what David and the dying prisoner said, and figure the whole thing out.

'So tell me more about the grey zone,' I say to Gadya as we head over to grab some stew.

'Better yet, I'll draw you a map.'

'Really?'

'Well, not a map of the zone. No one's mapped the whole thing yet. It's huge. But a map of where our journey's gonna take us.'

We reach some wooden tables and sit down. Torches provide us with flickering light. I look for Rika, but I don't see her. There's a long line of kids snaking around the edge of the clearing, lining up with bowls.

Gadya takes a chewed-up pencil and a piece of tattered paper from her pocket. She draws a rough circle to indicate the island.

'Here we are now, see?' she asks, starting to fill in parts of the circle. 'This is our village by the river, and this is our whole sector.' I watch as she sketches out the rough dimensions of the thin sliver of the blue sector. 'And here are all the sectors the Monk controls.' She starts sketching other sectors of the wheel and labelling them.

'Our sector's that small?' I ask.

'Pretty much.' Then she draws an oddly shaped area about ten times larger, bordering the north shore of the island. 'And this is the grey zone.'

As I scrutinise her primitive map, I realise something terrible. 'Wait, the grey zone's there?' I place my finger on it. 'Way up top?'

She nods.

'But that means we have to cross part of the Monk's territory!' Indeed, due to the size, location and fluctuating boundaries of each sector, a portion of the orange sector sits between us and the southern boundary of the grey zone. I hadn't realised the spokes of the wheel were so inexact.

'It's impossible to get to the grey zone without sneaking through the Monk's territory. I thought you knew that. I thought everyone did.'

'I've only been on the wheel a few days. I had no clue!' I want to put my head in my hands and sob. This mission is going to become a death march. 'I didn't know we'd have to cross enemy territory – and to get to what? *More* enemy territory?'

'That's life on the wheel for you.' She looks me square in the face. 'Having second thoughts?'

'Definitely! But I'm still going.'

'Then, back to the map.' Gadya continues drawing. 'The grey zone is where we think the aircrafts, landing strips and docks are. Right on the shore in some kind of industrialised city.'

'How do you know all this stuff?'

'From interrogating prisoners. Veidman's serum. And from Liam and the other hunters, before the tunnel collapsed.' She scratches her nose with the tip of her pencil. 'Hey, look. Chow line's finally moving.' She gets up. I do the same.

Soon we have our stew, and we're sitting back down at one of the tables. I'm still trying to recover from the revelation that if I go on the expedition, I'll be heading straight into the Monk's territory.

I finally see Rika nearby, sweaty from cooking, and Gadya and I both call out to her. She comes over and sits down next to me with a bowl, across from Gadya.

'So did Alenna tell you about her decision?' Gadya asks. 'She's becoming one of us. A hunter, I mean. She's joining Operation Tiger Strike.'

Rika looks at me, strangely unsurprised. 'I thought you might.'

'Really? I didn't even know myself until today.'

'Something in your eyes gave it away. There's a fire in them. Not as plain to see as Gadya's. But it's there.'

I feel embarrassed. 'I'm not so sure about that.'

'Oh, I am,' Rika says confidently. 'I know these things.' She takes a bite of the stew. Furrows her brow. 'Too much salt. Tastes like seawater.' She looks at me again. 'Just be sure to send me a postcard when you get there, OK?'

I laugh. I'd almost forgotten that postcards existed. The

wheel has a way of wiping out time and memory. I feel like I could be living two hundred years in the past – or two hundred years in the future.

A shadow falls over our table, blocking the light from the nearby torches. I look up and see Markus.

'We're eating here,' Gadya says impatiently. 'What?'

'Veidman sent me to get Alenna.'

I suddenly feel nervous. 'Is this about earlier today?'

'He didn't say. He's waiting for you in his cabin.'

I stand up, extracting my legs from the bench.

'Follow me.' Markus starts heading away from the table. Faking a nonchalant shrug at Gadya and Rika, I follow. *Could Veidman have found out about me and David somehow? If David really was a spy, does Veidman think that I'm involved?*

Markus is ominously silent as he guides me to the cabin. All around, I hear the noises of the forest at night: the thrum of insects, the crackling of twigs and the whisper of the wind through tree branches.

We quickly reach our destination. The metal roof of Veidman's cabin is corroded, and one side is now propped up with a broken tree branch. A few hunters whose names I don't know are sitting on fallen trees outside. They're scarfing hoofer meat, gnawing it right off the bone and washing it down with juice from hollowed-out melons. Liam is not among them.

'Vei?' Markus calls out, pausing in front of the cabin's flimsy wooden door.

'Come in,' Veidman's voice answers.

Markus swings the door open, and I step inside. Veidman sits at a makeshift desk – a wooden board propped up on piles of rock. A clutch of tallow candles burns on a window ledge. The cabin is warm and smells like hoofer fat.

'Hey, Alenna,' Veidman says, smiling. Even in the dim light, he still seems to possess his peculiar glow. He looks calmer and more relaxed now than he did at the fire pit. I feel relieved. Markus shuts the door behind me, and I hear his footsteps heading away.

I take a seat across from Veidman on a strange chair that feels as soft and comfortable as a beanbag. I look down and realise it's made from dried hoofer skins wrapped around a bunch of ferns.

'I need to ask you a favour,' Veidman says.

'Sure. Anything.'

He presses his hands together. 'I want you to consider joining the expedition and coming with us.'

I startle him by smiling. 'Actually, I already decided that I'm going.' He looks a little surprised, so I feel like I have to give him a reason. Obviously I don't mention anything about David or my parents. 'It's because of Gadya,' I explain. 'She's my friend. And she's the one who rescued me and brought me to the village. I want to become a warrior like her.'

He nods. 'That's great news.' I'm thinking, *So that's it? That's the favour?* But Veidman isn't done yet. 'There's something else.'

'What?'

'With Meira staying behind, I need someone to keep

a lookout for me on the journey. Who lets me know if anyone says or does anything suspicious. That kind of thing. Understand?'

'You want me to be your snitch, basically.'

He leans forward. Cups his hands under his chin. 'Basically.'

I don't know if I should feel flattered or offended. 'Why me? I'm one of the newest kids here. And after what happened with David, why do you trust me? I mean, he passed the truth serum test, but you still didn't trust him.'

'Unlike David, you passed the truth test with flying colours. There were questions he answered too smoothly and quickly. He didn't act like other kids do when they're given the serum. You're a known quantity. Not everyone else is. But beyond that, I can tell that you're smart. Honest. You have a good heart. You volunteered to get to work after the first feeler attack, and you brought food to the prisoners. That's not a job many kids volunteer for. I see how you interact with people. So far, everyone likes you and—'

He stops talking, because I've started laughing. I can't help it.

'What's so funny?' he asks.

'It's just that back home, it was the exact opposite. I never really felt like I fit in with a group, even when it seemed like I did.'

'That's one thing we all have in common on the wheel.' He leans back in his chair. 'So will you do it for me?' He grins. 'Be my spy?'

'I guess so.'

He pauses and looks at me sideways in the candlelight. 'You remind me of Meira sometimes, you know that?'

'Really?' I glance away, embarrassed. He must mean my personality or something, because I know I look nothing like her. I don't have perfect blonde hair and perfect skin. And I'm not supersmart. I'm just me.

His words have made me blush. What does it mean that he thinks that? And why should I even care? He's probably just saying it so he can manipulate me. I know he lied about how much the prisoners know, and I'm guessing he's keeping a whole lot of information from me and most of the other villagers as well.

'I'm looking forward to our journey,' he finally says.

He stands up, and I do the same. He walks around me and swings open the door, letting in the night breeze.

'If anyone asks why I summoned you here, just tell them I wanted to ask you about the raid today. If you saw anything.'

I nod. 'Sure.'

I exit the cabin. The hunters are still gorging on food as I walk past them. I'm struck by the irony that even though Veidman is trusting me to be his spy, I'm actually keeping a huge secret from him.

I see the light of the fire pit ahead of me. I vow to keep my promise. I will be a good spy for Veidman, at least on the surface. But I'll be a much better spy for myself. I will trust no one, and focus on learning the truth about what happened to my parents.

'Alenna!' I hear a voice blurt out, right before I reach the fire pit. 'Hey.' It's Liam.

'Hey, yourself,' I reply.

'So, I heard you're going with us?'

'Yeah, I figured I only have my life to lose.'

We stand there for a moment, kind of awkwardly. Gadya's warning keeps echoing in my head. *Stay away from this boy.*

'You wanna see something cool?' Liam finally asks.

'That depends.'

Unexpectedly, he takes my hand in his. 'Just come with me. It's right this way.' Before I can even resist, he starts leading me along a narrow dirt trail I haven't been down yet.

'Where are we going?' I ask, intrigued, despite myself. I pull my hand gently out of his.

'Don't you like surprises?'

'Only the good kind, but I haven't seen too many of those on the wheel.'

Liam keeps walking. The path finally ends at a small ravine with water at the bottom. I realise it's another shallow tributary of the main river.

But the water isn't what catches my attention. In fact, I barely notice it, because hovering above the surface are thousands of tiny glowing butterflies – all different sizes and colours, from pink and white to silver and blue.

'They're beautiful,' I breathe. I've never seen butterflies like these before. They respond to my voice, darting upwards in delicate multicoloured clouds as they whirl around in the night breeze.

One flutters down towards me, so I hold out my hand. It alights on my knuckles, shimmering there, opening and closing its purple and gold wings.

I turn to Liam. 'You probably take all the new girls here, don't you?'

'Only the cute ones,' he replies. Then, turning serious, he adds, 'I usually only come here by myself. To get away from everyone. To plan battle strategies without getting distracted by the other guys.'

I turn back to watch the butterflies, conscious of Liam's gaze on me. The butterfly on my hand departs, rising upwards on a draught of warm air. I hold out my hand again, hoping another will land on me.

'So, do you have a boyfriend back home?' Liam asks from behind me, completely out of the blue.

The moment is ruined.

I turn and face him. 'Are you for real?'

He looks surprised by my reaction. 'What do you mean?'

'First of all, why would that even matter at this point? It's not like I'm ever going back home. And second, don't you and Gadya have some kind of thing for each other? I'm not gonna get in the way of that.'

It's clear he didn't expect this response. 'I just thought I'd ask. I like you. And for the record, Gadya and I are done. She dumped me, actually.'

I can feel my heart beating faster. Even though it's girly and stupid, I admit I feel a thrill that Liam said he likes me. But at the same time absolutely nothing is going to happen between us. 'Look, I like you, too. But I don't have time for a relationship, or any drama. I'm too busy trying to stay alive.'

We're standing only a few inches away from each other. My words are one thing, but I keep feeling like I can't breathe, like all my nerve endings are tingling. I sense Liam's gaze intensifying. I look up into his warm eyes and see myself and the world of butterflies reflected back at me.

Just as I'm thinking, *Am I deluded, or is this boy actually going to try to kiss me?* he leans in and presses his lips against mine.

I'm in shock.

This is my first kiss, and I still can't believe it's actually happening. His touch is almost too much for me. I press my chest against his, as his hands hold me tight, moving against my body –

Then, coming to my senses, I shove him away from me.

'Ow!' he says. 'What's wrong?'

'You're what's wrong,' I snap at him. 'This can't happen. It doesn't matter how I feel about you. I promised Gadya I wouldn't get involved.'

'Gadya,' he says. 'First she dumped me and now she's trying to stop me from liking another girl?'

'Exactly.' I cross my arms.

He sighs. 'You girls always stick together.'

'She said the same thing about you and the other hunters.' I try to compose myself. 'Don't kiss me again.'

Liam looks disappointed, embarrassed and bemused all

at once. 'Well, I guess it's good you're loyal to your friends,' he finally says, brushing back his hair. 'So, I feel kind of stupid right now...' His words trail off. He smiles sheepishly. 'Make that *really* stupid.'

'It's no big deal.'

'It's just that since I first saw you, I felt kind of comfortable around you. Like maybe we had some kind of connection? I know that sounds pretty weird, huh?'

He turns away.

'Wait,' I suddenly say, speaking before I can stop myself. 'There's something you should know. The day before I got sent here, when I toured the Harka Museum in New Providence, I saw you on the screen.'

He turns back to me. '*What?*'

'You were talking to the camera. You were trying to send a message, and then you got attacked.'

'I can't believe you saw that! I didn't think anyone was watching.' He pauses. 'It's something I usually do every time I head into the grey zone, or on a mission. I swing by the camera and try to signal to my family. Just in case they're out there watching somehow. It's a long shot, I know. I was using sign language 'cause my little brother Gabriel is deaf.' He pauses. 'The drones often hang out there, so it's a dangerous place. Why didn't you tell me earlier?'

'Because I didn't want you to think I was crazy. And I don't know if it means anything or not, or if it's just coincidence.'

A loud crashing noise makes both of us startle. I turn to see a figure lumbering between the trees, down the trail towards us. It's Markus again. I wonder if he just constantly prowls the forest.

'Hey, man,' Liam calls out.

Markus stops walking. I realise he didn't see us. 'Sorry,' he says. 'Just checking for drones.' He stumbles away, averting his eyes, like he caught us hooking up or something.

Once he's gone, Liam and I look at each other again.

'We better get back to the village,' he says. 'I've got guard duty in a few minutes.'

We start up the narrow path, which barely gives us room to walk side by side. He takes hold of my hand to help me navigate around a tree branch, and squeezes it. For an instant, I squeeze his hand back, like we're passing a secret signal between us. Then I let go, dropping my arm to my side.

I knew I felt something for him – even that first time I saw him on-screen in the museum. I still feel like I could fall for a boy like him. But I promised Gadya I wouldn't. And I'm not about to backstab the girl who saved my life.

There are so many other things to worry about on the wheel that love would probably be a liability here. I tell myself I'll have to keep my guard up around Liam, despite my feelings. Still, it's going to be hard, and I know it.

EXODUS

For the next several days, I don't see as much of Liam as I hoped. I kind of expected that he'd try to kiss me again. But he's busy training and strategising with the hunters. I don't know whether to be relieved or disappointed. I guess I feel a bit of both. So I put myself in Gadya's hands, turning my schedule over to her.

She gets Veidman's approval to spend her days training me. She's happy to have found another girl who wants to be a warrior, and I'm happy to have found someone to teach me. Of course, I don't mention anything to her about my moment with Liam, because I feel so guilty about it. We also don't talk about what happened with David. It's just become another mystery of the wheel.

Gadya doesn't go easy on me in training. 'We're gonna run five miles today,' she announces on the first morning. She has woken me up before sunrise, when the dew is still thick on the grass underneath our hammocks. 'I gotta get your heart pumping. Turn some of that blubber into muscle.'

'Blubber?' I say, wounded.

'You're not fat, but you're not toned either. Still, there's no time for magic. We'll have to focus on skills. I'll teach you a condensed version of everything I know – if you can handle it.'

For the next few days, I'm at her mercy. We go through endless drills in the heat, mostly running and sparring, sometimes so hard I throw up. My hair gets soaked with sweat, and so does my ragged, disintegrating bra.

But Gadya does what she promised. She teaches me how to notch an arrow into a bow. How to pull the arrow back and release it, so that it flies fast and true with a snap of the bowstring.

The bow reminds me of my guitar – except the notes its string plays are violent and deadly. We use trees as targets, peppering their trunks with arrows. Slowly, very slowly, my aim improves, until I can hit a one-inch mark from a hundred feet away. Gadya's initial frustration with my ineptitude gives way to grudging satisfaction. She jokes that I've finally found an instrument worth playing.

Gadya also shows me simple defensive moves I can use with a stick or spear. She shows me how to throw a punch like a boy, with my thumb outside my fist, supporting my index finger. And how to throw a rock like a boy too. How to wrestle. How to grip a knife the right way, with the tip of the blade pointing down, so I can slice upwards at my opponents, using my full strength.

I admit to myself now that I was secretly jealous of athletic girls back home. They always seemed so carefree. It was probably an illusion, due to their thought-pill consumption. But still. I missed out on a lot of fun because I was afraid to try new things. Now I don't feel so afraid any more. Or rather, I guess now I'm afraid of more serious things – like death – so the little things don't matter as much. I've been forced to stop being a coward and start taking responsibility for myself. And to start caring again – for the first time since my parents got taken.

As I train, I think about finding the messages my parents supposedly left for me in the grey zone. I imagine that my secrets make me seem preoccupied. If so, Gadya doesn't notice. She's too busy yelling at me, 'Think on your feet!' and, 'Push yourself harder!'

Our training sessions attract attention, mostly from the boys. A few of the girls seem curious too. I'm hoping others might join us, but none do. In the village, hunting is mostly a male activity. Gadya is an anomaly. But now there are two of us.

Of course many of the kids are getting ready for the expedition in other ways. The hunters are frequently off in the deep forest of the blue sector, practising routines of their own. The drones launch a few minor attacks on us, but nothing like the ones prior to the burning of the prisoners.

When Liam isn't training, he occasionally stops by to watch us with his friends. At those times Gadya becomes harsher, barking out orders like she's trying to impress him. I still haven't found the nerve to tell her about Liam's kiss.

I wish we weren't all so busy. Liam never seems to be around when I want to talk to him in private. Maybe he regrets trying to kiss me. Or maybe he just doesn't want to be friends any more. In some ways, I understand. I don't want to be tempted by him into betraying Gadya. But there is no denying our connection, even if we refuse to act on how we feel.

One night after dinner, I overhear Sinxen talking to another hunter about Liam, near one of the huts around the fire pit. I linger behind the hut, trying to catch the words.

'He's gonna lose his edge, getting distracted over that girl,' the other hunter is saying.

'Yeah, it's not like him to talk so much about a chick,' Sinxen agrees. 'I heard that Markus saw them together down by the river.'

It takes me a moment to realise that they're talking about me. I freeze.

'Usually girls have crushes on him, not the other way around,' the other hunter muses. 'He's gotta remember to stay focused.'

Their voices start growing fainter, like they're walking away. I strain to hear, moving sideways around the hut. But I can't make out any more words. I just stand there for a while, heart racing, not sure what to think. I already knew Liam liked me. But I didn't know how unusual it was for him to feel that way about someone. And I don't know what to do about it.

Then, on the fifth day of training, I wake up early, and there's no sign of Gadya. It's unlike her to be late. I pick up my spear and go down to the grassy area that we use for our training ground. Minutes tick by as I wait.

I'm about to give up and go look for her, when I hear

footsteps behind me, and someone steps out of the trees. I turn around, expecting to finally see Gadya, or maybe just another villager who wants to chat.

Instead, I see some kind of unholy monstrosity.

A tall masked figure draped in hoofer skins stands before me, wielding a spear twice the size of mine.

Before I can scream, the figure lunges forward, swinging his weapon wildly. His mask is a scowling wooden atrocity.

My training kicks in immediately, and I parry the first blow as best I can. Then I spin around, like Gadya taught me, trying to stab my attacker in the flank.

But he's way faster than I am, and he knocks the spear out of my hand with barely any effort. I stumble back. He raises his weapon.

I'm about to scream for my life, when I hear a muffled voice say, 'Relax, Alenna! It's OK!'

The figure reaches up a hand and takes off the wooden mask, tossing it on to the grass.

It's Liam.

'What the hell!' I exclaim, both furious and relieved. 'What's wrong with you?'

'You've got a substitute teacher today.' I can see that he's trying to stifle a grin, and it makes me even madder.

'You really scared me, you jerk! It's not funny.'

'I wasn't trying to be funny. I wanted to see how you'd respond.'

'Why?'

'Because you gotta be prepared if you're really coming

with us.' He kicks at the mask. 'I got it off a drone. Ugly-looking, right?'

'I'm mad at you.'

'Sorry.'

I take a deep breath. 'What does Gadya think about all this?'

'It's cool. She's running errands today. Besides, who do you think trained her?'

'Are you serious?'

He nods. 'Yep. And I cleared it with Veidman, too. He agreed it's better if you have more than one instructor. That way you gain experience in different styles of fighting.' He pauses for a second. 'If you're coming on the expedition, I don't want you getting hurt.'

Is he being straight with me? Or did he just want to find a way to finally spend some time with me? Either way, I realise that by training me today, he's not hanging out with the other hunters, and I'm flattered. 'So what's with that creepy mask and the hoofer skins, anyway?' I ask.

'Element of surprise.' He starts putting down his weapon. 'You never know what to expect on the wheel.'

I suddenly reach down and pick up my own spear. 'Then who says this battle's over?'

His grins. 'That's the spirit.'

I lunge forward like Gadya taught me. For a second, I think I've caught him off guard. But then his spear is back in his hands, and he has knocked mine away from me again. My palms sting from the impact.

'Good attitude,' he muses, 'but we gotta work on your technique…'

We spend the rest of the day practising. Liam is a lot kinder than Gadya, but he's also a lot stronger and faster. Impossibly fast. By the end of the day, I'm more exhausted than I've ever been in my life.

We finally take a break just before dinner. I slump down on the grass. I'm panting for air and drenched with sweat. I lean back on my arms, stretching out my bruised, aching legs. Liam sits down nearby and hands me a water flask.

'I'm impressed. You're picking stuff up faster'n Gadya did.'

'I guess I should thank you for training me. But honestly? I feel like I'm gonna croak.'

He smiles. 'Then, I'm doing my job.'

I take a swig of water. Then I pass the flask back to Liam. We sit there in silence for a moment.

'Sorry about the other night,' he finally says. 'I mean, the part where I tried to kiss you.'

'You didn't just try. You actually *did* kiss me, remember?'

'Well, I'm sorry. I mean, if I came on too strong.'

'No big deal,' I tell him. I want him to know how much I like him, but I'm nervous, afraid I'll just complicate things even more if I speak, so I stay silent.

'You know how I feel about you,' he continues. 'I think you're awesome.' He pauses. 'I'm cool with just being friends, if that's all you want. OK?'

I'm still thinking about the fact that he called me awesome. 'Sounds like a deal,' I manage to say.

He sticks out his hand with an overly formal flourish, kidding around. 'Shake on it?'

I laugh and shake his hand. He holds it just a moment too long before he lets go.

When Gadya returns the next day, we don't even talk about what happened. But she works me harder than ever, and seems particularly gruff, so maybe she's angry. I get the feeling Liam and Veidman gave her no choice in taking a day off. Soon, however, things go back to normal, and we continue to spend our time sparring and running drills.

'You're getting good,' Gadya says grudgingly near the end of our training. 'Definitely better than most of the girls here – and even a few of the boys.'

I nod, realising this is probably the highest compliment she can pay me.

Then she adds, 'Just don't get complacent. 'Cause the grey zone's not gonna be a walk in the park.'

'No kidding.' I shoulder my spear. 'Thanks for teaching me.'

She squints in my direction. 'It was kind of fun, actually.'

Despite my new skills, I still feel incredibly nervous about what's going to happen to me. I'm trying not to think about all the awful things that might befall us on the journey.

Fortunately, my mind gets distracted from my worries on the night before we leave. Liam stops by my hammock before dinner. He's holding a small wooden crate.

'What have you got there?' I ask.

He opens the crate, revealing a small tureen, some apples

and a pair of bowls. I see a couple of unlit candles in there too. 'Want to have dinner with me?'

I smile. 'Only if you don't light those candles. We're just friends, or have you forgotten already?'

'I haven't forgotten.' He picks up the candles and tosses them out of the crate.

Then he leads me down to a nice part of the riverbank, where we sit on flat rocks next to each other as he dishes out the food.

'How are you feeling about everything?' he asks, as we start eating.

I'm not sure if he means about us or about the journey that lies ahead. So I just say, 'Fine.'

He takes a bite of stew. 'It'll be worth it to get off the wheel, just to have some real food again.'

'Don't let Rika hear you say that.'

He puts down his bowl. 'Hey, I got something for you. I mean, it's no big deal. I hid it here earlier, as a surprise.' He rummages behind the rocks and finally pulls out an object.

For a second, I think it's a weapon. It's just a long piece of wood with some nails at the top and metal wires running lengthwise down its surface.

Then I realise what it is, and I laugh in amazement and delight. 'Liam – How did you? It's—' I bring my hands up to my face. I feel like I'm about to cry.

'I remembered you said that you play music.' He hands the object to me, and I take it in my arms. 'I made it late at night, when I was supposed to be sleeping.'

I look down at the object in wonderment.

It's a homemade guitar.

Primitive, but definitely functional. Liam has strung six metal wires at different intervals on the plank and nailed them down at the top and bottom to keep them taut.

'You can spin the nails,' he explains. 'I've wrapped the wires around them, so you can actually tune it. I know it's crappy, and you deserve a lot better, but it's the first guitar I've ever made.'

'It's not crappy,' I say, looking up at him. 'It's perfect. I can't believe you did this for me.'

Then, impulsively, before I can stop myself, I lean up and kiss him.

I don't even know what I'm doing or thinking.

My lips find his and press against them. He kisses me back, his lips melting into mine, making me shiver for an instant.

Then I pull back from him. 'Wow,' I murmur. I feel confused. Hot and guilty. 'We shouldn't be doing this.'

'Yeah. I thought you said no kissing.' His voice is husky. I feel like I've surprised him. I've definitely surprised myself.

'I don't know what happened.' But the truth is, I do know. I've fallen for him, despite Gadya's warning. And I don't know what to do about it. Should I talk to her right away and confess everything? Or just try to end things with Liam instead of making everything worse? Neither decision sounds easy.

'It's OK,' he says, noticing my expression. 'I won't say anything, if that's what you're worried about.'

I look back down at the guitar. 'Thank you so much for this. You don't know what it means to me.' So many unspoken words hang between us.

'Well, I better get going,' Liam finally says. 'I got a night time training run. Tomorrow's the big day, right?'

I nod. 'Right.' As crazy as it sounds, I almost wish I'd gotten sent to the wheel earlier, so I could have had more time in the village with Liam, before the expedition. 'See you tomorrow,' I say.

With an awkward half-wave and a smile, Liam heads off for his training run.

I stare after him, watching his figure disappear. Then I sit there for a while, strumming the guitar strings with my fingers, spinning the nails automatically to get the instrument in tune. I start playing softly to myself, finger-picking melodies I remember from my dad back home. They're comforting to me, like lullabies. But they also make me nostalgic for a world that's gone forever. The only songs I was allowed to practise or learn at the orphanage were patriotic ones approved by the government.

When I finally walk back to my hammock, I rest the guitar under some leaves to keep it safe. Then I head over to the fire pit. There are still preparations I have to make for the journey.

Provisions are being packaged, and additional water flasks are being sewn from hoofer skins. According to Veidman's best guesses, the journey to the aircraft landing site might take several days. No one knows for sure. Because of the inexplicably frigid temperatures that exist in the grey zone, we've also assembled a bunch of old sweaters, jackets, gloves and hats to help keep us warm. They now have to be packed up in homemade hoofer-hide knapsacks.

I'm glad I'm going on the expedition. I want Gadya by my side. And Veidman too. And most of all, Liam, who I'm secretly aching to kiss again.

I'm thinking all these things as I go off into the nearby forest with a torch, to gather sapling branches to use to bundle our water flasks.

I'm still within shouting distance of the camp, when I see a robed figure crouching in the dark, illuminated by my flickering torchlight.

I stop walking right away.

Despite the robe, there's no way this can be a drone. Not so close to the village like this, and not all alone. They always run in packs. *Maybe it's Liam, testing me again.* But this robed figure looks too small to be him.

'Who's there?' I call out. I should probably feel more afraid, but I already have a knife in one hand and a torch in the other. Plus, I know that other villagers are nearby. 'Show me your face! What are you doing here?'

The figure slowly hobbles towards me, revealing his identity as he slips off his monk-like cowl.

'*David,*' I breathe in shock. 'You're alive!'

'Alenna.' He's found a new pair of wire-frame glasses, slightly too large, and he pushes them up his nose. 'Please, don't go. Just listen.'

On the one hand, I know I should believe what Gadya said. That David tricked me and that he's some high-level drone. But on the other, I remember that moment on the hillside when he shoved the drone out of the way and saved me. That wasn't planned, or faked. Neither were his emotions when he was imprisoned in the kennels.

He holds out both hands. 'Look. I'm unarmed. I snuck out and came here alone. And it was a long journey.'

'Why did you come at all?' I realise that my blade is still half-raised, so I lower it.

'To find you. Every single thing I told you is true.'

'Look at you. You're wearing robes. If anyone sees you, they'll say you're a drone now for sure! They'll try to kill you.'

'I'm just living with the drones to get answers. If I were a drone, I'd be drunk and lobbing fireworks at everyone – or planning ways to tear down your village. Instead I'm risking my life to help you.'

'How did you escape from your cell when the other prisoners got killed? You owe me some answers. Everyone says your people came and rescued you. That you set me up and tried to dupe me, so I'd help you become part of this village. So you could spy on us.'

He's shaking his head. 'That's crazy. That's not what happened.'

'I believe you, but others won't. And honestly, it's getting harder to tell whose side you're on, David.'

'I'm on my own side!' He moves even closer. 'Haven't you heard of individuality? Alenna, look, there are places on this island that are pretty much desolate. No drones, no villagers. Just lots of land. I've heard that sometimes kids just leave and go live on their own, or in small groups in the forest. There aren't any natural predators on this island. The only things to fear are other people. I came here to tell you that we could leave together, and just go somewhere and create our own society. Or find a group of kids who aren't fighting each other all the time.'

'We'd just get killed.' I pause. 'If you're for real, then come back with me to the village right now. Tell Veidman and the others everything you learned from the drones. I can offer you safe passage.'

He shakes his head. 'I'd get locked up again and drugged. At least at the drones' camp I can do whatever I want, pretty much. I lied and told them that I killed a villager, so now they think I've passed my initiation rite. But they're not all evil. Most of them are just running wild and don't know where to turn. That's what makes them so dangerous.'

'David, do you swear you're telling the truth about everything?'

'I swear it.'

'You still haven't explained how you escaped from the kennels,' I point out. 'Especially when all the other prisoners got torched.'

'I didn't escape.' He pushes his glasses up his nose again. 'All I know is that some drones turned up and opened my kennel, and I ran. Like anyone else would. I wanted to get away from Markus so he didn't beat me any more, and from

Veidman so he couldn't test his serums on me. I didn't find out until later that the drones burned the other prisoners alive. Maybe they didn't want me or anyone else talking to you. I'm as scared as you are. I'm just staying with the drones because there's no place else to go. I'd rather be here with you than with them, if I could.'

Before I can ask him any more questions, he speaks up again:

'I need to get back to my camp in the orange sector before they notice I'm gone – or before one of your perimeter guards finds me. I'll contact you again soon. Just be careful. Watch your back.'

I nod. 'I will.' I don't mention Operation Tiger Strike. I wonder if he even knows about it.

He raises his cowl and steps backwards. 'We could leave all this madness behind and start our own thing. Create a new New Providence on the wheel. That is, if you're willing to leave your little boyfriend behind and take a chance.'

'So you've been spying on me!'

'Looking out for you is more like it. Just think about what I said.'

I stare at him, my torch reflected in his glasses. His plan sounds suicidal. But I realise he might be one of the only kids on the wheel even making an attempt to straddle the two worlds of the village and the Monk's camp. I think back to when it was just the two of us. When we first woke up on the island and everything seemed so peaceful. No villagers or drones. Maybe David has a point after all.

He takes another step back, in between the trees. In the darkness, his robes make him nearly invisible.

'Remember, civilization is what we make it,' his disembodied voice says. 'It might turn out that Veidman and the Monk are equally wrong about how to approach life on the wheel.'

Before I can think of a good response, he's gone. Vanished back into the forest. I look for him, raising my torch. But there's no sign of him.

I want to run back and tell everyone in the village about David's return, but I know it could jeopardise their trust in me if they think I'm fraternising with the enemy.

As I start walking back to the safety of the main clearing, my encounter starts to seem like a mirage or hallucination. Or a ghost. I don't know who David really is – let alone what his agenda is any more. I could be in serious trouble. I quicken my pace, heading towards the fire pit.

That night I get only a few hours of sleep. As the sun rises over the island in the morning, the sky takes on a reddish hue. It's finally time for Operation Tiger Strike to take effect.

Veidman and Meira stand before us at the fire pit in the sun, surveying the entire village. Nearly everyone is here, except for the Ones Who Suffer and some guards. This is the last time all of us will be together for a while – possibly forever.

'Those of you staying may face tougher challenges than those leaving,' Veidman says, his voice ringing out in the silence. 'My thoughts will be with everyone who remains behind.' I notice he doesn't say 'prayers' or anything like that. There's no religious talk in the village, and there never has been. The Monk has usurped everything religious on the wheel by twisting it into something perverted. The closest thing to religion in the village is probably Rika's pacifism.

For once, kids don't chatter in response to Veidman's words.

'Say your goodbyes,' Veidman instructs sombrely. 'The hunters and I will be leaving in half an hour, heading north.'

A girl nearby breaks down crying, and she is quickly consoled by two of her friends. I feel a pang of longing for the village. It's the only safe place I know of on the wheel. Maybe I'm making the wrong choice. But I have to find out about my parents.

'Veidman's really dragging this nonsense out,' Gadya mutters in my ear impatiently. 'Let's get going already!' I glance at her and see that she's a war chest of weaponry. Along with her homemade pack, she's carrying two bows, a clutch of arrows and a spear that doubles as a walking stick. She sees me staring. 'Better safe than sorry.'

I just have my simple bow and a few arrows that Liam made. And my knife. I haven't brought the guitar. There's no room for it in my pack, and I know we're going into a place where making unnecessary noise could put lives in danger. I'm hoping Liam will understand. I wish I could think of something to do for him that is half as nice as making the guitar.

I glance up and see that now the group of male hunters is standing in a shirtless row. Liam, Markus, Sinxen and about ten other boys. All of them are carrying plenty of weapons, including some massive metal-tipped spears. The boys look fierce, and I'm glad they're on our side.

My eyes gravitate to Liam. He notices my gaze, and his face softens a little. He risks a subtle wink. My heart surges.

'We *will* find a way off the wheel,' Veidman is saying. 'We *can* find an answer...' He looks at Meira, faltering a little. 'I guess that's about it.'

Some of the kids applaud him.

'See you in half an hour,' he murmurs, and climbs down from the stump, followed by Meira.

'I guess we should say goodbye to Rika,' I tell Gadya.

'She'll just cry like a big baby. Let's not make a production out of it.'

'Gadya! We have to say goodbye. You guys are friends.'

'OK, OK,' she says, exasperated. Her eyes are watching Liam. I want to talk to her about him, but it never seems like the right time, and also, I'm chicken.

In any case, neither of us can find Rika. We search the cooking areas, but there's no sign of her.

'She's gone to help the Ones Who Suffer,' a girl tells us vaguely.

'Looking for Rika was a dumb idea,' Gadya snaps at me. 'She obviously doesn't care about us.'

We trudge back to the fire pit. The troops are amassing. I realise that roughly one tenth of the camp is leaving, and the rest are staying. That means nearly twenty of us will be forging ahead into the jungle. Other than the male hunters, there are a couple of hut builders, me and Gadya, and then Veidman.

The ones who are going are easy to spot, because of their weapons and their packs. Along with my bow and arrows, I have a pack too, slung over one shoulder and filled with cups and tallow candles. Others carry different provisions. Several of the sturdier boys are carrying our water tureens and flasks.

For security reasons involving the potential spy, no maps have been drawn of the bulk of our journey to the city on the shore of the grey zone. Those details have been committed to memory by Veidman, Liam and a few trusted others. They couldn't risk writing them down, which means we'll be relying on their mental notes to reach our goal – a pretty risky proposition.

We wave our final goodbyes to everyone as we follow Veidman on to a trail and into the verdant jungle. I'm surprised that Rika didn't say goodbye to us. Maybe it was too much for her. I'm lost in the sea of my own thoughts and emotions. I'm sad about leaving, but also filled with nervous excitement about what lies ahead.

Liam and some hunters walk at the front of our line, with a few of the other hunters bringing up the rear. Gadya and I are near the middle.

After just ten minutes of hiking through the thick vegetation, I already start feeling tired. I don't know how I'm going to manage too many miles.

'So, you didn't bring your guitar?' Gadya asks me out of the blue.

Startled, I turn to her. 'No.'

'You think I don't know about you and Liam.' She doesn't sound mad any more. Just sort of resigned. 'Well, I do. I've even talked to him about it.'

I stop walking for a second. 'You have? Liam never mentioned that.'

'Yeah. Well, don't worry. Everything's cool. I'm not going to flip out on you.'

I'm not sure what to say. 'I tried not to let anything happen. You have to believe me. All we did was kiss. Once. No, wait. Twice, technically.'

'I know how it is. Liam has an effect on people.' She laughs, but it sounds forced. 'Really, it's OK. It's time for me to move on anyway. It's not like there aren't enough other cute guys around.'

'You sure you're OK with this?'

'I'm trying to be.'

'Thanks, Gadya,' I tell her. I feel relieved that she knows the truth. But also really guilty, because I tried to hide something from her.

'Just remember what I told you about him,' she adds. 'Don't forget that I tried to warn you.'

'Sure.'

We keep walking.

An hour passes. Then another.

Sometimes we talk among ourselves, but mostly we're silent. Gadya doesn't mention Liam again. She also doesn't seem bothered by the weight of her pack and her weapons. Meanwhile, my pack is killing me.

Suddenly, our line comes to a stumbling halt.

'What—' I begin, but Gadya flashes me a concerned look.

'Listen,' she mouths, motioning at the forest to our left.

At first I hear nothing. Then comes a faint rustling in the trees. The sound of twigs snapping underneath feet. I know it's not a hoofer. Their hoofbeats are heavier, wilder.

Boys start raising their weapons. I'm not sure whether I should slot an arrow into my bow. Probably, but I don't want to risk making noise. Instead I unsheathe my knife with a shaking hand.

No one makes a move. We just stand there.

Veidman suddenly shouts, 'Show yourself!' His words ring out in the forest, loud and confident. Birds squawk and fly from the trees into the grey sky. 'We're from the blue sector. And we're armed.' He lies: 'There's a hundred of us!'

The footsteps increase their pace and volume. The person is heading straight at us. My pulse quickens. Bows are being drawn all around me, including Gadya's.

'Now there's a hundred and one of you, Veidman,' a girl's voice suddenly yells.

A second later, the girl crashes out of the foliage, skidding on to the path.

Rika.

'I almost killed you!' Gadya yells. 'Are you crazy?'

Veidman rushes over as I lower my knife and exhale. Rika seems oblivious to the fact that she nearly got skewered by a bevy of arrows and spears.

'I know I'm late. I know – but better late than never, right?'

'You gotta be more careful!' Liam says, helping her up.

'Sorry.' Rika climbs to her feet.

'Why'd it take you so long to make the right decision?' Markus grumbles. We're all gathering around Rika now as she brushes leaves and dirt off her clothes.

'Cooking's what I do. You all know that. I'm not a hunter or a builder.' She takes a breath, and then keeps going. 'But the more I thought about it, the more I realised that you need a cook.'

We all just stare at her blankly.

'You might work your magic with weapons,' she continues. 'But I work mine with roots, leaves and hoofer meat. There are plenty of cooks back at the village. But not a single one here. Until now.'

'How'd you even find us?' a hunter asks. 'You're not a tracker.'

'I have my ways,' she retorts. 'Don't underestimate me. I can smell hickory bark a quarter mile away, and a patch of mint even further than that. You think I can't find a slow-moving group of twenty kids hiking through the forest? Please.'

'It shouldn't be this easy to find us,' Gadya mutters. 'We need to do a better job of covering our tracks.'

A lot of the hunters don't know what to make of Rika's

sudden appearance. They're probably wondering if she'll be a liability. But the more I think about it, her decision makes perfect sense. Everyone will fight better with a full stomach.

'Someone help her with her pack,' Veidman instructs.

He says this because her pack is crammed with cooking pots and hollow wooden bowls. It's like she tried to cram her entire kitchen kit into there.

'No, I can carry it. Really,' she protests as a few hunters step forward and grab some items to lighten her load.

'Take this,' Liam says, giving her one of his spears.

'What am I gonna do with that? It's too big to stir a pot.' But she takes it anyway.

Markus moves over and says something softly to Veidman. Veidman nods in agreement. 'We need to keep moving. Each time we pause, we give the drones a chance to attack.'

As we start hiking again, Rika falls back and joins Gadya and me near the middle-rear of the line.

'We came looking for you to say goodbye,' I tell Rika, so she doesn't think we ditched her.

'If I knew you wanted to come, I would have trained you, too. Like I did with Alenna,' Gadya complains.

'Then I'm glad you didn't know.' Rika pokes Gadya's arm. 'I'm no athlete.'

'Neither is Alenna, believe me.'

'Hey, watch it!' I say, although I'm pretty sure Gadya's just teasing.

We continue hiking for the next hour. Rika's sunny disposition has lightened the burden in my heart. And now we have her stew to look forward to for lunch and dinner, instead of dried rations of cured hoofer meat.

Yet another hour passes. Then another. Time becomes fluid. At some point we pass the invisible boundary that divides the edge of the blue sector from the orange one, but no one makes a big deal out of it, which is probably for the best.

If you control your fear, then you keep your mind clear. That's a line I learned from Gadya.

I think about David. It's hard to believe he was serious about splitting with the two factions and doing his own thing. On this island, setting off on one's own might be the most courageous – or stupid – act of all. Crazier even than going to war or hiking into the grey zone.

The sun moves overhead, grilling us with its heat, even through the canopy of trees. It's hard to imagine the grey zone being cold. For now, all the coats, gloves and other winter wear are stowed inside our packs.

The hike is going well – so well that I start to get complacent, the very thing Gadya warned me against. But we all do. Our voices grow too loud, and even the hunters are lulled into the rhythm of the hike. They relax, their bows no longer at the ready. It's just too hard to stay that tense, hour after relentless hour.

Between lulls in the conversation, my thoughts drift to Liam. To David. To my parents. And most of all to the rocks that I'll be searching for once we find a way into the grey zone.

The last thing I'm worrying about is walking straight into an ambush.

THE ATTACK

We're still hiking when the first arrows hit. I'm just putting one tired leg in front of the other and listening to Rika tell us about the stew she's going to cook tonight.

But Gadya stops moving and looks distracted about a second before everyone else. I'm just about to ask if she's OK, when something whisks right past my face. It's so close it blows back a strand of my hair, and nearly grazes the tip of my nose. Stupefied, I stumble backwards. And when I turn my head, I see an arrow sticking out of a tree trunk about three feet away, still quivering.

'Close ranks!' Veidman immediately screams.

At the same moment I realise that my worst fears have come true.

We're under attack!

Everything Gadya taught me goes out of my mind instantly. It's like I'm frozen. Nothing seems real. Although I've been under siege twice already, both times were back at the safety of the village. This is different. Out here we're exposed. And we're technically in the Monk's territory.

'Alenna!' Gadya yells at me, getting right in my face. 'Pull yourself together! Grab an arrow!'

Her voice snaps me back to reality. I do what she says,

getting the arrow slotted, despite my trembling hands. My training slowly starts coming back. I crouch down low in the underbrush as more arrows whiz past my head.

The others do the same. We're all moving closer to one another. I stare out into the foliage. I can't see who's firing at us. Just faceless shadows leaping through the forest.

Gadya spots movement nearby and unleashes an arrow. She's already got another one loaded, a millisecond later.

I stare around wildly. Rika is hiding in the centre of the group. An arrow hits one of the pans sticking out of her pack, making it crash like a gong.

Liam races over to me. Other hunters are spreading to the sides now, trying to establish a perimeter and scare off the drones.

'Are you hit?' Liam asks, worry creasing his face.

'No. I'm OK,' I tell him.

'Just keep your head down. Use your pack as a shield. It'll be over soon.'

We crouch down, bows at the ready. Sinxen runs past with his spear. A few more arrows plough into nearby trees, barely missing us.

I peer into the dense jungle. The shadowy figures keep dancing and leaping, making unearthly whooping sounds.

'What are we going to do?' I ask, swallowing hard. I knew an ambush was possible. I just didn't think it would happen so soon.

'We fight back,' Liam responds, shooting off another arrow.

'I've got a bad feeling about this,' Gadya mutters. It's the first time I've actually heard her sound scared.

'Can we turn back?' I ask.

'Too late. The drones know we're here, and right now they're spreading the word. Probably telling every other drone in this sector to come and get us.'

More arrows hit trees around us. I hold my pack over my head. So far, I'm lucky. I haven't received a single hit yet.

But not everyone is so fortunate. Markus bears a bleeding gash on the side of his neck. It looks like a flesh wound, because he's still firing arrows, but I can't tell for sure. Some of the other hunters have been hit as well.

It's clear that we're seriously outnumbered. There are so many arrows coming our way, it's like being in a hailstorm. I figure there have to be at least fifty drones in the forest.

Then the random fireworks begin, even though it's daytime, blasting off into the sky. Their pops are deafening, disorienting.

Even with the noise, I can still hear kids yelling at one another. Veidman is barking orders, fighting against the chaos. He stands there without any sort of shield, his spear raised.

Abruptly, a lull comes. The frequency of the arrows inexplicably diminishes. Then they cease altogether.

'Heathens!' a voice cries out into the silence.

We swivel our weapons in the direction of the voice. It's coming from a drone hidden in the forest.

'You're trespassing,' the voice continues. 'The Monk controls this sector.'

I see Liam take aim with his arrow. He's honing in on the sound of the voice. Sinxen and two of the other hunters follow his lead.

But Veidman holds out his arm, signalling them to stop. 'We aren't here to fight,' he calls out to the voice in the trees. 'We're just passing through.'

'With twenty warriors, all bearing weapons?'

So they've been watching us. Tracking us. It's worse than I thought.

'I'm telling the truth,' Veidman insists.

'It's more likely you're here to attack our outpost.'

'We're not. We're from a village in the blue sector, a village that your people have been perpetually raiding. But I'm asking you to let us pass in peace. We're on an expedition into the grey zone, trying to find a way off the wheel. The knowledge we're seeking could help all of us – even you and your Monk.'

There's a long pause. For a second, I'm afraid arrows will rain down on us again. But then the voice speaks, and this time it's cold and flat. 'You're a liar.'

'No. We think the way off the wheel is hidden on the northern coast.'

I'm surprised Veidman is being so honest. Then I realise it's a solid strategy. He knows we need a valid reason to be here, or we'll all be slaughtered like hoofers.

'There's nothing inside the grey zone except death,' the voice intones. 'Is that what you're looking for, heathen?'

'We're looking for answers, numbnuts!' Gadya yells out.

Veidman motions angrily for her to be silent. 'Let me speak for the group.'

'Then make them understand,' she snaps back.

The voice speaks again. 'It doesn't matter if I believe you or not. Don't you know who I am?'

Veidman signals to some of the hunters to fan out. 'Tell me.'

'I'm a chief watcher for the Monk. I make sure that no heathens pass through this corner of the orange sector without permission.'

'Then give us permission,' Veidman says. He's trying to reason with this drone, but I'm not sure that's a good idea. It's clear the watcher doesn't trust us, and he definitely doesn't like us.

'No chance,' the voice continues. It seems to be everywhere. All around us, coming from the trees. The hunters spin and turn, still trying to track its source. 'The Monk depends on me to do my job. He is my lord and master.'

Gadya curses under her breath. 'Let's fill this brainwashed loser full of arrows.'

'I have an army of more than one hundred soldiers,' the watcher continues. 'And right now we've got you completely surrounded.'

'You're bluffing.'

'Am I?'

Lights immediately start flashing and twinkling in the trees around us. I realise they're coming from the drones. They're giving away their positions, but they're also revealing that they decisively outnumber us, at least five to one. The watcher is telling the truth.

'All of my soldiers are armed,' he says. 'All of them will fight to the death if I give the signal. They loathe heathens like you.'

'Then don't give them the signal! Let us go in peace.'

'Tell me, Matthieu Veidman – and yes, I know your name, so don't look so surprised – what would you do? If twenty of our soldiers turned up at your village with bows and arrows?'

'I'd talk to you. There's enough death on the wheel. This place breeds it. We should stop killing one another and start working together.'

'Your people and mine have been at war for as long as anyone can remember.'

'That's exactly why we should stop!' Veidman yells in frustration. 'We're at war because there's nothing else to do on the wheel. Because the UNA, or whoever runs this place, wants us to be at war! Don't you get it?'

The voice is silent for a moment. Finally it speaks. 'Surrender, then. Put down your weapons and packs. Let my people take you to our beloved Monk. We can trust him to work out our differences.'

'Your Monk is insane,' Gadya snarls.

'Enough, Gadya!' Veidman barks.

But this time, the hunters agree with her. 'We'll never surrender!' one yells into the trees.

'Never!' Sinxen seconds.

'Not to scum like you!' Markus cries out angrily.

Jeers and catcalls come back at us from the trees, like deranged echoes. These drones sound ready to fight. Our hunters start screaming insults right back at them.

Only Liam remains quiet, moving his bow back and forth. I can tell that he's locked on to the sound of the watcher's voice now.

'You have no faith,' the voice lectures us over the escalating noise. 'No belief. The Monk offers the one true path. Soon this entire island will be his.'

'I've heard that one before,' Gadya says through gritted teeth. 'Your Monk is a big fraud.'

The watcher isn't listening. 'If you refuse to surrender, then you'll pay with your lives.'

'Don't do this.' Veidman's voice is hard now. 'I'm begging you.' But he's not begging at all. He has just finally realised that the time for diplomacy is over. I see him making covert hand signals at the hunters. Bows and spears get raised again, and I follow the lead of my companions.

'You shouldn't have come here unless you expected to find trouble,' the watcher calls out, his voice rising into a hysterical whine. 'You're all simple heathens! Sent to kill us and hurt our Monk!'

Veidman shuts his eyes, his face twisted up. I know what's coming next, and so does he. We all do. 'Please—'

'Warriors, tear down these infidels!' the watcher suddenly screams at full volume.

There's a split second of silence. Then comes the roar of the watcher's men. It sounds more like a thousand drones than a hundred. They spill forward with their torches. Arrows fly at us in undulating waves. I dodge one, slip, and tumble on to the ground.

'I'm hit!' Rika screams as she collapses, pots and tins tumbling out of her pack with a crash. I see an arrow sticking through her pant leg. She sounds like she's in shock.

I start crawling towards her over the mud. What Gadya taught me is useless. Even she can't get a shot off because she's forced to take shelter behind a tree.

This battle isn't going to last very long, I realise. But it's going to leave a pile of corpses behind. *Our corpses.*

Just as I'm succumbing to despair, I suddenly hear a rumbling in the sky, followed by a high-pitched squealing noise. I look up. I'd almost forgotten that the drones aren't the only things to fear on this island. That something even worse lurks above us in the clouds.

'Alenna, stay low!' I hear Liam yelling. He's trying to run over to protect me, but the storm of arrows makes it impossible.

A second later, the first of the feelers shoots down from the heavens, ploughing into the earth about ten feet away from me. I scream, scrabbling away as fast as I can.

The feeler's tentacles snap, whir and grind as they throw up clods of dirt and tree roots. Then they whip into the air and slam downwards again. They're like coils of living rope. Black metallic snakes in search of prey. Malignant. Inhuman.

'Alenna, look out!' Liam yells. I hear a deafening noise

and roll sideways just in time. Another set of feelers strikes the ground right where I was crouching.

Our bows and arrows are obviously useless against these things. So are spears. But it also means the drones' weapons are useless too. I can see drones running away as the feelers go after them as well. The watcher and his drones apparently didn't anticipate this assault. Painted bodies flee in terror back into the trees.

I watch a drone get plucked as he scrambles away from us. He's tossed up into the sky by the feelers, disappearing so fast that only his screams linger behind.

Gadya races towards me and helps me up. Rika staggers to her feet too, despite her injury.

'We brought them on us when we crossed into this sector!' Gadya yells.

'How do we fight them?' I scream back.

'We don't! We run!'

'I can't move,' Rika yelps, gesturing at her leg.

'You have to!' Gadya lunges forward, grabbing her and supporting her weight. 'Alenna, cover us.'

I raise my bow and arrow. I can cover us against the few remaining drones, but not against the feelers. We lurch sideways as we hear the feelers making their terrible sounds. So far I've seen them take more of the Monk's drones than our people, and I'm grateful for that. But right then I see one descend and snatch up one of our builders.

I spot Liam. He's racing nimbly across the terrain towards us. At the same time, he's also spinning and twirling – a blur of constant motion – to avoid feelers diving down from the sky.

I continue firing arrows. Some hit tentacles, but the tips just ricochet off the metal without impact. The feelers are relentless. One tears a cypress tree right out of the ground, roots and all, in its attempt to snatch Liam.

I crouch back down on the ground in the dirt. The feelers haven't come after me in earnest yet. They seem more interested in the boys. But maybe that's just because the hunters are the ones running around exposed. I watch helplessly as they take another of our hunters. There's nothing we can do.

'Alenna—' I hear Veidman yell. I turn and see him on my left. He's trying to organise everyone.

'What do I do?' I call back, terrified but slotting another arrow into my bow.

'Stay put!'

Veidman rushes past. Feelers slam down a few feet behind him, knocking up a spray of dirt. He stumbles but keeps plunging forward. The feelers pull back up into the sky, preparing for another assault. I wonder how many are hovering above us. At least six or seven. Maybe more. And each one seems to possess at least eight individual tentacles.

Sinxen helps Gadya drag Rika to the shelter of a large tree. I know the feelers can still reach her there, but they're not paying her much attention. I wonder what draws the feelers. Maybe motion or body heat. I look back and see that Liam has paused to help pull another wounded hunter to safety in the forest.

That's when it happens.

I catch a glimpse of something fast and metallic, as fast as an arrow, slamming into the earth in front of me like a meteor. *It's a tentacle.* The ground shakes and I stagger back, getting pelted in the face with debris.

Then something hits the earth behind me. Another tentacle. I'm thrown forward and lose my balance between the two mechanical monstrosities.

I feel a vertiginous sensation of absolute liquid terror. My vision constricts like I'm looking through a tunnel.

I'm about to be taken!

I race sideways as fast as I can, letting myself be guided by instinct. I regain my footing and try to slip past the feelers, dodging them. But one of them lifts up and comes down hard to my left. I stumble and catch myself.

'Help!' I scream.

But no one hears me. I focus on a tree with a huge trunk and thick branches. It's much larger than the other trees around me, and I race towards it, thinking I can take refuge there.

As I run, the feelers keep plunging and swooping. Attacking. At any moment I expect their mechanical fronds to curl around my body and fling me upwards into the sky. I zigzag, refusing them an angle of attack. I'm getting close to the huge tree now, just ten paces away, closing the gap quickly.

Another tentacle comes down and slides under my foot

as I'm stepping forward. It jerks me off balance, and this time I can't recover. Before I can twist out of its grasp, it gets me around the ankle and throws me down.

'*No!*' I scream as loudly as I can.

I claw at the earth, its damp scent thick in my nostrils. My hands can't find purchase on anything. I hammer at the dirt and grass with my feet, trying to get the thing off me. The feeler starts pulling me up. Other tentacles slam down next to me and begin curling around my limbs, writhing and bucking.

I yank against them with all my strength, but I can't make them budge. I hear myself screaming, sobbing like a crazy person. I kick and hit at the metal.

Then I feel my body rising into the air.

My hands grasp at tree branches, tearing off fistfuls of leaves.

This is the end.

I know that I'm about to die, but I don't feel peaceful. My life doesn't flash before my eyes. I just feel furious and terrified.

'Get the hell off me!' I scream at the tentacles as I continue to rise. I'm four feet off the ground already. In a second, I'm going to get yanked all the way up above the clouds.

Then I feel something crash into my lower torso, slamming me sideways into a tree trunk. I hit the tree so hard I almost lose consciousness. One of the tentacles around my waist loosens and uncurls. Something crashes into me again, scraping the skin off my left arm.

Then the tentacles are gone, like they're retracting into the sky as the feeler departs.

And I'm falling . . .

I plunge through branches and leaves, trying to get my hands around my head to protect myself.

An instant later, I slam into the underbrush, and the breath explodes from my lungs. I choke for air, gasping. Everything goes numb from the impact. I can't feel my arms or legs.

I lie there, trying to figure out what happened. I wasn't taken; I've been let go. But why? I try to move. Slowly the feeling starts coming back. I struggle to sit up, terrified the feelers are going to seek me out again.

Then I realise that the feeler that grabbed me is still there. It's just preoccupied because someone else is doing battle with it.

Liam.

He's the one who rescued me. He must have thrown himself at it, not caring about his own life.

He's now wrestling the largest of the tentacles, using all his strength. Luckily, one of the feeler's other tentacles has gotten trapped between two tree trunks, so it can't get at him. The motors inside the tentacles whine as they go into overdrive. The noise from the feeler is nearly unbearable.

Liam is yelling to the other hunters. They're rushing over, including Gadya. I realise most of the feelers are gone now, except this one. The one that almost took me. I would have been the last person to get snatched.

I manage to get to my knees, shaking. Liam saved me. The surviving hunters have reached him, and they're attacking the feeler with everything they have – their entire arsenal of bows and spears, as well as their brute strength.

I remember what Rika said about how they cut off part of a feeler once. This time it looks like they're going to bring the whole machine down, and reveal the secret part that hovers above the clouds. They're pulling at its tentacles, keeping it earthbound. I struggle towards them to help.

But as I move, the tentacle that's been stuck between the trunks finally gets loose. With a massive flailing motion it tears down the trees that were trapping it, making us fall back for a second.

Liam still has hold of its other tentacle, and he's hacking away with his spear. He doesn't realise he's now in sudden danger.

'Liam, look out!' I scream at him. 'Behind you!'

Somehow he hears my voice over the racket and looks up. *But it's too late.*

The newly freed tentacle slices through the air. It curls itself around Liam's waist like a belt. He gasps as the tentacle whips his body backwards, slamming his head against a tree. The spear gets knocked from his hand.

I race forward. 'No!'

His eyes lock on to mine. I don't see fear in them. Only clarity and determination. But I also see the look of someone who knows his time is up.

'Alenna,' he mouths.

One simple word.

My name.

And then the tentacles pull him straight up through the branches and into the sky.

It happens so fast, I can't believe it. I continue moving forward. But Liam is gone. I look up. He's not even a speck. He has just disappeared. *This can't be real,* I tell myself frantically. *Oh, please no – Not Liam!*

Everyone looks shocked.

Liam is gone. Liam, the best hunter. The best tracker. My first kiss. Liam, who lost his life saving mine.

Liam, I think over and over, just repeating his name in a daze. I can't believe I've lost him.

My body stops moving. My legs feel weak, and I collapse to the ground. I wish the feeler had taken me instead of him. I'm useless on this island. *He should have just let it take me!*

Kids are shouting and yelling. No one can believe what just happened. The feelers have decimated our group. They've taken half our people. I shut my eyes, trying to wish the world away. *What am I going to do now?*

THE BOUNDARY

A few seconds later, a pair of hands yanks me to my feet. I open my eyes. It's Gadya.

I'm still in shock, the events replaying in my mind like a loop. But the battle is over now. The feelers are gone, and so is the Monk's watcher and his drones. 'Gadya,' I say.

Then I notice that her face is red. Furious. 'This is all your fault!' she yells at me as I stumble back in surprise. 'If it weren't for you, Liam wouldn't have got taken!'

'Wait, Gadya, stop.'

'He was trying to save your pathetic ass!'

'I know that!' But does she know how badly my heart is aching? 'I didn't ask him to.' I'm about to cry. 'I'm sorry!'

'Sorry?' she screams, turning around. 'Hey, everyone, did you hear that? Alenna is sorry she got Liam killed! Doesn't that make you feel so much better?'

'Leave it be,' Markus says glumly. 'Liam wasn't the only one who got taken today.'

'No, I will not leave it be!' she screams back at him.

'Gadya, don't do this,' Veidman cautions. He's at Rika's side, rolling up her pant leg to inspect her wound.

Gadya ignores him, turning back to me with blazing eyes. 'How does it feel to be a murderer?'

'C'mon. That's crazy, Gad. She's not a murderer,' Sinxen says, trying to get between us and failing.

'Yes, she is!' Gadya stares me down. 'You only came on this journey because of Liam! Admit it. You're deadweight.'

'That's not true!' I feel myself getting angry. 'This is not my fault. I came here to help. And earlier today you said you were cool with me and Liam! Were you lying?' I realise she must have been hiding her feelings from me. Now her true emotions are getting released in an angry torrent.

'You're a follower. Not like me or Liam. Not a real hunter. You caused his death.' Gadya shoves me in the chest, ready to fight. 'Now you're going to pay for it.'

'The feeler killed him!' I tell Gadya. 'Open your eyes!'

Gadya knows what I'm saying is true. For a moment I think she's going to back down. Then the moment passes, and all I see is steely determination and rage again. 'I wish I hadn't wasted my time on you. I wish I'd just spent it with Liam.'

'Maybe he didn't want to spend any more time with you,' I snap at her, knowing it's the wrong thing to say. 'Maybe you shouldn't have dumped him if you were still in love with him!'

Gadya rushes forward, like she's going to punch me in the face. I flinch, but I stand my ground. She stops, a few inches away.

'I know that you and Liam were hooking up,' she spits. 'That you went behind my back, even when I asked you not to. It was more than just a kiss. Markus told everyone he saw you two down by the butterfly river.'

'I never said they were doing anything,' Markus calls out, overhearing.

'But we both know that they were.'

I want to turn away from her, but I'm afraid she might leap on me and attack. All her sadness is coming out as blind fury.

'Gadya, calm down,' Veidman says wearily. 'Liam knew the risks. We all did. He died an honourable death.'

She spins to face him. 'Listen, Vei, we can't trust her. Alenna's the newest person here, right? I know she passed your truth test, but maybe she lied her way through it somehow! She and David have probably been playing all of us from the start. What if she's the spy? The high-level drone?'

I can't believe what she's saying. 'That's crap, and you know it!' I retort.

'Is it? Who's to say that you and David aren't in league with each other? Can you prove that you're not?'

I'm speechless. Where I once saw an ally, now I see only someone who hates me.

'Maybe it's not a coincidence that Liam is gone,' Gadya continues, addressing Veidman. 'After all, she's been trying to seduce him this whole time—'

'That's not true!' I say. 'I tried to stop my feelings for him!'

'Yeah, sure. All I know is that if it weren't for you, he'd still be alive.'

Veidman has finally had enough. 'Shut up!' he barks at Gadya, startling everyone, because he rarely yells. Silence falls, broken only by the cries of the wounded. He glares at her until she finally looks away. 'Alenna stared down death. Just like you and me, and the rest of us. But we got lucky today. Liam and some of the others didn't.' He sighs. 'You girls are on the same side. All of us are. Start acting like it.'

'Yeah, and who knows if the feelers are gonna come back?' Rika calls out. 'Or the drones? Please be friends again. Gadya, we're all hurting about Liam.'

Even the mention of his name makes my heart ache. *How am I going to find the strength to keep on hiking, when I just want to give up?*

'OK, fine.' Gadya laughs bitterly. 'I guess the rest of you don't care.'

I know I must be in shock because I still feel disconnected from my own emotions. The only boy I ever cared about is gone. Dead. I should be sobbing.

I turn away from the group. Maybe there's some truth to what Gadya's saying. Liam probably would be alive if I hadn't come along.

I risk a glance behind me and see that Gadya has stalked over to the remnants of a tree. The one near where Liam got taken. I wonder what she's doing, and then I see that her shoulders are shaking. She's crying hard, her chest silently heaving. She's hiding her face so no one will see. I look away.

Rika walks up behind me, limping. 'You OK?' I ask her, swallowing hard.

'The arrow just grazed me. It hurts, but Veidman said I'll be fine.' She pauses. 'It's you I'm worried about.'

'Why?' I mutter. But I'm still wondering why I'm not crying as hard as Gadya. Shouldn't I be just as upset as she is? Is it possible she had stronger feelings for Liam than I did?

Like she's reading my thoughts, Rika murmurs, 'People show their emotions in different ways. Gadya's been on the wheel much longer than you. She's crying for all the friends she's lost – not just Liam.'

I nod, still feeling shattered.

'Besides, she never meant to break up with him. That's her big secret. The night she dumped him, she just got mad and overreacted. She thought they'd be back together the next day. But it didn't work out that way. And her stupid pride prevented her from begging him to forgive her.'

We walk over to the underbrush together, joining the others, gathering our scattered packs and possessions. We sit down, and Rika rolls her pant leg up. Her leg is still bleeding a little, but it looks more like a deep scratch than a puncture wound.

'So Liam is really—' I pause. I can't bring myself to say the word 'dead'. It seems so final. So I just say, 'It's hard to believe, that's all.'

Rika looks down at the underbrush. 'We don't know what happens when someone gets taken. Not for sure.'

'You're trying to make me feel better.'

'Well, look at it this way – no one back home in the UNA ever sees *us* again, and we're not dead.' Then she adds, 'At least not yet.'

I look around. Obviously everyone thinks Liam and the

other kids who got taken are dead. I see it stamped on their faces.

'If you really care about Liam, then you won't give up,' Rika continues. 'Not in your heart, where it counts.'

I nod. I think about the time that Liam and I spent together. How he helped me train, and made me the guitar. How we joked around with each other. What kissing him felt like. I can't think about it too much or the pain will make it impossible to keep going.

Veidman calls out to everyone, 'Gather round!'

We stumble towards him, bloody and bruised. The surviving hunters have found most of our backpacks. We'll have to abandon some supplies, because there aren't enough of us left to carry all of them. Gadya pushes herself away from the tree and walks over. I avoid her gaze.

'I wish today had never happened,' Veidman says, surveying our ragged crew. 'Now there are only ten of us left. We'll mourn our companions later, when we're out of danger. I know some of you got hurt, but we can't give up.'

His strained pep talk isn't having any effect on me or anyone else. I wonder how many of us will even be alive when we reach our destination.

'What matters is that we get inside the grey zone and find the city where the aircrafts are.' Veidman glances around. 'We've got a ways to go,' he continues. 'But at least we'll be out of the orange sector soon.'

'And then things'll be even worse, 'cause we'll be in the grey zone,' Markus points out.

'No, we'll be at the barrier,' Veidman corrects him. 'We have to get through that first, remember?' He looks up. 'I don't think the drones will come after us for a while. The feelers scared them off. But we need to move fast. So let's get going.'

Soon we're all hiking again. Gadya keeps her own company, staring out into the trees.

Rika and I walk next to each other. She's breathing hard, and I know her leg must be killing her. But she shakes off any offers of assistance, refusing to let me help with her pack.

We keep hiking, and I keep thinking about Liam. The pain feels like a physical wound in my chest. Raw and throbbing.

'What do you think the barrier's like?' Rika asks me, trying to coax me out of my despair, despite her own injury. 'Everyone's got a theory.'

'Who cares?' I know the barrier should interest me, but I just figured Veidman would think of some way around it. 'Isn't it just a big fence or something?'

'"Or something" is right. Supposedly you can see through it, but you can't cross over. If you try, it's like getting stuck forever, in invisible syrup. Before the tunnel collapsed, none of us ever had to worry about it.'

'Great.' I step sideways on a slippery tree trunk and almost fall. Rika grabs my arm to steady me. 'Can't you just dig a new tunnel?' I ask.

'We didn't build the tunnel,' she explains. 'It was here

when we arrived. We don't have the equipment or manpower to build something like that. It was really deep. All brick and concrete.'

I think about the tunnel, and the other buildings on the island that I saw on the museum screen. It's definitely an indication that other people lived on the island once. And hopefully a sign that David told the truth about my parents and the prison colony.

I glance up at the trees ahead and see we're making steady progress. There's no sign of the drones or the feelers, but I know it's just a temporary reprieve. They'll come for us again and again. Until no one's left. Without Liam, I feel depressed and alone.

The ground gets slippery again, and I slow my pace. I glance down and see that I'm stepping on one of those strange plastic bags. The ones with the chemical formulas printed on them.

'These are everywhere now,' Rika says, noticing it. 'Especially after a feeler attack.'

I kick it aside with my foot. I don't want more mysteries. *Only answers.*

'Stop!' Veidman calls from up ahead. The line stops moving.

'What?' someone else whispers. My body tenses up. I don't think I can handle another attack this soon.

'We're close to the barrier!' Veidman calls out. 'Come and look.'

We walk forward and gather around him.

'We're near the southern perimeter of the grey zone,' Veidman explains. He stares off into the forest, like he's scanning for secret landmarks. 'The barrier should be about five miles ahead.' Veidman peers up at the sky. Clouds are moving in, and grey light filters down to us through the trees. 'Rain's coming. We better get moving.'

We slowly shoulder our packs and continue the journey.

I try not to think about Liam as we hike. I know I'll crumple in a heap at the side of the trail if I let my emotions overwhelm me. I compartmentalise my feelings, packing them away in the back of my mind until I can deal with them later. It's a skill I learned after my parents got taken. A skill that all orphans must learn.

I just focus on the grey zone. Getting past the mysterious barrier – if we even can – will only mark the beginning of my real journey. Inside the grey zone, I plan to seek any trace of my parents. I'll leave the safety of the group if I have to. I'm glad I didn't tell Gadya my secret; it's best that no one knows my real motives. That way I won't endanger anyone except myself.

I feel a droplet on my forehead, and then another. Soon it's raining lightly. I just keep hiking, and so do my companions.

'There it is!' Sinxen finally yells as the trees start to thin. 'The barrier!' He rushes forward.

We follow him, stepping out of the trees into a clearing.

'Crap,' Rika mutters despondently. Some of the hunters, including Markus, curse and throw down their packs.

I don't blame them. Before us looms the surreal,

impenetrable barrier to the grey zone. I'm surprised by how massive it is – about sixty feet high, and at least several feet thick. It's nearly translucent, and slightly pearly, like an oil slick. To me it looks like solidified water standing upright to form a huge monolithic wall. I've never seen anything like it before.

Veidman strides right up to the barrier. I watch as he reaches out a hand and presses it against the surface. The rain makes the barrier easier to see, spattering off its edges, defining its shape.

'You sure it's safe to touch?' Sinxen calls out, sounding worried.

'Why don't you go find out for yourself?' Gadya snaps.

I'm still watching Veidman. His hand remains on the barrier, fingers splayed. He's pushing inwards, gouging at the material.

Rika and I slowly walk closer. She squints at it through the rain. 'It looks kind of like jelly or something.'

She's right. Like quasi-transparent jelly.

I'm almost there now. My feet make sloshing sounds with every step, because the rain has already filled my boots with water. I've taken my jacket out and put it on. I'm miserable, exhausted and in mourning for Liam.

I glance over at Veidman, who's ten feet to my left. Gadya walks over to the other side of him with Markus and the remaining hunters.

I watch Veidman's hand slowly sink into the barrier. It doesn't seem to be causing him any pain, but it looks like it's taking a lot of strength. He's leaning against the surface, using the force of his body to ram his hand inside.

'It's warm!' Rika exclaims. She's placed her palm on it too. 'I thought it'd be cold.'

I reach out and graze it with my fingertips. It's the temperature of freshly baked bread. Oddly pliable and organic.

I push against it, and the material pushes back. It's spongy, gelatinous. I realise it's going to be hard to fight our way through this, but I suppose that's why it's an effective barrier. I rake it with my chipped fingernails, but I barely make any impact. Each indentation I create just gets filled back in by the strange substance.

I look at Veidman. His fingers have formed a fist, and he's got his hand most of the way inside now. 'Ouch,' he suddenly mutters through clenched teeth. 'Too much pressure.' He starts sliding his hand back out, but he's stuck, as though the barrier is made of vertical quicksand. 'Someone help me.'

Sinxen and another hunter rush over and help him pull his arm out. The whole thing happens incredibly slowly, and everyone pauses to watch. Eventually, Veidman reclaims his hand. It's bone white, all the blood having been forced out of it.

'My fingers are numb,' he says, swinging his arm back and forth to get the circulation to return. We're all looking at him for guidance, but none is forthcoming.

'Move aside!' I suddenly hear Gadya yell. I look back over at her. She has walked off a little bit and is standing twenty paces behind us in the tree line. She raises her bow and arrow, about to fire at the barrier.

Veidman holds up a hand. 'Gadya, stop! We don't know what we're dealing with yet.'

Although Veidman is clearly the leader, and I've never seen anyone disobey him, Gadya's now playing by her own set of rules. 'I'm a warrior!' she calls back wildly. 'This is what I do!'

Before Veidman can stop her, she pulls back the arrow and lets it fly with a twang of the bow. It zooms through the air so fast, I barely see it. Then it slams into the surface of the barrier.

When it hits, it creates a ripple effect. Circles of shimmering liquid reverberate outwards from the point of impact. But it's a remarkably languorous ripple, like time is slowed down inside the barrier. I see the arrow's tip sliding through the liquid, decelerating rapidly with every millisecond.

And then it stops partway through, trapped.

We all stare at the arrow suspended in the strange substance. It made it only about a foot before getting stuck. A few colourful feathers stick out and mock us, like some kind of exotic flower.

'You won't be getting *that* arrow back,' Sinxen remarks.

But Gadya's already got another one ready, and it looks like she's about to try again.

This time Veidman won't let her. 'Hold your fire!' he snaps. 'That's an order.'

She hesitates.

'We need to conserve our arrows,' he explains. 'Besides, they're not going to work. We need another way.'

'Can we dig under it?' I ask.

Everyone looks at me, except Gadya, who's pretending I no longer exist.

'Not enough time,' Veidman says. 'Plus, we don't have shovels. And I'm guessing it goes deep enough underground that we couldn't get through, anyway.'

'What about going over it?' Markus asks.

'Won't work either.' Veidman is staring at the barrier. 'We can't climb up that high. We'd get stuck on top.'

I wonder to myself, *What the hell is this barrier made of? And who would build such a wall?*

Then I think that there must really be something worth hiding behind it – just like David said. But how will I ever find the section where the drones cross over? And the messages on the rocks inside? Will I really have the courage to leave the group if I need to?

I take a few steps back, trying to survey a larger section of the barrier. How do the drones get through this thing and into the grey zone so easily?

'Let's walk around it,' Veidman instructs. 'See if we can find a place where it gets thinner.'

I trudge after Veidman with a heavy heart. Not only is Liam gone, but his death was in vain. We're not going to be able to get past this barrier.

I can't imagine the trek back. I wonder if our village will still be standing, or if it has already been reduced to rubble by drones, and annexed by the Monk.

'Quick!' a voice suddenly screams out. 'Over here!'

I freeze.

It's the surviving builder, whom I don't know too well. He keeps screaming hysterically. 'Oh God, I found someone! It's a boy! And he's stuck inside the wall...'

RECKONING

We catch up a moment later. The rain has started coming down harder now. Cold drops pound the top of my head, and rivulets run down my cheeks and the back of my neck. I wipe rain from my eyes, struggling to make sense of what I'm seeing.

A skinny boy in black robes hangs before us, several feet off the ground. He's partially engulfed by the wall like a bug in an old paperweight.

'Keep your distance!' Veidman cautions.

Gadya and the hunters already have their bows out, all aimed at the same spot. I get mine out too.

The drone looks to be about my age, with long dark hair. He's short and thin, with a little peach fuzz stubble. His head, one shoulder, and one clawed hand are sticking out of the barrier. So is part of a leg and a foot. The rest of him is fully encased inside the translucent material.

His eyes are shut and his mouth is closed in a thin, tight line. Crimson blood has crusted around the edges of his nostrils and lips, as though squeezed out of him. He's not moving.

'Is he dead?' I whisper.

Sinxen hears and glances back. 'I think so.'

We stand there in the cold rain, scrutinising this drone, none of us eager to touch him. His exposed skin is alabaster white.

'Who do you think did this to him?' Rika finally asks.

Markus shrugs. 'Maybe he did it to himself, trying to get through.'

'But the pressure...' I murmur. 'Could he really make it that far? And why is he turned around, facing us?'

I'm still watching the boy's face, thinking to myself how awful it would be to die this way. To end up a frozen corpse inside the gelatinous barrier.

Then the boy's eyelids flicker open.

'He's alive!' voices start yelling.

Veidman steps forward. Gadya, Markus, Sinxen and the others follow him with their bows. The boy's pupils roll into position, fixing us with a bleary gaze. His eyes are pale blue, and I can see the pain in them. *The loss of hope.*

'What's your name?' Veidman asks.

The boy struggles to open his mouth, licking his cracked lips. Then he tries to take a huge breath. But he just gasps instead, like a fish on dry land. I realise that his chest must be under incredible pressure. 'Help,' he whispers. 'Can't breathe...'

"Can't breathe'? That's not a name!' Gadya taunts viciously. His eyes swivel towards her.

'Don't look at me, drone! I'll cut out your eyeballs and feed 'em to a hoofer!'

'Ignore her,' Veidman interrupts. 'Talk to me. Maybe I can help.'

'Please…' The boy can barely utter more than one word at a time. I realise if it weren't for us, he never would have been rescued.

Veidman looks around at our small group. 'We need to get him out. He might be useful.'

'He's the enemy,' Markus says. 'Let him rot. If he knew anything about how to get through the barrier, he wouldn't be stuck.' For a moment, even Veidman hesitates.

'What if this were one of you?' Rika pleads, her voice ringing out over the patter of the rain. 'Not every single drone is bad. They can't be! Some just chose the wrong path. And this drone doesn't pose a threat to us right now. We can afford to be kind, for once.'

Is she right? I think about David. About how he saved my life, and shared secrets with me. 'I think I'm with Rika,' I begin softly.

'You and Rika can go stuff your kindness!' Gadya yells, cutting me off. 'The wheel doesn't respect kindness. Look what happened to Liam! And the others! And you just don't care.'

'The drones didn't take Liam, a feeler did,' I say. 'Maybe a feeler did this to the boy.'

'Alenna's right,' Veidman speaks up, before Gadya can shout over me again. 'We have to get some answers from this drone.'

'And if he doesn't have any, we can always put him back in the wall,' Markus says ominously.

Veidman and the others walk forward and grab hold of

the boy's free arm and leg. Gadya hangs back with her bow, covering the group.

I try to help by walking forward, crouching down and yanking on the drone's foot. I wonder how long he's been trapped in here. The parts of his body inside the barrier are as white as a sheet of paper.

Gadya sees us having trouble. 'You need me to do it right,' she says in frustration, tossing down her bow and joining the fray.

Progress is slow. First we get the rest of the drone's shoulder out. Then another portion of his leg. Then part of his neck and chest. He starts to gasp as more air finally reaches his lungs. 'Please, please,' he keeps whimpering in a high-pitched voice.

'We're almost there,' Veidman tells him. Indeed, I can feel the jelly of the barrier loosening as we keep working.

Finally, with an explosive pop, the boy is pulled free from the wall.

He sprawls facedown on the dirt as we cluster around him. His body is slimy with the substance of the barrier. For an instant, a large indentation remains where his body was. But then the jelly surges forward and the hole slowly disappears.

I look down at the drone. Now that he's been liberated, we're all a little wary of him. Gadya picks up her bow again. We stand in a semicircle, watching and waiting to hear what he says. The rain is finally letting up.

The drone takes deep, shuddering breaths. He coughs,

gurgles. Hacks up phlegm. His limbs look thin and weak.

'Tell us your name,' Veidman gently instructs.

The boy can't even raise his head. 'They call me…Jump.'

'Dumb name,' Sinxen snickers.

'You're one to talk,' Gadya retorts.

Veidman silences them both with a look. But the boy has heard.

'You're right,' he manages in a breathy whisper. 'It's dumb… But they call me Jump 'cause that's what I do.'

'Is that how you ended up stuck in the barrier?' Markus calls out. 'Jumping around like a monkey? Why doesn't that surprise me?'

The drone has another coughing fit, and Veidman leans in closer to talk to him. 'My name's Matthieu Veidman. We're from a village in the blue sector, near the big river. We're searching for a way through this barrier and off the wheel.'

'Then you're infidels… You don't believe in our Monk's eternal powers.'

'No, we don't. But we'll give you water and food. And a chance to rest. In return you have to tell us everything you know. About this barrier, and about why you're here. About your Monk, too.'

'Why?'

'*Why?*' Gadya cuts in, sounding incredulous. 'Because if you don't, we'll leave you here to die! That's why. We just lost most of our friends. You mean nothing to us.'

'Jump, do we have a deal?' Veidman asks. Jump squirms around, like he's trying to sit up. 'Someone help him,' Veidman adds, but the drone waves everyone off with his good arm.

'I can manage,' he gasps, although it's pretty clear that he can't.

Veidman glances at Rika. 'Get some water and food from my pack.' Then he looks at me. 'Alenna, grab some blankets.' He peers back down at Jump. 'We're going to help you, and you're going to help us. We don't have to be enemies.'

Jump presses himself off the ground a few inches, using his good arm and shoulder.

'OK. I'll tell you what you want to know.'

'I'm listening.'

'Come closer,' Jump pleads. 'I don't want everyone to hear. What I have to say is just for you. You're the leader, right?'

Veidman reluctantly crouches down next to the fallen drone. 'Fine,' he says. 'Whisper it to me, then.'

I strain to listen, and everyone else does too. I hear Jump start whispering. I can't see his face, only Veidman's. But Veidman's expression is blank. Emotionless.

And then everything changes.

Jump emits a gurgling shriek, like his lungs are imploding. Veidman instantly lurches up, eyes filled with total inexplicable horror.

At first I don't understand.

But then I look down.

Sticking out of Veidman's chest, at the level of his heart, is a silver dagger. And Jump's hand is wrapped around the other end of it. 'I sure got the jump...on *you*!' he says, cackling madly, bloody saliva dribbling from his lips.

Before I have time to scream, an arrow flies straight from Gadya's bow right through one side of Jump's neck. The impact snaps his head back.

'It's a trap!' Sinxen yells.

Everyone explodes into action.

Sinxen grabs Veidman, whose shirt is already soaked with blood, and pulls him to safety. Jump lurches to his feet, displaying more energy than I thought possible. He yanks at the arrow impaling his Adam's apple, and gurgles blood.

'*Death to all infidels!*' he hisses, his voice a chilling, mutilated rasp, barely audible because of the hole in his throat.

I stand there paralysed.

An instant later, Markus and the other hunters come down on Jump like a ton of bricks, their fists battering his face. I catch a glimpse as his head lolls back. I see that he's laughing like a maniac, blood dripping off his chiselled teeth.

'Don't kill him,' Veidman calls out weakly. He sways, going into shock. He glances down at the dagger sticking out of his chest. 'We need him alive.'

Everyone hears, but nobody listens. Markus brutally rips the arrow right out of Jump's throat. Blood sprays up and paints the barrier red.

Markus steps back.

Jump is dying now. His throat is torn out, leaving a gaping hole. But a satisfied smile lingers on his lips.

Then a final arrow flies through the air from Gadya's bow,

striking him right between the eyes. His body tenses, hands seizing up, and then he relaxes again. Drooping. The life is gone from him now for good. And so is his smile.

'A dirty trap!' Gadya rants, brandishing her bow. 'The Monk probably sent him here and stuck him in the wall. He was waiting to get us!'

'I bet they've been putting drones in the barrier as sentries, ever since the tunnel collapse,' Sinxen mutters glumly.

Gadya flings down her bow in anger. 'This never would have happened if Liam were here. He would have protected Vei.'

Sinxen is sitting down now, cradling Veidman's head. Blood wells from Veidman's mouth, coming up from inside him. The knife is still in his chest. I know that if we try to remove it, it will just make things worse.

'Keep his head elevated,' Rika warns.

We all crowd around our fallen leader. I understand that Veidman is probably going to die because he tried to save someone. *Just like Liam.* Generosity is clearly a character flaw in the twisted microcosm of the wheel. Gadya was right.

Veidman's breath hitches in his chest. His neck arches.

'He needs air! Give him room!' Gadya yells.

'If you get back to the village, tell Meira what happened,' Veidman murmurs. He sounds sleepy. I feel an overwhelming sense of dread. 'Tell Meira that I love her.' He coughs, his chest rattling. The knife handle moves up and down.

'Fight!' Markus says. I see tears running down his face. 'Don't give up!'

'Tell Meira she has to forget about me. And continue our mission alone…' His words disintegrate into a breathy gasp. His mouth remains open. I think he's about to start talking again, but then I realise he's dead.

'Veidman!' Gadya yells. 'No!' Everyone starts screaming and yelling. *Liam and Veidman were not supposed to die.* Without them, we have no real leaders.

In desperation, Markus pulls out the knife and tries to breathe life back into Veidman's body, giving him CPR. But it doesn't work. More blood flows from Veidman's corpse on to the grass and dirt.

Rika wipes at her eyes.

'It's not fair!' Sinxen yells at no one in particular. He looks around, frantic.

'Damn this place forever!' the builder curses.

It's then that we hear the rumbling noises.

They emanate from the thick wall of forest that we stumbled out of just minutes earlier. It sounds like an army is marching towards us.

We've all been preoccupied with Veidman's death. For once even Gadya doesn't have her bow ready. Most of our weapons are down, scattered on the grass.

I spin towards the trees. The others hear the noises too, and grab for their weapons.

But it's too late.

Armed drones step from the forest in all directions.

At least fifty of them. All of them have arrows and spears pointed directly at us. We're outnumbered, backed against the barrier, and there's no time to run.

A few hunters race for their bows anyway, but arrows fly and strike them instantly. They fall at once, screaming in agony. The builder dashes for a spear, but gets an arrow through his back.

All movement ceases. The drones watch the rest of us silently. For once they don't shriek and yell, or toss fireworks. I'm in shock. There are only a handful of us villagers left standing now: Gadya, Rika, Markus, Sinxen and me. Everyone else is dead or dying.

None of us dares move or speak. If these drones fire more arrows, we're done for. Maybe we can take a few of them out with us, but it won't matter.

I don't want to die. Not before finding the signs of my parents, and the rocks with their messages on them. Not after I've come so far, and after Liam sacrificed himself for me. I stand as still as a statue.

Then I notice something strange beginning to happen.

Four drones with painted faces slowly emerge from the trees. They aren't clutching weapons. Instead, they carry a cushioned platform on their shoulders. On top of the platform is a reclining chair, ornately carved from black oak. A small, dark figure sits inside it, bundled in heavy woollen blankets up to his neck.

I stare at the terrible sight unfolding before me.

Where the figure's face should be is a malevolent wooden

mask, with two eyeholes and a twisted grin carved into it. It looks like some sort of ritualistic death mask from a lost primitive tribe. In fact, I'm not sure if this figure is alive or dead. He looks so old and hunched over. The drones carrying the chair walk closer.

I stand there, still afraid that arrows are about to fly through the air towards my heart. We are the victims of a perfectly executed ambush.

The four drones bring the chair even closer, just fifteen paces away. Then, as if hearing the same silent signal at once, they gently place the chair down on the grass and step back.

The masked head suddenly moves, swivelling in our direction.

I gasp, despite myself.

Behind the eyeholes, I see demented-looking eyes, burning red with fever and sickness. I flash back to what Gadya told me all those days ago about the Monk. That he never talks, never walks. Gets carried everywhere.

Could this monstrous, disintegrating figure be him? It must be. *But why is he showing himself to us now?*

The head moves again, panning stiffly like a camera on a tripod. Taking everything in. All the drones are eerily quiet, like they're waiting for something crucial to happen.

'Checkmate,' a raspy voice finally intones from behind the mask. It sounds like this man's larynx has been burned away. Or maybe he just hasn't spoken in a very long time.

'*Who are you?*' Gadya growls. I hear the fear and anger in

her voice, intertwined like the vines that grow all around us on the trees.

'You're the Can—' Markus begins softly, but then stops. Backtracks. He almost said 'cannibal' by accident. 'You're the Monk, aren't you?' I hear horrified awe in his voice.

The mask turns to stare at him. It's like his head is the only part of his body that moves. 'Some call me that, yes.'

I shut my eyes.

So this is the bogeyman.

Finally, right here in front of me. A myth made into flesh. I feel the blood rushing from my head. I think about what David said, that the Monk's drones know my name. I wonder if the Monk himself knows it. Should I speak, or stay silent?

'We're not here to fight,' Markus finally says. 'We're headed into the grey zone—'

Sinxen interrupts, his voice tense, 'Please don't kill any more of us, OK?'

I chime in, finding my own voice at last. 'We'll leave your sector. Honest. We were just trying to get through the barrier.'

The Monk's head swivels in my direction. 'I know. We've been following your group. Watching.' His words are stiff but oddly authoritative, and he speaks in clipped sentences.

'What do you want with us?' Gadya asks. 'Why are you here? To massacre us?'

'I know about your plan. To find the aircrafts.' He pauses. 'I need your help to reach them. Behind that barrier lies salvation.' I assume he means a way off the wheel, but then he elaborates. 'Salvation for the sickness that ails me.'

Then I understand.

The Monk has the Suffering.

That's why he wears the mask. Why he can't move. Why his eyes burn so red. His face has probably rotted away in the tropical heat.

Gadya instantly voices my thought: 'You're infected.'

The Monk laughs, low and throaty. He slowly raises a shaky hand from under his blankets. He's just skin and bones, his flesh dotted with sores like an old man with leprosy. The Suffering has ravaged his body. Most people this sick just die. But not the Monk.

At his signal, a drone rushes forward, flask in hand. He kneels before the Monk and dribbles water into the mask's mouth hole.

'I'm going to kill you when I get the chance,' Gadya says to the Monk, with cold fury.

I flinch, terrified of all the weapons pointed at us. It's clear the Monk's drones won't hesitate to kill every last one of us if he gives the order.

'Gadya—' Rika warns. 'Not smart.'

The Monk waves his drone away and licks the wooden lips of the mask, lapping up the water. The wood around his mouth is a darker colour now, stained by the liquid.

'You have information that I need,' the Monk continues. 'Yes, I have eyes inside your village. I know that your hunters mapped the grey zone well. Better than my drones have managed. I need you to take me to the city in the grey zone. I don't have long to live.'

Markus glares at him. 'Why should we help you?'

'First, you have no choice. Second, I alone know how to get through this barrier. Without my help, you will fail.'

'I don't trust you,' Gadya tells him. 'You're a maniac. A killer.' She glances down at the bodies of Veidman and the others.

He nods. 'Yet we share a common goal. You want to leave this island. And I want to cure my condition, so I can resume leading my flock.' He clears his throat. It's a wet, horrible sound. 'In addition to the aircrafts, there is a laboratory inside the grey zone. Staffed with doctors who can help me. So let us go into the zone together.'

There is something seductive and vaguely hypnotic about his deranged rasp. His cadence sounds almost familiar, but I can't place it.

'Why did you kill Veidman?' I ask.

'To get your attention.' I sense a sick, cruel smile behind the mask. 'Besides, if our groups join forces, we only need one person in charge.'

'You took his life for no reason!' Gadya begins, but the others hush her. I sense her barely repressed hatred for the Monk bubbling underneath the surface. Like me, Gadya is a mass of churning emotions: grief, fear and fury.

'We need to talk about this among ourselves,' Sinxen says. I know he's stalling for time. 'Just us villagers.'

'No,' the Monk says bluntly. 'If you don't obey me, my men will torture you until you do.' He pauses. 'We will make our assault on the barrier in the morning. But tonight you will be my guests.'

I exchange glances with the others. *Guests?*

'My devotees have a camp half a mile north of here,' the Monk continues, 'further along the barrier. You will accompany us there at once.'

The Monk raises his hand again and signals to his followers. The four drones step forward and pick up his platform.

His mask looks down at us. 'Shoulder your weapons. There will be no more fighting today. And no more deaths. Unless you demand them.'

Obviously, if we take a stand and resist, we risk getting killed like the others. There are five of us, and fifty of them.

All of a sudden, I feel like I'm ten years old again and back in my bedroom with the old man in the suit. I didn't take a stand when my parents were snatched, and I've regretted it ever since.

Here is another chance!

I glance around. There's no time to slot an arrow, but I could grab a spear. Throw it at this monstrosity. But what would that accomplish? I'd probably miss, and then I'd be dead, and all for nothing. I feel thwarted. Powerless. And I hate it.

'We can't leave our people's bodies here,' Gadya says loudly. 'Not like animals in the dirt.'

'My men will bring the bodies of your fallen. We will bury them for you, in a sacred place at our camp.'

I think about Meira. Who's going to tell her about Veidman's death? Then I realise that most likely none of us will make it back to the village. She'll never know what became of him.

I wonder how long the Monk can survive in his condition. The Suffering makes him dangerous – and desperate. He never would have shown himself to us if his need for a cure weren't urgent. But I'm afraid he'll just use us to lead him to his destination, and then tell his drones to kill us. Still, we have to play along. *For now.*

'Fine,' Markus says. 'We'll go with you.'

Gadya stares at the Monk defiantly, but she doesn't disagree with Markus.

The Monk doesn't say a word. Just nods. Then his four men bear him away back into the forest. As soon as he's gone, his army of drones converges on our group, screaming angrily:

'Drop your spears and bows!'

'Don't speak! Don't move!'

'On your knees!'

We do what they say. They make us kneel with our hands behind our heads as they confiscate our bows, arrows, knives, spears and packs. I burn with anger and frustration. We've been whittled down to just a motley crew of misfits and hunters, at the mercy of the most evil force on the island.

Soon our weapons are gone, and our provisions stowed. We're finally allowed to stand up again.

'Our Monk considers you his guests,' a long-haired drone with a scarred face intones, 'but I consider you our prisoners. I wish I could kill the rest of you right here and now.'

Another drone steps up. His face is painted with a psychedelic rainbow of colours, distorting his features. 'You will walk single file! You will remain silent! You will do as you're told!' His violent, brusque tone reminds me of the police back home in the UNA. 'You are in this predicament because you are godless heathens who believe in nothing!'

'What's your name?' I hear a timid voice ask. I realise that it's Rika.

At first I don't realise why she's asking him that question, because what does this ugly, insane drone's name even matter? Then I realise she's trying to reach out to him, to establish some kind of human connection.

It doesn't work. 'Call me Master!' the drone screeches at her. 'We are your betters! You're just faithless infidels from the corrupt blue sector! Call all of us Master, and you can't go wrong.'

Rika looks like she's been slapped.

'One day I'll make them pay for this,' I hear Gadya whisper under her breath.

'What'd you just say?' the long-haired drone asks ominously.

'Nothing, *Master*,' Gadya replies, her voice dripping with sarcasm. The drone is either too stupid or too power-drunk to detect it.

'Follow me, heathens!' he bellows, as the rough hands of anonymous drones force us into line. 'You belong to the Monk now. Freedom is a thing of the past!'

We start hiking as he leads the way. There are drones in

front of us, behind us, and some to the sides, moving noisily through the trees. They have enough weapons trained on our group to defeat an army ten times our size. The drones are taking every precaution so that we don't run or fight back. Not that we would, after watching them casually slaughter our friends and companions.

I walk with my head down, trying to look docile and complacent. But my mind is racing as I start recovering from the shock of the ambush. I'm planning how I can escape from these drones – because nothing is going to stop me from accomplishing my mission and learning the fate of my parents.

FAITHLESS

We stumble into the Monk's makeshift camp twenty minutes later. I'm scared, tired and thirsty. The drones have berated us the entire way. I've noticed that there aren't any female warriors in this group. Maybe the Monk doesn't believe that girls can make effective hunters, unless they're nearly mutants like the big girl who attacked me and Gadya.

The orange sun is low in the sky when we arrive at the camp. I instantly see how different it is from our village. Multiple ragged fire pits burn everywhere. Garbage is strewn all over the ground – old food, plastic chemical wrappers, broken furniture and unidentifiable charred remnants. It looks worse than the New Providence city dump.

Here at the camp, I finally see the girls. Most of them are half naked, tending to boys, and a lot of them look drunk. Their skin is grimy with ingrained dirt, like they've forgotten how to bathe. Some dance together by the fires, bruised and cackling. A few have shaved heads. I see girls in the shadows, bent over boys, seductively writhing against them. They arch their necks and backs as filthy male hands grope them.

So much for the Monk being holy. Or maybe this is a different kind of holiness – the holiness of despair, filth and depravity. I don't know why anyone would follow the Monk.

But I guess he offers freedom from rules and civilization. Freedom from the pressures of being human.

The drones sneer at us openly. Most of their teeth are filed down into points, girls and boys alike. Many look like they have the Suffering themselves, but they're not separated from the others. The camp is just a festering pit of disease, like some plague-riddled village from the Middle Ages that we studied about in New History class.

Our group is led to a small dirt clearing under a thicket of trees, near one of the larger fire pits. Drones are roasting hunks of hoofer meat on long sticks nearby. The air is filled with smoke and the odour of burning flesh and animal hair. There are no spices or cooking pots here. Just people living like savages.

I think about David. It doesn't seem possible that he could come from this world, or even bear to live in it. I search around for him in vain, wishing I could find him.

Then I look at Gadya. Her mouth is set in a tight line of revulsion like she's trying to block out the entire world. I wish she and I hadn't argued so fiercely earlier about Liam. I really need my friend back.

'This is insane,' Rika whispers to me, her voice trembling. I clasp her hand in mine.

A tall drone carrying an axe passes by, and we fall silent. Eventually we sit down on rocks and dirt in the clearing.

Has Operation Tiger Strike been worth it so far?

We've lost Liam. And Veidman. And so many others. And now we've been taken prisoner by the Cannibal Monk himself. I wonder again if what David said to me about my parents was a lie. I cling to any shred of hope I have left.

'Hey there!' a squat, hairy drone yells as he approaches us, sneering. He's wearing a necklace made from hoofer teeth. We all look over at him. 'You thirsty? Hungry?'

None of us want to admit that we are. Markus finally speaks. 'What do you think?'

'Personally, I don't think you deserve anything to eat or drink. But I do the bidding of the Monk. My brain is a vessel of his greater good.' I see a glazed, zealous look in his eyes. 'Bring these heathens water and meat!' he calls out to a nearby group of girls.

'I'm not eating anything of yours,' Gadya snarls.

'Then don't. I hope you starve. But the Monk told me to take care of you. So that's what I'm doing.' He turns away for a second. Then he turns back. 'The Monk also wanted me to tell you about tonight's *entertainment.*'

None of us say anything. The horror we see before us doesn't leave much room for entertainment.

'Tonight's death battle, that is.' His pink tongue flicks between his blackened, pointed teeth. 'Don't worry about getting a good seat – 'cause you're gonna be centre stage. Nothing beats a death battle.'

'Death battle?' Sinxen asks. 'The Monk said no more fighting. That if we came here, we'd work together with him.'

'A battle isn't a fight. A battle is a challenge of wills and strength.'

I don't like the sound of this. It's clear the Monk's followers are even more bloodthirsty than he is. I dare to speak up. 'Can we talk to the Monk?'

'You're talking to him now. Like I said, we are all his vessels.'

'If he breaks his word about fighting us—' Markus starts to bluster.

'You'll do what?' the drone asks. Markus looks away. We have no weapons. We're just a handful of stragglers in the heart of this enemy camp. The drone turns from us in contempt.

For the next several hours we sit and watch the camp around us. It's impossible for us to talk and strategise among ourselves, because drones stand guard, silently listening to everything we say. Girls bring us cold lumps of meat and a couple of bowls of brackish water.

The more I see of the camp, the more disgusted I get. For all their supposed devotion to the Monk, these kids act like they have no morals whatsoever. The larger boys dominate everything ruthlessly, running around, acting wild, throwing their ubiquitous fireworks into the sky as they shove and kick the smaller boys.

Girls are second-class citizens for the most part. I see a few pregnant ones, and some tending to small, dirty children. Many have scars and brands marring their cheeks and arms. Some nearly topless girls gyrate wildly by the fire pits, trying to attract boys.

I've never seen anything like this. Not on the wheel, and definitely not in the UNA. I'm lucky that Gadya found me, or I might have ended up here and not known there was any alternative.

Would I have become one of these desperate girls? This camp is exactly what I expected the island to be like – a violent, depraved colony of Unanchored Souls. *Maybe the GPPT works after all, and the other villagers and I are just statistical anomalies.*

As we sit and wait, I see a few girls watching us curiously, like they want to approach. The few kids that do get near us spit and heckle us angrily. Some recite incomprehensible prayers that sound like exorcisms. Maybe they think we're demons from the forest, instead of fellow exiles on the wheel.

Finally, once the sky has been dark for at least an hour, the long-haired drone in the hoofer-skin vest reappears, clutching a spear. 'Heathens!' he shrieks at us, striding into the clearing. 'It's time for you to amuse us! Time for your death battle!'

'Screw off, loser,' Gadya snaps.

Unexpectedly, he laughs. He's drunk. 'Look at you. You're feisty. A hellion. Look at your hair.' He gestures at her wild blue-streaked mane. 'That's the hair of a heathen, all right!'

He leans in closer. For a moment, I think he's going to stroke her hair. Gadya does too, and she recoils. Then his hand lashes out and grabs a fistful, yanking hard.

'*Ow!*'

The drone cuffs Gadya's ear as he pulls her to her feet. She is snapping and flailing, and I know she wants to fight back and kick his face in. And she's on the verge of doing so. But the drones guarding us have at least three sets of arrows aimed directly at her heart.

'I was gonna ask for a volunteer,' the long-haired drone tells Gadya. 'But your hair just volunteered you!'

He finally releases his grip and steps back, grinning. Gadya swipes at her hair where he touched her.

'Your turn now, girlie. Your turn to chose,' the drone tells her.

'What the hell are you talking about?'

'Our entertainment is to watch you battle someone else.'

'The Monk didn't say anything about this!' Markus calls out angrily.

'He's right,' I second. 'If he makes us fight, how can we help him tomorrow?'

'This isn't for the Monk. It's for us, although he permits it. Watching heathens do battle brightens our day.'

'I'd love to battle you,' Gadya says to the drone. 'I'd rip your tongue right out of your mouth.'

The drone chuckles. 'You don't get to battle *us*. Heathens must battle other heathens. That's our custom.' He gestures at our group as we sit there, huddled against the quickening chill of the night. 'You must chose one of your friends.'

'To fight?'

'Yes – to the death. You might want to pick a girl. The crowd likes that best. Girls are weak.'

Gadya's face is saying, *Oh, really?* But she doesn't speak. Just glowers. Meanwhile, I'm trying to come to terms with the awfulness of our predicament.

I notice that a large crowd has started gathering around our clearing, lit by the fire. Drones leer at us like we're animals in a zoo. *Did the Monk lie? Are we going to die here tonight?*

'What if I refuse to fight?' Gadya asks.

She gets her answer immediately. The crowd starts to boo and jeer. A rock flies past her head, smashing into a tree behind her. She spins around, trying to see who threw it.

An object hits the ground near me, kicking up dirt and splattering my face. For a sickening moment I think it's a firework, about to detonate. But then I see it's just a mouldy coconut. The mob gets louder.

'We don't like it when heathens refuse,' the drone hisses. 'The crowd will tear you to pieces like hoofer meat.'

Gadya looks at our group, eyes wide.

'Choose! Choose!' an anonymous male drone in the crowd begins yelling. Soon his words are taken up as a chant. The chant picks up steam. Drones begin pounding their spears on the ground.

'Choose! Choose! Choose!'

I hear the anger and excitement of a thousand deranged kids. The expectation of delight, and the frustration of pleasures being thwarted. They really are going to rip us apart with their hands unless we do what they want. The Monk must be permitting this as a way to demonstrate his power. But why? He's already won.

The drone presses the sharp tip of his spear to Gadya's throat. 'Choose now, girlie,' he says beneath the roar of the crowd. 'Or I'll make you kneel in front of me – before I slit your throat!'

'Choose! Choose!' the crowd keeps screaming, like one giant hive-mind.

I know that Gadya's choices are limited if she picks a girl. There's only me and Rika. And I'm the one she has a grudge against. That's why I know exactly what she's going to say before the words leave her mouth.

'I choose her!' Gadya yells, her roving eyes finding mine. She points directly at me.

The crowd roars its approval. Drones rush up behind me and grab my arms, dragging me forward. Everyone is screaming in my ears. The sounds just run together, becoming a deafening sonic blur.

As I'm pushed and pulled, I catch glimpses of individual drones within the crazed mob:

A one-eyed girl clutching a hairless baby.

A boy with scars across his neck, wielding a barbed club as he shrieks and wails at the moon.

A grotesquely fat boy with raw meat in his hand, bloody juice dripping down his slack jaw.

Then fireworks start exploding above us again, and these impressionistic images get burned into my mind forever.

I'm yanked forward in front of a fire pit, and placed directly across from Gadya. She stares at me with a cold expression I can't read. I stare back. The crowd is still screaming, pleased with Gadya's choice.

I realise that here, we are the monsters. We are the different ones. The infidels, the heathens. Reduced to entertainment for a mindless mob.

Markus, Sinxen and Rika are watching nearby. I know they want to intervene. Yet if they do, they'll instantly be struck with arrows and spears.

Gadya's face tenses as a drone hands her a spear. She's going to bring everything she has against me because she doesn't have a choice.

I know that my feelings for Liam are partly what brought me to this point. Anger has been building inside Gadya for a long time, and I understand why. But I don't regret anything I've done. If I have to die now at Gadya's hands because I ended up falling for Liam, then so be it.

A spear gets thrust into my hands. I hold it for a moment. Then I look at Gadya, and drop it on to the muddy ground. The crowd pelts me with stinking garbage and roars its displeasure.

'Pick it up!' Gadya yells.

I stare back at her. Foolishly, I decide to try reasoning one last time. 'We don't have to fight! Maybe they won't kill us if we refuse.'

Before she can reply, a skinny drone darts forward and picks up the spear. He shoves it into my hands and snarls, 'Drop it again, and I'll carve up your pretty face like prime rib!' There's enough menace in his voice to let me know he means it.

I clutch the spear nervously. Other than the day Liam sparred with me, most of what I learned about combat, I learned from

Gadya. There's no way I can defeat her. The crowd is in throes of ecstasy.

'Heathens, begin your death battle!' the drone with the psychedelic face paint screams. The volume of the crowd explodes, louder than the fireworks. 'The battle ends when only one of you is left alive!'

Gadya sinks into her warrior stance, bending her knees, keeping her centre of gravity low. She holds her spear lightly with both hands so that the weapon remains flexible. The iron tip is angled in my direction. She never takes her eyes off my face.

I try to mirror her stance, but I feel clumsy and awkward. My knuckles are white around the spear because I'm gripping it too tightly. Am I really going to die? Killed by the very person who saved my life here? Everything is starting to get slow and dreamlike.

Gadya advances, moving rapidly on the balls of her feet like a dancer. I'm immediately forced into a defensive pose. I decide to use my spear as a shield, holding the shaft in front of my face, hoping to deflect the inevitable blows coming my way.

Gadya always told me to watch my opponent for signs that they're about to strike. She told me that faces, eyes and posture can help you gauge what you're up against. Give you an advantage.

Most warriors have a 'tell', Gadya once explained during one of our training sessions. *That's how you knew to throw your spear at the big girl. You sensed what she was about to do. Always be on the lookout for subtle movements and adjustments, ones that accidentally reveal your opponent's true intentions.*

I have fought with Gadya at my side. And I've practised with her in mock battles back at the village. But the only tell I've ever observed is a slight widening of her eyes before she makes her first assault on an opponent. Other than that? Nothing. And here, in the firelight, I can't even see her eyes well enough to read them.

Gadya must also know all of my tells. But hopefully I won't give my plans away today, because I'm not going to be attacking. I'm going to be defending. She must strike first, because I refuse to strike her.

Gadya dances closer, and I raise my spear a split second before she lunges forward. My spear catches the tip of hers, deflecting the blow. She has hit me hard. My arms reverberate with the impact, my palms aching and burning. I stagger backwards, almost falling down.

I know I should lunge at her now and strike back. That's what the roaring crowd wants, and probably what Gadya wants too. It's what I'm supposed to do. But I just crouch in my defensive posture. Waiting for the next blow to arrive.

The whole time, food, trash and spittle are flying past both of us. It's like being in a storm of garbage. I can smell the stench coming off the crowd. Fireworks explode above us continually, leaving acrid grey trails behind them.

Gadya comes at me again. This time she aims lower, but I deflect the blow once more. Her spear slides up mine.

I move my hand at the last second to avoid getting my fingers sliced off. Our spear tips lock at the top for a moment.

We're breathing hard, our heads close together. Gadya hisses something at me. I barely catch it.

'What?' I whisper back, startled, thinking I heard her wrong. She's pushing as hard as she can with her weapon. My muscles strain. I struggle not to get pressed down to the earth.

'Quit fighting!' she spits again. No one else can hear us. They're just excited that we're in such close combat. 'I've got a plan!'

Can I trust her? Or is she messing with my mind? Sweat runs into my eyes, stinging them, but I can't wipe the droplets away. 'What are you talking about?'

The crowd is still screaming. They probably think we're hurling insults at each other.

'I picked you because you can fight!' Gadya whispers. 'I need you.' Her mouth is pressed against my ear as we struggle – although I'm slowly starting to understand that it's a mock struggle. Just for show.

'What do we do?' I whisper back.

'We turn around,' she continues. 'Each of us stabs the drone behind us. Markus knows what to do next. I've signalled to him secretly.' We're both straining to breathe. The crowd is getting louder. I know we can't keep talking, because they want to see blood.

Gadya starts to release the pressure on my spear. 'We attack on the count of three. After that, we get into the forest and run!'

I know she's right. If we keep playing by the rules of the Monk's drones, one of us is going to die. And neither of us deserves to. Weirdly, I'm not scared any more. I'm just relieved that Gadya is still my friend.

Gadya begins whispering the count as we continue to lock spears and fake like we're fighting.

A million thoughts race through my mind in those final seconds. I don't know what's going to happen when I spin around and plunge my weapon into the nearest drone behind me. *I've never stabbed anyone, let alone killed someone!* Will I be able to do it?

Gadya said that Markus and the others will rise up, but I know they don't have weapons. There's just too many drones, and way too few of us.

'Three!' I hear Gadya scream, and all thought leaves my mind as I transform into a creature of pure action. I twirl around and lunge at the long-haired drone behind me.

He's taken off guard.

He is careless.

The tip of my spear disappears right into his stomach, making him wail. He topples back into the crowd, screaming as I yank the weapon out. I hear cries behind me. I spin and see that Gadya has skewered her drone too. The shaft of her spear sticks right through his chest. When she jerks it out, a geyser of blood spews from the hole.

Markus and Sinxen are leaping on the other drones. I see Markus grab a knife and begin stabbing the very person he took it from.

The glee of the drones at seeing me and Gadya battle each other has now turned into terror. Some run screaming. Some stand there openmouthed. I know that any second, they're going to recover their wits and end our lives. But for one brief moment, we're in control again.

Then a blow hits me hard between my shoulder blades, and I drop to the ground. As I roll on to my back, I see the fat boy coming at me. He has dropped his chunk of raw meat along the way. He doesn't have a spear, just two big pummelling fists.

I slide sideways as the boy's right fist slams into the dirt, an inch from my face. He's big but he's slow. He comes at me again. I clamber to my feet, clutching my bloody spear. He hesitates.

'Touch me and I'll kill you!' I scream, baring my teeth and brandishing the spear.

He starts backing away.

I hear Gadya call my name. She's right behind me. We move into formation, each of us getting the other person's back. Markus, Sinxen and Rika stand with us now, clutching bloodstained weapons. This was obviously not the kind of death battle the drones expected.

Of course we're still massively outnumbered. We've injured or killed about ten drones at most. But hundreds more surround us in every direction. There's no chance to run into the forest.

I feel Gadya's hand grasp my arm. 'You did good.'

'So did you.'

Our group gathers even closer together. It's clear we'll be overwhelmed soon. These are probably our final moments together.

'I'm sorry I blamed you for Liam,' Gadya whispers, gripping me even tighter. 'It's not your fault, I know. Friends?'

'Friends,' I whisper back. 'I'm sorry for everything too.'

In these last seconds, I need her more than ever.

At least after they kill us, we won't be on the wheel any more, I think bleakly. Who knows. Maybe death is the only solution. That's something I never considered when my dad told me about Sisyphus. Maybe death is what Sisyphus spent his time daydreaming about; maybe death was the only thing that could truly set him free.

'Come get us, you cowards!' Markus screams at the assembled throng. There are no more fireworks. The drones just stare at us in outrage.

Sinxen notches an arrow into a stolen bow. He takes aim at the crowd. All of our weapons are drawn.

'Attack, why don't you?' Gadya yells.

But they don't attack, and I don't understand why. The drones have the advantage. And they don't really seem like cowards. They're too stupid, drunk and brainwashed to be scared of death.

There's total quiet now. I hear only the crackling of the fire pits. And then I hear a lone, strange sound.

The sound of laughter.

I peer past the flames into the darkness and see the crowd parting reverently, as a drifting object moves towards us.

I realise it's the Monk in his cushioned chair, carried by his drones. He practically floats through the air, like he's defying gravity.

He draws closer, clapping his crippled hands together in unabashed delight. All the drones stand silent in his presence. He glides up to us, his mask looking ghoulish in the firelight.

'You betrayed us!' Markus cries out. 'We trusted you!'

His laugh gives way to a hacking cough. His men lower his platform, so he can gaze at us at eye level. I have never hated anyone so much as I hate this deranged, terrifying figure.

Then he speaks. 'You passed. All of you. You passed my test.'

'What the hell are you babbling about?' Gadya spits.

'I was watching.' His voice grows louder. 'I was judging you. And you have pleased me.'

'I don't understand,' I call out, my voice shaking.

'My devotees follow me unquestioningly. They believe in my powers as a messiah, and in the glorious afterlife that awaits them off the wheel. But now I know that even you – the faithless, the infidels – can act as one as well. For the benefit of your group.' His head turns from side to side. 'You can put down your weapons.'

'How do we know this isn't another test?' Gadya challenges.

The Monk's wooden mask gives only its implacable smile. 'You don't.'

'Then we're not going to surrender!' Markus tells him.

The Monk swivels his head back and forth lazily again. 'You don't need to. My devotees will surrender to you.'

At his words, the members of his camp begin lowering their weapons and putting them on the ground. Hundreds of them. I glance at my companions, but they're as puzzled as I am. I want to rip the mask off the Monk's face and see who's behind that wooden façade. But all I can see are his eyes. They're dancing crazily again. *Dancing happily.*

We stand there, not sure what to do. The drones are all unarmed now.

'See?' the Monk says. 'They do as I ask, because they know I can save their eternal souls. My followers pose no threat to you any more.' He claps his hands together. His four throne bearers hoist him up even higher. 'Disperse, my faithful ones!' he rasps loudly.

The drones begin to shamble away. A few of them drag their injured or dead companions with them. Most of them resume their previous activities like zombies, like nothing happened. Meanwhile I stand there, totally panicked inside. I thought I was about to die.

I watch as drones return to the fire pits, to their feasting and dancing. Other than a few lingering stares, it's like no one cares about us any more. Or the fact that we hurt and killed so many of them.

I realise this camp truly is a hive, with the Monk as queen bee. They follow his orders without thinking. *Where is their free will?* Maybe they don't think free will is important, just like our government back home clearly didn't.

The Monk stares down at us from his chair. 'I will explain how to get through the barrier tomorrow. There's only one way it can be breached. But tonight you must rest. You must gather strength. The journey beyond the barrier will be... challenging.'

None of us can think of anything to say in response. He claps again, and his bearers take him away back into the forest. The trees and the darkness close around him. He's just a spectre. We finally start lowering our weapons. The threat is over for now.

My legs feel shaky.

'He's insane, isn't he?' Rika whispers. Her face is ashen. She still hasn't lowered her spear. Gadya notices.

'It's OK, Rika. You can put that down now.'

Rika is still staring after the Monk.

Gadya takes Rika's spear and gently lowers it for her. 'If they make us fight again, I'll protect you.'

'We'll protect each other,' Sinxen adds. 'We just have to live through this.'

Markus nods. 'If the Monk is telling the truth, then he'll help us get through the barrier. But we're the ones with a map of the grey zone in our heads. He needs us more than we need him. We'll get our revenge on the other side.'

I don't know what's in store for us. But I think of the Monk's word – 'challenging'. It carries an air of menace. On the wheel, 'challenging' can mean only 'life-threatening'. But it's too late to turn back.

'Let's get some food and try to sleep,' I say to the others, shouldering my weapon with aching arms. 'It's going to be a long night.'

THE GREY ZONE

The light of morning eventually finds us, illuminating our ravaged faces. None of us got more than a couple of hours of sleep. Despite the Monk's promise that we would be safe, two of us kept watch at a time, just in case. We're all exhausted and chilled to the bone. What little sleep I got was haunted by dreams of Liam being taken.

The Monk's people don't have shelters or hammocks. They just sleep outside by the fires in the filthy mud. From what I've observed, they don't care about themselves, or about anyone except the Monk. They only survive because there are so many of them. I'm guessing that when a drone dies in battle, or is taken by the feelers, more flood in to replace him.

I still don't know why they come to the Monk, why they're drawn to him like children to the Pied Piper. I suppose they're seeking meaning and structure, like Gadya said. But anything the Monk has to offer is just an illusion.

There's still no sign of David. Maybe he's at another camp, or maybe he fled and lit off on his own. I guess part of me was hoping he'd turn up and help us, but I guess we didn't treat him too well when he came to our village. Maybe he's somewhere watching all of this.

In the morning light, Gadya stretches. 'I wish we didn't

need these maniacs,' she mutters. 'I wish we had more time to figure out a way through the barrier on our own.'

Sinxen brushes dirt off his elbows. 'Well, we don't. So stay cool and don't piss anyone off.'

Soon a crowd of thirty or more drones comes to get us, some carrying mysterious crates and others carrying weapons. They're dirty and grubby, stinking of alcohol. Some wear metal masks, presumably to scare us. 'This way, heathens,' a haggard drone sneers. Black circles ring his sunken eyes.

The drones surround us, weapons in their hands, although I don't sense any immediate danger. And if I'm wrong, there are still weapons in our hands too, left over from the night before.

We're guided down a mud path towards the barrier. I can tell it's well-travelled because of all the footprints. I wonder whether this is the place that David was talking about. *The place where the drones cross over into the grey zone.* If it is, then at least one good thing came from getting captured by the Monk, because now I'm closer to where I need to be.

When we reach the barrier, it looks exactly like it did before, like a wall of clear jelly. The drones stop moving, and I see that we're not the first to arrive. The Monk and his bearers are already there, resting under a tree. The bearers hoist the Monk up and move towards us as soon as they see us.

'Greetings, friends,' the Monk says. There's no mistaking his mocking tone. He knows we're not his friends, and never will be.

Gadya pulls back her hair. 'Enough games. Tell us how to get through this damn wall.'

The Monk pauses and gazes at us, licking the wooden lips of his mask. 'I thought you would have already figured it out by now.'

'Enlighten us,' Markus snaps.

The Monk blinks. 'This wall is made of synthetic filaments. The substance was developed by the UNA military years ago, as a potential weapon of mass destruction.' He pauses. 'Yet they found it was most effective at containing harmful contaminants, like petroleum spills. And also, at containing people. The UNA built this barrier to keep everyone out of the grey zone.'

'How could you even know this stuff?' Sinxen asks.

'Who cares!' Gadya yells. 'We just need to get through it.'

The Monk raises one thin arm and points at the wall. His men move him forward. 'Watch and learn.'

Some of his drones bend down, opening up the crates they've been carrying. I see now that the crates are loaded with fireworks. Massive ones, like miniature rockets on rusty spring-loaded launchers. The drones start taking them out and setting them up.

I have no clue where so many fireworks could come from. As far as I know, the UNA doesn't drop any provisions on to the wheel, except perhaps for their chemicals. The Monk's people must have found a gigantic stash of fireworks, perhaps left over from the days before the wheel was a prison island.

'Are you serious? Fireworks?' Rika mutters.

'They contain barium and antimony sulphide... Those

heavy metals, plus the heat generated by their powder, break down the synthetic filaments.'

So this is why the Monk's people are so obsessed with fireworks, I think. *They've been using them to get through the barrier and into the grey zone.* And if they're so casual about using them in their attacks on us as well, they must have a nearly inexhaustible supply.

The fireworks explain why there were always so many drones inside the grey zone, just like Liam said. For all I know, maybe they destroyed the tunnel themselves, knowing that we didn't have another way to get in.

'The fireworks stick inside the barrier and begin to burn,' the Monk continues. 'They melt the fibres, and the wall becomes fluid. Sticky. Then it's possible to get through – at least temporarily.'

'What do you mean?' I ask.

'Once holes appear, the barrier tries to close them, like skin growing over an open wound. You must enter the barrier quickly and fight your way to the other side, before the holes seal themselves and the barrier envelops you. This place is where we commonly pass through, so the barrier is weakest here. Easiest to penetrate.'

So I am in the right place to find the rocks.

'Show us what you mean,' Gadya says to the Monk.

He raises a hand again. His drones start lifting the fireworks and begin extracting matches, lighting wicks. I jam my fingers into my ears.

'Begin!' the Monk rasps to his army of drones. 'Open the

Blessed Wall and show the heathens the beauty within!'

Drones run past us in a dizzying blur up to the barrier. They jam and thrust lit fireworks into the jelly. Then they leave them there and run back to get more.

Meanwhile, other drones use launchers, slings and even bows to fire more lit fireworks directly into the wall. A few bounce off, but most penetrate and hang inside the gelatinous substance. I can see tiny air bubbles appear around their burning wicks, which remain lit even inside the barrier.

All of us are watching in expectation, and we're not disappointed by what happens next.

The first firework inside the wall detonates almost soundlessly. There's an odd, uncanny beauty to the sight. It looks like an exotic red flower unfurling its coloured petals in slow motion. Wormlike sparks of light sluggishly explode outwards, trapped inside the barrier.

Another firework goes off. Then another. The wall starts rippling. Air bubbles are growing larger. A few burning, buzzing embers reach the surface, where they fizzle and die out in puffs of smoke. Holes are opening up everywhere.

'The barrier is like an ocean. A vertical one with a very slow current,' the Monk calls out in his raspy voice. 'Like a pane of glass. Once the holes are large enough, run towards them. Pry them open. Force your way through.'

I stare into the barrier, which is now filled with glittering multicoloured lights and rising air bubbles. Beyond is the monochromatic forest. I wonder what it will feel like to enter that icy world. I miss Liam.

'It's almost time,' the Monk says. I look back at him. One of his men clasps him around the chest while another gets his legs. They carry him off the platform. His head lolls back and his limbs hang weakly. He looks so vulnerable, but holds so much power. 'I will lead the way. Don't bring your weapons. You will not need them in the grey zone, and they will hinder your passage through the barrier... I'm not bringing my devotees, except one to carry me.'

I wonder what would happen if one of us lunged forward right now and struck the Monk down. Would killing him loosen his hold on his followers? Maybe we'd just create a martyr for them to worship even more.

Gadya is at my ear, voicing the thought I just had. 'We could take him! Kill the bastard. Rip that mask right off him.'

'I know,' I whisper back. But neither of us move. The risk is too great.

The Monk's men reach the wall and press him against the pulsing membrane of the barrier. They begin moving him into the holes and air pockets that the fireworks have opened up. The Monk's mask is forced tightly against his face, but his drones keep pushing. It's a surreal sight – like watching someone give birth in reverse.

'What happens if he doesn't make it?' I whisper to Gadya.

'Look. He's almost out.'

Indeed, I watch as the Monk reaches the other side of the weakened barrier. His outstretched fingers emerge into air. Followed by his hand, and then his forearm.

One of his drones pushes forward violently, accompanying

him. The drone explodes out the other side of the barrier like he's bursting free from an avalanche, just in time to catch the Monk as he tumbles out. He takes hold of his body and places him gently on the ground.

The Monk weakly waves a hand to show his followers that he's OK. Then his fingers curl into a claw, beckoning us. Other drones are busy pushing our backpacks through the holes, so we'll have them on the other side.

The barrier is trying to repair itself, the holes quickly closing as the material cools and starts pooling together like syrup. The drones begin assaulting it with fireworks and flares again, trying to open up new passageways.

'I don't know if I can do this,' Rika says, sounding shell-shocked.

'You have to,' I say. My eyes are fixed on the Monk and the grey zone beyond. His drone is putting a thick coat around him, and getting gloves on his hands.

'Let's go as a group,' Sinxen says. 'Just make a run at the barrier when the fireworks stop and the holes are big enough. Claw our way through together.'

We all agree to try it.

Soon the barrier is filled with burning holes again. It looks like melting Swiss cheese. The drones stare at us expectantly. We clutch one another's hands. Then we head straight towards the bizarre obstacle standing between us and the grey zone.

I aim for one of the largest holes, even though it's already closing rapidly. My body slams into the barrier, and I push at the viscous material, burrowing my way inside. It's warm and pliant, like congealed custard mixed with glue. It pushes on my eyelids, making patterns dance and arc in the blackness. Then I feel it pushing into my ears, blocking out all sounds except the beating of my heart.

I feel hot, and I can't move.

For a second, I can't even feel my body any more, and I start to panic.

Something's gone wrong!

I begin flailing and struggling, but my limbs are completely immobilised. I must have misjudged the holes, and the wall is surging up around me. Closing. I see nothing, feel nothing, hear nothing. I'm going to be trapped inside here forever.

I start screaming.

And then I feel an icy blast race across the fingertips of my left hand.

Fresh air.

I strain forward, like I'm running in syrup. I feel more cold air. A breeze never felt this good. I get my other hand free, and then tumble out of the barrier, sinking from the wall on to the forest floor, reborn in a puddle of jellied liquid into the grey zone.

I open my eyes and gasp for air, shivering. Liam was right. It's freezing in here, and as silent as a tomb. No birds, no insects, no animals. Gadya is next to me, coughing and swearing.

I glance around, afraid I'll see that one of our group got stuck inside the barrier. But no, all of us are here. The wall is rapidly closing up, with the Monk's drones on the other side. We made it just in time. I cough up bits of stray jelly, gagging until my throat and chest are free and loose again.

But then something unexpected happens. One of the masked drones on the other side of the barrier races forward awkwardly with a muffled yell. It's like he's come out of nowhere – he's not one of the drones who was lighting fireworks. I'm not sure what's going on, and I instantly get my guard up.

The screaming drone on the other side flings himself at the barrier, right at one of the last remaining holes. His momentum carries him forward, and he plunges into the opening, grasping and kicking against the translucent material with his hands and feet. Other drones rush towards him. Not to aid him, but to try to pull him back out. They're not fast enough, and he kicks their hands away.

He scrabbles forward through the hole, like he's battling jelly. I'm not sure if he's going to make it or if he's going to get stuck. The drones on the other side are all yelling and running around, like this wasn't part of the plan. Maybe he's just a drone who got overcome with emotion and passion to be with his Monk.

Even the Monk's eyes look startled.

Gadya stands up fast. I do the same.

This stray drone, who seems to be acting all on his own, finally makes it through the barrier. He sprawls on to the forest floor, gagging.

I look behind him at the barrier. The area that we all broke through has almost repaired itself completely. There is no trace that anything passed through it, other than some debris from the fireworks floating inside, and a few weapons that got stranded by those of us who tried to bring them.

I look at the final person who has joined our group. Even before his shaking hands rip off his mask, I suddenly have a feeling that I know who it is.

David.

'What are you doing here?' Gadya screams when she sees his face, sounding furious. 'We don't need a backstabbing spy on our journey! I was hoping you were dead.' She turns to the Monk. 'You said you weren't bringing anyone else! Why is *he* here?'

'Ask him,' the Monk replies, still struggling to recover from the journey through the barrier. 'I didn't intend for him to come.'

Gadya, Markus, and Sinxen start moving ominously towards David as he begins getting to his feet. Rika just looks shocked, like me. Markus's hands are balling into fists.

David holds up a hand, coughing. 'Wait – I know what you think about me. You have every right.'

'Damn straight we do,' Markus says. 'You're the reason all those prisoners got burned! You're a high-level drone. A spy full of lies.'

Gadya looms over David. 'You're here to help the Monk.'

'No – wait! Alenna, make them understand!'

Gadya spins towards me, eyes narrowing. 'What does Alenna have to do with this?'

'I talked to her—' David stutters. 'After I got out of the kennels—'

'He burst out of the forest the night before we left,' I interrupt, because now everyone is eyeing me suspiciously. 'He babbled some crazy stuff about setting up his own colony somewhere, not part of either group. He wanted me to join him. I didn't tell anyone because I knew I'd probably get interrogated.' Everyone keeps staring at me. 'That's the truth! I don't know any more than that.'

Markus looks at David hard. 'So why are you here now?'

'Because I want to come with you guys. I know where you're headed. Into the grey zone to find the aircrafts. I want to get off Island Alpha, and I'm sure you can use an extra body to help.' His dark eyes fix on to mine. 'I'm not a spy. I'm just trying to unravel the mysteries and save myself.'

'You're playing both sides, David,' Gadya accuses. 'I haven't figured out your angle yet, but I will. And I already know I'm not gonna like what I find.'

'Let's just make a new hole in the barrier and send him back,' Sinxen proposes.

'Yeah, dead or alive,' Markus adds.

The Monk waves his hand in annoyance at our debate. 'It doesn't matter. If he wishes to come, then so be it.'

Gadya speaks directly to the Monk. 'Of course you want him with you. He's one of your kind. But you realise we outnumber you now? Even with David tagging along?'

'Yes.'

'You aren't afraid we'll kill all three of you? Hurt you?'

'You can't hurt me as much as the wheel already has.' The Monk raises a ragged arm as if to prove his point. 'I could have brought fifty drones with me. A hundred. A thousand.' He pauses. 'I didn't want to. Inevitably, they would go wild and make noise. I control their minds. Not their bodies. Sometimes a body is stronger than a mind.' He makes a sound close to a sigh. 'Besides, the truth is, I have tired of them. They worship me only because they have nothing better to do. They are weak-minded… Unstable.' He raises a shaky hand again. 'They are a burden. I've been waiting for a group like you. Kids who can think for themselves.'

'So you're trusting us because we're better, smarter fighters? Is that what you're saying?' Gadya asks. 'And because we know the way to where you want to go? You don't even believe in your own cult any more?'

I know that if Gadya had a weapon on her, she might use it. Her voice is low and cold. If she ever blamed me for my role in Liam's death, she must blame the Monk a million times more. He can't know this, yet he senses her raw hatred.

'No, I still believe in the power of my cult. Their faith kept me alive all these long years. But their devotion sickens and wearies me. I lost my freedom to their numbers. Their love became my shackles, and I became a prisoner of their worship.' He looks around. 'Now, for the first time, I feel free again.' He coughs. 'Remember, I am not a villain. I shared my knowledge about the barrier with you. I didn't have to.'

'Only because you needed our help,' I point out.

'Friendship is always a case of mutual exploitation.' His

drone lovingly brushes back a tuft of the Monk's hair, which is sticking out behind his mask. It's like the drone didn't even hear what the crazy Monk said about being sick of his own followers.

David takes that moment to rip off his robe, throw it on to the ground, and stamp on it. Underneath he's wearing normal street clothes and a winter jacket. He also has a homemade splint around his ankle to support his foot. 'Look! See! I'm not a drone. I'm one of you.'

'You'll never be one of us,' Gadya snaps at him. 'And whether you're a drone or not, out here you're just a liability. You're weak. You're not prepared for this journey.'

Markus jabs a finger at David. 'I know you're a spy. I don't trust you, and I never will. Maybe I can thrash out of you what Veidman's truth serum couldn't.' He moves forward.

'Markus, no more violence,' I say. 'Better David turned up than a feeler. I don't know if he's a spy or not any more, but he's here now, and we can't send him back. We might as well take him along.'

'Guys, I'm freezing,' Rika interrupts in a small voice. 'Can we stop arguing?'

'Good idea,' the Monk rasps.

'David, if you come with us, you're walking in front,' Markus says. 'In case there are any booby traps.'

'Yeah, consider yourself our prisoner,' Gadya adds.

'Call me whatever you want,' David mutters.

We rummage through our packs and put on jackets, gloves, scarves and hats. We're trying to stay warm in the painfully cold weather. There must be a forty-degree difference on either side of the barrier. We've gone from eighty-odd degrees to just above freezing.

Of course, I don't see any sign of the rocks that David mentioned earlier. He said they'd be inside the barrier where the drones always cross over. Seemingly right where we are now. But there's nothing here.

I try to quell my rising panic. I know I haven't really looked yet. I obviously don't want to mention the rocks out loud. Not only will it reveal that I talked to David more than the others can imagine, but it also seems worth keeping secret. Right now I don't want to draw any extra attention to myself.

I gaze around at the trees, searching for any large rocks. The trees look odd – slightly crystalline, like they're frozen, or fossilised. I touch a branch above me, and it feels cold and brittle. Everything here seems dead, even when it's still alive.

Back on the other side of the barrier, I can see the sun and the emerald colours of the vivid landscape we left behind. I never thought I'd feel nostalgic for the horrors of the orange sector. But at least I knew what to expect there. I have no clue what awaits us in the grey zone.

I hear Gadya, Markus, and Sinxen still arguing with David

'I need to pee,' I say suddenly, startling everyone. The truth is, I need a chance to be alone to search for the rocks, but I can't let them know that. 'I'll be right back.'

'Alenna?' David calls out, probably suspecting what I'm up to. 'I'll come with you!' I'm not sure whether he actually wants to help or if he's just afraid to be left alone with the others. I ignore him and keep walking, pretending I didn't hear. I know the others won't hurt him, at least for now.

I plunge off to my right, into the forest, before anyone can stop me. I don't know exactly what I'm looking for. I'm afraid the rocks with 'Shawcross' on them are going to turn out to be gravestones, although at least then I'd have some closure. But I'm hoping for more. I'm hoping to find a secret message.

I know I don't have long until my companions get worried, or suspicious, and come after me. I tromp through the underbrush, staring around. *Maybe this is the wrong place entirely.*

Then I see an object, partially hidden by dead branches, rising up from the forest floor. It looks like a large rock, and my hopes soar. I rush towards it, excited and elated to have found so quickly what I was seeking.

But when I reach it, my heart sinks. It's not a rock at all. It's just the splintered stump of a large fallen tree, half buried in the underbrush, speckled with grey lichens.

I look around. I see more mysterious shapes in the brush, but most of them look like decaying tree trunks or random debris. I start to realise that finding one of these rocks might be much harder than I thought. I expected them to be bigger. More obvious. And David said there were a lot of them.

I start moving again, going deeper, searching desperately for a sign.

I find nothing.

Finally, I just stop walking. I rub my arms. Even with my

jacket and gloves, I'm freezing. I don't want to get lost out here in the cold. I realise I'll have to return to the others and try to keep searching for the rocks later on. But I know that the further we move away from the place where we crossed the barrier, the less likely it is that I'll find them – unless I can get more information out of David.

I turn and head back towards my companions, retracing my route.

It's only then that I spot something I missed, standing shrouded in the shadows of a cluster of nearby trees.

It's a granite slab, like a monolith – nearly twice my height and about six feet wide. I stumble towards it rapidly.

But when I get there, I don't see anything carved on its surface, let alone my last name. The surface is mostly overgrown with icy vines and hanging moss. I shove the vines away with my gloved hand, trying to see if anything is hidden underneath. I find nothing but jagged granite.

Time is running out, and I don't see any other rocks around anywhere.

Wait – maybe the message is on the other side.

The underbrush is thicker there, but I wade through it, trying to get around the rock, just in case. My breath is as visible as smoke in the frigid air.

As I turn the corner, at first I don't see anything. But then as I quickly pick my way around it, I see that a flat area has indeed been chiselled on to the surface of the rock.

My heart starts pounding as I swiftly move toward it.

I see letters.

Then the letters coalesce into words.

I stand there in the underbrush, swaying slightly in disbelief.

'*Shawcross Rock*,' I murmur in shock, reading the letters chiselled into the granite surface.

David was telling the truth.

Underneath are two names, 'Thomas & Leah Shawcross'. *The names of my parents.*

I fight back tears.

Underneath their names is a date and a dash: '16 June, 2026–'

That's two months after they got taken!

And underneath that is my own name, just as David said it would be.

I sink to my knees in the brush, feeling light-headed. My parents must have ended up here somehow. *But what does that dash mean?*

The rock doesn't seem to be a tombstone, because there's no second date. No record of their death. It seems more like a marker to signify their presence. Of course, I realise that someone else could have chiselled their names into the stone. Someone who knew them, a friend of theirs. So maybe it doesn't mean as much as I think it does.

But then I see some lines chiselled next to the names, obscured by vines. I brush the vines back with one hand.

What I see beneath them makes me know once and for all that my parents were actually here. It's not a message consisting of words. Instead, it's a pictogram. Probably most of the drones who saw it couldn't make sense of the image. But I can. In fact, I know exactly what it means.

On the rock face is a primitive carving of a steep hill, with a human being – barely more than a stick figure – pushing a circular object up the sharply angled plane. The figure is smiling.

It's Sisyphus.

I know that my dad carved this, and that he did it for me. Somehow, as impossible as it sounds, he must have known I would be sent to the wheel one day. Why, or how, or when is a mystery. I take off one of my gloves and push the vines back further, hoping there are more images, but there is only one:

An arrow, pointing north-east.

Just as I lean in closer, trying to figure out what the arrow means, I hear Gadya bellowing my name in the distance, sounding worried. But I'm not ready to leave yet.

I place my hand flat against the rock face, tracing the chiselled lines of the arrow with my fingertips. It's some kind of instruction, left years ago by my dad.

I hear Gadya yell my name again, louder, so I push myself off the rock, letting the vines swing back into place. I wipe my eyes. I don't want to leave, but I have to keep my secret safe. I don't want anyone – not even Gadya – seeing this rock. It's too personal. Too painful. I need time to deal with it myself before I show it to anyone else.

With a backwards glance at the granite monument, I hurry back through the forest to the clearing. I wish I had time to search for more rocks that might carry other messages for me.

My head is flooding with thoughts and images of my parents – their faces, their clothes, their voices. How they smelled. It's like the rock in the forest is giving me my memories back.

When I reach the group, Gadya is standing up at one edge, peering around. 'Took you long enough!' she says when she spots me. 'What the hell's wrong with you, running off like that?'

David is sitting against a low stone, with Markus and Sinxen standing over him like guards.

'Sorry,' I mutter. I sit down on a rock, trying to keep my turbulent emotions to myself. I'm not sure whether I feel like crying or laughing. I don't want anyone to know what I've found. I don't even know what my discovery means. I try to catch David's eye, but he's looking down, seemingly afraid of Markus and Sinxen.

The rock is a sign. A trace of my parents' existence. Proof that they survived deportation from the UNA and made some kind of life here, at least for a while. I will head in the direction of the arrow, no matter where it leads – even if I have to break away from the group for good.

I gaze around at my companions. Everyone looks so sombre in the cold grey light, exhausted and bedraggled.

'We've got a long hike ahead of us,' Markus finally says. 'Better get started before something bad happens.'

The Monk chuckles. 'Time has no meaning in the grey zone.' He chuckles creepily again, like he knows something we don't. He doesn't seem threatened at all by the fact that we outnumber him. What's going on here exactly?

I stand up, joining the others. 'Time still has meaning to me.'

Markus pulls David to his feet.

Rika stays slumped on the grass. 'I need longer to rest.'

'Rika, you're one of the nicest people I know,' Gadya says, 'and the best cook around here for sure. But you're also a wimp. No offence. *We have to move.*'

Rika looks up at Gadya. A tear runs down her cheek. 'I don't think I can.'

'We're not leaving you, so you don't have a choice,' I tell her, thinking about that arrow carved on the rock. 'Maybe we'll find some fruit along the way, despite the cold. Or a hoofer. We can make a meal.'

'There's nothing edible in this zone,' the Monk says flatly.

We turn to him.

'Nothing at all. No food. Only frozen water. This isn't a zone that sustains life.'

'Are you serious?' Sinxen asks, stamping his feet for warmth as he scowls. He's so different now from the frolicking, teasing boy I first met. 'Why didn't you tell us that? We could have brought more food and water with us.'

David steps away from Markus. He opens his coat to reveal two large flasks of water. 'Now who isn't prepared?' he asks.

Markus looks disgusted. Spits on the icy ground in David's direction. 'Figures.'

'I'll share it with you,' David replies. He holds out a flask to Markus. 'See?'

Markus doesn't take it. 'It's probably poisoned.'

For some reason, this strikes the Monk as humourous, and he chuckles, like he's enjoying a private joke.

Gadya steps menacingly towards him. 'Stop playing games with us.' His drone stands up to protect him. 'I can take you!' she snaps, undaunted. 'Bring it on!'

The Monk stops chuckling. 'I thought you knew about this zone already,' he says. 'It's true we must start moving. Soon they will know that we're here.'

'"They"?' I ask.

'The ones who run things. The ones who really control this island.'

I wonder if that's where the arrow leads, to the city, and the aircrafts we're already seeking. *To the people in control of this terrible place.*

All of us are standing now except for Rika. Finally even she pushes herself up, because we haven't given her much choice.

The drone hoists the Monk on to his back. The Monk wraps his arms around the drone's neck, like he's strangling him, but the drone doesn't seem to care. I see that underneath the drone's robes is a backpacklike apparatus, with loops of twine sticking through slits in the cloth. The drone reaches around and positions the Monk's limbs in the apparatus, like a pack animal shouldering its own load. I shudder against the cold air, my teeth chattering.

'We head north-east,' Markus says.

The same direction my father's arrow pointed.

Now that Liam and Veidman are gone, Markus is the only

one left who knows the route, as far as I know. I guess at this point, he should write it down for us, in case he gets killed or taken, but he doesn't volunteer to do that. Instead he just points. 'This way.'

We gather our belongings, preparing for the hike. I pull my scarf up higher and my cap down lower, wishing I had warmer clothes.

'How far?' Sinxen asks Markus.

'Roughly six miles.'

'Yeah, and then we all live happily ever after,' Gadya mutters.

'Not all of us,' Markus replies, eyeing the Monk and David. I suspect Markus has got a nasty plan in store for them, and the Monk probably has one in store for us, too. But for now there is a tense, fragile peace.

'Let's start walking,' I say loudly, before friction can erupt into outright confrontation. I wish I could go back to the Shawcross rock once more and study it, but there's no time. I stomp my feet and swing my arms, trying to warm up.

With a final glance back at the barrier, we begin hiking again. Markus takes the lead, prodding David along in front of him.

'Hey, don't touch me,' David says, turning back, shoving Markus's hand away.

Markus shoves him right back. 'You better keep your mouth shut if you know what's good for you.'

'I don't have to do what you say. We're not in the kennels any more,' David replies.

'No, we're someplace worse, which is why you both need to quit it!' Rika admonishes.

But Markus has basically made David his prisoner again, and continues shoving him along roughly, no matter what Rika or I say. I wonder what secrets the grey zone has in store for us, and I desperately hope we can survive them.

I think of my father's carving of Sisyphus. I know exactly what it means – to keep going at all costs. To never give up. And to find meaning in the journey.

FROZEN

We move slowly, travelling through a nightmarish landscape that looks like it's been devastated by aerial bombings. The trees are twisted and stunted. Everything is off-kilter. Even the frigid air smells oddly sterile, antiseptic.

Liam has been through this zone, I tell myself, curling my fingers in my gloves. He explored parts of the grey zone more than any of the other hunters. I try to calm myself and find some familiar trace of him in the landscape to cling to. But I find nothing.

The drone carrying the Monk seems to barely notice his master's weight. But Rika is having trouble walking. In addition to her injuries, the barrier took something out of her. I feel it too, a numbing exhaustion that saps my strength.

Gadya and I settle into a rhythm, hiking next to each other. I wonder if she's thinking about Liam too. I'm certain that she is.

There aren't any paths here, but the trees are so thinly spaced in places that we can walk between them, creating our own trails. Our feet crunch on the icy grass.

'So Markus knows where he's going?' I ask Gadya.

'He better. Veidman told him the directions as a fail-safe. And Veidman was pretty meticulous.'

'What if something happens to Markus?'

'Then we're screwed.'

I wonder for a moment if Gadya knows the way too, and just isn't admitting it. *There has to be another fail-safe among us.* I think back to Veidman's strange request that I spy on the others for him. So far, no one has done anything suspicious, but I'm guessing I'm not the only one on this journey with secrets.

We trudge along. The Monk's drone should be getting tired from carrying him, but it looks like his misguided faith still keeps him going. I wish I had some of that energy. I feel cold, exhausted and afraid. To keep going without that kind of faith is harder, but it feels more honest to me.

I wonder how cold it'll get inside this zone, because the temperature keeps dropping the deeper we go. The sky seems grayer too. Not darker, just a deeper shade of grey, as though I've stepped inside an old, flickering black-and-white movie. The kind my dad used to watch on contraband videodiscs, late at night.

Our line abruptly comes to a halt, as Markus stops walking. He barks at David to halt as well.

'We got a problem?' Gadya calls out. She's shivering but trying to hide it.

'No,' Markus replies. He's looking around, like he's seeking landmarks to guide him.

'I'm freezing my butt off,' Gadya says. 'You better not be lost.'

I realise that the barrier must somehow divide two

completely separate ecosystems. The sectors we left behind were all hot, humid and intensely tropical. But here in the grey zone, everything is cold and dry, as though the water and heat are slowly being leeched out of the air. I have no idea what kind of island geography, or even government technology, could create this effect. It's completely unnatural. But then again, so is everything about the wheel.

I'm struck by a terrible thought, so I voice it to Gadya softly. 'What if it just keeps getting colder and colder in this zone until we end up freezing to death?'

She turns to me. 'You want to go back? Be a big wimp? It's just cold weather, so bundle up and tough it out.'

'I will. But I also want to be smart and plan ahead.'

A cackle interrupts me. It's the Monk. He's heard us talking, and his drone has carried him closer. 'Plan ahead?' he rasps.

'Just shut up!' Gadya says to him. 'Or I'll smash your ugly face in. I'll turn your mask into splinters and use 'em as toothpicks.'

'Gadya!' Markus calls out, ready to start hiking again. 'No fighting. Not yet. Let's go.' He shoves David forward. 'Move it!'

Gadya turns away from the Monk and starts heading through the trees. I follow, catching up. I don't want to talk to the Monk. His drones might have faith in him, but the only thing he has faith in is himself. He even abandoned his own flock.

But the Monk does have an uncanny knack for knowing things. I wonder if he knows that David told me about

Shawcross Rock. *How long has the Monk even been on this island? Where did he even come from?*

I continue hiking, placing one heavy foot in front of the other. We bunch up, the cold driving us together, like a herd of animals. Even the Monk and his drone don't stray far from us now. There's no chance to talk to David alone, because Markus keeps guarding him.

In the cold grey landscape, I've lost track of time, and of how far we've travelled. We could have walked five miles, or we could have walked fifty. I can barely keep my legs moving any more. The cold has made all of us silent and introspective.

Finally, I see a break in the forest ahead, where the trees inexplicably thin out into nothingness.

'Look!' I yell, my words loud in the silence. The others see it too. Everyone starts walking faster.

'Are we there?' Rika asks, sounding a little dazed.

I reach the opening in the trees and stumble cautiously out of the forest, right behind Markus and David.

For a moment, I'm speechless. Then I feel a wave of dizziness, and I crouch to my knees, wanting to sob. Markus is cursing angrily. David looks confused. The others step out behind us.

This can't be possible!

My hopes of finding the city and the aircrafts anytime soon have been obliterated.

We've been following all of Markus's directions, not to mention the arrow that my father drew. But they've taken us to an unexpected place.

We stand at the edge of a huge frozen lake that sits in glacial silence. The surface is perfectly smooth, like a sheet of treacherous glass.

The lake is so massive, it stretches out on either side as far as I can see. There's no way to walk around it, unless we want to add twenty or thirty miles to our journey – miles that we wouldn't survive in these temperatures.

On the other side of the lake, which looks about half a mile away at most, I can see the forest resume. That means the only way to get past this lake is to walk across the ice – an incredibly risky move that will leave us exposed to anyone watching.

'I'm guessing this wasn't part of the plan,' I mutter.

Markus shakes his head grimly.

'We're lost?' Rika dares to ask in a small voice. 'For real?' No one answers.

For once even the Monk isn't chuckling. It looks like he can barely move. His thin, twisted fingers have curled into icy gloved claws that grip the robed shoulders of his drone.

'Markus, we need answers,' Gadya prompts.

'I don't think we're lost,' Markus begins. 'But this frozen lake doesn't make any sense. The directions I memorised didn't take us to any lake. The other landmarks match up perfectly. Just not this one.'

'How is that possible?' Sinxen asks, sounding panicked.

'Maybe it's man-made. Maybe it's been flooded since this area was scouted,' Markus offers.

'Now I wish I were a spy, so I could help us all out,' David begins. 'I thought you guys knew the way.'

Markus glares at him. I just stare across the lake in despair.

It's then that I finally notice something in the trees on the other side. It's an odd shimmering of the light that almost looks like a mirage. It rises up above the tree line by about fifty feet or more.

Gadya notices it too. 'What the hell is that?'

We all squint, but it's impossible to make out what we're seeing. It almost looks like there's another translucent barrier on the other side of the lake. A barely visible one, flickering in the forest. *Without fireworks we won't be able to get through it.*

'We're not lost,' the Monk suddenly rasps, catching us by surprise.

'I thought you didn't know how to get where we're going!' Gadya says. 'I thought that's what you needed us for.'

'I don't know the way, but I do know what we're looking for.' His mask has patches of frost on it. 'What you're seeing across the lake is an illusion…created by a system of cameras, projecting images of the sky and forest on to a gossamer screen. Designed to fool anyone who gets this far. Behind it lies the city…and a way off the wheel.'

'Is he lying?' Gadya asks Markus.

'Probably.' Markus gazes around. 'Only one way to find out, though.'

'This ice better be thick, or we're all gonna drown,' Sinxen points out.

I glance up at the sky. I wonder if it's going to start snowing; the air has that strange expectant feeling. How is it possible that just a few hours ago, on the other side of the barrier, it was eighty degrees?

'We're gonna die if we stop moving,' I say, hoisting my pack with freezing arms.

'So we're just gonna walk across the ice?' Rika asks, repressed hysteria in her voice. 'What if it does crack? I can't swim.'

'Why didn't Liam say anything about this lake?' Sinxen broods uneasily. 'He was here too, right? He gave Veidman info about the grey zone.' His question raises another one that is left unspoken. *What if Liam was a spy?*

Gadya stares at him. 'Maybe Liam took a different route.'

'Or maybe there wasn't any water in this lake when he came through,' I point out. 'I mean, if it's man-made. We don't know how anything works in this zone.'

Markus looks at David. 'You sure there's nothing you want to tell us?'

He shakes his head. 'I'm as clueless as you guys.'

Gadya takes a step closer to the icy surface, so I walk up next to her. 'We'll have to spread out,' she says. 'Distribute our weight.'

I watch as Markus steps on to the ice. It creaks, but it holds.

'Pretty thick.' He taps his foot. The ice doesn't splinter. It just groans a little more.

I start walking forward. If the ice is this thick all the way across, then we'll be able to make it to the other side without much of a problem. I exhale with relief as I edge my way onto the surface, shivering.

I know we have to cross this lake quickly. If the temperature is low enough to freeze ice this thick, it must be very cold out here now. How long will we last in our shabby coats, hats and boots? I can see that there's a hole in one of Sinxen's gloves. He's probably going to get frostbite on his hand.

But none of us are in as bad a shape as the Monk. He doesn't scare me so much any more. In fact, there's something pathetic about him, like a broken old man. All his megalomaniacal plans of conquering the wheel and enslaving kids with his lies have brought him to this place – an icy, barren wilderness far from his sectors. Here, he has no one except his drone. Here, in the barren cold, he will soon succumb to the Suffering and the elements.

The others fan out behind me. I peer over at Markus, who is pointing the way forward, still trying to guard David.

As a scattered group, we begin to walk and slide across the icy surface of the lake. It's slippery, but all of us move cautiously, and none of us fall, not even the drone carrying the Monk.

The ice is thick enough that it feels like I'm walking on solid earth, but I know we can't risk congregating on it. Our combined weight might shatter the ice and send us all plunging into the water. So we continue to keep our distance from one another.

The further we go, the more frigid the air becomes. I can't feel my toes, and I can barely feel my fingers. My nose and cheeks are numb. I tell myself that everything will feel better when we're off the ice and back in the forest. Maybe we can risk starting a fire then.

We're right in the middle of the lake when I hear the first faint buzzing noise.

Bzzzzzzzzzzzzzz.

My heart seizes up in panic. The sound is so soft, and the place is so silent that it almost seems like it's coming from inside my own ears. But I know it's not.

'Gadya!' I whisper. She doesn't hear me, so I wave my arms. 'Do you hear that?'

Gadya looks over at me, just as Rika stops walking. I can tell she has heard it too.

I look up. I don't see anything, but the noise is growing louder. I know exactly what's headed our way.

'*We've been spotted!*' I yell. '*It's a feeler!*'

Everyone stops walking instantly.

'We better run!' Rika yells.

'There's no time!' Markus screams back.

He's right. We're in the centre of the lake. The feeler is going to get here much faster than we can reach the other side. We all look back and forth at one another with panicked, desperate eyes.

'We have to fight it here!' Gadya yells.

'It's going to take one of us!' Rika replies. The noise of the feeler is becoming even louder, a whining sound far above the clouds. Based on the other feeler attacks, I'm guessing it's only sixty seconds away from us now. And I know that more feelers will probably follow in its wake. We're going to be forced to take a stand on the ice.

Sinxen turns to the Monk. 'Any bright ideas?'

The Monk shakes his masked head.

'Let's fight it!' Gadya yells again. 'I'd rather die in battle than get picked off helplessly, like a bug!'

I wish Liam were here, because he'd know what to do. And I wish Veidman were here too. *But they're not – it's just us.*

I look at David.

'What if we each grab one of the feeler's tentacles?' I yell, trying to think of a strategy. 'Maybe we could outweigh it and bring it down.'

'I don't know if the ice will hold!' David yells back.

Gadya's eyes burn with the expectation of battle. 'No, it's a good idea!'

'I've never seen a feeler take more than one person at a time,' Sinxen calls out. 'Maybe we'd be heavy enough to crash it. Then we could run, before the other feelers come. At least we'd have a chance.'

The rotor sounds get even louder, as though the feeler is directly above us now, hidden in the clouds. Heads snap up, and we stare at the grey sky. *Why can't we see it yet?*

We draw even closer, and for the first time I hear the ice creak loudly under our feet, making ominous sounds like it's about to give way. For a second, I'm afraid it will start cracking. But it holds.

I feel a hand on my shoulder. It's David.

'You found the rocks, didn't you?' he whispers beneath the noise of the rotors. 'I could tell from your face earlier.'

'Maybe.'

'Then you know I'm telling the truth. You gotta help me deal with Markus, and you have to trust me, Alenna. It's been you and me from the start, and we—'

'Look sharp!' Markus barks, knocking David's hand off my shoulder. 'Here it comes!'

Rika starts crying. She's shaking uncontrollably, from fear and from the cold. I hear the Monk's laboured breathing behind his mask.

'Hand-to-hand combat,' Gadya is saying to Sinxen. 'It's the only way.'

I tilt my head back again, eyes glued to the sky. I'm terrified. I wonder if all warriors feel this fear, if Liam ever felt it. Maybe real warriors don't get scared like this. It's a stomach-clenching, breath-stealing fear. The kind that comes from facing down your worst nightmares.

'Almost here,' I whisper, clenching my frozen hands into fists inside my gloves. I've never fought with my bare hands before, but now I'm going to be fighting those metal tentacles with everything I have.

The noise of the rotors becomes a screaming roar, and a stiff wind kicks up on the ice. 'Let's grab this thing and kill it!' Gadya screams, as the first three metal tentacles shoot down towards us from the feeler with frightening velocity.

I don't know which one of us the feeler is going after. Tentacles crack down on the ice all around me like gunshots.

I explode into action, racing forward, trying to grab the nearest tentacle. The others do the same.

I see the Monk's drone step forward, with the Monk still hanging on to his back. A long metal blade suddenly extends from the drone's wrist, a hidden sword under his robes. *So this is what the Monk had in store for us.* But now he'll never have a chance to use it. As all of us clutch at the tentacles, even Rika, the drone attacks the feeler with the sword, sparks flying as metal hits metal.

Then a tentacle curls down right in front of my face. Instead of fleeing from it, I go straight for it, getting both of my gloved hands around its circumference. My right hand catches on some sort of hydraulic nozzle, and the tentacle starts curling around my wrist.

Then I hear a wailing scream from the drone. A tentacle has whipped the blade right out of his hand and sent him crashing down, headfirst. The Monk has toppled off him and is lying unprotected on the ice.

More tentacles zoom down at us from the feeler hovering in the clouds.

'Keep fighting!' Gadya yells. The ice is creaking so loudly, I can tell it's going to splinter soon. Then it'll all be over. We'll die, just like everyone else.

I tear at the tentacle, ripping my gloves and bloodying my hands. I try to pull it around my arm, like a coil of rope, but it resists. It is a cold, dead thing. Designed to take lives and keep us from ever getting off the wheel. I hate it passionately. But I know it doesn't hate me, even though it's probably going to kill me. It feels nothing. *I refuse to let it win.*

I glance around in a terrified haze. I can't see the Monk or his drone any more. But I see that all of us – even Rika and David – are hanging on to different tentacles, trying to pull the thing right out of the sky.

At first I don't think it's ever going to work. We're not heavy enough. I remember seeing feelers uproot entire trees. Even if our weight is enough to destabilise it, I'm guessing it has some means of disentangling itself from us.

But maybe not, because I hear the rotors screaming as the tentacles try to pull us upwards. We're tenacious, and the feeler can't get away.

The noise becomes an intolerable high-pitched cry of mechanical agony. Suddenly the feeler's spotlight turns on, and we're blasted with white light. I shut my eyes, temporarily blinded.

I lose my balance and feel myself getting pulled sideways across the ice. I realise that the feeler is trying to get away now, but it can't lift off with our weight still on it. And so far, none of its companions have arrived.

We actually have a chance!

The thought gives me a burst of energy, and I try to get traction on the ice. But the tentacle is intertwined with my gloves and hands, and I'm flung down hard. The impact jars my jaw and knocks the breath from my lungs. I get dragged across the ice, still struggling and fighting.

'We're going to beat you!' I scream at the tentacle. 'We're going to win!'

I get flipped over, so I'm staring up at the sky. The back

of my head keeps slamming down on the ice as I get pulled along. I hear everyone screaming and shouting over the sounds of the engine.

And then I see it.

The thing above the clouds.

I just catch a glimpse. It's black and round, like a small helicopter. It's got a spotlight and a hatch mounted to its undercarriage between the attached tentacles, like an octopus's mouth. I don't know if there's a person inside or if it's some sort of automated device like Gadya said. I just know that I want to destroy it. When the spotlight moves out of my eyes, I can see a red UNA logo painted on the hatch.

Then I see Gadya slide past, fighting two tentacles, trying to wrap herself up in them. The bright spotlight cuts off completely, like the feeler is conserving its power.

I see the underside of the helicopter again, and then the full shape emerges, its blades spinning wildly. Smoke is rising from it, like we've overloaded its capacity.

The tip of my tentacle whips across my face, bloodying my lips, but I don't let go. Nothing will make me let go. This is the thing that killed Liam, and so many others. For all I know, a feeler killed my own parents.

Now I will get my revenge.

The helicopter-thing finally loses control. It veers sideways, still pulling us along with it. My head cracks against the ice so hard that I almost pass out for a second. I smell burning oil and see clouds of smoke billowing from the helicopter's rotor.

The feeler begins emitting beeping sounds. I realise that the noise is the death throes of a machine. It makes me happy to hear that sound, almost like it can feel pain. The tentacles start to spasm as though they're having a seizure. Everyone's screaming.

Then the tentacle whips sideways, right out of my hands, as the helicopter-thing starts falling from the sky. I slide for several yards on the ice until my momentum finally slows.

I watch as the feeler and its dead tentacles plummet on to the ice about a hundred yards away. The helicopter blades hit the surface first and break off, spinning away past my head. The body of the helicopter crashes through the ice in an explosion of freezing water and tentacles. Bits of metal and wire shoot through the air like bullets, eventually skittering on to the ice and sliding away into oblivion.

I stagger up, feeling tremors underneath my feet as the ice starts cracking all around us.

'No!' Rika screams. I look over and see that she's OK. But Sinxen is standing near her, swaying, as red liquid bubbles from his mouth. A shard of metal is sticking out of his chest.

I realise that in the feeler's death throes, a stray tentacle must have skewered him. He falls to his knees, turning the ice around him red as his eyes roll up in their sockets.

I can't believe it.

Sinxen.

Another death – and for what?

Gadya races to his side. I follow right behind and see that she's bleeding too. Deep slices from the tentacles run down both her arms, cutting through the down of her jacket.

I gaze around wildly. The drone is back at the Monk's side, hoisting him up. He's recovered his secret blade, but it's gnarled and chipped now. Markus is crawling across the buckling ice. He was closest to the impact site, yet looks relatively unscathed. David is also on his feet, swaying unsteadily.

But the crash has set off a slow-motion chain reaction – a destabilising effect that is now cascading across the surface of the frozen lake.

We start sprinting and limping towards the bank ahead of us. All except for Gadya, who is trying to drag Sinxen's body along with her.

'We have to run!' I scream at her. 'The ice is breaking!' The cracking noises are deafening under our feet. A jet of water suddenly sprays up between us. I feel the ice shift and move, like sections are about to break apart and give way. I know that if we tumble into the water, we'll be swept under the ice and trapped there.

I turn back to see Rika lagging even further behind me, along with the drone carrying the Monk.

'Faster!' I yell.

Gadya finally lets go of Sinxen, because there's nothing she can do for him any more. The life is gone from his body.

I feel a weird sliding sensation underneath me. Suddenly, a sheet of ice breaks free right in front of me. I veer sideways in panic.

While I avoid the ice, I get slapped in the face by a wall of freezing water. I stumble and fall, hands slapping on to the ice. Then I pick myself up, blinking ice out of my eyes, trying to see clearly.

Maybe the feeler is going to be victorious after all, I think, as I start moving again. *Maybe I'm going to drown.* I stare at the bank ahead and tell myself that I have to make it.

Water slams against the side of my head again like an icy wave, stinging my ear. Large chunks of ice are breaking up everywhere. I struggle to outrun them as water seeps and surges between moving slabs of ice.

Ahead of me, I see Markus reach land, sliding on to the frozen mud at the shore. He stands at the edge of the lake, yelling for us to run. David is hopping and jumping over chunks of ice, desperately trying to make it too, despite the splint on his foot.

I ignore the terrifying cracking and snapping noises, and just focus on the edge of the bank. My eyes fix on an icy crystalline oak tree, its frozen boughs shimmering in the grey light. *If I can make it to that tree, then I'm going to be OK,* I tell myself. *I just have to keep moving.*

But my body is barely responding to my commands any more. I try to move my feet, but I'm so cold, it feels like I'm running in molasses.

I glance back to see the others struggling forward. The lake has claimed Sinxen's body already. I see his pale hand slip off a slab of ice and into the water.

Gone forever.

The feeler has completely disappeared too, its tentacles sucked into the ever-widening hole created by the impact.

Now there are only five of us left, plus the Monk and his drone.

I keep my eyes locked on that icy oak tree. I'm getting closer as I dodge ice chunks and dance over pools of water. Underneath the ice, the lake is far from placid. It's roiling and dark, like an ocean. I feel its currents wanting to suck me in and pull me under.

Then I hear frenzied screaming, and I chance a final look back.

While Gadya is practically alongside me, and the Monk and his drone are off to my left near David, Rika is now lagging badly. She's trapped on an ice floe, with water spraying up all around her.

'Rika!' I yell. I don't want to stop moving, but I pause for an instant as the ice cracks around me.

'Help!' she calls back, too scared to move in any direction. More water cascades upwards, and she almost loses her balance. The piece of ice she's stuck on tilts sideways and she screams again.

My survival depends on getting to the bank. I spin around and see that Gadya and Markus haven't heard Rika's screams. No one else is going to save her.

Suppressing my fear, I realise that I don't have a choice. *Not if I want to live with myself.* I'm only alive because Gadya brought me to the village, with David's help, and because Liam saved me during the feeler attack in the orange sector. Our survival depends on helping one another. So I race back across the ice, lunging towards Rika.

I slip across the surface, which is disintegrating under my feet. I inch as close to her as I dare, and hold out my hand, swaying as the ice moves with me. 'Come on!' I yell. 'Jump towards me!'

She's crouched on all fours, pressing herself against the stray piece of ice so she doesn't get tossed off into the water.

I creep a bit closer, still hearing those explosive cracks. If any more ice breaks up, I won't be able to get to the shore either.

'Grab my hand!' I scream.

'I'm scared!'

'Me too!' I stretch my arm out as far as I can, while water billows up around me. I'm so cold, I don't feel any pain. My whole body has gone numb.

I don't think my plan is going to work. I think Rika is just going to sit down on the ice and give up. But then I hear footsteps next to me, and a voice yells my name. It's David. He has turned around and come back to help us.

'Give me your hand!' he calls out to Rika. 'You can do it.'

She's sobbing hysterically. 'I can't.'

David looks at me. 'I'm going to get her.'

'How?'

'Watch.'

He takes a few steps back and then runs forward, leaping up and throwing himself over the water. He barely makes it, landing on Rika's sheet of ice with a crash, flailing to keep his balance. Wincing in pain from his foot.

She turns to him, shocked.

'If I can do it, so can you,' he yells, grabbing her. 'Look at Alenna, OK? You're going to have to jump. Just like I did.'

Rika starts to whimper, but David forces her forward.

I lean down, stretching out my arms. 'C'mon, Rika!' I yell. 'I'll catch you.'

David whispers something into her ear. Maybe words of encouragement. Maybe even a threat. Rika looks at me. She shuts her eyes, and then pushes herself off the sheet of ice, right at me.

For a terrifying moment, I think she's going to fall into the widening abyss between the two sheets of ice. She lands right at the edge, and is about to teeter backwards into the water.

'No!' I howl, lunging forward to grab her.

And then her hand catches mine, and I'm yanking her forward to safety. Her feet and legs get soaked, but her body makes it on to the ice.

She tumbles into me, and we lurch backwards. By now, Gadya and Markus have realised something is wrong, and I can hear their voices yelling at us.

I roll sideways. I sit up, dazed.

'David!' I scream, as I see the sheet of ice he's on starting to disintegrate. He's looking around wildly. His sheet of ice and ours are separating, with only freezing water left between them. 'Jump! Do it now!'

David hears me and runs forward. He has enough momentum that at first it looks like it'll carry him over the water. Then his injured foot slips at the last second and he stumbles.

'David!' I scream, automatically moving forward.

He falls straight into the water. His hands claw at my sheet of ice for an instant and then they let go. He disappears completely. Then his head reappears, choking and gasping.

I lay down on the sheet of ice, aware that our lives could end at any second, and throw out my arms. He grabs my wrists, hard. I start moving backwards using my elbows, pulling him out of the water as his feet kick violently.

Within a couple of seconds, he's back on the ice with me and Rika, shivering and soaking wet. He's so cold, he can't even speak. I know that without him, Rika probably would have died.

'We still have to run,' I tell him and Rika firmly. They both look like they're going into shock.

We start hobbling towards the bank. Everything goes all strange and distant, too surreal to actually be happening. The only sound I hear is the noise of my own frantic heartbeat, blotting out everything else.

We move as rapidly as we can. I look for my icy oak tree on the bank, but I don't see it any more. My vision is just a blurry frozen haze.

I can barely make out Gadya, standing on the bank with Markus. The Monk and his drone are almost there too. I run towards them, half-dragging Rika and David along with me.

Somehow we make it off the lake, through a combination of luck and perseverance. A few moments later, we're out of danger, collapsing on to the frozen shore next to the others.

I fall to the ground near Rika, chest heaving for air. David is coughing up water. Gadya and Markus crouch over our shivering bodies.

'Oh God, that was close,' Rika says.

Markus and Gadya are trying to get us warm. David is soaked from head to toe. He's not going to make it long out here unless he gets warmed up. None of us are. Hypothermia is going to kick in soon.

'We need to start a fire,' I say, teeth chattering. 'David fell in saving Rika.'

'I saw,' Gadya says. She's looking at David in a new way now, with new respect. Like she's re-evaluating her opinion of him.

'I'll get the fire started,' Markus says. 'I have a lighter.'

It's too cold to stay lying down, so I stagger to my feet, colder than I've ever been in my entire life. I glance over and see the Monk sprawled on the icy mud of the beach. His drone is sitting next to him. Somehow in the chaos of escaping the lake, the drone lost his blade again.

Gadya looks at me, her face ghostly white. I think she's going to say something about David and his act of heroism, but instead she says, 'The Monk is dying, from the cold and his wounds. He can't survive here. We need to find out everything he knows before it's too late.'

She looks over at the drone, studying him. But the drone doesn't notice, because he's too busy attending to his master. Ice crystals have formed on the Monk's mask.

'I can't believe Sinxen is dead,' I murmur, looking back out at the water and ice. This awful lake has become his grave.

Gadya just nods, trying to hide her pain. I know the emotions are too much for her. She turns away from the lake and gestures at the weird shimmering wall about a thousand feet beyond us, in the forest ahead. 'If the Monk's right, then we've almost made it to our destination. We might still find a way off the wheel.'

Off the wheel. It's what I thought I wanted. That, and information about my parents. 'Unless we get warm and dry, I don't think we're going to make it,' I reply.

Markus has gathered a few pieces of wood and is trying to get them lit. It's going to be hard, because everything is cold and wet. David is trying to move around, swinging his arms and legs so they don't freeze up.

'Please—' I suddenly hear a voice say. To my surprise, I realise it's the Monk's drone. We all stare at him.

'You can speak?' Gadya says derisively, her voice as cold as the ground under our feet.

'The Monk needs my help.' The drone looks away for a moment. 'I need to take off his mask. Ice got underneath.'

'Then do it,' I tell him.

He hesitates. If I didn't know better, I'd think the drone felt sheepish. 'Can you please not look?'

'Why not?' Gadya asks. 'He's gonna die anyway, just like my friend Sinxen did. And before he does, I plan on interrogating him.' Her hands become fists. 'You can't stop me any more.'

The drone blanches. 'You know he has the Suffering. We can't gaze upon his holy face. No one can.' He knots his fingers together nervously.

'You're completely nuts,' Markus says. 'Are you aware of that?'

'And you really thought I was one of them?' David mutters, his whole body trembling from the cold. 'You couldn't see the difference between me and some brainwashed lunatic?'

Markus doesn't reply. He just keeps trying to get the fire started.

'If you gaze upon the Monk's naked face, you'll be blinded forever by the sight!' the drone continues gibbering. 'It is our way. It's our belief.'

'OK, fine, whatever,' Gadya says, sounding disgusted. 'Do what you want. We won't look.'

So we turn away to give the Monk his undeserved privacy. I hear latches clicking, as the drone removes the Monk's mask and starts uttering soft, soothing words.

Right then, Gadya spins back around and leaps at the drone, kicking him off the Monk and pinning him to the ground. The Monk's mask was in the drone's hand, and it goes flying across the icy mud.

I turn, startled. Gadya is crouching over the drone with a small knife at his throat. She took it out of her ankle sheath, where it must have been hidden this whole time. 'I'll kill you right now!' she snarls, teeth bared. The drone looks shocked. The Monk curls up, covering his ruined face so we can't see it.

Markus moves forward. 'Gadya, I hate the Monk too, but we might need him later.'

'Stop!' she snaps. When Markus pauses, she turns her attention back to the drone. 'You have two choices. I can cut your throat right now. Or I can let you go – if you promise not to stand in my way.'

'The Monk is the one true path to salvation,' the drone murmurs in a well-worn litany. 'He is the doorway to life after death. He is the eye of the needle, and we are the threads! The multicoloured threads!' He shuts his eyes and starts muttering faster and faster, his lips moving with increasing speed. It takes me a second to realise that he's praying ferociously, maybe even speaking in tongues.

Gadya leans back and slaps him across his freezing cheek. His eyes snap open. 'There's no time for that nonsense! Do you want to live? Or do you want to die? I know you believe in the Monk, but I can make your death incredibly long and painful. Do you want my knife carving your throat out, slice by slice? Besides, we'll probably all die out here anyway. Do you really want to get killed right now? By a girl? What would your Monk think of that? At least wait a while. Maybe you can die a glorious death in battle later on.'

The drone hesitates for a moment.

Gadya presses the knife tight against his throat. 'It's your call.'

I notice that David does nothing to intervene. He certainly doesn't seem interested in helping the Monk or the drone. *He has obviously been telling the truth about his identity the whole time. No drone or spy would risk their life like he did for Rika.* I just hope that Markus finally sees this.

'I want to live,' the drone finally gasps, as he starts crying. It's clear the choice is incredibly painful for him.

'Good.' Gadya pulls back her knife and slowly gets up. The drone shuts his eyes. 'That's right. You don't have to watch if you don't want to.'

'Gadya—' I begin, worried.

'I'm just gonna ask the Monk a few questions. He owes us some truth.'

Gadya steps towards the Monk's cowering body as all of us watch, except for the drone. He remains on the ground, eyes still tightly shut.

I follow Gadya and stand with her, Markus, David and Rika around the Monk's shrunken body. For a moment, I think he's already dead, but then I see his arm twitch slightly.

'Uncover your face,' Gadya instructs, because he still has both hands over it.

'You might not like…what you see…' He breathes haltingly, between his fingers. Some blood comes up with each word.

'Do it,' Markus commands.

Slowly, the Monk lets his hands slip away from his face, down to his side.

'No freaking way!' I hear Gadya gasp.

When I see the Monk's face for myself, I stumble sideways, like I've been punched in the gut.

I go down to my knees. The others aren't far behind me. All except David, who murmurs, 'So the rumours are true.'

I'm not just shocked because the Monk's face is grotesquely

blackened and scarred, which it is. And it's not because of the mocking sadistic smile he wears on his blistered lips.

It's because, against all odds, I recognise his face. And I realise why his voice sounded weirdly familiar.

Despite his grievous injuries, an older, deeper mark gives his identity away. A unique diamond-shaped white scar on his left temple.

The Monk is Minister Harka.

THE HOUSE OF ICE

Rika starts wailing behind me, in horror and disbelief. We have all seen this man's face thousands of times back home – on posters at school, on billboards, in government-sanctioned textbooks. It's the face of the UNA's totalitarian regime. We all know exactly who this man is, despite his disfigurement.

But it doesn't make any sense that he would be here on the wheel with us.

'I don't understand,' I hear Gadya saying, her voice just a gasp.

Markus leans over, gagging.

I stand up again. 'How is this possible?' I ask in a barely audible voice. If Minister Harka is here, then who is actually running things back home? I dare to look down at Minister Harka again. No wonder he hid his face all this time.

He doesn't even have the Suffering, I slowly realise. It's true his face is deformed – as though someone doused his head with gasoline and then put a match to it – but up close I can see that he doesn't bear the sores and pockmarks of disease. In fact, what I thought were sores on his arms are actually old scars.

He has been pretending to have the Suffering so that

he never had to show his face. I guess that explains how he has lived so long with a disease that usually kills its victims within a few months. It's not because he has supernatural powers. It's because he was lying all along.

His eyes catch mine. 'I came here…six years ago.' He chokes out the words around his cynical smile.

'But how?' Markus manages. His eyes look dazed and far away. Rika has stopped screaming.

'I was condemned and sent here. Just like you,' Minister Harka rasps. He coughs, and more blood bubbles up. He doesn't have long to live, and he knows it. He doesn't seem to care, though. Maybe he's even glad that he can finally reveal his true identity. My mind is filled with a million questions, but there's only time to ask a few.

'Why did they send *you* here? You run everything! You're the prime minister!'

'In the end I was disposable. My staff betrayed me when I tried to make changes…when I told them the UNA had become too corrupt. I was arrested and tortured by men more cunning than myself. Men who feared I was growing soft… I woke up here on the island.'

'But we saw you back home. You can't be in two places at once!' Gadya says.

'Lookalikes and body doubles, am I right?' David asks. 'That's what they always said. In my resistance cell.'

Resistance cell? I'm not sure what he's talking about.

'Yes,' Minister Harka answers, his smile finally fading. 'I always had them. For security. Now they use them as my stand-ins. As human puppets to make people believe I'm still in charge.'

'Couldn't you get off this island?' I ask, realising that the lookalikes and body doubles explain why he seemed so ageless. 'It's a government island. As far as we know, you practically designed it! Why didn't you find the way off? Why did you need us? And why did you start a crazy cult?'

He's coughing, his chest making strange sounds. 'I never even knew this island existed,' he whispers. 'It was a secret colony, set up years before. By another regime in Old America, at the dawn of the twenty-first century. For political prisoners. They told me it had been abolished.' His lips curl upwards again as more blood seeps out. 'I know less about its geography than you do.'

David is nodding.

Minister Harka keeps talking, and we listen, riveted: 'When I got here, the prisoners recognised me and burned me alive. They hated me…and I deserved it. But others rescued me and kept me alive. Made me part of their encampment. Then everyone started getting sick. Dying. Teenagers began turning up. I pretended to be sick…but because I knew so much, and because I never died, they thought I had mystical powers. That I was a supernatural being. I played along—'

Minister Harka is gripped by another coughing fit. I glance over at the drone. His face is a rictus of agony and disbelief. His world has been shattered.

Even though Gadya and Markus are right there, I have to ask about my parents. This is probably my final opportunity to get any answers from Minister Harka. I lean in close. 'My name's Alenna Shawcross.' I glance at David. 'David said that my parents got sent here?'

Minster Harka's eyes are shut. So much blood is coming up now, it's like he's haemorrhaging from the inside. 'Shawcross,' he breathes. 'Of course. It's you. You look like your mother.' The breath instantly gets caught in my chest. *Minister Harka knew my parents?* 'Your parents were both here. They were among the kind ones – the ones who helped me when others would not.'

'What happened to them? Where did they go?'

'Now they are free. They are—'

His body abruptly seizes, as though he's plugged a finger into an electrical socket. Gadya rushes to my side.

'We have to do something!' I yell at her. 'He can't die! Not now!'

David runs over to him and tries to help.

But I know the life is leaving his body. I can tell. And there's nothing we can do about it. We try to keep his arms from flailing, and eventually the seizure stops. No more blood comes out. But for him, the long journey is finally over.

Minster Harka is dead.

I can't accept it.

'Wake up!' I yell at him, straddling his corpse. I'm crying, but my tears come from anger, not sorrow. 'Wake up and tell me about my parents!'

I feel hands on my shoulder, pulling me off him. I struggle against them, but I finally get torn from his body. I look up.

It's Gadya. 'He's gone, Alenna.'

I nod. Slowly, I get to my feet. I know that everyone is watching me.

'You never told me about your parents being here,' Gadya says softly.

It all seems so unimportant now. All the little secrets each of us has kept from one another. 'I know.'

'Is that the reason you wanted to come on this expedition?' She doesn't sound suspicious of me like I expected she would. She just sounds tired.

I nod.

She looks at me. 'I wish you'd told me that. I thought it was all about Liam.'

The drone staggers up behind Markus.

Gadya and I turn to him.

'You can come with us if you want,' Gadya says. 'Now that you know your Monk is a fraud. He tricked all of you, understand? And us, too.'

The drone just nods wanly. He still can't look down at the body near our feet. Neither can Rika. She's been rendered mute by shock.

Five minutes later, Markus has somehow managed to get a few branches lit. They emit a dull yellow glow, and little heat. 'I hated Minister Harka for so many years,' he mutters. 'But it wasn't even him I was hating. It was some stupid body double.' He laughs grimly. 'Now I don't know who to hate.' He turns to David, as he tends the fire. 'How did you know?'

'I first heard the rumour two years ago. My resistance cell in New Providence—' He pauses, looking around. He can barely talk because he's so cold. He moves over towards the burgeoning fire. 'I better start from the beginning, I guess. Back home I'm part of a youth resistance movement. Against the UNA and Minister Harka's regime. It's secret, passed on by word of mouth. We noticed Minister Harka never aged, and looked different in certain photos. We started to suspect something like this had to be going on.'

'Wait, slow down. A resistance cell?' Gadya asks him.

'Yes. Trying to sabotage the UNA and restore order instead of tyranny.' He bends in closer to the fire, letting the heat play over him as Markus fans the flames. 'I was always on your side. The side of freedom. And there are a whole lot more like me back home.' We stare at him. 'That's how I could move so easily between worlds on the wheel. I'm used to it. Used to acting one way, then another. I was recruited by the resistance cell when I was thirteen, by a friend's older brother. I'd been putting up antigovernment flyers in my building. Secretly, at night, while my parents were asleep. I knew I'd probably get sent to Island Alpha all along – either because the GPPT is real or, more likely, because I was under surveillance by the government already. I just didn't know what to do about it, so I figured I'd make the best of it and try to figure out how everything worked once I got here.'

Gadya scrutinises him. 'You're telling the truth, aren't you?'

He nods.

We stand there for a moment in silence. So much starts to make sense now. 'Sorry,' Gadya finally murmurs. 'For not believing you. Anyone in a resistance cell is a friend of mine.'

'It's OK.'

The others chime in with apologies too.

'We need to keep hiking,' Gadya finally says, after we've warmed ourselves around the fire for a long time. We've swapped some items of clothing around so that David and Rika have dry clothes. It means all of us are even colder, but at least they're not wet any more. 'We'll just leave Minister Harka here. There's no way to bury him. The ground's too hard.'

'Can I—' the drone begins. 'Can I put his mask back on?'

'Make it fast,' Markus tells him.

So Minister Harka is dead, I think as the drone reattaches the mask. And we're the only ones on the entire planet who know it. Of course, for the citizens back home, he's still alive. He'll probably be alive as long as the UNA exists, an ageless cipher of a corrupt regime.

The drone walks back over to us, in a trance.

I realise that this whole time, no one has even asked him what his name is. 'Hey,' I say softly, trying to be nice. In a weird way, I feel sorry for him. 'What's your name?'

He looks at me. 'I don't...' He pauses. 'I don't remember.'

Gadya makes a scoffing noise. Maybe she thinks he's lying, but I can tell from his eyes that he's telling the truth.

'I've been with the Monk a long time. Three winters. I think my name was John. Or James. Or—'

'Doesn't matter,' Gadya interrupts. 'Pick one, and that's what we'll call you.'

'James,' the drone says. He repeats it, his voice getting stronger. 'Call me that.'

So we leave Minister Harka's body there by the frozen lake after we've warmed ourselves as best we can by the fire. We head up the desolate beach from the shore, into the forest. I don't look back, and neither do any of the others, not even James.

I don't know how long we can survive out here without succumbing to the elements. We're all going to end up like Minister Harka sooner or later, unless we find some way out of this cold. I thought I'd enjoy watching him die, but I didn't – not after I learned the truth. Of course he took most of his mysteries with him to the grave. I still don't know what he was going to say about my parents.

I look around at my ragged band of companions. David is no longer Markus's prisoner. The others trust him now. Still, that doesn't matter if we can't achieve our goal. So many of us are already dead. Maybe none of us will make it all the way to the end.

I force the negative thoughts away. I can't afford to think that way.

We limp up a hill, getting closer to that shimmering mirage that supposedly masks a city beyond it. This hidden city must hold the secret to our escape – assuming Minister Harka was telling the truth, which is a pretty big assumption.

I keep walking. I wonder what will happen if more feelers

spot us now. I'm surprised that others didn't come when we got trapped on the lake, but maybe the fact that we killed one of them scared the rest off. Of course, we won't be able to fight like that again. There's not enough of us left, and we're too weak now.

I think of my dad and his Greek myths for the millionth time. *To imagine Sisyphus happy.* Sometimes I wish I could get that phrase out of my head, because I just can't do it yet. It's a contradiction to imagine him happy when he has to suffer so much.

But I do know one thing: Sisyphus must have been one hell of a survivor. He didn't give up, whether he was happy or not. Focusing my mind on that thought, I start walking even faster, leading the pack with Gadya and David as we move through the forest towards our unknowable destiny.

By the time we finally reach the base of what is indeed a bizarrely shimmering wall, I can't feel much below my knees. I'm stumbling forward unsteadily. The others crowd around me. The air is so cold and still here that it's like being inside a vacuum. The tips of Rika's ears look like they're crusting and turning black. I probably look even worse.

'Minster Harka wasn't lying,' I say, as I look up at the wall. It's thin like a sheet of silk fabric, nearly translucent. Behind it, something is projecting images of trees and sky on to the material so that it camouflages whatever sits beyond. The screen creates the illusion that the forest continues forever.

Gadya pushes at the fabric tentatively. It sways slightly,

like a giant movie screen suspended on hundred-foot poles. I reach out and push it too.

I look closer at the material. I see small holes and tears in it, like it's been hanging here a long time and is starting to fall apart. Still, it creates a relatively convincing illusion, at least from a distance.

'We have to cut our way through,' I say.

Then I see that Gadya already has her knife out. She holds it up and slices downwards in one clean motion. The blade shears the material, opening up a slit in the fabric. A coloured light shines through, like we've exposed part of the projection mechanism.

'Who wants to go first?' Gadya asks.

Markus lumbers forward, barging his way through the opening. I follow, with David, Gadya, Rika, and James at my heels.

Within seconds, we're all standing there at the top of a grassy hill. Bright projector lights shine into our faces. I hold my hand above my eyes, trying to block the lights out. Behind the lights, I can see buildings, and my heart leaps.

We've found the hidden city!

But 'city' isn't the best word to describe it, because it looks nothing like New Boston or New Providence.

From our angle, I mostly see the black roofs of gigantic industrial buildings stretching out for miles in either direction. It's a mix of warehouses and factories. They're all dotted with massive silver ducts, venting white puffs of steam into the frigid air. Tangles of white pipes connect many of the buildings to one another and run off into the surrounding forest at oblique angles.

Beyond the city is the shore of the grey zone. Blue-green ocean stretches out for miles, and I can smell the tang of briny salt water.

I can't believe we're actually here.

We walk forward, passing underneath the projectors. They sit in vertical rows on acres of metal scaffolding, projecting images on to the undulating fabric. This scaffolding appears to surround the entire inland side of the city, shielding it from view.

Every single building is ugly and monolithic. Rail lines stretch off to our left, heading further up the coast. I don't see any sign of landing strips for aircrafts, but they could be hidden too. I also don't see any feelers – at least not yet.

Weirdest of all, I don't see any people. Everything looks deserted. The only sign of life is the smoke that rises from the chimneys and vents, forming low-lying clouds of steam and pollution in the sky.

'How do we get down there and inside the buildings?' I ask.

'We hike.' Markus sounds completely wiped out. 'David, you know anything about this place?'

'Not yet.' He's scanning it with his eyes.

'See that one building?' Rika asks faintly. 'Near the centre of the city.' It's the first time she's spoken in a while. 'The round one with the silver paint on it?'

We follow her gaze. The building is one of the largest ones

I've ever seen in my life. Perhaps twice the size of the GPPT scanning arena in New Providence.

'Yeah,' David says.

'Well, that's the one,' Rika replies. 'The place we need to get to.'

Gadya looks at her. 'And why do you think that?'

Rika peers down at the ground, suddenly shy. 'Because I'm a fail-safe... In case everyone else died.' I look at her, startled. 'Veidman knew I was coming the whole time. He asked me to. He said no one would expect me to know anything. That no one would question me.'

'Unbelievable,' Gadya says, shaking her head.

Just as I'm wondering how Veidman could know which building we had to get to – apparently without knowing about the screen and the projectors – Rika adds, 'He also wanted me to spy on everyone. Tell him if anyone acted weird.'

'He asked me to do the same thing,' I confess. I'm starting to realise that Veidman probably asked each of us to spy on one another and report back to him. Maybe he thought that was the only way to figure out who the real spy was.

'Rika's correct about the building,' Markus adds softly. 'According to all the data we've gathered, I think that's the nerve centre of this entire place. We have to get down there and find a way in. From there we can figure out how to locate the aircraft hangars. They could be underground.'

James is silent, his face grim. He probably thinks we're all going to die.

As a group, we start walking down the hill towards the

city. I know that we're exposed out here, but we don't have another option.

For some reason, no feelers come out to greet us. Then I have a depressing thought: maybe there are no feelers here because they don't need to swoop in and kill us any more. Maybe whoever runs this island knows we're going to die anyway, and they just don't want to run the risk that we'll destroy another precious feeler.

As we keep hiking, getting closer to the industrial city, I realise that the central building presents a kind of illusion. It looked so sleek and massive from a distance. But up close, I see cracks and holes in its curved exoskeleton. Peeling silver paint, and white fissures like marbled slabs of meat, run up and down its side. It clearly hasn't been maintained in years.

'How can this place be in such bad shape?' I whisper to Gadya, who's walking right next to me. 'What does it mean?'

'No clue,' she mutters.

'Me neither,' David adds. 'This is uncharted territory.'

We walk closer, until finally we're standing on a slab of cracked concrete at the bottom of the hill, several hundred feet from the buildings. The entire place is still deserted and silent, except for the sounds of distant machinery hidden behind thick walls. All of us are on guard.

We cautiously head towards the massive silver building. When we finally reach it, Gadya moves up to one of the largest cracks in the building's wall. 'Air's coming out,' she says. She presses her face up to the crack, trying to see inside, but then recoils violently.

'It's freezing!' she yelps. I can see a white, bubbling welt on her cheek. A raw blister. 'It's even colder inside than it is out here! It's like dry ice.' She raises her hand and touches the blister, wincing.

'Must be some kind of cooling plant inside,' David conjectures. 'I don't know for what. Maybe they need it so their machines don't overheat.' He crosses his arms, trying to stay warm against the biting cold. Trying to figure things out.

I'm just surprised this place is so dilapidated. I expected anything but this.

Gadya's blister is already fading from a white pustule into angry redness. 'We can't break inside this place. It's too cold. We'll die.'

'Then let's keep walking,' Rika says dully.

Markus nods. James just stares at the ground.

I'm looking around, suddenly realising there could be cameras anywhere on these buildings. I should have thought of that sooner. 'You think we're being watched?' I ask out loud.

'Probably,' David says. 'The UNA loves to watch people, so it can control them.'

'Then why's no one stopping us?'

'We're either lucky or it's a trap,' Gadya guesses.

Markus is still scanning the silver building. 'This way,' he says. 'We need to find a door, or some kind of way inside. Rika, you got any more information that we need to know?'

'I wish I did.'

We start heading east, along the curved edge of the building. It's incredibly cold here, as if the building itself emanates the frigid air permeating the grey zone. I'm glad for the numbness, or else I'd probably be in more pain. I don't care any more if I get frostbite. I just want to get off the wheel.

So I walk. Occasionally we pass holes in the building that are as large as my fist, and I try to sneak glances inside, dodging streams of icy air. I can't really see inside because it's so dark, but I hear the distant rumble of machinery and occasionally catch glimpses of large metallic shapes moving around.

It reminds me of video footage of a factory that we were forced to watch in New History class a year ago. The footage was about the UNA's military prowess, of course, and how we were the greatest superpower the world had ever known. It showed tanks and airplanes being constructed in massive hangars, and rows of gleaming war machinery that kept our enemies frightened of us. *That's what this place looks like to me – some kind of military installation.*

I glance inside another jagged hole as we pass. But when I try to see more, I suddenly get a blast of cold air straight to my eyeballs.

'Crap!' I twist away, blinking madly, temporarily blinded.

'You OK?' Gadya asks.

'Fine,' I tell her, rubbing my stinging eyes. My sight comes back, blurry at first but then slowly clearing. I keep blinking, breathing warm air into my gloved hands and cupping them over my face.

'You gotta be careful,' David says. 'We don't know what we're up against. This city might be a testing ground for new weapons, or the place where new weapons get built. Either one is possible, and equally dangerous.'

We keep walking, our feet crunching on the icy broken pavement. Our journey has become an endurance test. There's no end to this building, or so it seems. It looks the same no matter how far we walk. I glance back and see it stretching endlessly behind us, like a mechanical wave constructed from steel and brick, frozen in space and time right here at the edge of the wheel.

'Up ahead!' Gadya suddenly calls out.

I stop walking and squint.

In the distance, I see a break in the monotony. We've come upon a thicket of the large white plastic pipes, each one taller than a person. Each one covered in ice. They stick out the side of the building and run directly across our concrete path in a thick mazelike tangle.

David comes to a halt too and stares into the distance. 'Some kind of venting system?' he guesses. Here and there, steam rises from small gasket holes in the pipes. 'What are they trying to keep so cold in this place?'

Rika looks despondent. 'More important, how are we going to get through these pipes?'

'We might have to backtrack,' Markus replies. 'I don't know if people are meant to be here. It looks too industrial. Like it's only meant for machines or something.'

'It's too cold to go back,' Gadya says. 'We have to go forward.'

'Then we'll have to go over and under the pipes,' I say.

'Like it's a jungle gym.'

David nods in agreement.

We all walk closer. It takes another fifteen minutes to even reach the tangle of pipes, which looms large ahead of us. At least sixty pipes extend out of the wall at different heights, leading away from the structure, forming an oddly impassible barrier.

We pause when we reach the pipes, standing a few paces away. I hear whooshing noises, like there's air or water passing through them. I gaze up. The pipes rise about twenty feet into the air at their highest peak.

To get past these pipes, we're going to have to slide our stiff, wounded bodies through small gaps between some of them, and then climb up others – all the while evading occasional jets of cold air from the pipes' valves.

I'd take Sisyphus's task over this, I think desperately.

I imagine if I could get a bird's-eye view, the layout of the pipes might make more sense, but from my perspective it almost looks like they've grown organically across the landscape. They spread out at different angles, forming a surreal obstacle course.

'What if we get trapped here?' Rika asks. 'Stuck between the pipes?'

'Then we're going to die,' I hear James murmur, sounding resigned.

'Shut your face!' Gadya snaps. 'If it wasn't for Minister Harka and the rest of you loonies, we wouldn't even be in this place.'

'Quit fighting,' I break in, swallowing my fear. 'I've been studying the pipes. If we get stuck, we can follow one back to the silver building and then keep looking for another way through the maze.'

'Exactly,' David says. 'We just gotta be careful. Don't touch the pipes with your bare flesh.'

Gadya and I nod, although Rika still looks terrified. James just stands there until he finally nods wanly too. He's just blindly following our orders now instead of the Monk's.

I look up, nervously checking the sky for feelers.

'Let's go,' Markus says.

As a group, we step over the first small duct and cautiously enter the maze of pipes.

There are pipes behind, in front of us, and running over our heads. We duck and crouch to get under them in places. Most are freezing, but I can feel intense heat coming off a few of them.

We make good progress at first, despite our injuries and the temperature. I'm in the lead, narrowly ahead of Gadya and David. I'm starting to think we'll be through this maze in another minute or so.

Of course, right then I reach a pipe that I can't circumvent.

It's huge, about eight feet in diameter, and crusted in places with frost and jagged icicles. Gadya and David crawl out from under the pipe behind me, and we all gaze up at the pipe blocking our way.

There's no way to pass underneath it because it's resting right on the ground. And we can't walk sideways along it because other pipes descend from above and block the path.

Rika, Markus and James emerge behind us.

I'm still staring at the pipe. 'I guess we have to climb over it? Even if we don't know what's on the other side.'

'Agreed,' Gadya says.

'I can help everyone up,' Markus declares. 'But who's gonna help me?'

'Once the last person's on top of the pipe, they can lean down and pull you up,' David points out. 'It's not gonna be easy, though.'

Markus nods. He moves closer to the pipe and kneels, making a cradle for someone's foot. I step forward first. It was my idea to climb over the pipe. I'm willing to be the one to face whatever's on the other side.

'Put your foot in my hands and I'll hoist you up,' Markus instructs. I do what he says. One frozen boot goes into his hand. The other lodges on the side of the pipe, as do my hands. The pipe is freezing, but my gloves and clothes protect my skin.

For a second, I sway there awkwardly. Then I lean forward, clawing my way on to the top of the pipe as Markus pushes my boot up with his hands. I feel the icy thrumming pipe beneath me, the cold instantly penetrating my jacket.

Once I get on top, I try to peer around from my new vantage point, but all I see are more pipes and buildings stretching ahead of us. My stomach sinks. It looks impassable.

I glance back at the curved silver building and see that there might be a way back around to it, if we can get over this pipe and then squeeze under a couple of thinner pipes to our left. We could huddle and regroup there.

I hear Gadya yell, 'Hurry up, Alenna!' I look down at the patch of ground I'll be landing on, and I get into a squat. It's just icy concrete at the bottom, and I'm going to be coming down hard.

Here goes nothing. I take a breath and then I jump, pushing off from the pipe with the soles of my feet.

I hit the ground, stagger, and almost fall. But somehow I manage to keep my balance. 'I made it!' I call back.

'I'm next!' Gadya yells.

I hustle off to one side, so I'm out of the way when she jumps. Ahead of me, I catch a glimpse of the silver building, stretching onwards beyond the pipes. As I keep staring, squinting between the pipes, I think I see some variations in its surface, way in the distance.

It almost looks like there could be a doorway up ahead.

Of course, even if it is a doorway, I know we have a huge struggle ahead of us. How are we going to get the door open? And how are we going to find whatever vehicles brought us to the wheel, let alone hijack one of them? I wonder if Rika knows more than she's saying.

I almost wish we could turn back around now and get home to the village. With our knowledge, we could assemble a new party for a second expedition – one that might have a better chance of succeeding.

But there's no way to turn back, even if we wanted to. The frozen lake, now turned into hundreds of icy slabs, would make that impossible. And the undulating barrier would trap us on the wrong side of the grey zone, with no fireworks to help us get through.

So I give up on that idea and keep staring at the silver building, trying to figure out if what I see in the distance really is a door. Or if it's just wishful thinking. I hear David and Markus start helping Gadya on to the pipe behind me.

'Gadya—' I begin loudly, about to yell back to her about the possible doorway.

But then I hear a distant buzzing sound.

One that strikes dread in my heart.

'No!' I scream at my companions, who are still stuck on the other side of the pipe. 'Feeler attack!'

I suppose I knew the feelers would find us again. I hoped they wouldn't, but the whole time I've been afraid of this. Maybe they were just waiting until we got trapped in the pipes, so they could pick us off one by one.

The others hear the sound too, and their desperate screams mingle with the noise of the rotors. Gadya's head suddenly appears over the pipe, unleashing a litany of curses.

I stare up at the sky, paralysed. I spot the feeler within half a second. It's like a distant black helicopter zooming towards us, not even trying to stay hidden in the clouds any more.

'Gadya, hurry!' I scream. On top of the pipe, she's the most exposed. If this feeler gets any of us, it's going to get her. I lunge at the pipe, trying to help pull her down, as I hear another sound. I look up.

A second feeler is behind the first one.

And behind that one is a third.

They've lifted off from someplace nearby, and all three are making a beeline towards us.

They must have known we were here all along, I realise. The feelers are probably as vast in numbers as the drones. It doesn't matter that we tore one of them out of the sky. Our lives must be nothing more than a game to whoever controls the wheel.

I stretch up and grab Gadya's hands. The whine of the feelers becomes overwhelming as they hover overhead. I pull with all my strength, leaning back, and she slithers over the top of the pipe.

She topples forward on to me, and we tumble back on to the icy ground. My head slams down, making my vision sparkle. I taste copper – I've bitten my tongue. The noise of the feelers roars in.

Gadya gets to her feet unsteadily. 'I think I sprained my ankle when I landed!' she yells.

I scrabble upwards too, reeling with dizziness. Beneath the sounds of the rotors, I still hear screaming on the other side of the pipe.

'Run!' Gadya yells in my face.

'Wait – the others! David!'

She grabs my arm. 'No time! They'd want us to keep going.' I pull back, because I've seen something she hasn't – another pair of hands appearing over the top of the pipe. I realise that Markus and David, in the last moments before they're taken, are trying to heave someone else over. I see that the hands are small. Female. And I know that it's Rika.

Gadya is still trying to drag me along, even with her sprained ankle, but I yank her shoulder as hard as I can. She doesn't understand, and she spins around, looking furious.

'It's Rika!' I yell, pointing at the pipe.

Gadya finally sees her. A look drifts into Gadya's eyes. It's the look of a divided soul. She wants to help save her friend. But she also knows that if we all get taken, our entire journey will have been for nothing.

I understand where she's coming from, but there's no way I can leave Rika. Not the girl who's been so kind to me. Who counselled me after Liam's death. Who probably has the biggest heart of anyone in the village. And, as one of Veidman's fail-safes, also probably knows more about this city than me and Gadya combined.

'We don't have a choice!' I yell at Gadya. 'We've gotta help her!'

For a second, I think Gadya's going to bail on me and stagger off, squeezing under the pipes to get away. But then her eyes narrow and she yells, 'Let's go for it!'

We both race forward and leap up at the pipe again. By now, the feelers are overhead. I expect their mechanical limbs to wrap around my torso at any second. I won't have the energy to fight this time. But for some reason that doesn't happen – maybe because it's too hard for the tentacles to get a good angle between the pipes.

Rika is sobbing hysterically. Gadya gets a foothold on some ice and manages to climb all the way back on to the pipe, despite her ankle. She grabs one of Rika's hands. I reach up, trying to grab the other one, but it's too high.

Gadya starts pulling Rika forward on to our side. We're being battered by the noise and wind of the rotors. Tentacles finally start slamming down and slapping against the pipes.

I get hold of the arm of Rika's jacket, and Gadya and I start pulling her over the edge of the pipe. The world contracts to my immediate surroundings as I tune out the noise of the feelers.

But then they start descending all at once.

I manage to grab Rika and pull her down to the ground at the last second, falling next to her with a thump. Two tentacles lash out at the pipe, inches away from us. Rika panics and tries to get up, but I press her head down. 'Don't move!' I yell. 'Not yet!' I feel wind whip above my hair as another tentacle whisks past, probing for flesh.

I look up at the pipe and realise that Gadya is still stuck up there from trying to rescue Rika. She's sprawled across the pipe as a feeler hovers directly above her, the wind from its blades ruffling her hair. I see that the second feeler is just a hundred yards away, moving with horrifying speed and accuracy.

The feeler above the pipe spirals upwards for a moment, like it's trying to see the big picture. I know we can't stay here. It'll figure out how to get all of us within seconds, despite the pipes.

'Ready?' I whisper at Rika. 'We're gonna have to run!' She doesn't answer. But I know she heard me. Time has run out.

I glance back at Gadya, catching her eyes. She knows what she has to do.

I burst up, lunging forward, and Rika follows, leaping up from the icy concrete alongside me. I hear Gadya fling herself off the pipe and down on to the ground. I spin around. She's a few paces behind us, gasping and limping.

'Go!' she yells. 'Under the pipes!'

We race for the nearest ones and slide beneath them, slithering through the narrow space under the cold tubes. The tentacles are just a few feet above us, slamming against the pipes and making them rattle.

'We gotta get to the building and find shelter,' I gasp. 'I think there's a door ahead. I'm not sure.' Another tentacle whips past above us. I don't know what's going to happen to the boys.

Then we're on our feet again, running.

I scramble under another pipe, and when I re-emerge, I finally see the doorway unobstructed. It's a large white hatch about a hundred feet ahead in the side of the curved silver building. Tentacles start descending again, their whirring noises loud as they slice through the air like swords. One glances off my shoulder, almost knocking me off balance. I shriek and zigzag.

I can hear Markus and David screaming in the distance, doing battle against the other feelers, trying to buy us time.

I run and slip on patches of ice, attempting to avoid the feeler hovering above us. It seems like its tentacles are everywhere. We leap and stagger over pipes, trying to reach the hatch in the wall. It resembles a door for some kind of airlock.

Of course it won't be unlocked, I realise. Why would it be? I doubt the people who control this island would be so careless. *And if it's not unlocked, we're all going to die.* The only thing that gives me hope is that this entire city is in total disrepair and seems abandoned. Maybe the hatch will just open right up, like the door to some empty tenement back in the UNA. And if it isn't too cold in this part of the building, we can run inside and hide.

We're almost there, having successfully navigated the pipes, when I hear a rattling noise behind me, followed by the ear-piercing shriek of a descending feeler. At the same time, I hear Gadya yell.

But when I turn, I see that it's Rika who's in trouble.

The feeler has got her, and it's already pulling her upwards, its metal limbs intertwined with hers. The feeler's spotlight has turned on. Harsh light reflects off the icy pipes and ground, blinding us as its noise deafens us.

'*Help!*' Rika cries, pulling against the tentacles encircling her waist and chest.

I turn back and flail at her, beating on the tentacles, trying to keep the monstrous things from taking her. But truthfully, I don't have any more strength left than Rika does. Everything is happening faster and faster. The tentacles tighten around Rika's arms and legs, preparing to take her away for good.

'No!' I rail at the feeler. 'It's not fair! Let her go!'

My anger is infectious. 'You son of a bitch!' Rika yells at

the feelers. It's the first time I've ever heard her curse. '*You can't have me! Not now! Not ever!*'

Gadya joins me in attacking the feeler with our frozen hands. Miniature gears grind inside the tentacles. For a moment, I think the feeler is going to give up because we're dragging it down a little. Maybe the three of us can outweigh it after all. Get it to the ground and destroy it, like we did to the one on the lake.

But then a look passes across Rika's eyes, and I know the tentacles have tightened too far, squeezing her ribs, constricting her chest. Her mouth opens. She looks down at us as the feeler starts rising. 'Gadya. Alenna...'

The noise of the rotor increases, like it has received a massive surge of energy. I grip Rika's foot, trying to keep her from vanishing into the sky. Gadya grabs her other leg.

'Don't give up!' Gadya yells. 'Fight the damn thing!'

But this time there will be no victory for us.

The tentacles coil like elastic bands. And then suddenly, Rika's foot is ripped right out of my hands. The force is unbelievable. I'm thrown back on to the ground, stunned, holding her empty boot.

I look up just in time to see the feeler hurl Rika upwards, towards the clouds. It begins zooming away, with Rika's limp body dangling beneath it.

Gadya falls back. Her hands are bleeding again, more flesh ripped from her fingers. My hands are stinging, so I look down at them. They're bleeding through the gloves too. Lacerations mark my palms like stigmata.

Gadya and I stare at each other.

Rika is gone.

And Markus, David and James are trapped behind the big pipe, probably about to be taken.

There are only two of us left.

I want to cry. I want to shut my eyes and make this whole terrible place disappear. But there's no time for self-pity. We're easy targets, and there are other feelers on the loose.

'The hatch!' I call out, breaking the spell. Gadya and I start moving towards it. Gadya can barely walk, cursing as she limps and hobbles her way forward. I put my arm around her shoulders, trying to support her.

I'm certain the other feelers are going to chase us, but when I look over my shoulder, I see they're still battling David, Markus and James. I turn back around and keep moving with Gadya.

Seconds later, I hear the awful sound of someone being taken.

And then someone else.

I turn again, just in time to see Markus being pulled up into the sky. Then I catch a glimpse of another feeler heaving James into the heavens, his black robes flapping, his mouth open in a frightened, disbelieving *O*.

There is nothing we can do for them. Gadya and I keep heading towards the hatch.

Another feeler has descended behind us. I hear David yelling as he tries to fight it off alone. I can't stand feeling so powerless any more.

'David!' I scream, looking back one last time. I see the feeler pulling his struggling body up into the sky. He has sacrificed everything so that Gadya and I have a chance to survive. I turn back around. I can't watch any more – the pain is too great.

Gadya and I reach the hatch within seconds. Up close I see that it's huge and round, nearly the width and height of a single-car garage door. The words 'MAINTENANCE HATCH No. 12' are stencilled on it in red paint.

I throw out my hands, grabbing the large hydraulic wheel that serves as its handle. I desperately hope we'll find refuge from the feelers in this building, even if we just curl up and freeze to death inside it.

Gadya grabs the wheel too. We both crank the handle with all our strength, screaming as we hear more feelers in the sky above us, getting louder. The metal wheel feels locked and immobilised at first.

Then, with a sudden hiss, the wheel slowly starts to turn...

SELECTED

'It's open!' I yell, barely believing our good fortune. Part of me thinks I'm hallucinating. Another part thinks it's a trap and an army of feelers is going to burst out and fly us up into the void.

'Go, go, go!' Gadya screams at me.

We yank the hatch wide open. As pressurised air pours out, we fling ourselves inside.

I don't know where we're headed, or who or what we'll find there. I just tell myself it can't be worse than what's outside.

Gadya sprawls to the floor, clutching her damaged ankle as I slam the huge door shut. I spin the handle, trying to lock us inside and keep the feelers out. I hear a clank, and the handle stops turning.

I'm gasping for air. I lean over, heaving, trying to listen for the feelers. There's nothing but silence.

I gaze around. We're inside a frigid, square cement chamber. It's cold but doesn't have the dry-ice feeling. It's dimly lit by a few recessed fluorescent bulbs, and the concrete walls are slick with ice.

Three large metal doorways to our left appear to lead into further catacombs. I can see icy stalactites hanging down

340

from the high ceiling, as though pipes have leaked and the water has frozen. The floor is pretty much a sheet of ice, as slippery as the frozen lake.

'Where is everyone?' Gadya asks, trying to get a look at her ankle. Indeed, the space is deserted, like it was abandoned long ago.

'I don't know.' I can barely speak, and not just because I'm out of breath. I'm mourning all of our friends. I failed to help David – after he saved me so many times. Just like I couldn't save Liam. And now there's no way to ever make it up to them.

'I thought there'd be people in here,' Gadya says, her voice rising in a groan of desperation. Her fists are clenched, but there's no one around for her to fight. 'None of this makes any sense!'

'It looks like no one's been here for years.'

'How is that possible?'

I hear the raw panic in her voice. This is not the place either of us expected. It's not the gleaming nerve centre of a city. It's just an empty hole inside an old industrial building.

'Liam, Sinxen, Markus,' Gadya says. 'David, too. They died for this? *For this?*'

I gaze around. 'At least they have lights in here. That means they've got power. Which is more than we had at the village.'

Gadya doesn't respond. I see a bank of dusty computer monitors embedded in one of the walls. They're all dead, their LCD screens cracked and frozen.

Gadya sinks against a concrete pillar. 'I think my ankle's broken from jumping off that pipe. I can't move it any more. Not even a little.'

'We have to go deeper and find somewhere to hide,' I tell her urgently. 'Then we can rest.'

Gadya nods. She sits there wincing in pain as I start trying to open the metal doors closest to us. The first two are either locked or I'm not strong enough to open them. Then I come to the final one, the largest of the three, which has a huge concrete arch above it. A sign next to the door reads BALCONY DELTA OPENING: PORTAL TWELVE.

Gadya watches me with hooded eyes.

'It's not over until we give up,' I tell her. 'And I haven't given up yet. Have you?'

'Never,' she spits back.

I grip the third door's chrome wheel handle. It's freezing, and my gloves are in tatters. I put all my strength into it as I try to crank the wheel. At first I think it's never going to turn, that it's either locked or frozen shut.

And then it gives.

I turn the handle faster, spinning it. The door begins to move. I leap back as it starts opening outwards, under its own power.

Gadya is startled too. She pushes herself off the floor. We know that anything could come through this door.

But nothing does, except stale air. It's like we've broken into a mausoleum. Inside is blackness, with a few small lights burning white in the darkness like electric candles.

Neither Gadya nor I say anything. We just stand there for a moment, completely puzzled.

'It's deserted,' Gadya finally says. 'Like the rest of this place.'

We creep closer to the entrance, trying to understand what's going on. My teeth are chattering so hard, my jaw hurts.

I take one step forward and then another, passing through the archway with Gadya at my side.

Immediately, I sense that we've walked into a much larger space. One that is slightly warmer than the outside. But it's hard to get oriented here. The scattered white lights don't make sense to me. They seem to float in the air, like fallen stars.

'Alenna,' Gadya says. I feel her fingers grasping for my sleeve. 'I can't see you.'

I slow down, and we find each other's hands. I take one more step and put my foot down.

I hear a strange echoing click, like I've triggered something. I stop dead in my tracks.

A millisecond later, the entire space explodes in a blaze of white light.

I reel back, as light glares at us from all directions. I press my hands against my eyes and sink to the icy floor.

For a sickening moment I think maybe I'm dead. That I stepped on a mine or booby trap meant to thwart intruders. Then I realise I can still hear Gadya trying to talk to me. So I can't be dead. *Not yet.*

I open my eyes, but I keep my hands over them, peeking out through my fingers. I still can't see anything because the room is impossibly, overwhelmingly bright.

'Alenna – it's OK,' Gadya tells me.

I open my fingers a little bit more, still squinting through the gaps.

As my eyes adjust, I'm surprised at what I see. We seem to be at one end of a colossal semicircular chamber, curving off to our left like a horseshoe. From here, it appears to have no end.

I turn to Gadya. She has lowered her hands from her eyes. I slowly do the same.

Along one side of the chamber is a curved white wall with an endless array of video monitors on it. Unlike the ones in the maintenance antechamber, these look unbroken, although none of them is turned on.

I get up and tentatively step towards the nearest one. Electronic buttons are recessed into the wall everywhere – thousands of them, as though we're in a gigantic control room. *Maybe this is the place we've been seeking!*

I realise that the blinding whiteness is emanating from banks of glaring fluorescent lights. They're on the ceiling, the wall, and even on the floor, encased in translucent tiles underneath our feet.

Opposite the white wall is a massive curved window made from huge panes of thick glass. I can't see what's behind it because it's so dark out there. All we see are our own reflections. I notice additional computer consoles jutting up from the floor in front of the window, covered with dials and controls.

'What is all this stuff?' Gadya asks, leaning against the wall to take the weight off her wounded ankle.

Before I can even begin to speculate, I'm interrupted:

'Hello there!' a female voice crackles loudly above my head, making both of us shriek. The voice ricochets off the floor and the glass wall like a sonic bullet.

I look up, staring directly into a circular loudspeaker in the ceiling. I see more speakers stretching off into the distance around the curve.

'Someone else is here!' I yell at Gadya excitedly. Of course I realise that they'll inevitably want to punish us for escaping our sector and breaking into their city. Maybe they'll even kill us. But at this point, anything is better than getting massacred by the feelers or freezing to death.

Gadya tilts her head back. 'Help us!' she demands. 'We're from the blue sector!'

'It's a pleasure to welcome you to the Silver Shore Terminal on Prison Island Alpha,' the voice replies stridently, loaded with forced optimism. 'I was not expecting guests today, but our staff will do our best to accommodate you—'

'Just send someone down to get us!' I yell, barely listening. 'We're freezing and we're injured! We surrender, but we need help—'

The voice keeps talking over me.

'A staff member will be with you shortly,' it informs us in bright tones. 'If you require a beverage, please ask one of our receptionists for assistance.'

Receptionists? Beverages? I look at Gadya, thinking, *What the hell is this lady talking about?* There's nothing here but ice.

'We need your help, damn it!' Gadya screams at the speaker above her.

'If you require rest after your journey, you're welcome to take seats in the waiting area on concourse B,' the voice continues blithely. 'Just follow the dotted lights.' As if by magic, a pathway of red-lighted panels brightens the floor, leading off down the curve of the horseshoe. 'A tour guide will be with you shortly. If you have a prearranged appointment, please speak the letters of your guide's last name, and I will page your contact.'

I spin to face Gadya, finally understanding. 'It's not real!' I say. 'It's a recording. A computer program.'

Gadya's face reflects my emotions.

Total, absolute despair.

'Because at the Silver Shore Terminal,' the voice continues babbling, 'your comfort and satisfaction are our primary goals.'

I have no clue what this building is, or why this automated voice is speaking to us now, but it continues, undeterred.

'My video feed indicates that no staff members are currently available. So I invite you to take your seats in the waiting area.' The lighted panels on the floor start flashing more insistently.

'Video feed,' Gadya mutters. 'Did you hear that?' We immediately start looking around for cameras.

Finally I see one, up high on the ceiling above the door. It's the first camera I've seen since the one near the spiral staircase, the first day I arrived on the wheel. Gadya and I both start waving at it. Even though this voice is automated, maybe there's a human somewhere out there in the darkness, watching us.

'I notice that you are signalling to me,' the voice says. 'If you have a request, please speak to the receptionist. Remember, a staff member will be with you shortly.'

'Screw you!' Gadya screams, head tilted up at the speakers again, her voice raw. 'Rot in hell!'

I stop waving at the camera. The voice is just saying the same things over and over. I was hoping I could ask it questions and get some answers. Clearly, that's not going to happen.

Or so I think – until the voice abruptly changes in pitch. It's still female, but now it sounds deeper and more serious. 'I apologise for the delay. We here at the Silver Shore Terminal take pride in our punctuality. It is possible your guide has been unexpectedly detained. If you wish, you may request the automated tour function. Just say "automatic mode".'

I do what the voice says.

The lights dim slightly, and I try to see out of that huge, mysterious window. But beyond all the reflections, it still looks blacker than the night sky.

'Welcome. I will be your automated tour guide this afternoon,' the new voice continues. 'My name is Clara. C-L-A-R-A. At any time you may interrupt this tour, and

I will do my best to answer any questions.'

I take that as my invitation. 'Where are we?'

'You are on Balcony Delta.'

'No, I mean, what is this place?'

'Balcony Delta,' the voice repeats, with the exact same inflection.

'What does that even mean?' Gadya presses. 'What does Balcony Delta do? Where are the aircrafts?'

There's no answer this time.

I stare at Gadya helplessly. Under the lights, I see how dirty and grimy she is. Her piercings are dull and encrusted with blood. I see my own reflection in the glass wall and realise I look just as haggard. I barely recognise the filthy, skinny girl staring back at me. I look like a wild animal.

'This isn't working,' Gadya mutters.

'What's behind all those windows?' I ask the robotic voice, trying another tactic.

'Windows?' It's like the voice just recognises certain words and ignores the rest of the sentence. 'This gallery window is the focal point of Balcony Delta, which is one of twelve viewing portals in the Silver Shore Terminal. The windows are made from a Plexiglas-silicone hybrid, fourteen inches thick, to provide maximum viewer protection.'

'Protection from what?'

My question throws the voice. 'I'm sorry. I do not understand.'

Gadya speaks up. 'She means, what the hell's behind that glass?'

For some reason, the voice likes her phrasing more than mine. 'Behind the glass is the Silver Shore specimen archive. We've processed more than fifty per cent of the island's specimens, making this the largest processing facility on Island Alpha—'

'The island!' I jump in. 'How do we get off it?'

I don't think there's any chance the voice will answer that one. But to my shock, it does. 'The helipads and aircraft landing strips are located on the roof level of Terminal C. Please contact a staff member to request all relevant scheduling data.'

'Can we get off this island without a helicopter or an airplane?' Gadya asks.

'I'm sorry. I do not understand.'

I leap in. 'Is there a boat? A bridge? *Anything?*'

'I'm sorry. I do not understand.'

Gadya yells and kicks at the wall with her good foot. Her boot leaves a dark smudge on the white surface. We stand there, freezing and dirty, not sure what to do next.

'Hey, what did it mean by "specimens"?' Gadya finally asks me. 'It said that earlier. Did you hear?'

The voice decides to answer before I can. 'All specimen test subjects are flash frozen in a cryoprotectant solution, and held at minus fifty degrees Fahrenheit, to minimise cellular decay.' It pauses. 'Do you wish to view the specimens?'

'Yes,' Gadya and I say, at the exact same moment.

The fluorescent lights start dimming again, and our

horseshoe-shaped room grows darker until there's barely any light at all.

'Please step forward to the observation window,' the voice instructs.

Finally, as the lights in our horseshoe fade to total blackness and the ambient light beyond the window begins to rise, I'm able to see through the glass.

'This facility is currently running at ninety-three point seven per cent capacity.'

I ignore the voice for a moment and struggle to make sense of the strange shapes emerging from the darkness. The glass is as cold as ice. Way too cold to touch. I feel it trying to burn the tip of my nose when I lean forward.

'The specimen archive is the heart of this facility,' the voice continues. 'More than one hundred test subjects are processed here every day. That includes harvesting, freezing and transportation to their position in the grid. The specimens are then held until they get recalled to Mexico City Three in the UNA, for clinical tissue biopsies and live dissection...'

Live dissection? Tissue biopsies? I'm still just trying to figure out what I'm looking at. Then, as the lights within the massive black space are adjusted more precisely, I finally realise what is being held inside it.

'*No!*' I gasp.

My legs turn to jelly as the air is sucked out of my lungs. I get a strange floaty feeling, like I'm about to faint.

Gadya claws at me, clutching on to my arm. I grab her

back, holding her close. I literally cannot believe what we are seeing beyond the glass.

'The archive currently houses more than ten thousand specimens,' the voice burbles, oblivious to our horror. 'Our efficiency rate is the highest of any station. We are proud to be the number one processing plant on Island Alpha, for the second consecutive year.'

'Burn in hell!' Gadya suddenly screams, kicking at one of the monitors, splintering its glass screen.

'I'm sorry. I do not understand.'

Tears run down my face. I know that Gadya is crying too, wracking sobs that make her shoulders shake.

'Don't look,' I whisper. 'We don't have to look.'

'No, I want to.' She leans back up to stare down through the glass. I do the same, because I can't help myself.

What I see are human bodies.

Ten thousand of them, hanging on vertical metal beams inside an incredibly vast subterranean space, descending hundreds of feet deep.

The bodies are strung up inside semitranslucent pods that appear to be made of metal and plastic, stretching into infinity. Only the people's heads are visible through small portholes. The pods are filled with fluid, circulated by plastic tubing that flows back into the beams that support them. Catwalks and metal stairways run beneath each row of bodies, like internal scaffolding.

I know these frozen bodies are alive, but they have the grey pallor of corpses. It's like a nightmare cemetery, one in which the bodies are denied any respect or grace.

These are the 'specimens'.

They're just kids from the wheel. Kids like us. Exiles.

And given what the voice said about it being the number one processing facility, there must be other places like it on the wheel.

'How—' I begin. 'How did this happen?'

'I'm sorry. I do not understand.'

I want to kill the repetitive blandly innocuous voice. Want to find whatever computer controls it and smash it into a million pieces.

But we need answers, and right now this voice is the only hope we have of getting some. 'How did these kids –' I can't bring myself to say 'specimens' – end up here?'

'All specimens run free-range on this island. Each one has been individually acquired by our automatic UNA-51 High Altitude Selection Units, with minimal tissue damage. All selection units are equipped with flight capabilities, and the capacity to acquire and disable uncooperative subjects with minor energy expenditure.'

'Selection units. That's what the feelers are,' I mutter to Gadya tiredly.

We are just test subjects. Specimens. *But why?*

'Our selection units have an eighty-four per cent success rate in accurately acquiring their target samples,' the voice regales us proudly. It doesn't understand or care that it's talking about human beings. 'Our staff can brief you on the latest data.'

'You have no staff,' I finally say, my voice echoing in my ears. 'The staff you keep talking about? They're gone. No one's here but you, and all these frozen bodies.'

It picks up on the word 'you'. 'Yes, I am Clara, your automated guide—'

'Your staff has left you here, but you don't care,' I continue. 'And you never will. Because you're not human. You're a machine. The UNA has automated mass murder.'

The voice doesn't have an answer for that one. Maybe I've finally confounded it.

I stare out the window, looking at all those bodies again. I imagine being frozen is like being in a coma, but worse.

I struggle to keep control over my sanity. More questions occur to me, creeping into my mind like dark tendrils of thought.

'Where do you think all the people running things went?' I whisper to Gadya. 'I mean, the scientists or doctors, or police. Or whoever built this place?'

'They left.' She can barely speak.

'Maybe there was an accident,' I whisper back. 'Everything's automated, but it's in shambles, and it's so cold in this zone. That can't be normal. Maybe there's a crack in the cooling mechanism.' I pause. 'It just seems like things are still running, but no one's around to check on them any more.'

'Maybe no one's around because they don't need to be. Everything's probably functioning fine.' She laughs bitterly. 'It's just us *specimens* here. And selection units – whipping us off to get dissected. This place isn't running by mistake.'

'But why? Why are we worth testing?'

The lights on the other side of the window begin to dim again, as the horseshoe lights around us are raised. In a way I'm relieved, because we won't have to keep staring at the awful sight of ten thousand frozen bodies.

Then I'm suddenly thinking about something else. *Liam.*

My dad's message carved on the rock meant 'Never give up'. He'd want me to find the meaning when there seems to be none.

Although it seems unlikely, if these bodies are being held alive, maybe there's some way of unfreezing and resuscitating them before they get shipped off the wheel.

'Hello?' I call out to the voice, eager to communicate with it again. 'Is there a way to find out who—' I break off, trying to reformulate my question. 'Is there a way to track individual specimens being held in the archive? Can you do that?'

'Tracking test subjects is possible through our data link.' A touch-screen panel lights up nearby. I step over to it, followed by a limping Gadya. 'Enter the UNA identity number of your required specimen.'

'We don't know their identity numbers!' Gadya calls out angrily. 'They have names! Not numbers! Liam, Markus, Rika, David!'

'What about dates of capture?' I ask suddenly. 'I mean the date the specimens were "harvested". Can you search by date?'

'Affirmative,' the voice replies blithely. 'Please use two digits for the day, two for the month, and four digits for the year.'

Before the voice has finished talking, I'm already punching in numbers for yesterday's date. 10-20-2032. The day Liam was taken.

It takes me only a second to input the digits.

'Processing…' the voice says. Then it asks, 'Male or female?'

'Male.'

'Height and weight?'

Gadya and I guess as best we can, blurting out words, talking over each other.

'Five eleven—'

'Wait, six feet—'

'One hundred and fifty pounds—'

'No, one forty—'

Then the voice declares, 'Possible subject located.' A nearby computer screen flares to life. On it is a blurred photograph of Liam's face, with a stream of data running up the right-hand side in a dizzying column.

'That's him!' I yell. I run to the window, Gadya at my side. 'Where is he? Tell us!' I'm sick with excitement. 'Is he still in the archive? *Is he still alive?*'

It picks up on my final word. 'All specimens are alive, and suitable for shipping.'

'Where is he, then!' I yell, feeling like my chest is about to burst. If I know where he is, I can try to get to him.

'Specimen number 112-782-B is currently being held on level twenty, which is viewable from this gallery window. That specimen has not been shipped for processing yet.' The voice pauses. 'However, his pod is scheduled to depart this station in fifty-six minutes, on Airbus Gamma.'

I barely hear what the voice is saying.

Liam is still here.

Alive.

There is hope.

Gadya and I clutch each other.

'We have to save him!' I yell.

'I know.'

Then, as we look out the window, I see a light begin to glow in the distance. It's very faint, way out there in the rows of bodies, hanging in endless darkness. The light is about two hundred feet down, and slightly off to our left.

'I have illuminated your requested specimen,' the voice tell us, sounding pleased with itself. For once I don't mind.

'Liam,' I murmur, staring out the window at the distant light far below us. 'They haven't dissected him yet. But we've only got fifty-six minutes.'

'I can't believe it.' Gadya looks like she's going to cry.

'We have to get to him,' I say, swallowing over the lump in my throat. 'Then try to rescue the others, too.'

Gadya and I start rapidly punching in dates, giving information and physical descriptions as fast as we can. Rika. Markus. David. Even James. Everyone we can think of.

Scattered dots light up in the vast dark space, as images of their faces flit past on the computer screen. None of them have time restrictions like Liam does. He's the only one whose pod is scheduled to leave the wheel today.

But one of the four is completely absent.

David.

'How can he not be here?' I ask. Neither the computer nor Gadya knows. It's like there's no trace of him. 'Has he already been taken to another facility?' I wonder out loud, scared for him.

We try everything, but the computer refuses to recognise anything we say. There is no match for David whatsoever. It's another mystery. Where else could the feeler have taken him but here?

'How long do we have until Liam – I mean, the first specimen – departs?' I ask, desperate to keep track of the time, trying to focus on what's most important to me now.

'Forty-nine minutes and thirty-five seconds,' the voice replies. I stare out at Liam's faint light, shining like a star in the darkness.

'We need to thaw him out and bring him back,' Gadya tells the voice. 'How do we do that?'

There's a brief silence.

Then the words crash in. 'Thawing is only possible using the manual controls on each pod.'

'Then we need to get down there.'

'Your request cannot be granted.'

'Why not?' I challenge.

'Guests cannot enter the specimen archive without authorised supervision,' the voice replies. 'The subzero temperature necessitates the use of an LS-8 zone suit inside, which can only be operated by a qualified staff member.'

'Like we told you, there aren't any staff members,' I say. 'There's just you and there's us. It's an emergency!'

'I'm sorry,' the voice begins again, but I'm already looking around. *A zone suit*, I'm thinking. *What is that, and where can I find one?*

Gadya and I quickly answer that question once we start exploring. There are a number of white doors further around the curve of the horseshoe. One of them is marked LS-8's/ SERVICE ELEVATOR FIVE. I rush over to it and put my hands on its wheel handle, trying to turn it. But just as I reach it, I hear clicking noises and realise that it has just been locked. By Clara.

'Open this door right now!' I yell.

'I'm sorry,' the voice says sharply. 'You are attempting to enter a restricted area.'

I begin yanking harder on the wheel. Gadya hobbles over and joins me.

'Cease your actions immediately,' the voice admonishes us. 'If you do not, I will be forced to request security personnel.'

'Good luck with that,' I mutter as we keep trying to open the door. But it remains locked.

'You are breaking Silver Shore protocol. I will enact security measures if you do not desist.'

Gadya grabs my arm. I turn to her, and she puts a finger to her lips. I don't understand at first. Then she points at a red switch a few feet away, encased in a glass-panelled box on the wall. I hadn't noticed it before, because there are so many switches and buttons everywhere. 'What?'

'Look closer,' she mouths silently.

I stop trying to crank the wheel. I slowly walk over and stare at the switch for a second, reading the words printed next to it:

MANUAL OVERRIDE: FOR LS-8'S
AND SERVICE ELEVATOR FIVE
EMERGENCY USE ONLY

In smaller type below is written the words:

WARNING! WILL DISABLE C.L.A.R.A.
OPERATING SYSTEM.

I raise my hand and curl my fingers into a fist as Gadya watches, nodding her approval. It's time to put the voice to sleep and get to work saving our friends.

'Do *not* touch that box!' Clara's voice begins, rising into an angry whine. 'Please! Stop. Do not—'

Without thinking about it, I pull back my arm, smash the glass with my fist, and then yank the switch down as hard and fast as I can.

THE ARCHIVE

The switch makes a loud snap, and my knuckles start oozing blood from the broken glass, through my gloves. I clutch my hand, trying to staunch the bleeding.

I don't know what I expected. Maybe lights to start flashing, or for a siren to go off. Or maybe for the observation deck to flood with nerve gas, as punishment for our transgressions. But nothing happens.

'I think we killed it,' Gadya finally says.

I pause, waiting to see if the voice will pipe up. There's only silence. 'Hey!' I call up at the ceiling, just to make sure. 'You still there, Clara? You still gonna stop us?'

No response.

I walk back over to the door. 'Think it'll open now?' I start pulling on the wheel again with Gadya. This time it begins to turn.

It takes both our strength to get the door open, but we manage it. Our frostbitten fingers are barely able to move. The wounds on my knuckles are deep, but because of the cold, I feel barely any pain. I guess that's good, for now.

We stare into the room beyond the door. It's large. Well lit. There's a row of what look like space suits hanging against one wall on hooks – four thin silver one-piece outfits that resemble empty sleeping bags.

These must be the LS-8 zone suits.

Next to them are huge bulbous helmets. On the other side of the room is the metal scaffolding of a freight elevator – no doubt one that descends into the abyss of the specimen archive.

'We have to put the suits on and go down there,' I say. 'And walk until we find Liam. Then figure out how to unthaw him. We're gonna have to bring an extra zone suit to put him in, or he won't make it back up here alive.' I know I'm probably deluded in my optimism, but the fact that Liam is still alive – at least for the next forty minutes or so – makes anything seem possible again.

'Alenna?' I hear Gadya ask. I glance over at her, and see that there's blood seeping out of her boot now. A piece of bone must have finally poked through the skin of her broken ankle. I don't know how she has the strength to ignore that kind of pain. 'Must be a compound fracture. I've been trying to walk around on it, making it worse…' She's swaying, unable to put any weight on it.

I help her sit down, worried. She's injured far worse than I thought. The cold is preventing us from feeling the true extent of our wounds.

'You don't have to come with me,' I tell her, although the thought of being alone down there terrifies me. 'You can stay here. Cover me from the window and make sure everything's OK.'

'I want to go.' Gadya looks at me, eyes burning with pain and frustration. 'I just don't want my ankle to collapse down there and jeopardise it for everyone.'

'Don't worry. It'll be fine.'

She nods grimly, leaning back against the wall. 'I'll keep a good lookout.'

I want to stay and help her, but there's no time. I need to get to Liam.

I walk over to the nearest LS-8 suit and grab it off the wall. It's surprisingly thin and loose; the material feels silky, even though it looks like aluminum foil. The suit's sleeves end in large gloves. I glance at the helmets, which are the opposite of the suit – heavy and cumbersome, like diving helmets.

I start stepping into one of the suits as Gadya watches me. 'You're not gonna win any beauty contests in that thing,' she cracks weakly.

I hoist a helmet up. It's painfully heavy. I take a deep breath and shut my eyes. Then I duck down, putting my head inside the claustrophobic dome.

A second later, I'm staring at Gadya from behind the helmet's glass visor, taking shallow breaths. The helmet is musty and dank, like it hasn't been used in a long time, maybe years. I smell the tang of ancient sweat. I start zipping the suit up and around the base of the helmet, where it makes a seal.

'How's it feel?' Gadya asks, her voice muffled.

'Warmer.' The helmet starts to fog up for a moment, but then it clears. I want to sit down and rest, but I have to keep moving. By now we probably only have half an hour left until Liam's pod departs the Silver Shore for good.

I rapidly take down a suit for Gadya, so she can put it on and try to warm up too.

'I'll be back soon,' I tell her as I help get the suit over her clothes and injured ankle. The swelling is obvious, even through her boot, although at least the bleeding seems to have stopped now that she's not standing up. 'Hopefully with Liam.'

Gadya nods weakly. 'Do the best you can. For both of us.'

'I will.'

I clamber over to the elevator. The whole structure is made of metal wire, like a chicken coop – walls, floor and ceiling. Walking in the suit is difficult because of the helmet, which adds at least twenty pounds. In my right hand, I'm holding the spare suit for Liam, and in my left, a spare helmet. If I can figure out how to save Liam first, then we can ferry our other friends back one by one.

I glance behind me and see Gadya watching. I never thought it would be me right at the end like this. I would have guessed anyone else: Liam, Gadya, Markus, Sinxen, David, or even Rika. I can't let them down.

I pull back the metal grating that serves as the elevator's door, and peer at the touch-screen display hanging on one of the walls. The buttons on the screen are large, designed to accommodate the clunky gloves of the zone suit. I raise my arm and push the button marked LEVEL 20. A second later, the elevator begins to move.

I expected the ride to be smooth. Instead, I hear a grinding squeal as the elevator lurches downwards a few feet and then just hangs there.

I stumble sideways, banging my helmet on the metal grating, trying to keep my balance in the rickety cage. I drop the extra suit and helmet. In my haste, it hadn't occurred to me that the elevator wouldn't work.

It's probably falling apart, like everything else in this abandoned city, I think. My mind flashes with terrible images. What if I get stuck? Or what if the cable snaps, and I plummet straight to the bottom?

Then the elevator lurches again, heading downwards. I clutch at the railings, but it's too hard to grasp them with the gloves on. I press myself against the intersection of two walls. The elevator moves faster, metal still screeching.

Gadya is now many levels above me. I can't see her any more when I look up through the grating, because the angle is too severe. So I peer down at my destination – the sprawling blackness that lies beyond me in every direction except for the few dots of light.

I glance at the elevator panel. Judging from the buttons, there are sixty-six levels. It's like descending into some frozen version of hell. I focus on those twinkling lights in the distance. I don't know how much time I have left before Liam's pod is taken. I'm guessing it's not long.

The elevator finally arrives on level twenty with a juddering halt. I slide the door open with a clatter and stare into the darkness.

For a moment, I wish Clara were still around, so I could ask her where to go. From here, it's harder to see the lighted pod that holds Liam's body. I can barely make out faint traces of illumination around the corner of a narrow walkway, about a quarter of a mile ahead.

I pick up the extra suit and helmet, and lug them out of the elevator. The sound of my breath is loud in my ears.

I sense frigid temperatures beyond the confines of the suit. I can only wonder in horror what it would be like to get flash frozen like Liam. One second you're alive – warm and human – and the next, you're encapsulated in an airless icy pod for the rest of eternity. *Or until you get dissected.*

Dragging the suit and helmet behind me, I start walking along the metal catwalk leading towards rows of pods. I turn back occasionally to stare up at the lighted horseshoe of windows way above me. I feel like I'm at the bottom of the ocean. There's no sign of Gadya.

It's so dark that it seems like a dream. There are levels below me, levels above. But there is nothing to guide me. I can barely see my gloved hand in front of my face, and can only make out the faintest outlines of the pods as I grow closer to them.

When I finally reach the first row, I have to stop and rest for a second to catch my breath. Up close, the pods look like vertical coffins with rounded edges. Egglike, made of some sort of smooth white material. Each one hangs a foot off the catwalk.

A very faint cyan glow comes from underneath them.

I see pipes running into each individual pod. They seem to be part of the massive cooling system. I peer into the nearest pod, but its viewing portal is dark, so I can't see anyone inside.

I run my gloves over its surface as I prepare to resume my journey. It's all buttons and knobs. I'm just about to take my hand away, when my thumb brushes against a stray switch.

A square of light suddenly blazes into my face, refracted into prisms by my glass visor. I realise that I'm looking at a video monitor instead of an actual porthole – and it's showing a live video feed from inside the pod, displaying the face of its occupant.

It's a boy I don't know. A random drone. His painted face looks like it's been carved out of wax. A mechanism is locked around his head like a medical halo, keeping him immobilised. His eyes are shut, and he's wearing an oxygen mask.

The bottom of the video monitor displays a row of red numbers. An additional series of moving lines is tracking his vital signs. All the lines are flat, but no alarms are going off.

I realise the pod is like a reverse life support system. There is a problem only if the boy starts heating up and his heart begins beating again. *A flat line in this terrible place means that everything is in great shape.*

I tear myself away from the capsule, pick up the extra suit and helmet, and start moving rapidly down the catwalk again. I can see Liam's light in the distance, blinking and flickering. Calling to me.

I suppose that here, in a weird way, I've found the Fountain of Youth. None of these kids will ever age. But it's a terrible fountain, because it sucks your life away. These kids are preserved just as surely as if they were dead and embalmed.

I walk for what seems like forever. Without the suit it might have taken me only two more minutes to reach Liam. But with the suit on, it's more like ten minutes, and I'm well aware that our time is running out. On either side of me are unending rows of pods. They're dark, but I know that almost every single one of them is filled with a frozen body.

It's so silent with the helmet on that between breaths I hear faint static in my ears. It's like the sounds of the island are still inside my head, keeping me company. I wonder if I'll ever be rid of them.

I continue walking.

By the time I reach the illuminated pod that holds Liam's body, I'm drenched with sweat, even though the air outside my suit is far below zero. My hair is soaking, and I blink strands out of my eyes.

I manoeuver myself awkwardly along the catwalk in front of Liam's pod. Beams of white light are pouring out from behind it, like miniature spotlights, delineating its contours.

I've been trying not to think too much about what I'm going to do. I'm not sure what buttons to push, or if I can thaw him in time.

I long to see his blue eyes open. To hear his voice again. To feel his touch on my skin. Plus, I could use his help right about now.

Because his pod is so well lit, it's easy for me to decipher the controls on the front of it. I see a switch marked VIEW, so I flick that one first.

The video screen activates, and Liam's face appears with crystal clarity. I stand there staring at him in awe. His eyes are shut, and the oxygen mask obscures part of his face. His brown hair drifts in the fluid. My breath gets frozen for a moment like the air. It's almost too much for me to take.

He's alive after all.

The very thought is shocking; I guess part of me didn't really believe it.

'Liam,' I murmur. He looks peaceful. Uninjured. I'd think he was sleeping, except for the halo and the oxygen mask.

I quickly pull the lever marked MANUAL OVERRIDE. I'm expecting an instant reaction from the pod, but nothing happens.

I spot a number on the upper corner of the screen, like a countdown clock. It reads '–15:49'. I assume that's how many minutes I have left until Liam gets taken from me again. *I'm not going to let that happen.*

I glance down at all the dials and knobs on the pod. I was hoping that the process of thawing people out would be more intuitive. But most of these knobs might as well be labelled with hieroglyphics.

I flick the manual switch up and down again, but there's still no response.

Suddenly the static in my ears gets louder, and I hear an electronic squealing noise that makes me wince. It's followed by a faint voice:

'Alenna?'

'Gadya!' I reply. There must be some kind of speaker system in the helmet.

'I can hear you,' she says through the static. 'I just found a microphone up here.'

'And I found Liam – he's alive! But we don't have long. Fifteen minutes.'

'I can see you down there. I'm watching you right now.'

'I don't know what to do! I can't figure out how to rescue him. This was a crazy idea.' Hot tears of frustration well up in my eyes, and I fight them back down. One escapes and rolls down my cheek. 'Can you help me?'

'I don't know what to do either—' A burst of static cuts her off.

I'm looking all over Liam's pod for a way to thaw him. If there is one, I don't see it. I can't believe the manual override switch didn't work. The clock on his pod now tells me I have only twelve minutes left.

'We have to put Clara back online,' I say finally, still furious at myself for thinking there would just be a button I could push that would solve everything. My luck has finally run out.

'I'm not sure that's a good idea,' Gadya's voice drifts back to me. I can hear the pain and fear in it.

'I know. But can you try? Or we're going to lose him.'

After a pause: 'OK.'

I'm still staring at Liam's face on the monitor. He looks ghostly. Otherworldly.

'I'll do it right now,' Gadya says. 'I found some instructions on the wall. It's a sequence of buttons.'

A moment later, I hear a high-pitched electronic squeal. It's definitely not coming from Gadya this time. I crouch down on the metal grid by the pod.

'Activating localised neural network,' the computer's bland voice says in my ear. Then, a beat later, 'Hello. I am Clara, your electronic tour guide to the Silver Shore facility. We are sorry for the interruption in service. How may I assist you?' The voice trails away. Almost like it's trying to remember what happened.

'We need your help!' I blurt out.

'You are in a restricted area,' the voice volleys back. But there's no edge to it now, just manufactured concern. 'You must have become lost. A security team will escort you to safety. You are in danger.'

'Tell me something I don't know!' I interrupt. 'Look, how do I unthaw this pod? Give me instructions.'

I only have ten minutes left.

The voice ignores my request. 'Please wait for the security team.'

'Maybe next time,' I snap, still looking over the buttons and dials. So far Clara hasn't been very helpful. I'm about to ask Gadya to shut her back down, when something occurs to me.

I have to do something drastic.

In a burst of deranged inspiration, I decide that maybe if I act like there's something terribly wrong with the pod, I can get Clara's attention off me and on to Liam. 'Hey – wait!' I yell, as I rake my hands up and down over the pod's buttons and levers. 'There's a problem down here! Emergency! Emergency!'

'Running diagnostic check now,' the voice replies smoothly. 'Please step away from the pod.'

So I was right in guessing the computer would prioritise the contents of the pods above everything else. The voice probably thinks that its long-defunct security teams will handle any other problem that comes up.

'Diagnostics complete,' it continues. 'No anomalies detected. Please state the nature of the emergency.'

I am the problem, of course, but the voice doesn't seem to know that. My hands are busily fiddling with all the dials, trying to wreak temporary havoc on Liam's pod, despite the risk to him.

I know I'm gambling with his life, but that might be the only way to save him. He's going to die anyway unless I take action.

'Check the pod again!' I yell. I have eight minutes left. 'How do I manually thaw this thing out?' I slam my hands on the knobs one last time. I toggle the manual override switch up and down, over and over, like a crazy person.

I'm watching the pod's video screen. Liam is still completely frozen, and so far nothing I've done has affected him in the slightest. But apparently it has finally affected whatever data stream Clara monitors.

I suddenly hear a distant beeping noise, getting louder. It

almost sounds like something's coming towards me. I twist sideways.

'Warning! Error!' a voice starts intoning. It's not Clara – it's a different voice. Deep and robotic. Simpler. I'm confused, until I realise this voice is emanating from the pod itself.

'See?' I yell. Lights start flashing all over the pod. The light on Liam's face suddenly switches from white to stroboscopic red. 'Do something, Clara!'

'To activate emergency thawing procedure, please press sequence three-seven-four-two-eight on the red keys, followed by the enter key,' Clara finally explains over the voice of the pod. I pound in the numbers and press enter.

The two machines are both talking at once now, yammering at each other. The beeping continues too, drilling into my skull like the buzzing of an angry hornet. And somewhere in the cacophony I hear Gadya's voice, trying to yell over the clattering din.

I scream in frustration. Nothing is happening. *Are my actions killing Liam?* Am I going to accidentally murder the first boy I've ever fallen for? The voices and the lights grow to an almost unbearable level. *Six minutes left.* I sink to my knees.

Then, everything changes.

The noises cut out.

The light dims.

And it's over as quickly as it began.

I see steam rising within the pod, blotting out Liam's face on the screen. Then the screen goes black.

'Emergency thawing procedure on specimen number 112-782-B initiated,' Clara tells me. 'Do not interact with this unit. Keep away from it for your safety. An armed security team will be there shortly.'

I ignore the voice, standing up to stare at the pod's dark video screen. I press my helmet against it, despite the cold. Then I hear cracking and snapping sounds.

Clara is still talking. About temperatures, and radiation, and safety risks. But I don't care. I'm repeating Liam's name over and over again in my head like a silent prayer. I don't know if he can be thawed in time.

A minute passes. It seems like an hour.

Then the front section of the pod unlatches and swings forward on automated hinges. I step back, startled. Thick white steam billows out in a cloud, along with a gush of liquid, and for a second I'm afraid Liam's corpse is just going to tumble on to the metal at my feet.

Then I hear a gasp from inside.

The sound of someone fighting for air.

A hand emerges, followed by Liam's masked face. He's pulled himself free of the metal halo. He yanks the oxygen mask off and shoves it to one side. The liquid slime covering his body is already drying in the cold, and turning into a white, powdery substance that flakes off him like dead skin.

I stand there, too stunned to do anything.

I'm afraid this is all a dream. Afraid that if I speak, or move, I'll wake up.

Liam takes a tentative step out of the pod. He hasn't

seen me yet. He puts an arm on the pod's exoskeleton to steady himself, as he extricates his body. But then he slips, crumpling to the icy floor.

'Liam!' I gasp. I try to yell his name again, but it comes out as a hushed whisper – partly because of the suit and partly because I'm choked up.

He looks up and finally sees me standing there. For a second, a flicker of dazed anger passes across his face. Then he sees past the reflections in my visor and realises who I am. His face floods with relief.

Then he realises something else.

'Crap.' His voice is a slow rasp. He looks at me with a crooked grin. 'I'm naked, aren't I?' He is, but I just want to grab him and hug him anyway. 'It's so cold… Where am I?'

'Liam, you're alive!' I babble, feeling the tears start cascading down my face like raindrops. The tears break my torpor, and I rush forward, embracing him as hard as I can in my freezing zone suit. He hugs me back, shivering violently.

I never want to let him go. I want to stay here forever, even with the cold and the computer voices and the alarms blaring.

'What happened to me?' he asks. I'm amazed he's recovering so fast. He reaches for the spare suit and starts putting it on quickly, trying to insulate himself against the unbearable cold. 'The last thing I remember, we were fighting the drones. Then the feelers came and—' He breaks off, coughing.

'You got taken, and this is where you ended up. We're at

the city in the grey zone. I thought you were dead.'

'I guess I thought I was too.'

I help him up. The suit is on. I help pull the spare helmet over his head. I can see frostbite on his ears, but other than that, it looks like he's OK. I realise the liquid in the pod probably had some kind of insulating effect to prevent damage.

'Wow.' I can hear his voice loudly now over the radio in my helmet, crackling in my ears. Liam is taking in the massive scale of the cavernous chamber, eyes filled with horrified wonder as he scans the seemingly infinite rows of pods. 'What are these things?'

'Hibernation pods,' I tell him. 'Whoever runs this island freezes the kids who get taken by feelers, and puts them inside these pods to dissect later in the UNA. They call us their specimens, and they call this place their archive.'

I'm suddenly interrupted by Clara, whom I'd nearly forgotten about. 'You are in violation of the terms of the Silver Shore facility.'

'Ignore her,' I tell Liam. 'It's a computerised system that controls this place and keeps things running. There's only computers here – no people any more.'

The voice keeps talking, but Liam and I only have eyes for each other, standing there in our helmets and zone suits. 'You saved my life,' Liam says.

'And you saved mine.'

Then another voice bursts through the static: 'Alenna! Liam! Hurry up.'

It's Gadya. Liam looks surprised.

'Gadya's here too,' I explain, 'but she broke her ankle. She's in the observation deck.' I point up at the curved glass window that seems to hover a mile above us.

'Gadya, is that you?' Liam says into his helmet's microphone.

'Yeah,' her voice comes back weakly. 'So get your butts back here, OK? The time on Liam's pod is almost up, and it's going to leave the archive soon. I don't really know what'll happen next. Stop messing around.'

'Same old Gadya,' Liam says. I hear the smile in his voice.

Then Gadya speaks again, and this time her voice sounds even more concerned. 'Guys? We've got another problem.'

'What?' I ask.

'I just heard a noise.'

I try not to panic. 'What kind?'

'Something metal. Scraping. Like a feeler's trying to get in. I can't tell if it's at the door or if I'm hearing it over the radio.'

Liam and I stare up at the glass windows of the observation deck. 'We better get up there.' He's still recovering, but eager to start moving.

Right then, I hear a terrified scream over the radio.

'No!' Gadya starts yelling. 'Not now!'

My blood goes cold and shivery. I've never heard her sound like this. I know we can't get to her fast enough to help. Not if something's already in the observation deck with her.

'What's going on?' I call out, staring up at the lighted

windows far above us. I can't see anything clearly up there.

'It's a feeler!' her distorted voice screams back. 'A miniature one! Some kind of robot!'

'Find a place to hide!' Liam yells.

'In the room where we found the suits!' I add. 'Climb in there. Lock the door!'

'No!' Gadya's voice comes back. 'You don't understand! It's not up here with me. *It's down there with you and Liam! In the specimen archive!*'

And then I hear the horrifying whisking of thin metal limbs on the catwalk, and I realise that Liam and I are about to get attacked.

ESCAPE

Liam grabs my arm, trying to put himself between me and whatever's headed in our direction.

'What do we do?' I yell.

'I can hear it, but I can't see it!' Liam says, staring into the blackness of this terrible void. 'Use your ears.'

I spin around, trying to locate the increasingly loud whisking sounds. The visor makes it hard to see and hear. My breath grows faster and more ragged. I'm starting to hyperventilate, and I can't stop.

The miniature feeler must have been summoned by Clara after I tampered with Liam's pod. I forgot that they appeared each time we crossed a zone or boundary. *What could be more of a boundary than the line between life and death?* It just never occurred to me there could be smaller indoor variants.

'On your left!' Gadya yells in our headphones. Liam and I both turn in that direction just as a thin tentacle flashes through the darkness, barely missing my helmet. Liam tries to reach out and swat it away, but it evades him in the darkness.

What will happen if this robot gets us? It might not kill us, but it might stuff us into pods and freeze us, like week-old hamburger meat. That's all we are to it. Meat for dissection. And I still don't know why.

Honour can be found in death. I learned that on the wheel during our battles with the drones. But what honour is found by being frozen alive in perpetual hibernation, in a seemingly abandoned warehouse? Eternal stasis is worse than death.

'Oh no,' Gadya's voice says in my ear. She isn't screaming any more, which makes me even more afraid. 'There's more than one of them.'

'Where?' Liam asks.

'Everywhere. On all sides, closing in. At least five. They're floating like jellyfish.'

It's funny. I thought Gadya would be the one who wouldn't make it. Because she got injured, and because she's up in the observation deck, closer to the surface of the island. I thought Liam and I were safe down here.

But I was wrong.

'Talk to the computer,' Liam says. 'Make it stop them somehow.'

'Clara!' I yell. 'Tell these selection units, or whatever they are, to leave us alone! You don't have to do this.'

The voice is coolly efficient. 'Earlier, I requested that you move to the observation deck, but you did not follow my suggestion. You will therefore be removed and placed in protective custody until the staff of this station returns.'

'They're never coming back!' I scream. 'Don't you get it?' I hear more metallic noises now, coming from every direction, just like Gadya said. She's trying to tell us which way to go. But her voice is breaking up into electronic crackles. I'm yelling at her to shut Clara down again, but she can't hear.

'We want out of here,' Liam tells Clara. 'Just let us get back to the observation deck and we'll leave peacefully, OK?'

'I am following Silver Shore protocol,' the voice tells us. 'I must detain you because of your actions.'

I feel something grab my arm. I yank it back instinctively, thinking it's a tentacle. But it's Liam.

I look at him. Our eyes meet through the glass of our visors. 'There's probably no way out of this one, Alenna,' he says with surprising calm. 'Those things are going to collect us, put us into pods, and freeze us. And no one's ever going to come and find us.'

'I know that!' I yell. We only have a few seconds left before the tentacles grab us.

'I'm not getting frozen again. No way. And I'm not letting it happen to you, either.'

'Then we need to run!'

'Run where? These things can move way faster than us.'

I don't have an answer.

'What if we don't run?' Liam suddenly says. 'What if we do exactly what we're not supposed to do.'

I stare at him through my visor. 'Which is?'

'Get these helmets off and climb back into my pod together. And let it take us out of here on schedule. Hijack their mechanisms. Get off the wheel that way.'

I don't need time to think about his idea. It's crazy, ill-thought out, and probably doomed to fail. 'Let's do it!' I yell.

Gadya's been listening, and now she speaks over the radio: 'Move fast. Less than one minute left!'

Then I realise that if we leave, we'll be stranding Gadya. Leaving her to either bleed to death, or get taken by an indoor feeler. 'Wait, we can't go!' I suddenly yell. 'I can't leave you.'

'You have to! They'll probably just find me and freeze me... I'll be here waiting when you come back and rescue me, along with everyone else.'

I know she's just saying that to help us make the decision to leave. I hesitate for a second.

'Do it!' Gadya screams over a burst of static. 'Or we're all going to die. Every single villager on the wheel. You and Liam are our only chance!'

Before she can say another word, I'm already tearing off my helmet. The cold is unbearable, like a living entity surrounding me, trying to flay the skin off my face. Outer space couldn't be much colder. I don't know how Liam was able to withstand it even for a second.

'We'll come back for you!' Liam yells to Gadya.

I want to cry. Gadya is the one person who saw me through this entire journey, and now I feel like I'm ditching her. But she's right. If we don't get off the wheel, no one else will either. At least not for a very long time.

The countdown clock on the pod is still running.

Thirty-two seconds left.

'Go, you idiots!' Gadya yells.

I know her sacrifice is for the sake of all of us villagers. It's not just for me and Liam. I vow that if I survive, I will do everything I can to get everyone off this island and back to civilisation.

Liam has torn his helmet off too, with a wild glint in his eyes. 'This might actually work!' he yells at me. 'Go! Go!'

I yank open the door to the pod and climb inside first. He follows. With the liquid turned to powder, there's room enough for the two of us. But only barely.

I knock the halo out of the way, and we cram our bodies together, pressing against each other side by side, as tightly as possible. Liam grabs the pod door and closes it. I hear a hiss as it begins to pressurise. He passes me the oxygen mask. We're going to have to share it.

I'm worried Clara will put a stop to our escape, or that the pod will malfunction because we're not frozen. But I'm hoping that because everything is so regimented and automated, the pod will stick to its timetable no matter what.

With a reverberating clang, a tentacle slams down on the metal catwalk outside where we were standing just seconds earlier. *Does it know we're in here?*

I grab Liam harder, pressing my head into his shoulder as I hand him the oxygen mask.

Another tentacle slams down, cracking across the front of our living coffin like a whip. This time the pod rocks back and forth, twisting and tumbling us into each other.

Then something starts lifting us into the air.

I shriek because I think it's one of the miniature feelers at first, but the motion is too smooth. Then I realise our pod has been hoisted up by some sort of crane.

I'm guessing that we're about to be taken to whatever vehicle is going to ship us off the wheel. I wish I could see where we're headed, but of course there's no video screen on the inside of the pod.

I hold on to Liam so tightly, my nails feel like they're going to rip through his suit and into his skin. His strong arms are wrapped around me, holding and protecting me. We keep passing the mask back and forth, but there's enough air trapped in the pod that we can breathe without the mask. At least for now.

I wonder what's happening to Gadya. If she's fighting for her life. My mind can find no safe place.

Our pod sways and then stabilises again.

'We're going to be OK,' Liam murmurs into my ear. He's trying to keep me calm.

I know this could be the end. I sense that we're swinging high up in the air, probably still somewhere inside the huge domed structure of the specimen archive.

I shut my eyes.

Then, with a jolt and a clank, our pod comes to an abrupt, puzzling halt.

I hear a clicking noise, as though our pod has docked on to something. Perhaps we're inside another, larger vehicle. Then, a moment later, I hear another click. Then another.

'Where are we?' I whisper to Liam.

'Not sure. Maybe in a transport aircraft?'

'I hope so.' I wonder how the aircraft will leave the archive.

Maybe through a subterranean runway, or even a retractable opening in the roof.

I hear the muffled roar of jet engines starting up outside the pod. Everything starts shaking. *We really must be inside a larger aircraft now.* There's no way to know for sure, of course, but that's the sensation I get. It's terrifying but exhilarating. I grab Liam tighter as the noise of the engines grows louder.

'I think I've fallen in love with you,' I say to him, suddenly blurting the words into his shoulder. I had to say it, in case our pod blows up or something. It's the first time I've told anyone I love them, other than my mum or dad when I was little. But I don't know if he heard me or not, because the words got muffled, and he doesn't say anything back.

Our pod starts shaking like it's falling to pieces, as the aircraft – or whatever vehicle we're inside – starts picking up speed. My body is so tight against Liam that it hurts. Are we going to survive without the protective fluid?

'Alenna!' I hear Liam yell. 'Hold on!'

A second later, the roar reaches a deafening pitch and the vehicle surges forward, like we're blazing up some steep runway out of the archive.

I can't see. I can't hear. And I can't breathe. But I feel a sense of calm wash over me. *I did my best. I didn't give up. And in the end I found Liam again.*

If we're about to die, I guess I'm OK with it.

Then, sickeningly, we're off the ground and rocketing through the air. Everything is shaking, vibrating and churning. I'm still wrapped around Liam, my arms and legs entwined with his.

There's a loud boom as we continue shooting forward. I feel crushing pressure against my chest and my face. We're moving incredibly fast.

The journey has begun, and there's no stopping it.

I cease screaming. I'm still alive. I feel something underneath us shift. We're spinning forward as the aircraft containing our pod cuts through the air like a blade.

Please let us live, I think. *Please let us make it out of here, so we can help the others.*

The aircraft finally stabilises. The air is feeling thinner, and we pass the oxygen mask between us. My body feels bruised. Just as I start relaxing for an instant, Liam begins kicking at the pod's door.

'What are you doing?' I ask, startled.

'We have to find out where we are. Get a look around. If we're on one of the transport airplanes like I hope, maybe we can take control of it. Free the other kids.'

He kicks at the base of the door so hard that it springs open, no match for an unfrozen occupant. I grab on to him and follow, as he staggers out of the pod.

I immediately see that we are indeed inside a cavernous, rattling aircraft, like some sort of ancient cargo plane. Just as Liam predicted. The air is thin and cold here, and my chest burns with every breath.

All around us are rows of other pods, locked on to circular metal devices to keep them from bouncing around.

There are about forty pods total on this aircraft. No sign of any other people. I imagine the plane is automated, like everything else in the Silver Shore.

'Liam, I'm scared,' I tell him, struggling for air.

He grabs my hand. 'Me too, but we're gonna be fine.'

The plane has no windows, just sloping metal sides. But then I spot a small video monitor screen near the front. There's no access to the cockpit. I'm not sure this aircraft even has one. There's merely a large metal bulkhead blocking our path. We rush up the aisle towards the monitor together, clutching at metal railings.

'Look at this,' I hear Liam yell.

I stare at the screen as I steady myself. On it, I see what looks like a field of blue. It takes me a second to realise that it's sky.

Wisps of clouds shoot past, like tendrils of cigarette smoke. I don't know how fast we're going, but it's faster than I've ever moved before in my life.

The plane judders. The video screen suddenly flares with static and then shifts its position. I realise the camera has randomly pivoted downwards by about ninety degrees. Now I can see a verdant landmass directly below us.

'It's the wheel,' I breathe.

I see it now, in all its harsh splendour. The island sprawls out below us as we zoom overhead, acres of trees flying past at breathtaking velocity. It looks so green and lush from up here. So tropical, and weirdly peaceful. We must have already passed over the grey zone. It's hard to imagine there are so many friends and enemies still running around below us, fighting and killing one another over nothing.

I wonder if David managed to escape getting frozen, given his resourcefulness. *Maybe he's still out there somewhere.* I hope that he is, and that somehow he's OK.

It's amazing to get this vantage point of the place where I've spent the last few weeks. From above, it doesn't look scary and terrible. But Liam and I know the truth.

Even though I'm transfixed by the island view, I can't wait to be over open water. Until then, I'll keep thinking that a feeler is going to fly up from the wheel and battle our aircraft.

As we move faster and faster, the trees give way to white sand and blue-green ocean. The aircraft starts rising higher, the ocean's choppy whitecaps dropping further below us. I feel dizzy. We're probably the first kids to make this journey awake.

I realise that our chances of finding help are slim. Wherever we're headed, the people there intend to dissect our bodies. No doubt we'll face more battles.

The video screen shifts to straight ahead again, seemingly of its own will, and now the camera just shows blue skies and clouds. I wonder if this plane is how we were taken to the island, while we were still unconscious after the ECT, but before the feelers dispersed us across its surface. Even now that I understand some of the island's mechanics, the purpose of the wheel is still a mystery to me.

Liam and I continue to hold each other as the plane blasts its way through the air. There's almost something comforting about the noise of this airplane, like being in a giant womb. Except for the part where we could crash and die at any second.

But we don't crash. Instead we stand there watching the screen.

Liam finally turns to me. 'I heard what you said earlier. In the pod, I mean.'

I start to blush. *So he heard me after all, but he didn't say anything back.* I feel a little embarrassed. 'I thought we were going to die. That's why I said it.'

He takes my hand as I look up at him. 'It's OK. You know I feel the same way.' I hug him tightly. 'Right before the feeler took me, at the very last instant, you were the only person I was thinking about. And then when I woke up, you were right there. The first face that I saw.' He kisses the top of my forehead. 'I never thought I'd fall in love on the wheel.'

I shut my eyes. 'Me neither.'

We hold each other for a long time.

It finally becomes clear we're not going to be landing anytime soon. Yet neither of us wants to go back into the pod, because we don't want to lose our connection to the outside world. I tell Liam everything that happened since he got taken: about Veidman, Sinxen and the barrier, and the Monk being Minister Harka. Liam listens in sadness, horror and amazement.

Eventually, we explore the entire aircraft and survey the other sealed pods, coming back to the aircraft's view screen every few minutes to make sure everything looks OK. We're unable to thaw the other occupants, even though we try all kinds of different methods. But what worked in the specimen archive doesn't work here, and without Clara's intervention, the occupants remain frozen.

We also search for any items we can use as weapons when we land, but the plane yields nothing that isn't bolted or welded down.

'I think we're losing altitude,' Liam finally calls over the engine noise.

I tilt my head to look at the monitor but still see only blue sky. I'm guessing we've been airborne for several hours. 'We're coming down?' I feel my gut clench up. I'm not ready.

'We're moving hyperfast. We might have gone a couple of thousand miles already. We'd better get back into the pod, so we're safe when we land.' I can hear the tension in his voice.

I wish we could stay in the air forever. Suspended in the clouds, like a twinkling star, or like one of those butterflies from the island river, never having to face what's in store for us. Never having to face the consequences for leaving the wheel.

The images on the video screen suddenly start sliding, and I realise the camera is moving again.

'Whoa!' I yell, not understanding what I'm seeing. Now we're just staring at a rippling golden surface.

Liam leans forward, scrutinising the image. 'I think those are sand dunes.'

'What? We're already over land?' I stare at the monitor, perplexed and scared.

The image starts to make more sense the further we go, and I realise that, inexplicably, we're flying over an unbroken stretch of desert. It's unpopulated and completely sparse. I've never seen anything like it. It's like the water just turned into sand underneath the aircraft without us noticing.

More desert unfurls, like an endless stretch of unrolled canvas. Somewhere in the distance is the horizon.

'Let's go back now,' Liam says. We tentatively move down the centre of the plane and find our pod.

I take one final glance back at the view screen. We're so low now that I can see dust clouds rising up from the sand, like banks of fog.

My ears get stuffy for a second, and then they clear as we keep descending. Wherever we're going, I sense that we're almost there. Maybe just a few minutes away.

'There's gotta be some kind of landing strip or runway around here,' I yell into Liam's ear as we climb into the pod, curling up again and closing the pod door as best we can. 'We're their specimens! It doesn't make sense for them to let us crash and die in a desert.'

The aircraft slows even more, like it's coming in low. I clutch at Liam.

The roar of the engines becomes deafening again. The plane is going to touch down soon, whether there's a runway around here or not.

'What happens when we land?' I ask Liam, refusing to acknowledge the fact that crashing seems far more likely. 'Do we fight?'

'If we have to.'

I can barely hear him because of the noise. I curl up against him tighter. I try to get some air from the oxygen mask, but it doesn't seem to be working any more.

Then I hear a noise halfway between a thud and a pop, and we start to slow even more. 'What was that?' I ask, panicked.

'Wing flaps, maybe?' Liam's body tenses, preparing for whatever lies ahead. 'Grab on to me hard.'

'I already am.'

'Harder. Keep your head down.'

I do as he says. He moves his arm around me, trying to protect me better.

'Alenna?'

'Yeah?'

'I think we're going to crash.'

I nod and whisper, 'I already know that.'

Maybe Clara is responsible, or maybe the pod finally sensed we weren't frozen and the entire aircraft is doing some weird self-destruct thing.

I feel our altitude and speed decreasing. We can't be far from the ground now. I wish I could see what was happening. We're probably going to hit one of those sand dunes soon. I brace for the impact.

'Liam,' I say.

And then we hit.

The airplane smashes down against the sand with such force that I black out for a second, cracking my head against the plastic hull of the pod as my teeth snap together.

Then I'm conscious again, and the plane is sliding over the sand, out of control. Sparks shower on to us as hidden wires short out inside the pod's shell. Liam is calling my name.

We hit the ground again and bounce hard. My head whips back and then forward. The plane is spinning and sliding as the engines scream. I smell acrid smoke as more sparks shower down on us. I can't tell if we're airborne again or still on the ground.

There's a jolting thump as we hit something. Then another. *Must be a ridge of dunes.*

I know we can't withstand much more of this. The aircraft is going to tear itself to pieces and fling our pod out of it. *We're going to die!*

But we don't die. That would be too easy.

We just keep bouncing and getting pounded. The padding on the interior of the pod is all that keeps me from hitting the hard siding. That and Liam's protective body wrapped around mine.

The crash landing seems to go on forever, every second elongated into an hour. But it probably hasn't been even a minute since we clipped the top of the first dune. Time slows down and everything moves at a crawl, like it did in the awful, unearthly barrier around the grey zone.

But eventually our journey comes to an abrupt end.

The plane careens sideways, losing power, like it's slipping down one side of a dune. We just keep holding each other.

Bruised and battered, we finally come to a dead stop. I've lost all sense of direction inside the pod. I can't tell what's up or down. My whole body hurts. Even though I know we're stationary, my balance is screwed up, and it feels like I'm still moving.

'We're alive,' Liam says faintly. Then louder, as if to reassure both of us: 'We're still alive!'

We lie there for a moment, gasping. I still smell something burning. It could be fuel. I realise we need to get out of the pod and off this aircraft. Liam does too. He starts grappling with the door of the pod, but it's broken now and doesn't budge.

He starts kicking at it again, but there's no room for him to get enough leverage. The frame doesn't give way.

'We're stuck,' I say. *In a pod, inside a crashed airplane that's probably leaking fuel, in the middle of a desert.*

Liam suddenly stops moving and grabs my hands. 'Did you hear that?'

'What?'

'Voices.'

I don't hear anything other than the crackling of the cooling engines and the settling of the aircraft into sand.

I dare to whisper, 'Should we…?'

But then I hear something else too. A faint swooshing sound, right outside. I hold my breath. The noises increase, sounding like rapid footsteps, as though people are already boarding the wrecked plane. Can that be possible? I put my lips against Liam's ear. 'I'm scared,' I whisper.

'Be strong,' he mouths back.

Then we hear a clank, and I flinch. It's the sound of

something metal hitting the base of our pod. Like someone's trying to free our pod from the plane.

'What's the plan?' I breathe into Liam's ear.

'We've got the element of surprise,' he whispers back. 'Whoever they are, they'll think we're frozen.' Both of us are as still as corpses. 'Just stay behind me if the pod gets opened.'

'I'll fight too,' I whisper.

'I know. I'm counting on it.'

The noises outside grow louder, but I still can't make out any words. Another clank comes. Then another. I feel our pod start to move, like it's being dragged out of the plane with us inside.

I grip Liam tighter.

I know that these people will probably open our pod soon. I can feel Liam flex his muscles. His body has become hard and taut, like the string of a bow. He is a warrior preparing for battle. I feel at one with him.

Our pod starts moving faster. We get slammed against the hull of the plane. I hear a clatter, and the world starts spinning as our pod begins to rotate. I realise we're probably being rolled down a ramp, out of the aircraft and on to the sand.

The pod keeps moving. The motion goes on for several minutes, until we finally come to a sudden, brutal stop, as though we've hit a wall.

The jarring impact makes me cry out loudly.

I bite my lip.

But it's too late.

I hear startled voices yelling. Footsteps running towards us.

Oh no – they heard me!

'It's OK,' Liam whispers into my ear.

And then comes an awful wrenching sound, as the roof of our pod is torn back in one piece by a gigantic pair of metal shears.

The sun hits my eyes, blotting everything out in a blaze of white light. Except for the shadowy figures that loom over us with guns, screaming wildly.

DESTINY STATION

Liam explodes upwards with surprising energy, clawing his way right out of our pod. He's yelling, trying to scare these people.

But as my eyes adjust to the light, I see that they already look scared enough. 'These kids are awake!' one of them yells, stumbling back from the opening.

I'm right behind Liam, staggering up and out. Our silver zone suits sparkle under the harsh glare of the desert sun. I flail, trying to clear my vision.

I realise that at least thirty adults are now amassing around our pod. We're pressed right up against the edge of a dune. To our right, I see a mountainous, red-coloured sandstone rock formation, the size of several city blocks, towering two hundred feet above the dunes. It has a flattened top, like a mesa, and it's the only visible landmark, other than sand.

'Oh my God!' another voice yells. I turn in her direction. It's a middle-aged woman with dark curly hair.

She's not particularly threatening-looking, but I still scream at her: 'Get the hell away from us!'

She backs off rapidly, as do the others.

Liam crouches on the sand in his warrior stance. We're both trying to make sense of where we've landed and who these people are. They don't look like UNA scientists or soldiers, that's for sure.

They're just a mix of regular men and women, all dressed in loose white desert tunics. On their faces, I see looks ranging from surprise to catatonic shock.

I move over to Liam and stand back-to-back with him. The group has formed a wide circle around us. Behind them I see the aircraft that brought us here. It looks like an old slate-grey UNA bomber, large and cumbersome. It's missing part of a wing from our landing.

'Who are you?' Liam yells. 'What is this place?'

A tall, lanky man with thinning grey hair and glasses takes a step forward.

'Keep your distance!' Liam barks. 'Don't come near us, or I'll kill you.'

Liam sounds both ferocious and believable. The man stops moving and stretches out his empty hands, presumably to show that he's unarmed and means no harm.

'What's your name, son?' he asks. He has a strange accent. Maybe British or Australian.

'Don't call me "son"!' Liam snaps. 'I said stay back!'

I glance around at the group of adults. If these really are the technicians who intended to dissect us, then I hate them with a passion that I've never felt before.

Yet I see looks of compassion and pity on some of their faces, now that their shock is wearing off. It's hard to imagine that these rumpled desert dwellers are murderous UNA scientists. I don't even think we're in the UNA any more.

I hear one woman murmur to another, 'The first ones who are awake! And there's more than one of them.' When she sees me glaring at her, she stops talking pretty fast.

'I'm Dr Terry Elliott,' the tall man says to us.

'*Doctor?*' Liam asks, his face darkening. 'So you want to cut us up and study our corpses? Sorry we aren't frozen enough for you.'

'No, no.' The man shakes his head. 'Not that kind of doctor. I'm an anthropologist, originally from Old Melbourne, Victoria. Do you even know where you are?'

I don't reply.

'What's your name, hon?' the middle-aged woman calls out in my direction. I don't respond. These strangers will have to earn our trust.

'You're safe now,' Dr Elliott continues, running a hand through what's left of his hair. 'Look, I know you might not believe it, but you've been rescued.' He takes a hesitant half-step forward. 'I understand why you're so angry. You've been on that bloody island too long and—'

'You don't know anything about us!' Liam snarls.

The man nods slowly. 'True. But we want to learn. That's why we brought you here.'

'*You* brought us here?' I ask.

'Yes. Me and the other rebel scientists at Destiny Station.'

'What are you talking about?' Liam asks the man. 'Alenna rescued me, then we hijacked a pod, and after that, the transport plane crashed here. You didn't do crap.' Liam looks like he's ready to lunge forward and attack.

'Let me explain.' Dr Elliott wipes sweat from his eyes. 'We've been tracking radio signals emitted by the Island Alpha airplanes. I guess you could say we've been doing some hijacking of our own.' He glances at his silent companions, and then back at us. 'For the past month, we've been intercepting guidance signals for each plane that leaves the island. The planes are remotely operated by computers, all automated, so we've been able to take over the controls and guide the planes here, and land them in this desert. The landings are rough, but if the occupants of the pods are frozen and preserved in fluid, they're generally well protected. You two are complete anomalies.' He pauses. 'Right now, the UNA just thinks there's a temporary glitch in their system. They can afford the steep losses because they have plenty of planes from their wars, and a current backlog of thousands of bodies. They can't even keep up with their own research.'

'Keep talking,' Liam prompts the doctor warily.

'We've managed to rescue more than three hundred of you inmates, and bring you all here to our settlement.'

I fold my arms. 'Settlement?'

'Yes, on the northern ridge of Australia. Thousands of miles from where you should be right now.' He pushes down his glasses and scratches the bridge of his nose. 'If it weren't for us, you'd be in the processing centre on a UNA naval base. From there, you'd be shipped to a medical facility, where – as you seem to already know – you'd eventually be dissected.'

'Why?' I ask. 'Why are we worth dissecting?'

'Because the UNA wants to analyse your brains and your

DNA. To determine why you're immune to the sedating chemicals that your government puts in your thought-pills and pumps through the veins of its entire populace.'

I digest this information slowly. Liam and I look at each other. Things are beginning to swim into focus. 'Immune to chemicals?' I ask. *That explains so much – the vague feeling of always being an outsider in the UNA.* The feeling that so many of us shared on the wheel.

'That's the real reason you got sent to Prison Island Alpha. You and all the other kids like you. A genetic mutation protects your minds from being pacified by the chemicals in the thought-pills. The UNA also secretly infuses most of its food and water with chemicals, to keep the populace docile. Your government uses Island Alpha to test new drugs on those of you who are resistant to the drugs they already have. They go after kids who cross the zones because those are generally the most active and rebellious ones. They want to learn how to break the minds of teenagers like you. Kids who think for themselves, and might grow up to question their system.'

I stare back at him, horrified.

'We're all dissidents ourselves from an earlier era, when the UNA exiled the scientists who didn't agree with its policies and research,' Dr Elliott continues. He gestures to the huge sandstone formation. 'We've built tunnels and chambers inside that rock over there, like a honeycomb. We call the place Destiny Station. More than two thousand of us live inside it, trying to fight the UNA and countries like it.'

I look at Liam. He still seems wary. But I believe this man.

I've been watching the people who are with him. They're more afraid of us than we are of them.

'When we misdirect a plane here, we're used to finding the occupants frozen, and then thawing them out in the temperature chambers in our lab,' Dr Elliott continues. 'I'm glad you two aren't frozen. It's a sign that the system on Island Alpha is finally crumbling. We know that the UNA is spending all its money on new war machinery. They can't maintain the island any more, so they're in the process of abandoning it. They've put a containment wall around their entire cooling zone, because of all the leaks and spills. We think at some point they're going to exterminate everyone on the island – unless they can find a drug soon that will defeat your genetic immunity, and brainwash you.'

The middle-aged woman steps up next to him. 'I know both of you probably have questions. We have answers. Some but not all.' She's looking right at me with intelligent eyes. 'My name is Dr Angeline Vargas-Ruiz. I'm an anthropologist too. Most of us are scientists here.' She holds out her hand.

My head is a jumble of data. *Anthropologists. Australia. An outpost in the desert.* I take Dr Vargas-Ruiz's hand and shake it. 'My name's Alenna Shawcross.'

I see a strange look pass across her eyes. She knows my name – I can tell. But how? Nothing makes sense to me any more.

Liam looks at me, then at the woman. Grudgingly he says, 'Liam Bernal.'

'Nice to meet you,' she replies.

I feel so tired that I just want to curl up in the sand and sleep for a thousand years. I see Liam's shoulders slump, and his fists start to uncurl.

'Come with us. I bet you're dying of thirst,' Dr. Vargas-Ruiz says. 'We have water and food, and fresh clothes too. Soft beds.' Everyone's watching us. 'You're safe.'

Safe. It almost sounds like a joke.

'You believe them, right?' Liam whispers to me. I hear the longing in his voice. I feel it as well, my chest aching with hope.

'I think it's OK,' I whisper back.

'Come, come,' Dr Elliott says. 'We have to get back inside the station as soon as possible.' The group starts to encircle us.

I don't feel fear, just relief tempered with confusion. I look up at the sun. It's hot enough to burn my face, but the heat feels wonderful after being inside the specimen archive.

I see men break off from the group and surround our fallen pod, as well as the other pods, which are scattered everywhere. Muscles heaving, they start dragging and pulling them across the sand like they're taking them with us. I know these other pods must contain the frozen bodies of both villagers and drones.

'Let's keep talking as we head back to Destiny Station,' Dr Vargas-Ruiz says, hurrying along. 'We don't want our movement to get picked up on satellite.'

'Someone's still watching us?' I ask as Liam grabs my

hand. We begin walking quickly across the sand with the group, heading towards Destiny Station.

'Someone's always watching,' Dr. Vargas-Ruiz replies with a faint, sad smile.

As we walk, her companions start introducing themselves one by one. Their names wash over me. I'm thinking about how great it will feel to get a hot meal and a soft bed.

Then I feel guilty.

What about Gadya? And David, Rika, Sinxen, Veidman and Markus? Didn't they deserve to get rescued too? How will we even find David?

I think about all the others still stuck back on the wheel, either dead or entombed in the specimen archive. Liam and I didn't abandon them by choice, yet I still feel like we've betrayed them.

Liam tightens his grip. 'You OK?'

'Just thinking about everyone we left behind.'

He nods.

'How are we going to get back and save them?' I ask.

'I don't know. Not until we learn more about what's going on here.'

My eyes tear up, but I turn my face away so he doesn't see.

Dr Vargas-Ruiz slows her pace so she's even with us. 'That's the opening to our base right there.'

She points at the clifflike face of the rock. I stare in the direction of her fingertip, wiping my eyes. The sandstone shimmers with diffraction patterns in the heat, and I don't see anything. For a moment, I wonder if this whole thing –

our escape, our landing, and our rescue – is just a delusion on my part.

'What are we supposed to be looking at?' Liam asks.

Dr Vargas-Ruiz smiles. 'Nothing, actually. We're not meant to be seen.'

'Everything's hidden inside,' Dr Elliott says from nearby. He's supervising the moving of the pods. Liam and I turn to look at him. 'Not by choice, but we have to stay off satellite and radar. And out in the desert, it's cooler inside the rock formation. We've built tunnels and rooms throughout it at all different levels, and buttressed them with steel. There's practically a city in there.'

The group starts slowing down. I'm still scrutinising the sandstone for any signs of life. Dr Vargas-Ruiz notices. 'Closer to your left.'

She gestures again. I squint against the brightness.

Finally, I see an almost invisible indentation in the base of the rock. It looks like it's been eroded into the side of the sandstone by the wind, but it's more than that. It's small and square, like there's something hidden behind it.

A secret doorway.

'That's the entrance to our labyrinth,' she tells me and Liam as the group heads towards it, trailing through the sand, dragging the pods. I glance back and see others rolling the rest of the pods out of the aircraft. A light wind kicks up, blowing sand into my eyes. 'We'll have the entire plane disassembled by night time.'

We keep trudging towards the rock wall. Liam has his

arm around me. I'm so glad I'm with him that in some ways, nothing else matters.

'How are you holding up?' he whispers.

'Good.'

He laughs softly and hugs me tight. 'You're a trouper.'

Dr Elliott finally reaches the sandstone indentation, and the rest of the men put down the pods. Some of them spit on their blistered hands to cool them off, because the exteriors of the pods are being superheated by the sun.

Dr Elliott takes out an old-fashioned key from his back pocket, nearly the length of a screwdriver. He drives it into the rock, slotting it into a hidden lock with an audible click. Chunks of crusted sand fall away. I catch a glimpse of chrome beneath the sandstone.

Then I hear a grinding sound. Instinctively, I startle. A huge section of the rock face slowly and methodically starts opening outwards. I see a series of large metal pistons pushing it, and realise that this entire twenty-foot portion of the sandstone wall is fake – hollow and plastic. But it's very convincing.

As it opens, it reveals a huge industrial elevator, large enough for a truck to drive on to. It's definitely large enough to carry all of us, and some of the pods as well.

'How did you build all of this in here?' Liam asks Dr Vargas-Ruiz.

'Remember, most of us are scientists and thinkers. We like to design and build things. It's our passion. Still, it took several years. We constructed drills and cutters to bore through the sandstone, and to excavate all the tunnels and ventilation shafts. Then the real work began. Building generators and making it livable inside.'

Adults flow past us, rolling the pods again. Dr. Vargas-Ruiz leads us towards the elevator opening and on to the metal floor.

'Where'd you get your materials?' I ask.

'Mostly scrap metal. It's amazing what you can find. Most of what the UNA and other nations consider trash can be recycled and reused. We've also recycled metal from some of the pods and planes we've brought here. We just melt it down.'

I notice a small keypad in one corner of the elevator, and flashing lights on its electronic display screen. Dr Elliott taps in a code, and we rapidly start our ascent, up into the mysterious interior of the rock.

I look up through the metal grate above us and just see darkness. By the time I look back down, the light from outside has narrowed to a two-foot band as the false wall closes. Then just a slit.

And then there's nothing but the dim light of the elevator's digital display, as the dune seals with a clattering crash.

The elevator continues moving upwards. *Is it really over?* I can't come to terms with that idea. I feel more tired than I've ever felt before.

'How high does it go?' Liam asks. He sounds exhausted now, just like me. Neither of us expected that a place like this would exist at the end of our journey.

'Eight levels,' Dr Elliott says.

'And tunnels branch off at each one,' another man with a long beard adds. 'Don't worry. There are plenty of safe rooms inside here. The rock won't collapse on you.'

We keep ascending. I'm still hot and sweaty, but I feel a chill pass over me. The makeshift elevator clangs and groans as it bears us upwards. 'We need to rescue our friends,' I say. 'We have to go back to the wheel.'

'We can talk about that later,' Dr. Vargas-Ruiz replies. 'First you need water, food, and rest – in that order. Then you'll be briefed on the Destiny Station and our mission here. You'll meet the other kids that we've rescued from Island Alpha. And hopefully, you'll help us work to bring down the UNA and establish a fair society in its place.'

I sense from her voice that she's not telling us everything about her agenda. But I don't want any more surprises or secrets.

'So that's it?' I ask. 'We just get to live here from now on? There's got to be a catch.'

Suddenly, Minister Harka's terrifying visage flashes across my mind. I tighten my grip on Liam's hand.

What if this is all a trap, and we're being set up somehow?

But Minister Harka is dead. I saw him die on the wheel. So if there is some dark surprise that awaits us in the heart of Destiny Station, it has to be something else. But what?

The elevator interrupts my thoughts with a jolt, as it comes to rest.

'Level three,' a woman in the back declares. 'We'll take

the occupied pods up to level six and start thawing them.'

Dr Elliott nods.

'This is where you two get off,' Dr. Vargas-Ruiz tells us. 'The other kids your age from the island live on levels one and two. You'll meet them soon enough.'

We follow her out of the elevator and into a wide tunnel carved through the rock, supported by metal beams. A few other people disembark behind us, heading off down another passage. Yellow utility lights hang along one side of each tunnel. They make it bright enough to see but cast odd, gloomy shadows.

'Watch your step and watch your heads,' Dr Vargas-Ruiz cautions us. Behind me, I hear the elevator start up again.

I feel nervous because I don't know what's coming next. If things go wrong, Liam and I are trapped in here, and there's no place to run. This rock could be our tomb.

But as we walk, I can hear the tunnels buzzing with life. The distant sounds of conversation and laughter echo off the walls, coming from small rooms attached to the main tunnel. I even hear faint strains of acoustic music every now and then, and realise they must have instruments up here.

Soon more adults emerge, as our tunnel intersects with a larger one. Like an ant colony, this intricate maze seems to be created from a series of tight crisscrossing tunnels.

'You'll get to know everyone eventually,' Dr Vargas-Ruiz tells us. 'Two thousand people isn't as many as you'd think. In a week or two, it'll seem like home.'

'Are there any windows in this place?' I ask.

'There are some rock crevices to look out of, on the highest levels. We mainly use them to keep watch. We've built an access tunnel to the top of the rock as well. At night we often go out there for air.'

As we pass people in the tunnels, they wave and smile at me and Liam. I wave back. It's clear they know we're new arrivals. I realise that almost everyone here probably went through an experience similar to ours, assuming Dr Vargas-Ruiz is telling us the truth.

We are the rebels now, I think, hardly believing that I've become the very thing the GPPT purportedly tested for. Our government's paranoia and fascism has created exactly what it feared the most.

I think back to how I was in New Providence: shy, quiet and a little mousy. An orphan shut inside the confines of her own mind within a society that ultimately didn't understand her.

But that was before Gadya taught me how to stand up for myself.

Before David and Veidman taught me to question the reality around me.

Before Rika reminded me of the importance of being generous and kind.

And most of all, it was before Liam taught me how to fall in love.

Three boys roughly my age stream right past us. No one jostles anyone. Everyone seems polite and respectful.

'This way,' Dr Vargas-Ruiz says, steering us onwards, past more kids.

I'm suddenly self-conscious. Everyone here looks so clean and normal that it's almost shocking. I can smell their soap and freshly laundered clothes. I can't wait to get out of my zone suit.

'Where are you taking us?' Liam asks, as we navigate another tunnel, going slightly upwards.

'To your rooms. After thawing, we generally make new arrivals spend three days in a very informal quarantine – mostly to get them adjusted to life in the station.' She pauses. 'We also need to debrief you further, and get you medical checkups.'

She turns a corner, and we follow. A moment later, we reach a large metal door positioned flush in the rock wall. A plaque on it reads QUARANTINE ROOM 2.

Dr Vargas-Ruiz opens the door. Beyond it, I see a huge space carved into the sandstone, with rows of lights hanging overhead. There are about ten different cubicles inside, separated by glass walls rising nearly to the ceiling. Each one appears to have a narrow mattress inside it, along with a table and a chair. There are curtains inside each room to pull around the walls for privacy, like in a hospital.

I feel nauseous for a second. These rooms remind me a little of the scanning cells in New Providence.

'It's just for a few days,' Dr Vargas-Ruiz says, noticing the looks on our faces. 'You'll each get your own cubicle. And it's not like we're going to lock you in or anything – although

I'd prefer if you stayed in here for the next three days, for your own safety.' She walks forward and opens up another metal door in the side of the rock wall, displaying a primitive bathroom with a toilet and a shower stall inside. 'There are towels on the rack. Fresh tunics and pants as well. You might want to clean up.'

'Definitely,' I say.

She gestures at the cubicles. 'You can each pick your own. In a few days, when we've thawed out the other pods from your plane, this place will be filled with more kids from the island.'

'What about the Monk's people?' Liam asks, concerned. 'On the island, there are two tribes of us—'

'I know,' she interrupts. 'There's your kind and those you call the drones. The drones are generally just kids whose minds get more affected by the chemicals on the wheel. We tend to keep the different groups separated at first. Just so there's no fighting. But pretty soon all of that goes away.' She pauses. 'Here at Destiny Station, we're all equals. United by a common cause.'

Liam nods.

'I'll send a doctor to check on you both tonight,' she says. 'To make sure you don't have any tropical fever, parasites or other medical conditions.' She eyes us. 'Do you both feel OK?'

'We're fine,' I tell her as Liam nods again.

She moves back over to the main door and opens it. 'Someone will be in shortly with food.'

She steps into the tunnel and closes the metal door firmly

behind her. Liam walks over to it and checks the handle. Indeed, it isn't locked. He swings the door open and then shuts it again. For a moment, Liam and I just stand there in silence, like we can't believe everything that's happened to us. Or that we're still alive.

Then, inexplicably, we both start laughing.

It comes out of nowhere. It's the sound of being safe. The sound of being overwhelmed. The sound of relief that for the first time in as long as I can remember, we're not facing imminent death.

But then my laughter slowly fades as I remember that despite our good fortune, our friends are still in jeopardy back on the wheel. Not to mention all the other kids in the UNA just like us.

'Which room do you want?' Liam finally says, gesturing around. 'I think they're all identical.'

We end up taking two cubicles across from each other, so we can leave the glass doors open and talk.

I sprawl back on my narrow mattress. Liam does the same on his. Although our journey is over for the moment, I know that many more challenges await us.

I'm just about to say something to Liam, when the door to the room suddenly opens again. I sit up, expecting to see someone bringing a tray of food. Instead, I see Dr Vargas-Ruiz.

'Back already?' Liam asks.

'Yes.' She turns to me. 'Alenna, there's someone here who wants to see you.'

I start to feel nervous again. 'What? I haven't even showered yet or anything. And what about our checkups?'

'Those can wait. I thought you could meet with her tomorrow, but she demanded that I fetch you right away.'

'Who?' Liam asks, standing up protectively.

'It's not my place to say,' she tells him, sounding mysterious. 'Besides, this meeting is really for Alenna.' She gazes at Liam with an unreadable look in her dark eyes. 'I can't explain why. Not yet. But it's her choice whether you come with her or not. If she wants you to, you can.'

'Oh, he's coming,' I say. There's no way I'm going to let anyone separate us.

Liam speaks up in agreement. 'I go where she goes.'

Dr Vargas-Ruiz nods. 'Fine. I'm actually coming too. These meetings can be stressful. It's best if I'm present to mitigate any issues.'

Issues? I'm too tired to even want to know what she's talking about. But I figure as long as Liam is with me, everything will be OK. I stand up, Liam already at my side.

'Come with me, then,' Dr Vargas-Ruiz says.

We follow her out of the chamber and back into the hall, wending our way through the network of tunnels. My pulse is racing faster. Liam and I hold hands.

Dr Vargas-Ruiz finally stops at a wide door. This one is made of burnished wood. It has a handmade sign hanging on it that reads RECONCILIATION ROOM 6.

Her fingers tighten around the doorknob. 'Alenna, are you ready?'

'Probably not,' I tell her honestly. 'Can't you just tell me who's in there?'

Liam steps in front of me. 'Let me go inside first,' he says.

'You're worried there's something scary in the room,' Dr Vargas-Ruiz intuits. 'A threat.'

'Just being cautious.' He glances back at me. 'Alenna saved my life in the specimen archive. We watch out for each other.'

'Good. We need people like you and Alenna here.' Dr Vargas-Ruiz turns the doorknob and pushes the door open. 'Just take it slowly, OK?'

Liam steps forward, and I follow him into the room.

The room is small and has a warm yellow lightbulb jerry-built on to the ceiling. There's a wooden table inside, with a plastic pitcher of water on it and two mugs. In one corner sits a pathetic fake rose in a homemade clay vase. Dr Vargas-Ruiz moves into the room behind me.

But it's the person sitting in the chair at the table, looking up at me, who makes my heart skip a beat.

'You…' I breathe, feeling my legs start to give way.

It's not possible. I must finally be losing my mind. That's the only explanation.

I've cracked.

Liam grabs at me, keeping me steady.

'Easy,' he says, but I can barely hear his voice over the rush of blood to my head. 'Who is she?' he asks.

The woman in the chair is someone I never expected to see again. Someone I haven't seen in a very long time.

'Alenna,' she says, still looking up at me.

Now I know I must be going crazy, because her voice hasn't changed in all the years since I last saw her. It's the same voice that has played over and over in my head.

A voice I could never forget.

Her hair is short and greying at the temples, and she has a lot more wrinkles. Otherwise, she looks pretty much the same. I just keep staring at her.

'C'mon, tell me who she is,' Liam is saying, sounding worried.

I can only manage a single word before the emotions overwhelm me, and I go crashing to the floor.

'Mum.'

HOMECOMING

I'm crying so hard that my words catch not only in my throat, but also in the jumble of my mind. Thoughts crash down like waves breaking on jagged rocks. Liam has his arms around me as we crouch on the floor together.

'Your mum?' Liam whispers into my ear. 'But I thought you were an orphan.'

I still can't speak. Not even to him.

My mum half-rises from her chair. 'Alenna,' she says again.

Then she rushes around the table towards me. I fall forward into her arms. She feels different from how I remember. Smaller and frailer. But she smells the same: the warm scent of home that has lingered in the corners of my dreams and tattered memories ever since she and my dad were taken.

'It's really you?' I whisper past the tears.

'It's me.'

'But—' I'm so confused, torn between laughter and hysterical tears. 'How?'

'The thought of seeing you again is what kept me alive,' she murmurs.

I pull back from our embrace, and I scrutinise her face.

Yes, it is her. I have no doubt. Her eyes are the same shade as mine, like they always were.

I glance back. Liam is right behind me. Dr Vargas-Ruiz places a pale hand on his shoulder.

'I thought you and Dad were dead,' I tell my mum, turning back to her, wiping my nose with the back of my hand. 'I mean, I always secretly hoped I was wrong.'

'I was sent to the wheel too,' she says. 'It was an internment camp for UNA political dissidents, before it became the abomination it is today. Your father and I were both sent there after we were arrested, along with anyone else who the government thought was a threat and couldn't coerce into joining them. We did nothing wrong, other than disagree with the UNA's policies.'

'Minister Harka told us you helped him on the wheel, before he died.' I pause, wondering if she even knows that Minister Harka is dead. This should be major news to her. But she doesn't look surprised, so maybe the inhabitants of Destiny Station already know somehow. Perhaps from tapping into the network of hidden cameras, or from other sources. 'And I found one of the rocks with our name on it,' I add. 'So, is Dad here somewhere?'

She can see the yearning in my eyes, and a look of pain flashes across her face. 'Your father—'

I can guess what's coming next. I shut my eyes. My scarred heart aches so much that the grief is hard to bear.

'He passed away three years ago.'

I put my head against her chest again.

'Don't be sad,' my mum says. She pulls back, staring into my eyes. 'He died fighting for a cause he believed in. If it weren't for him, we never would have been able to build this place, or even get off Island Alpha. Your dad is a hero.'

I don't know what to say. He was always a hero to me. I just wish he were still alive. 'His stories about Sisyphus kept me going,' I say. 'And his carvings in the rocks as well.'

My mum nods. It's weird to have a mother again after I've become so used to being on my own. I wonder if she feels weird about it too. 'What do we do now?' I ask.

'Your being sent here wasn't a coincidence,' she tells me. 'We've figured out how to intercept some of the video feeds from the museum camera, and other cameras hidden around the island. I watched your arrival. I suspected you'd fail the GPPT and end up on Island Alpha, because the gift we have – the ability of our brains to repel the government neurotoxins – has a genetic component, and that's primarily what the GPPT tests for. Of course, given your family history, they probably identified you as one of us from the start.'

'So we're, like…mutants?'

She smiles. 'No. We just have something inside our heads that won't let the government in. We don't know what it is, and they don't either. A quirk of our genetic codes. Maybe Dr Elliott told you, but that's why the island is a testing ground for all their new variant drugs. They spray them in the atmosphere. Then hidden motion detectors around the sector boundaries alert the feelers to come and pick up the most energetic inhabitants. The sickness – what you call the Suffering – is what happens when their new drugs cause unwanted side-effects. Some people are susceptible to them sooner than others. In time, almost everyone falls prey to their effects.'

'But what about the others? My friends?'

I glance back to see what Liam thinks, but Dr Vargas-Ruiz is escorting him out of the room. I feel a sudden pang of fear. 'Wait,' I call out.

Liam turns.

'We should give you some privacy,' Dr. Vargas-Ruiz says.

'It's OK. You can stay,' I tell Liam. To my mum, I add, 'This is Liam Bernal. My...' I feel more fluttering in my stomach. 'My boyfriend.'

Liam smiles.

'Nice to meet you,' my mum says to him, sounding a little awkward. But that makes sense, because the last time she saw me, I was a ten-year-old with pigtails. But then she adds, 'Actually, we've met before, Liam. A long time ago.'

I'm startled, and so is Liam.

'What do you mean?' he asks her.

'Unless I'm mistaken, your father's name is Octavio Bernal. He was a famous rebel leader.'

Liam now looks completely shocked. 'How do you know that?'

'Alenna's father and I were friends with your parents many years ago, in the chaos before the UNA was formed. You and Alenna played together sometimes when you were little kids. We took a trip together to Old Florida once. You probably don't even remember it.'

She's right. I don't remember.

But it explains so much. The instant connection I felt with Liam from the first moment I saw him on-screen.

I turn to him, my surprise reflected in his face. It's clear he doesn't remember either.

'Wow,' he says, sounding as stunned as I feel. 'That's crazy.'

To me it seems like fate. That we would know each other as children and then be reunited again on the wheel.

'I watched your arrival on the island as well, Liam,' my mum adds.

Dr Vargas-Ruiz puts a hand on his shoulder again. 'Let's give Alenna and her mother some time alone together. Besides, there's a lot more you need to know about your father.'

Liam looks at me and asks, 'Is it all right if I go?'

'Yes,' I tell him, still reeling from everything I've learned.

'We'll be waiting right outside,' Dr Vargas-Ruiz assures me, as she leads Liam from the room.

I turn back to my mum. 'Tell me everything.'

'You mean about this place?'

'No, I mean *everything*. The whole story. What happened when you and Dad got taken. I need to know.'

I hear the door close. It's just me and my mum now. 'I'll try. But I don't remember all of it.'

For the next hour we sit there, holding hands. She tells me a condensed version of everything she went through. How she and my dad were interrogated for days. Starved and denied water. Beaten and chained.

Then they were shipped across the country to the West

Coast, and then onwards to Island Alpha – a desolate, unpopulated island in the Pacific, located halfway between Hawaii and Australia. My mum explains that the UNA established its prison islands far from the mainland because of fears of rebellion – especially Island Alpha, the largest and harshest of its prison colonies. Other smaller, secret islands apparently exist elsewhere.

Back then, Island Alpha was a different place from the one I encountered – with dissidents, criminals, vagabonds and intellectuals mixed together, forced to battle for the small population of hoofers released on to the island to provide food for the prisoners. The coloured sectors for each part of the wheel were already established by the UNA, and were initially meant to demarcate zones for different kinds of prisoners.

The ubiquitous fireworks were already present back then too – apparently because the island used to be a layover for cruise ships in the early years of the twenty-first century. Giant buried crates of fireworks, some the size of trailers, still exist on the island, providing the drones with a seemingly inexhaustible supply.

My parents and their fellow dissidents began building a new society on the island, complete with a primitive power station and a huge lookout tower. The ruins of the spiral staircase are all that remain of it. This is because the government soon began bombing the island. After that, the chemical testing began, and people started dying.

Eventually, my parents and some other islanders, mostly

scientists, came up with a plan to attack one of the UNA freighters that was shipping prisoners there back then. They battled the crew and eventually took over the boat. Then they piloted it all the way to Australia and started building Destiny Station inside the sandstone formation, deciding to use their knowledge to find a way to defeat the UNA.

Australia had just become an enemy of the UNA at that time, and the Australians were also embroiled in bloody civil conflicts in their own cities. They did nothing to intervene and stop these refugees from arriving. So the city inside the rock grew and grew, unchecked.

'Tell me about Dad,' I say. I can tell that's the part she doesn't want to talk about, but it's the part I need to know about most of all.

'There was a bombing raid. For a while, the UNA thought it might be able to take advantage of Australia's unrest and occupy the country. They briefly tried to turn it into a colony of the UNA, until the Australians fought back. UNA warplanes used to bomb the dunes occasionally, mostly at night. Parts of our rock shelter were hit a few times, but we rebuilt any sections that got damaged. Your father was outside one night, trying to save some children playing in the dunes and bring them back into the station. A bomb landed nearby...' Her voice falters. 'The children survived, but the shock wave from the blast took his life.'

I wipe away tears. All these years I assumed that my dad was dead, but hearing this story makes the pain feel fresh again. 'How did you keep going?'

'Because as long as you were alive, there was hope. That's all people need in order to do amazing things, Alenna. Hope is the great human motivator. It always has been.'

She pulls away gently and then stands up. I know there's so much more she wants to say, and so much more I need to ask her. 'Look, I don't want to overwhelm you,' she says. 'The doctors asked me not to. You're dehydrated, probably starving, and you need sleep. There's plenty of time now. I'm not going anywhere, and neither are you and Liam.' She pauses. 'At least not right away.'

'What do you mean?'

'For the moment, we'll be staying here. But we're not alone at Destiny Station. Other rebel colonies of UNA refugees exist, hidden across the globe. One in the Highveld of South Africa. One in the Arctic, under the ice. And others on remote islands off the coast of India. We're in touch with them by radio. Armies are being trained. We're going to join together with them in a year or so. And return to the UNA to fight, and take back our freedom.'

She leads me over to the door as I try to digest her words.

'Get some rest now,' she says. 'We'll talk more in the morning.'

Liam is still waiting in the tunnel, standing there with Dr Vargas-Ruiz. They both look up as the door opens. I can tell they've been having an intense conversation.

'Things will be different from now on. Your new life is beginning,' my mum tells me. In some ways, she's a stranger, but in other ways, she's the most familiar person in the world to me.

'God, I missed you,' I say, as she leans in and hugs me.

Dr Vargas-Ruiz touches my arm. 'I need to take you and Liam back to your quarters.'

'And I've got guard duty now,' my mum adds. 'We all have to pull our weight around here.' She kisses my cheek.

I realise I haven't said 'I love you' to her yet. I want to say it, but I still feel too awkward – I don't know why. I guess it's just because I haven't seen her for so long. Or maybe it's because it feels like it would be rushing things to say it. *It's like she has come back from the dead.* But I decide to risk it anyway.

'I love you, Mum,' I tell her.

She smiles, eyes damp. 'I love you, too.' We hug one more time before my mum lets go of me and heads off down the tunnel.

'This way,' Dr Vargas-Ruiz prompts, as I stare after my mum's retreating figure.

'This place is incredible!' Liam whispers as we start walking. 'I talked to Vargas-Ruiz. They've got a plan to liberate the wheel from the UNA and unfreeze all the pods. They're going to meet up with some other rebel stations. She even thinks it's possible my dad is still alive, at one of the other bases somewhere. That he might have been taken in the raid but escaped being killed. They're going to try to find out more info for me. I still can't believe we met each other when we were little kids…'

I nod like I'm following his rush of words, but I feel like my mind is fading in and out. Right now, I just need to lie down and sleep.

'Oh yeah, and something else.' Liam looks troubled. 'She said they think Veidman was a spy. Him and Meira. Not David. That the UNA put Vei and Meira in the blue sector and gave them fake names and identities, as a way to keep us in line and stop us from trying to escape. We weren't supposed to succeed in getting off the wheel. We were meant to fail and go back to the village. I don't know if it's true or not.'

Veidman a spy. And Meira, too?

I think about how they always seemed to have things. The serum, the coffee, clean clothes. And about how Veidman was so obsessed with finding the spy. Was that all for show? It's possible, but I still find it hard to believe.

'I don't know what to think,' I tell Liam. 'Veidman's dead. If he was a spy, then it doesn't matter any more. And Meira could be dead by now too. I'm more worried about rescuing our friends in the archive, and finding David.'

We finally reach our quarantine room again and head inside, as Dr Vargas-Ruiz leaves us. I can barely believe everything that's happened to us.

I'm not the same person I was before I got sent to the wheel. I will fight side by side with the people from Destiny Station. With Liam. With my mum. And if there's any way to do it, Liam and I will try to rescue Gadya, David, Rika and everyone else. I'll do whatever it takes to liberate the wheel and ultimately destroy the UNA itself, so that no one else has to go through what we've been through.

I see myself reflected in a mirror hanging on the wall

opposite the bathroom. With my tousled hair and wild stare, I look more like a warrior than I ever thought possible.

Liam walks over to me and holds me from behind, brushing back my hair. 'Everything's going to be OK,' he says.

I laugh a little.

'What? You don't believe me?'

'I've heard those words before. But right now, here with you? It's the first time I actually believe them.' I nestle against his body, feeling his heat and his strength. 'This is only the beginning,' I tell him. 'You know that, right?'

'Yeah,' he says. I turn around to face him and gaze into his blue eyes. 'There's no one else I'd rather have fighting by my side than you,' he tells me.

We kiss passionately, standing there in the empty room. The kiss that got interrupted the night he gave me the guitar.

I used to think my life was over when I got sent to the wheel, but now I see that my life is just about to start. The next time we set foot on Island Alpha – if that ever happens – I know that we'll be the ones in control.

I shut my eyes and hug Liam tight, listening to the comforting thrum of Destiny Station all around us. I know that no matter what happens next, at least for this moment, I have finally found a home.

ACKNOWLEDGEMENTS

I am hugely grateful to my agent, Mollie Glick, whose enthusiasm and inspiration made this novel a reality. Thanks also to Hannah Brown Gordon, Stéphanie Abou, and the entire team at Foundry Literary & Media.

My fantastic editor, Courtney Bongiolatti, helped shape this book every step of the way, and I'm so glad that she took a chance on me. Thanks also to Julia Maguire and everyone else at Simon & Schuster for their support.

Much thanks and love to my family for always believing in my dreams.

ANNA DRESSED IN BLOOD

KENDARE BLAKE

Cas Lowood is no ordinary guy -
he hunts dead people.

People like Anna Dressed in Blood.
A beautiful, murderous ghost entangled
in curses and rage.

Cas knows he must destroy her, but as
her tragic past is revealed, he starts to
understand why Anna has killed
everyone who's ever dared to enter
her spooky home.

Everyone, that is, except Cas...

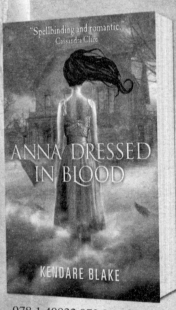

978 1 40832 072 3 £6.99 pbk
978 1 40831 945 1 £6.98 eBook

ORCHARD
www.orchardbooks.co.uk

HEAVEN

BY CHRISTOPH MARZI

THEY'D KILL
FOR HER HEART

OUT NOW

978 1 40831 466 1 £6.99 pbk
978 1 40831 657 3 £6.98 eBook

ORCHARD

www.orchardbooks.co.uk

SLATED

TERI TERRY

Sixteen-year-old Kyla has been Slated: all of her past memories erased, her entire personality wiped blank.

She has been assigned a new name, a new date of birth and even new parents. The government that did this to her claim she was a terrorist, and that she has been given a second chance.

But somehow, Kyla knows that the government is lying …

978 1 40831 946 8 £6.99 pbk
978 1 40831 947 5 £6.98 eBook

ORCHARD BOOKS
www.orchardbooks.co.uk